Travel Page

Every publication from Rippple Books has this special page to document where the book travels, who has it and when.

Hunter

A Novel

Campbell Jefferys

Rippple
Books

The right of Campbell Jefferys to be identified as the Author of the Work has been asserted in accordance with the Copyright, Designs and Patents Act 1988.

First published in 2008 by arima publishing

This edition published in 2012 by Rippple Books
Cover design: www.simoneflorell.de
Layout: Susanne Hock

Rippple Books
Postfach 304263
20325 Hamburg
Germany
www.rippplebooks.com

A CIP catalogue record for this book is available from the British Library.
ISBN: 978-3-9814585-4-1

One

He was still alive and that was bad. He had volunteered for the scouting group, hoping that if he ventured close enough to the enemy line, a sniper would take him down and all this madness would be over. His sins would be absorbed by the scorched battlefield and he would float up to the paradise he had envisaged so vividly as a child. God would be there to absolve him for following the others, for not standing up and rebelling against the fanatics; He would understand and forgive, and walk with him through the gates of heaven.

But he was still alive and that was bad. He could hear his heart thumping against his ribs. His body had deteriorated, his soul poisoned, but still his heart pumped on, this time pounding out the shock of the explosion. His eyes were caked with dirt and dust, but he had no water to wash them with, so kept them closed. Maybe an enemy soldier would chance upon him, hear the drumming heart and put a bullet through it.

The bomb explosions sounded like the thunder of a mighty storm, like the ones back home in summer when the wind swirled and blew, and purple and black clouds filled the sky. Those morning storms when he lay in bed hoping that school would be cancelled, but knowing full well it wouldn't. Football practice would be on too, and they would go through their military-type drills with sharp hail driving at their heads and leaving round pink marks on their bare arms. Through the crashes of thunder would come the ever present whistle of the coach, blowing hard until his big round face turned red.

When these storms rolled in from the sea, he cowered in bed, pulling the blankets over his head. The thunder made the bed shake and the wind rifled through the thin walls of the small house his father dominated. Sometimes it was his father who shook the bed, thumping around the house, a big, heavy man, even heavier when angry or excited, forever opening and slamming doors, complaining loudly regardless of his mood. How he could make the furniture shake with his thumping steps. Then, the glasses would clink together in the cabinets and pictures would drift slightly askew on the walls, giving him another reason to complain about the state of the house. The hulking tyrant took up a lot of space, filling the room with his bulk and his loud voice but never with his presence. There was something pathetic about the way he dominated the house; only by right and circumstance.

The ground shook again and dirt rained down on him.

He was still young, but why did his youth seem so distant? What an ordinary thing to say, he thought, that war ages you. Old heroes would say it makes a man of you, but all it really does is hollow you out inside and makes whatever good memories you once had seem like a lifetime ago, memories belonging to a different person.

His youth hadn't been much fun. Or was it that his memory chose to see it that way? It didn't matter. Lying on the frozen ground with the thunder of explosions throwing earth and bodies in the air, he would have given everything to be back in that small house, with the blankets over his head, waiting for his father to go to the hospital. Then his mother would come into his bedroom, open the curtains and say something superfluous like, "It's just a few drops." The house would seem so empty without the old man, that you could know he was no longer there just from the silence and stillness that followed his departure.

He heard crying. Someone near him was still alive and that was bad. The flashes of light lit the bodies around him and he saw the shadowed outline of crows perched on top of them, already pecking away. The crying was muffled, with much sniffing; the crier sounded embarrassed, swallowing the sobs to prevent anyone from hearing him. Much the same way he himself had cried as a boy when hit by his father, who had reproached him for crying. He would try so hard to stop the tears, but they came anyway and his shame made it worse. But there was one reward. When it was over, his mother sometimes came into his room to comfort him, when his father was asleep or had left the house. She would climb into bed with him and put her cool hands to his bruises. He loved her smell, which had the freshness of cut grass after spring rain, a farm freshness; when the farmers went out before dawn to prepare their fields for planting and the whole village had a fresh quality that made you feel that life started over every year and you had new chances and new beginnings, and that which haunted and oppressed you last year was raked and ploughed away. Hope, that's what it was; his mother smelled like hope.

He had spent all his youth wanting to be an adult, big enough to protect his mother and fight back against his father. But now, as an adult, he wanted only to be a small boy asleep in his mother's arms,

2

crying softly so she would give him even more love and attention. He inhaled deeply through his nose, thinking that he might smell her again and that the smell would take him back to his youth. But the smells around him were rank.

Still alive, bad.

He opened his eyes again, feeling the dried dirt flaking against his eyelids. Bugs crawled over his chest and legs. His right arm felt asleep and throbbed with pain. His head was ringing from the explosion and the faint sound of crying was annoying. Couldn't they die in peace, he wondered. An army of men with the mentality of small boys, that's what we are. He tried to sit up. Someone was sharing his dirt bed, the body lying on his right arm. Thinking a corpse had landed on him, he tried to give the body a push with his free hand. The body rolled over and his arm was free.

The sky was putrid, thick with smoke and lit intermittently by the explosions of bombs and anti-tank missiles. They screeched overhead, the ground shook and dirt rained down. The earth was groaning, whining for mother, for relief, comfort and an end.

He looked at the body next to him. The whites of the boy's eyes glittered in the night, the blue startling and shiny like the buttons of a small boy's sailor's uniform. But there was desperation in the eyes, confusion too, the expression of a sheep before its throat is cut. The boy was crying in a muffled and childish way, the tears cutting clean streaks through the dirt on his face. The boy stared up at him, hoping for an explanation, for reasons. They hadn't said anything about this at training camp. No, it had been all glory and honour and territorial gains. Victory was only a matter of time, their evolutionary right. There had been nothing about your entrails seeping out of you while you died without dignity or honour on a wasted plain miles from home for someone else's cause; that no matter how brave and honourable you were, you could still die a miserable and meaningless death just the way your enemies did.

He looked at the boy, taking in this historical specimen which his country had manufactured. There were millions just like him, bred for battlefield sacrifice while the generals smoked real cigarettes and drank real coffee in heated bunkers.

Why hadn't I rebelled? he wondered. Not because of father, surely. I could never please him anyway, even if I rose to the rank of general; he would always find something to criticise.

The soldier got to his knees and tried to stand up. He knew he was a bad soldier, self-serving and never one to be a hero. The crying boy looked up at him hopefully, thinking that he was about to be picked up and carried back behind the line to the medical tent. But the soldier dropped his head and began to crawl away.

"Wait," the boy cried out. His voice was high pitched and cracked. "What about me?"

For the soldier, the voice was lost on the wind, and his hearing was still shot from the explosion that had blown him perhaps five or ten metres from where he had been when he was scouting. But he still stopped and turned to the boy. The youngster had his teeth gritted together in pain. With effort, he reached into his pocket and pulled out a stack of letters and papers.

"If you're gonna leave me here to die," he said with considerable spite, a bloody drool dribbling onto his chin, "at least take these with you."

Reluctantly, the soldier reached out and took the collection of letters and photographs. The boy nodded sarcastically and then winced with pain. He turned to the smoke and blood stained sky and screamed his anguish at those who had caused his suffering. He cursed and denounced the leaders and cried for his mother.

"Shoot me," he begged, his breath coming in short starts. "You heard what I just said. I'm a traitor now. You know how we deal with traitors." And then he shouted, "Deal with me."

The soldier shook his head. His dried-out tongue struggled to provide the means to produce the words he wanted. "I don't do that anymore."

The dying boy was appalled. "But you're one of us." He looked up at the soldier's collar. "I even out-rank you. I order you to shoot me."

The soldier unclipped his pistol and pointed it at the head of the boy with the higher rank. Maybe if he, the soldier, had killed more of his traitorous comrades, he would have been promoted, and then maybe he'd be the one lying on the ground dying. The boy closed his eyes, waiting for the end, a strange, thin-lipped expectant smile on his face. When the shot didn't come, his right eye squinted open. The soldier had put the gun to his own head.

"What are you doing? What about me?"

The soldier pulled the gun away and looked at it. He held it in his numb right hand and saw for the first time the damage; the last two fingers and half of his hand were gone, and he could see the jagged

4

outline of white bone sticking out of the remains of his glove. The pain hit and he dropped the gun.

The boy quickly reached for it, picked it up and pointed it at the soldier. There was the glimmer of madness in his eyes, the insanity of war painted in streaks across his pale face. The gun shook in his hand. The soldier looked down its narrow barrel and closed his eyes, smiling that his end had finally come. And could it be more fitting than at the hands of his own countryman, a pimple-faced fanatic who out-ranked him? The boy screamed their national catch-cry and fired the gun.

It seemed forever that the soldier stayed there, crouched on his knees, awaiting execution. He was still alive and that was bad. When he finally forced his eyes open, he looked down and saw the bloody mess the boy had made of his own head. Cowards to the end, he thought, all of us.

The missiles whistled overhead and scattered bullets dug into the dirt and into already dead soldiers who merely took the extra bullets like sandbags, their bodies shifting slightly, with no more blood to bleed. A leather book bound by a short belt lay on the ground. He picked it up and pocketed it along with the letters and photographs of the now dead boy. He started to crawl away and took refuge in a shallow bomb crater. There were bodies everywhere, in different stages of decomposition; some only recently dismembered and the life still steaming out of them.

He shrugged off his heavy pack and threw his rifle aside. With difficulty, he tore off his uniform and took the blood stained uniform of a regular soldier, and with it another community of lice and assorted bugs. The material was coarse and itched against his skin, but in the front pocket of the coat was a piece of chocolate. He couldn't believe his luck. He held it tightly in his left hand, melting it slightly and then swallowed all of it, too hungry to savour it.

The chocolate renewed his strength and he started to climb out of the crater, but he couldn't grip the earth with his ravaged right hand. Dirt got inside the wound and hot pain shot down his arm. He cried out, cursing. In response to his cry, he heard the dull monotones of the enemy. Good. He could just stay here and wait for them to find him. Then they would kill him. Or would they drag him off to one of their prisoner camps he had heard rumours about? Survival instinct made him jump to his feet, and he hauled himself out of the shallower front side of the crater. Bullets streaked past soundlessly. He turned and ran as fast as he could, pumping his arms until his lungs burned. Just run, he thought, run as far as your legs can carry you, across this scorched and lifeless plain and back to where the fields smell so fresh and new after spring rain, to where the cow dung stinks on hot summer days, where the autumn bathes the countryside in red and yellow and orange, where every year life starts again.

Strewn bodies broke his stride and tripped him over. He saw faces frozen in anguish and pain, their innocence gone. These were the men of his nation, bred for combat, promised glory, victory and the deserved utopia, but now fertiliser for the poisoned and punished lands they had tried so desperately to conquer. Some called for help, but he didn't stop. He just kept on running. Close to the line, he heard the guttural strains of his own language: "Hold the line. There must be no retreat."

He took a running jump over the barbed wire and landed in the arms of a young machine gunner. They both fell to the earthen floor. Some other soldiers helped them up and dusted them down.

The machine gunner had a bright, round face and a toothy smile which was even more striking in the darkness because his pearl-white teeth glittered. He took a close look at the soldier's face.

"You the lad that won the silver in Berlin?" he asked with a broad grin, showing his teeth.

The soldier managed a thin smile, his first in months, and shook his head. The machine gunner patted him on the back.

"You sure can jump."

"Man your gun, Corporal," ordered the commanding officer.

"When you give me some bullets to fire, sir, I will," the machine gunner said insolently.

The officer came over and snarled as he spoke. "I've had just about enough of your mouth, Schwarzer. No more warnings. And if we've got no more bullets then I'll throw you at the enemy."

The officer marched away. The machine gunner snarled in return, but in a funny way, and rolled his eyes. The soldier would have liked to stay by the gunner. The front lines were so devoid of humour. Everyone had grim expressions, the sallow faces of the hungry, the hopelessness that one normally saw in the faces of prisoners and those sent to die.

"You there," shouted the officer. "Take your place."

The soldier held up his bloodied hand and the officer sighed exasperatedly.

"All right," he said, rubbing his forehead. "Go get yourself patched up."

The soldier followed the lines of wounded to the medical tent, joining a collection of other men who had minor wounds. They waited and spoke together in low voices, drawing hard on thin cigarettes. One man had a bottle of something and was reluctantly letting others have a swig. The bottle came to the soldier. It was vodka, not the good stuff, but strong nonetheless and it dulled the pain. He kept his dirty head down in fear someone would recognise him. But he was sure none of his unit would be here; it was only the regular soldiers who had to wait for treatment.

The doctors' white coats were streaked with red, their gloved hands bloodied up to their elbows. Their faces poured with sweat under the strong lights and they maintained order with difficulty. They shouted until they were hoarse, but their voices were sometimes barely audible over the noises in the tent: men cried out in agony and others called out the names of their regiments hoping this would get them preferential treatment; low ranking officers with minor wounds surged forward, shoving the regular soldiers aside; intermittent gunshots rang out as soldiers chose to end their lives on their own terms, while others reproached them for their cowardice. The floor ran with a stream of blood, and with the earth already so full of it, he wondered if it would soon flow into a river of red.

When his turn came, the teenage orderly roughly cleaned his blown off hand and wrapped it with a soiled length of white cotton; it could well have been a dead man's undershirt and he was probably lucky to have that. The wounded kept arriving and the orderly was called away. Men were carried in on makeshift stretchers of blankets, with each soldier's condition more pressing than the last. And all around him the soldiers screamed: for water, for their families and their mothers, while others shouted out their sins deliriously in the hope they would be received more favourably on the other side. Strange, he thought. For a country which had frowned upon religion, there seemed to be a lot of God in this tent.

The great parades of their youth had marched them all here, their heads held high, a clear cause worth fighting and dying for, and all those smiling supporters had cheered them forward, the girls bright eyed and fanatical. But as their boots stomped proudly from their fatherland, none of them had pictured this: open wounds steaming

7

in the night, boys barely men blowing their heads off rather than submitting to having a leg removed, and the air stuffy and rank from the stink of remorse, guilt and rotting flesh. The soldier helped his bandaged hand into his coat and walked out of the tent.

The darkness was heavy, the sky an enormous mud-soaked blanket. He saw white eyes and the red glow of fast burning cigarettes. Few talked and nobody laughed. He looked around for the machine gunner but he was gone. The soldiers scratched hard at their uniforms and pulled their jackets tighter around themselves against the cold. How it had changed since the early days of the war, when the trenches had sparkled with laughter and the marches had been like afternoon walks in the forest. Sometimes, the officers had even spun records and broadcast them for all to hear. There had been girls around and plenty of food. The land had opened up with promise. The sun had always been out and one impressive victory had followed another. But now, the grim faces stared into the putrid, meagre contents of their food cans, with forks scraping against the metal to pick off every last morsel. There was not only the sense of doom, but also one of retribution; they deserved this and it was just the beginning.

The soldier walked away from these men towards the latrine to relieve himself. Hanging from the tree which supported half of the latrine was a man. A sign saying "I am a traitor" was draped around his neck. The soldier looked closer and recognised the pearl teeth of the machine gunner. He was smiling and grimacing at the same time, his eyes open and seemingly staring at the sign draped on him as if it was some kind of mistake.

"Where you going, soldier?"

He turned to face the voice, clicking his heels and raising his arm in automatic salute. The officer laughed at the bloodied, bandaged hand, a high-pitched squeal like one would hear at a bawdy stage show. The officer was small and weedy, slight through the chest and shoulders, and his uniform seemed several sizes too big. When he laughed, his shoulders bounced and the uniform fluttered like a wind-blown flag, with his medal for bravery swinging on its pin.

"Latrine," the soldier replied, lowering his arm. He wondered if the officer patrolled this area and was responsible for the previously jovial but now dead machine gunner swinging from the tree.

The officer laughed again, somehow extracting amusement from this macabre mockery. "Think you can?"

The soldier nodded and turned towards the stinking pit. Bugs had attached themselves to his pubic hairs and he was scared to look. He turned and looked at the machine gunner. Someone had already taken his boots and socks, and the soldier wondered if the man's blistered and scabbed feet might perhaps tempt someone delirious enough from hunger. Was it better swinging from a tree than lying dead in a bomb crater? Dead, either way. Just anything to make all the senseless brutality stop. The enemy would come and his nation would suffer. He could die here at the hands of his countrymen or at the hands of the enemy somewhere else. Did it matter? You were still dead, and your life was a meaningless digit in the great figure of lives lost to war. He felt the burden of the book in his inside pocket, the lump it made and how the metal buckle dug into his ribs. Got to get this home, he thought.

He looked around for the officer who had laughed at him, and when he didn't see him, began edging behind the latrine. In the distance, he heard the sounds of planes, buzzing like a swarm of mosquitoes. The buzzing grew louder and the planes plunged out of the clouds. The bombs fell and officers shouted orders. The medical tent disintegrated, the red and white cross blown apart. Body parts were thrown in all directions. A head sailed through the air, landed at his feet and bounced along the ground like a flat soccer ball. Another bomb fell near the latrine and its force threw him into the pit. He quickly climbed out and dry-retched on the ground, his head ringing from the explosion. He looked up to see soldiers streaming past him, taking the chance to desert. Bullets whistled past as the deserters were shot. They tried to run, but their weak legs couldn't carry them fast enough into the safety of darkness. They let out muffled cries and crashed to the ground hard. The soldier ducked behind the tree. The machine gunner was swinging from side to side, taking bullets the way a piñata takes hits from children. The soldier waited for the madness to stop before turning and disappearing into the blackness of the night.

***

He woke hungry. A soupy grey dawn was creeping across the sky and promised snow. He absently tried to scratch at the lice on his chest with his bandaged right hand and winced with pain. The fingers were gone, and that fact hurt more than the physical pain their departure

9

had caused. Perhaps some joyous crow was breakfasting on his pinkie finger, ripping the meagre flesh from the skinny bone.

He had slept sheltered from the wind between two rocks, but didn't remember sitting down there. There had been bombs, limbs thrown into the air all at once like men tossing hats in a crowd. He had jumped over the comrades who had been shot from behind and there had been a hill to climb. He looked down on the lifeless plain. The land was pockmarked, with perfect round holes that made him pine for a slice of Emmental cheese. It was a barren landscape, with no grass or trees, where nothing would ever grow again. Far in the distance, he saw slithers of smoke rising from the few functioning chimneys of a small village. The army could be down there, he thought, or is it too small and obvious? If there was no army, he could steal some civilian clothes and dispose of his uniform.

He scampered back to the top of the hill and peered from behind a rock at the lines of his army. The area smoked, but already shelters were being erected, including a makeshift medical tent, as the army sought to hold its position to the last as ordered. Dead bodies were being thrown into a large pit behind the latrine. His hunger made him consider walking back down, but the lifeless grey and black lumps, those who hadn't made it over the hill, made him think again. He turned and walked down to the village.

The ground was slippery, frozen in parts, and he stumbled and tripped, often breaking his fall with his injured hand, making him curse under his breath. He didn't have the strength to maintain his balance when his footing was unsure. This bumbling step was a far cry from the long stride he had marched off to war with. His father had seen him off that day, finally showing a glimmer of pride.

"It's a great day for you," his father had said, a meaty hand gripping his bony shoulder. "You'll come back fit and strong, a worldly man."

He had worn the black uniform with pride that day. After struggling his whole life to win his father's approval, it had taken this uniform, a gun and potential death for him to finally be close to the son his father wanted. The attention and pride made him forget the sobs of his mother. He would march off, fight for the cause of the nation and come back a hero. How proud his father would be then.

But war had not made him strong and fit; rather, he was weak, emaciated, hollowed-out, hunched-over and bitter. And he had proven himself certainly no hero. The rush to prove one's bravery often resulted in death or capture. His only goal had been to stay alive. Chances for heroism passed him by, and promotion was seldom forthcoming, happening with the passage of time and not from his leadership or soldiering ability. The pride his father had in him would most certainly dissipate when news of his desertion reached the old man. But it didn't matter. His life could hardly go back to normal after what he had seen and done, and his father had been a fervent supporter of it all from the beginning. As a traitor, he would return and once more disappoint his father. But he started the long walk in the hope that his pathetic effort at playing soldier might be forgiven in light of the horrific time he had lived through. Of course, it would all be made easier for him if his father was dead. He had not heard from his parents in over six months, and rumours of cities flattened by bombs with thousands of civilians dead had swept through the ranks.

Close to the village he saw the flag he had come to hate, the flag that had been the strongest image of his military childhood, to which millions had zealously attached and defined themselves, himself included. He recalled the rallies, the flags blood red and a million soldiers ready to die for one enigmatic screamer. It hung limp in the windless morning, its colours in stark contrast to the grey of the half-destroyed buildings of the village. What a pathetic little place, he thought, looking down on the low buildings and the overused dirt track that was the main road and which had been churned to sludge. This is why we walked half way across the continent? This is our promised land?

Skirting the main supply road that fed the wasted village, he headed into a nearby forest. The trees were leafless, but their trunks and branches were strong. Come spring, they would sprout buds and be covered in green by mid-summer. It was reassuring to still see strength in nature when all the land around him was bombed and burned.

He found burrows, dug in summer and now frozen in form, where soldiers had tried to hide from the special units who scoured the army for traitors. Some had been shot through the head while others had died of hunger or exposure, their skin drawn tight across their sallow faces, their cheek bones sticking out as if horns were about to grow from them. With his hands shaking and the bile burning his throat, he searched these rank and putrid corpses for food. After rummaging through several burrows and finding nothing, he thought about eating

11

a body, and in the dizziness of his hunger, it seemed a rational thing to do. He would stare for a long time at a leg, trying to picture himself hacking it off, his grubby teeth tearing at the raw and hairy flesh. Time and again he had to force himself out of a burrow and away from the sickening temptation.

The sound of engines drew him to the edge of the forest. A long column of soldiers knifed through the land en route to the front line. But there was no swagger about this group, no six-foot tall broad-shouldered examples of the master race; this was a death march, made up of the last remnants of manhood which could be thrust at the enemy. The war was lost and it was probably better for these men to die in glory on the battlefield than face life in a defeated and occupied land. They had shown their enemies no mercy and as victors, the enemies would surely do the same. He thought about staggering down to join the march, at least he might get some food that way, but was too weak to go any further. He slumped against the tree and watched the column pass. The soldiers turned their heads to the sky when snow began to fall and moaned collectively, hunching their shoulders against the cold. They walked without formation, with their heads down, struggling against the wind that was angling the snow into them. Soon, they were all white with snow, the colour adding a brightness to the scene.

The snow drove him back into the last burrow he had searched. He took a stinking greatcoat from a fallen soldier and wrapped it around himself. Before sitting down at the entrance to the burrow, a ration packet caught his eye. Hunger is painful, he knew too well, and the requirements of the body affect the thinking of the brain. Covering his nose, he crawled over and reached for the packet, thinking it would disappear. In order to hide his rations, the fallen soldier had put them down his pants. Would he reach out and grab only the man's penis? Then what? Would his hunger induced insanity make him think it was a sausage? But the ration packet was real, and he brushed away the bugs and hair and tore it open with his teeth. It wasn't much, but he ate all of it, feeling small ounces of strength returning with each mouthful. Soon his jaw hurt from the vigour of his chewing and he sat back to wait for the snow to stop. He would have loved a cigarette right then, not the army issued ones, but the ones he'd had before the war, real tobacco that took a good five minutes to smoke to the end.

To keep from falling asleep – he didn't want an extermination squad to find him in here – he dug into his pockets and took out the letters and photographs the boy had given him yesterday. He took out the leather book too and placed this gently on the earthen floor. The letters were written in diary form, giving day to day accounts of battles and the boy's reaction to events. Killings were described in detail, methodically. Like himself, this boy had been involved in his share of brutalities, but unlike himself, seemed to show no remorse, and recorded these shocking events as if he was writing home from summer holidays. He even bragged, thinking his execution of prisoners and civilians would make him a hero back home. He wrote with a fine script, in Sütterlin, an educated boy, perhaps a graduate of one of the elite schools. The soldier could feel the boy's happiness as he described the success of his operations, the promotions, the numbers killed, the vermin exterminated. The soldier shook his head as he read, marvelling once again at the depths his nation had sunk to, that their greatest minds had applied themselves so rigorously to a task so horrific. He wondered if the world would ever believe it. If they did, they would surely never forgive. The photographs the boy had were also startling, with bodies piled on streets or on the town square and soldiers posing next to them like students on holiday. The soldier put this photograph and others inside the leather book, pulling the buckle tight to hold all the contents inside. The letters he tore into small pieces and scattered them on the ground. He thought again about all the planning, the financing, the background work and research that must have taken place, the commitment and motivation, and the fervent followers who had carried it all out, the manpower committed to this evil cause; his entire nation was insane.

The snow had stopped and the ground was slushy and soft from it. Despite what he had learned at training camp, he took great handfuls of snow and shoved them into his mouth hoping to quench his thirst. He looked down at the road, churned into mud by vehicles and a thousand boots, and decided to walk along the edge of the forest until he was sure he was no longer near the supply road. His new freedom powered him forward and the rations had renewed his strength. The letters had convinced him he had to get home and show his mother what he had collected over the years; she would know what to do with it. She had never been a supporter and had often wondered, quietly, why all the women were so besotted with the leader.

The forest ended at a small farm. Through the trees he saw the flickering lights of candles in the windows. The stink of burning dung lingered in the air. A handful of pathetic animals limped around a yard that had no fence; the animals knew they had nowhere else to go. At the back of the yard was a half-destroyed barn. He headed towards it.

As darkness fell, a bitter wind blew over the valley and rifled through the barn. He was thankful for the greatcoat, despite the smell, and to be finally safe from the horrors of the front line. A hard wood floor had never felt so comfortable. The pillow of hay itched his neck, but he slept too deep to scratch.

***

The smell woke him first. The sun was streaming through the barn and it took a moment for his eyes to adjust. Some of the animals were in the barn. He could see the outline of a couple of pigs and an emaciated cow, and heard their noises. Eyes fully adjusted, he stared down the barrel of the rifle pointed at him.

Two

From the main highway, the turn-off heads toward the city centre. On this road there is a narrow side street, the first on the left. The buildings are hidden behind the trees and are easy to miss. The school itself is a broad expanse, spread out and seemingly hastily added to over the years, resulting in a mismatched set of buildings, classrooms and temporary solutions. There is a long walkway which cuts the school down the middle and to which most of the classrooms are attached. Other rooms, called demountables, are a short walk from this walkway.

It was neither a good school nor a bad school; just a school like any other. The children gathered in groups for protection, preyed on those weaker, sought shaky alliances with other groups, made false promises and spread damning rumours. Bullies were like corrupt police, celebrities and the beautiful were untouchable, and new students were always singled out. It was all about strength in numbers and the brand you wore. There were misunderstandings, complications, popularity contests, lying, betrayal, and kids could fall from grace just as fast as they could rise to it as a result of playground opinion. Reputation was everything, as was knowing and respecting your place. The school was ruled by a leadership principle, stemming down from the top according to age, size and beauty. It was a difficult place for some and the high point of their lives for others. Teasing was the worse torture, ganging up on someone typical. And the adults seemed not to notice any of it, or at least noticed but didn't care.

With the Christmas holidays approaching, the school was in a state of excitement. Energy levels were running high, with students and teachers eager for the six-week break. The year twelves were gone, having sweated and struggled through their final exams, and that meant the year elevens ruled the school. How they strutted down the walkway in their assorted groups, with nothing to fear, the younger students stepping aside as if parting for royalty. What a difference a year can make; that a fifteen year old cowers to a boy of sixteen but feels physically and mentally superior to a boy of fourteen.

The day was coming to an end. The joyous shouts of kids let out early echoed down the walkway. A free afternoon beckoned, and it was still warm enough to enjoy a swim at the beach or a quick surf before dinner.

Eric sat at the back of the classroom, gazing out the window. He watched the other kids form their groups, heard their shouts and teasing, saw the attempts to chide and humiliate, the extraordinary efforts to be cool. He wondered whether, at his old school, he had behaved the same way. Certainly, he had teased other kids, pushed around the younger ones, but it had all been just a joke, and he had never meant anything nasty. But now, outside the safety of a group, he understood just how brutal the violence – physical and verbal – of children could be.

The room was disgustingly warm and stuffy. There was no air conditioner, and it seemed the room shimmered like a hot desert highway, the heads of the other kids rippling in the haze. He could hear the windows softly banging inside their frames. The sea breeze was finding its wind, as it did every afternoon, but the windows remained closed and the sweat trickled from his armpits down his sides. Ever since hair had started to grow there, he found himself sweating much more, but he didn't wear deodorant in fear the kids would tease him for smelling like a girl. He was such a target here; the last thing he needed was to give them another excuse for teasing.

A crumpled piece of paper lay open on his desk. "Were gonna git you," it claimed, and two boys nearby were sneaking looks at him and trying to look mean; one pretended to slice his neck open with his fingers. The teacher was completely oblivious to this and stared absent-mindedly out the window, humming softly to herself, tapping her foot lightly on the floor to the rhythm. She even hummed as she checked her watch.

Eric continued to sweat, subconsciously tapping his foot in rhythm with his teacher, who seemed to be more eager for the Christmas break than the students. The clock crawled towards three. He tried to read his history book, to focus on the heroic Americans who, with the help of equally heroic Australians, had overcome all odds to defeat the evil Germans in the Second World War. They had earlier watched a boring documentary about the allies marching towards Berlin. Yanks on Tanks it should have been called, for most of the footage had the Americans sitting on their tanks, grinning broadly while handing chocolate to the children who ran alongside. All around them was utter destruction and they seemed proud of their work. Eric wondered how any Germans had even survived such bombing and devastation. Had the whole country been an army, women and children and old people too, so that the cities had needed to be bombed to smithereens?

As the minutes limped towards three, the kids slowly started to pack away their books and files, ready to shoot out the door the second the bell rang. Eric did the same so as not to appear bookish and add more fuel to the humiliation fire. A ball of paper hit him in the head, making him jump. The boys behind him snickered. He turned and a tubby boy, one of Josh's hoods, motioned for him to pick up the ball of paper. Eric did so and flattened it out on his desk. It was a crude drawing of a stick figure hanging from a tree by a rope. The round face had Xs for eyes and a drooping frown. There was an arrow pointing at the figure and the word "you". The boys snorted with laughter. Eric took his pencil and drew an enormous penis on the dead stick figure, rolled up the paper and threw it back. The tubby boy unrolled it and showed it to Josh. His mouth curled into a sinister smile, lifting his top lip and showing the gap in his front teeth.

In his first week at this new school, Eric had yet to discover the perfect getaway. One problem was that he lived on the other side of town, near the beach. Taking the bus was out of the question; they had teased him when he took it on his first day. There had been no way to escape and the driver seemed completely unaware of what was going on. Worse, everyone had seen his humiliation, so the next day the whole school knew about it and other groups teased him for being a wimp or a girl, or the friendless faggot, as Josh had labelled him.

The only method he had come up with was to linger behind after class and ask the teacher questions. Josh and his group were bloodthirsty but impatient. If he dawdled long enough with the teacher, perhaps a more immediate source of scorn would cross their path and they would forget about him. Even better was when he left the class with the teacher and talked to him or her as they walked down the walkway together. Then he was free to walk home, even though it took over an hour. But that method seemed no longer possible; the teachers were out the door faster than the students, and there was no more school work to discuss. His only chance was to try to out-run Josh and his group. Josh and another boy lived in his neighbourhood and it was those two who had first tormented him on the bus; wearing the school uniform had been a big mistake that day, but how was he to know the school was so lax on the compulsory uniform issue?

The bell shrieked and the kids scampered for the door. Eric continued to sit at his desk, even when all the other students had left.

He slowly packed his bag, thinking that the longer he delayed, the more chance he had.

"Come along, uh, young man," said the teacher. "Time to go home."

He stood up and met the teacher at the door. Up close, the history teacher was a withered bag of skin and bones, shrivelled up and dusty, as a history teacher should be. She had a thin, hawk-like face with a long nose that served as a beak, particularly well when she was profiled as a shadow, and she had wispy grey locks of hair like dried spider webs. Her reading glasses hung from a red chain draped around her neck. Every day she wore a different coloured cardigan that was made of the same mouldy wool. Eric guessed she knitted them herself, passing away the lonely spinster evening hours.

Hoping to delay the inevitable, Eric asked, "Why did the Germans kill the Jews?"

The teacher sighed. She took her horn-rimmed glasses from her face and let them hang limp against her flat chest. "A difficult question, but most historians say it was because they considered them inferior. But in reality, they were scared of them, and blamed them for all their problems. Quite xenophobic people, the Germans, afraid of anything unlike themselves."

Eric looked past the teacher. At the edge of the walkway, near the entrance to the library, Josh's group waited, collecting members from other classes. They leaned close together conspiratorially, pointing in Eric's direction, discussing strategy. They looked eager, hungry for violence. They called themselves the bikers because they all had 50cc motorbikes and they dressed accordingly with black jeans and matching desert boots. Eric had wondered last week that, if he got his own motorbike, the group would accept him as a member. From his life in the country, he already knew how to ride. Other groups of kids walked past: the sporties, musos, modes and goths. They all had their uniforms and lingoes, their places to sit at lunchtime and their own initiation rites. They're all safe, he thought. Why can't that be me?

He turned back to the teacher. "What does xenophobic mean?"

Another exasperated sigh. "Fear of anything different from yourself, as I just said." But she collected herself and continued rather grandly, "Run along, now. History isn't going anywhere. We can talk about all of this next year. It'll be history by then."

She let out a squawk of laughter and then stalked off, her dress billowing behind her. The bikers moved in. Eric turned and ran in the opposite direction, against the flow of kids moving down the walkway. The bikers struggled against this peak hour throng, pushing younger kids out of the way. Eric saw one of the bikers get floored by a year eleven sporty, whose group thought it extremely funny and slapped the hitter on the back. Eric heard their laughter as the fallen biker floundered on the ground. Not looking where he was going, he bumped into a few year ten surfers, a group he had admired from afar. Drew stepped forward.

"Sorry."

Drew smiled, and seeing the bikers rushing towards them, said, "Looks like you better run for it." The surfer group laughed and moved on, but Drew hung back and held out his right hand. "Gis ya bag."

Eric smiled and unloaded the bag on his neighbour. "Thanks. I owe ya."

Eric ran for the back of the school, to where the demountables stood like lost buildings from a military camp. They were raised, and if you didn't mind a few insects, could make a good hiding place. Eric hated spiders, but ducked under the science demountable, the same room where he sweated through biology. He saw some of the bikers kicking up dust as they ran past.

"He's gone," one of them shouted, and he stamped his foot childishly.

"Check under the demountables," Josh said. He wouldn't be so easily deterred.

From his vantage point, wedged in a dark corner with spider webs grabbing at his bare arms and legs, Eric watched the boys duck their heads under the nearby buildings. Maybe they won't see me, he thought; it's pretty dark under here.

From the other side of the building a head popped under and spotted him. Eric took a deep breath and cursed once again the horrible world that was childhood. Why the adults thought it was so wonderful to be a kid baffled him. His own adulthood, freedom from school and family, seemed a lifetime away.

"He's under the science demountable," the boy shouted.

Eric scampered to his feet, skinning a knee in the process, and ran for it. He sprinted across the sports field and towards the car park in the hope that he might know someone there who would give him a lift, or that a teacher might stop him and offer temporary safety. He knew his chances for either were slim, but he sprinted anyway.

Some of the bikers were good runners and were gaining on him. A few of the others, overweight and slow, fell away from the chase.

As he crossed the now almost deserted walkway, he thought about running for admin and the safety of the principal's office, but telling on Josh and his group would only make things worse. So he detoured across the grass area where kids sat in their groups during lunch, playing games or talking shit, anything to pass the idle time. At the far end of the grass was a small forest that was out of bounds; if you were caught there during school time, you were in big trouble. Eric followed a narrow trail that led to some deserted buildings where he knew tough kids smoked cigarettes between classes. Thinking he might encounter some older, more threatening but equally bored kids, he fought his way out of the forest and found himself on a wide street in a part of town he didn't know. He was quite a way inland now. The sea breeze was barely a waft. Unlike where he lived, here the houses were small and run down, and the gardens looked like they hadn't seen water or attention for years. He heard the bikers fighting through the bushes and started running down the street. Josh followed right behind him, and as they all ran down the street, it must have seemed to adults that they were having immense fun. But for Eric, it was like in those dreams where you run and run, pumping your arms until your lungs burned and your legs ached, but your relentless pursuer just keeps gaining.

It was over. He couldn't run any more, but he had given them a good chase; he hoped that the bikers might respect him for that and go easy. Just as they closed in, Eric ducked into a nearby supermarket to catch his breath. All the shoppers and workers looked at him, red-faced, doubled-over and breathing hard. The bikers waited outside, knowing Eric was trapped. Maybe they thought he was buying gifts to use as bribes. They pressed their faces to the windows, cupping their hands around the sides of their eyes to stop the glare, and watched Eric as he moved deeper into the store.

Mothers pushed heavy carts laden with this week's specials and babies with shiny, runny noses grabbed items from the cart and threw them to the floor. The checkout bells rang and cashiers called out for price checks.

He had no money. How he would have loved a cold drink right then, but his father didn't believe in pocket money. "Children only understand the value of a dollar when they've earned it," he often said.

And it was no argument for Eric to say that all the other kids got pocket money.

One of the shelf stackers, a balding man in a sweat stained shirt who looked like he was a career shelf stacker, was eyeing Eric suspiciously. So he pretended to be searching for something, reading from a short list cupped in his hand. In the frozen food section, the refrigerated air blew through his sweaty shirt, making it feel like a cooling towel, and for a moment, he forgot his troubles. He glanced down the aisle towards the entrance and saw Josh standing at the window, waving. Eric stopped and stared at him.

Arsehole, he thought. I'd take you out if it wasn't for your friends.

At the back of the supermarket was a double door made of two sheets of thick plastic. It led to a small storeroom and a loading area. Through the gap in the plastic, Eric could see daylight. The back roller door was open. A man came through pushing a trolley stacked high with boxes and Eric saw that the distance between the plastic door and the roller door was barely a few metres. As he ran for it, he heard someone shout at him from behind. He leapt from the loading area and disappeared around the first corner.

He was miles from home, but he didn't mind. His parents hardly seemed interested in him anymore, and he hated having to answer all their mundane questions. As long as he made it home before dark, as was the rule, he could say that he had worked longer at school and then played sport with some friends, and it wouldn't even be a lie; running was sport and he had spoken with the teacher about the Germans. But if he came back after dark, especially if his father was already home, then he would be in for it. His father hadn't hit him since the stealing episode two years ago, but punished him instead with sarcasm and insult in ways that hurt much more than physical blows. Given the choice, he would have preferred to be beaten.

Eric dawdled on his way home, stopping at a primary school and taking a long drink from a tap. The school was deserted and he was quickly reminded what frightening places schools were when all the kids had gone home, as if decades of fear and repression had seeped into the walls: the demonic souls of bullies lurking in the shadows of vacant corridors, spinster teachers circling the playground on broomsticks and cackling, and the ghosts of violent vice-principals, always small and weedy men, preying the halls for easy targets, belittling the weak and small to better themselves.

Eric looked around the playground, expecting the bikers or some other group to emerge from the shadows. The wind rustled down the long hallways, whistling through the smallest of gaps in the doors, and blowing scattered papers and chocolate wrappers into the air. Back in the country, he had been warned to stay away from the district school outside of school time. It was rumoured an old man in a white van drove around and offered kids sweets or some such. When he was younger, the stories had scared him, forcing him sometimes to sleep with the light on; even now, every time he saw a white van, he shivered.

He bent down for another drink and then walked across the playground. Coloured lines marked out tennis courts, hopscotch, four square, and even an assembly area. When he looked closely, he saw numbers painted on the bitumen, so the classes knew where they had to stand. He found an old marble, a cat's eye, and played with it in his fingers. He looked a few times over his shoulder. He had escaped the bikers today, but they would surely come after him tomorrow. And then it would be school holidays and tormenting him could become a full time activity. The bikers were probably already hatching plans to make his summer hell. He wished he was back in the country, where his friends were and the land held such adventure. He missed those flat lands, where you could work like a man on the farms and all the adults respected you. Making friends there had been easy; in this new town, it was impossible. He knew how to ride a motorbike, was good at sports and not such an academic to be considered bookish, but not stupid either. There was nothing that would make him an obvious target for teasing. The bikers simply made stuff up.

The centre of town was nice, he had to admit that. It wasn't dusty and dry like in the country, where the main road there was lined with fifties style buildings in different stages of disrepair and decay. Here, it was new and developed, the buildings modern and arty. There were parks with grass of deep green, with trees providing plenty of shade. The centre was located on an estuary where the river split wide to meet the ocean. As he crossed the bridge over the estuary, fishermen were setting themselves up for dusk, hoping to catch the fish that swam in from the ocean to dine on the weed growing on the bridge pillars. Sometimes, even dolphins came all the way in, chasing the fish. The men wore checked shirts in red and green, and had weather-worn hats with small hooks threaded through. They smiled at him as he walked past, but he couldn't guess if their smiles were friendly or sinister. Did they all drive white vans? They looked like retirees. He wondered if the evening's fishing was the high point of their dull day.

A further kilometre from the bridge was the walled suburb of Crescent Bay, his new neighbourhood. He passed through the gate and gave the security guard a placid wave. The house, which had come as part of his father's new job, was a couple of streets from the beach; when the surf was up, Eric could sometimes hear the waves crashing against the shore at night as he lay in bed. The salt rusted everything, and parts of the gutters had gaping holes from where the rust had eaten through the metal. It didn't matter if the gutters were broken; it felt like it never rained here. His father had been excited about the move – it had been his decision, after all – thinking that living in this coastal hamlet would be like having a permanent holiday. But he had yet to visit the beach and had only talked about joining the nearby golf club. Work took up too much time. That was okay for Eric, for the less he saw of the old man the better.

Guessing he had about an hour of daylight left, Eric walked past his house and headed for the beach, hoping to wash away the dirt and grime of the chase. He also wanted to clean the blood from his skinned knee so that his mother wouldn't have cause to ask questions and act all motherly.

A lifetime in the country had made him wary of the ocean, but his confidence grew with each swim he took. The sea breeze rifled the sand against his bare legs and there were white caps as far as he could see. The water was fresh and the undertow strong. He fought against it and realised how tired he was. The swell was decent but the wind was knocking the tops off waves before they could take any form. Nevertheless, a group of surfers rode the waves as best they could. Eric saw Drew and thought to call out, but decided against it. They briefly made eye contact. Eric turned away and self-consciously staggered out of the water. He walked up the beach path, feeling the whole time the eyes of the group on his back and imagining the jokes they were making at his expense.

**

Eric's mother was of middle height, with a head of striking blond curls. In a country full of women who dyed their hair blond and permed it and, Eric thought, looked ridiculous for it, his mother's Dutch descent ensured that her golden curls were real, and local women were often jealous of her. Eric knew it sometimes made it hard for her to make friends. Her most striking feature though was her face, with a strong, protruding jaw which kept her skin taught and unlined. Eric loved her maiden name, van der Mergen, and often said to himself what his name would be if his parents got divorced: Eric van der Mergen. It sounded so exotic, much more interesting than plain old Eric Messer.

The kitchen was his mother's domain, even if she wasn't proud of it. Before moving to Crescent Bay, she had worked at the local kindergarten; only during the mornings because his father was opposed to the idea of her working full time. But now she was a full time housewife.

Eric saw his school bag propped against a chair as he walked in. His mother turned around from her position at the stove.

"Ricky, what took you so long?" she said as she stirred a pot. "Why don't you call if you're going to be late?"

Another question. All his parents ever did was ask questions, menial ones that required pathetic answers, but answers nonetheless. They didn't care about his true feelings and just kept everything on the surface. They didn't even seem to care that they had dumped him in this town where he was everyone's easy target.

"Tookaswim."

"Drew said you ran off with some friends," she said brightly. "I'm so glad you're making friends here. I mean, we knew you'd have no trouble, but changing schools is hard."

Eric smiled sardonically, thinking of his new friends.

"Hungry?" she asked.

He nodded.

"We won't wait for your father," she said, looking into the contents of the pot. "He said he'd be late."

Eric ate his dinner quickly. He picked up his bag and went to his room. There were still unpacked boxes in the spare room next to his bedroom. His comic books were in the there somewhere, but he was too lazy to look for them, especially since his father had said it was childish for a fifteen year-old to read comics.

The bedroom was small and cramped, the spare room even smaller. A small window faced the back garden. When it was open, and the sliding door to the kitchen also, he could hear his parents talking, not that they had much to say to each other apart from the usual domestic topics. The room's only redeeming feature was the glow-in-the-dark stars the previous child had stuck to the ceiling, planets and comets too. Eric loved to look at them after he turned the light out and slowly drift off to sleep with visions of stars and planets and the big adventurous world that he imagined existed beyond his very small one. Out there somewhere were foreign countries, different races and languages, so much more than was locked inside the bubble of Western Australia. And there was his own heritage as well. He wanted to travel to Europe, to get away from his parents, away from school, away from Josh and the bikers, and do his own thing. They would come after him tomorrow and no one would help. He was alone like the stars on the ceiling. His throat went dry and he struggled to suppress his sobs. He wished he was back at his old school, where he had been one of the leaders of his group, and they had chased the smaller kids, teased those who had braces or wore glasses or were fat. Perhaps he was getting what he deserved. He needed a new group, and he thought of Drew and his surfing friends. But to get in with them, he would need a surfboard and all the cool surf clothing they wore. Maybe if he got some money for Christmas, he would be able to buy some of it.

The stars began to fade in the darkness, to the point where he could no longer look directly at them; but the larger planets held the light. If only he could jump from his bed and onto one of those planets where people didn't torment each other. Could there be such a place?

Three

The old man's hands were unsteady and the rusty barrel of the rifle shook slightly. Sensing the soldier's fear, the animals snorted and stamped their hooves, moving around inside the barn. The old man gripped the rifle tighter and motioned with the barrel for the soldier to stand. He did so, slowly raising his hands in the air. The eyes of the old man focussed on the bloodied and bandaged right hand and the small specks of bugs crawling over it. He sniffed the air and grimaced.

"It happens in war," said the soldier, following the old man's gaze.

The elder offered a quick smile, his dried face crumpling into a mess of lines and furrows. The body looked firm, but the face was old. And despite the rifle, the soldier thought the grey eyes were friendly. The old man took a withered and gnarled finger from the rifle and pointed at his right leg, where he had a thick wooden stump like a pirate.

"Some lose much more than that," the soldier said, remembering the head rolling in front of him after the medical tent was bombed.

The old man nodded, his face softening a little, but he kept the rifle pointed at the soldier's chest. "Where's your unit?"

Their common language gave the soldier confidence. He turned slightly and pointed in the direction of the forest he had walked through yesterday. "Maybe ten kilometres from here, on the other side of a hill. There's a village nearby too."

The old man chewed on this, clearly knowing the lay of the land there.

"But don't worry," the soldier added. "They won't retreat or come here. Their orders are to hold their position to the last man."

Quite suddenly, the soldier burst into heavy sobs, thinking of the comrades he had fought beside and the fast friends he had made and so quickly lost. He pictured all those nameless faces frozen in pain on the battlefield, the men of the country he loved with all of his heart, despite everything. If he had any pride, he would turn around and go back to the front and die an honourable death with them. The trenches would become their mass grave and the enemy would march on to victory; not because of superior skill or weaponry, but from sheer weight of numbers. With the reinforcements he had seen yesterday, they would perhaps hold out for another six or eight weeks, depending on how quickly the supplies came in. And there was always the constant fear of encirclement and then being abandoned.

He threw open his greatcoat to reach inside one of his pockets. The old man cocked the rifle, stopping the soldier in mid-movement. The loud noise startled the animals, and one frightened and extremely thin pig squealed and scampered from the barn.

"No," the soldier said, frozen to the spot. "I have no gun."

"Can't be a soldier without a gun," the old man said.

The soldier's head went down. He sniffed loudly. "I've deserted. I can't face it any more. You've no idea what we've done."

The pig came back into the barn and stood next to the soldier like a loyal dog. It brushed its snout against his pants and squealed. The soldier smiled down at the pig and then pulled the leather bound book out of his jacket pocket.

"Here," he said, reaching it out to the old man, "take it. It'll give you some idea of what I mean. There are documents and photographs. You can shoot me, I don't want to live any more anyway, but please, take the book."

The old man looked at it warily, but would not take it. The leather was worn and faded, the buckle burned orange with rust. With a sigh, he un-cocked the rifle and lowered it.

"Maybe you should be the one who takes it back," he said. "They may not believe a simple farmer. They might think I made it all up."

"I'm trying to get home. The enemy's coming, and when they come, we'll all be slaughtered. My mother will know what to do."

The old man looked at the bandaged hand. "Are you badly hurt?"

"I lost some fingers in an explosion."

"Can you still work?"

The soldier fumbled the book back into his pocket and tried to stand up straight and look strong. He pulled back his round shoulders and wiped away his tears, leaving streaks of dirt on his face.

"I come from a farming village. My father's a doctor, but I often worked on the farms when I was a boy. I'm not sure what good I'll be with this hand though." He looked at it sadly, trying to move his missing fingers and wincing with pain as the exposed skin scraped against the rough bandage.

"Maybe you'd like to stay and work for a while, until your hand's better," the old man suggested.

"I'd like that. Thank you."

27

"You're safe here." The old man seemed glad to sling the rifle back over his shoulder. "Come to the house and we'll change the bandage, and try to get rid of the smell, otherwise Wilhelmina might fall in love with you, if she hasn't already."

The pig squealed at the sound of her name and made to follow the soldier. The old man walked out of the barn, his leg thumping against the wooden floorboards. The soldier followed behind, Wilhelmina at his side, and the other animals started to come too until a shouted order forced them all back inside. The old man closed the door and the soldier smiled as the pig whined from behind it.

The house was made of an assortment of large greyish-black, mismatched stones. The thatched roof was covered in places by broad sheets of iron and in other places by tree branches. A retired tractor, orange with rust and wheel-less, stood like an overgrown toy next to the house. It had been painted over in places and the soldier could just see under the paint the symbol of his nation. Vandals as well as murderers, he thought, and thieves. An old bicycle, with a special strap on the right pedal to accommodate a wooden leg, leaned against the wall. But with the decrepit condition of the house, the way it creaked and groaned, the soldier wondered that if he took away the bicycle, the whole house would coming crashing down, sighing with relief. The walls looked weary with effort from standing upright and holding up the roof. The old man wasn't embarrassed; if anything, the soldier noticed that the old man opened the door and led him into the house with pride.

It was cold and musty inside, the stale air continuously reheated and breathed, but never circulated. An old woman looked up in alarm as the soldier entered.

"It's all right," the old man said softly. "He's not dangerous and he's alone."

The dialect was not unfamiliar to the soldier and he understood most of it, its structure and sound similar to his own language. He stood tentatively in the doorway, feeling unwelcome and knowing his smell was rank.

She was a small woman who looked thickset, though that could simply have been the layers of clothing she wore. She was slightly stooped, a lifetime of hard work and hunching over the fire and stove giving her back a curve, but her face had a round prettiness, a shadow of which remained in old age. Once, the soldier thought, there was a

28

beautiful young girl who had married this farmer and built a life on the land. He wondered if the work had hardened her or if the war had. She had shiny brown eyes and they bore into him as she looked him up and down. She frowned, making her face lined and bumpy, like a shrivelled apple, and she wrinkled her small nose at the smell.

"At least he's not one of them devils in black." She turned to her husband. 'What does he want?'

The old man smiled in a slow, calm way. "He looks to have deserted," he explained. "He could stay here and help us until the war's over. They can't hold out much longer. It'll be over soon enough."

"You've been saying that for years. This stupid war will never end." She turned to the soldier. "Take your boots off, you monster."

The soldier stared down at the woman. He was almost two heads taller than she was, and he felt too big for the house, crowding the doorway like an unwanted giant. Despite his own overpowering stink, he could smell her hair, dry and sweet like old dust.

"My what?" the soldier asked.

"Your boots," the old man added. "No boots in the house."

The woman nodded, and to force her point, bent down to help the soldier out of his boots. He stepped back, wedging himself against the closed door and bumping his head against the doorway. The woman jumped back, scared and shocked. He looked sheepishly at the woman, trying to show with his eyes he was no danger, and then looked with embarrassment at the old man.

"I've got lice," he said. "And my feet are a mess."

"What does he say, what does he say? Why does this demon act like a scared rabbit and why won't he take his boots off?"

I'm not a demon, the soldier thought.

The old man turned to his wife. "He's just shy, that's all. Better boil some water. We need to clean him up a bit. You remember what a wreck I was when I came back from the front."

"And that war was just as pointless as this one," she said. And as she busied herself about the room, darting around like a mouse, she muttered to herself. "We're just farmers. Why does all this rubbish have to concern us?" She stoked the fire and put on big pots of water. "I haven't had a bath in weeks and this devil walks in and gets the royal treatment."

The old man smiled and led the soldier back outside into the brisk, bright morning.

"Don't mind her. She always gets excited when we have visitors." He held out a canvas bag. "You can put your things in here. We'll have to burn the uniform, the boots too, because of the lice."

"It's all right. I don't want to wear it anymore."

The soldier put his meagre possessions into the bag, the few things he had salvaged and stolen, the small treasures he had found on the battlefield and in the trenches of the enemy. The old man watched him, frowning at the collection of gold rings and raising his eyebrows at the leather book bound with the short belt.

"Come on, underclothes too. Don't worry. I've seen a lot worse than you in my time."

The soldier was astonished by the condition of his body and by the rank smell of his feet; he had deteriorated to the point of being a walking skeleton, dirty and bug-invested as if he had been buried alive. The dirt had made intricate patterns around his ankles and he had a nice collection of bright red blisters on his heels and toes. He stood naked on the frozen earth and the cold wind was sharp against his raw skin. Already he felt cleaner and healthier. But he couldn't prevent his cynical side from wondering why this old couple were so eager to help him and take him in. He decided to tread carefully and not say too much.

The old man gently took hold of the soldier's right arm. "This will be painful," he said, unwrapping the bandage, "but I need to see it."

"Don't cut it off, please."

"They should use you in the propaganda posters," the old man said. "People never understand the reality of war."

He threw the bandage to the ground and recoiled slightly when he saw the mess of the hand. It was dark, the blood having clotted with dirt, and the side was missing from the wrist to the middle finger. Pearl tips of bone stuck out of the side and one remaining ligament dangled pink and rubbery like a dead earthworm.

"Ah, it's not so bad. We'll sew it up and you'll milk the cows again one day." He thumped his wooden leg on the ground. "The body falls apart. The important thing is to keep your soul together."

The soldier smiled. "My name is, uh, Peter."

The old man chuckled. He pulled the bugs from Peter's body, dropping them inside one of the discarded boots.

"What?" Peter asked.

"'Do not repay evil with evil, insult with insult, but with blessing.' You should heed the words of your namesake."

"Who said that?"

"Saint Peter." The old man sighed. "Sorry. I forgot. They wanted to give you new gods, didn't they? Some years ago, when your countrymen first marched through here, one of the doctors had been a religious man. He told me about it. But he was disillusioned, because the party said one thing and did another. He came back here a few times. He wanted to become a priest."

"Are you a priest?"

The old man frowned and took up a rough horse brush. He began to scour Peter's skin, somewhat viciously, causing Peter to work hard to hold his footing. His skin quickly turned bright pink.

"I was," the old man said at last. "Before the Great War. But the things I saw then convinced me that there is no God, or that if there is, and this is worse, He is not concerned with the suffering of His people."

Grimacing against the brush, Peter said, "I think I understand. I've also seen terrible things."

The old man stopped brushing and looked at Peter, waiting for him to say more. When he didn't, the old man said, "But it was Peter who also said, 'Submit yourselves to every authority instituted among men, whether to king or governors who are sent to punish those who do wrong and commend those who do right.'"

"Sounds like what we learned."

"And not just you, but all nations throughout history. It's just a question of the interpretation of what's right and what's wrong. The Bible is full of this concept of subservience."

They lapsed into silence. Peter shivered from the cold and submitted himself to the hard brush. It tore at the places where his skin was raw and he gritted his teeth. When the brush came close to the scar on his stomach, he turned his body away. The old woman opened the door and shrieked with laughter.

"Water's ready," she managed to say between cackles. "You make quite a pair. Going dancing later?"

The soldier smiled.

"We'll be a minute," the old man said. "I just need to cut his hair first."

"Well make sure you give it a nice curl and a wave. We want him to look his best for the ball."

Still laughing, she turned and went back inside the house. Peter noted that she had a musical, sing-song laugh. He liked it, but he also heard sadness, a reluctance to enjoy herself, that the laughter could just as quickly turn to tears.

"She sometimes likes to play the clown," the old man said, going at Peter's head with a blunt pair of shears, the kind used for shearing sheep. He took great chunks of matted hair in his hands, almost yanking it from its roots. "She was on the stage when she was younger," he added, smiling at the memory. "Only locally. That was how we met. She was a beauty, but she had a flair for comedy. Do you like the theatre?"

Peter's face turned red as he remembered the shows he and Ernst had gone to during their year of university together, the vaudeville comedies and the almost naked women. Then they had both been drafted, and with that, their youth was over. Where was Ernst now, back in Hamburg? At university? Watching the strip shows with faraway eyes, his soul crushed and his spirit broken by battle?

"Opera's a bit lost on me," Peter said at last, "but I like comedies."

"There are operatic comedies," the old man said. "Mozart, for example, but I guess you were raised on Beethoven and Wagner."

Peter frowned. His father loved Wagner, but his mother hated it, all the death and destruction and supposedly heroic and honourable endings. "Music for the proletarian masses," she had called it.

The old man put down the shears. "You're reborn. Now it's time for your christening."

Inside, the water was lukewarm and stung his cold feet and legs. He was too big for the bathtub, but the old woman forced him into it, so that his knees were wedged under his chin. He felt like a big baby. She talked to him while she cleaned him, rubbing his skin with an old, dry bar of soap, talking in a reproachful yet motherly tone: warnings, advice, mistakes, the lessons learned. But he thought he heard spite in her voice as well; no doubt it was justified, and she sometimes cleaned him with such vigour that the bath shook from side to side, spilling the soupy water onto the floor. He wanted to understand her, to explain, but it would have to wait. Right now, it was just good to be clean and to not be at the front. He looked around the room and took in the sparse furnishings: the ragged wooden chairs, the rickety table, the torn curtains. It all meant poverty, but there was a warmth to the room, a quiet happiness and satisfaction, the comfort of old and familiar things, a place well lived in. And as he looked closer, he saw small things of

32

value: an antique vase and gold-framed photographs of the old woman on the stage decades ago. They must have hidden these things when the soldiers came, he thought. Unlike his own home, the ceiling was high, and it made the whole room bigger and more comfortable. He thought it would take quite an effort for his father to fill this space, but the old bastard would probably find a way.

The old man came in and pulled a chair up next to the bath. He smelled of smoke.

"Now, Peter," he said, "you're going to have to be really strong." He produced a long needle and a thick line of thread. He bent the needle into a U and held both ends over a candle. "Elsie is going to clean your hand with alcohol and then I'm going to sew it up. Do you want something to bite on?"

Peter shook his head. Wedged in the bath, at the mercy of these two generous old farmers, he was in no position to argue. He watched Elsie prepare a small bowl with the clear alcohol inside. It had the smell of vodka and he wondered where they had got it.

"I suggest you think of home," the old man advised. "Think of the people you haven't seen for such a long time. We used to do that. Close your eyes and try to picture what the people look like. Get the details, blue eyes, long hair, big breasts."

"Josef!" Elsie exclaimed, giving him a resounding slap on the shoulder.

The old man cowered, but in a joking way. "She understands some of your language, the important words obviously, but can't speak it so well."

"I'd expect this monster to have a foul mouth like the others did, but not you, Josef," Elsie said.

"Your name is Josef?" Peter asked.

He nodded.

"My father's name is Josef."

The old man looked up, seemingly unsure whether to comment on this coincidence.

"Think of him," he offered, breaking the silence, "of your home, and the way the land looks and the colour of your mother's hair."

Elsie took Peter's hand roughly and forced it into the alcohol. It stung like an ice burn, firing white icicles of pain down his arm that froze his whole body. He splashed the water in the bath trying to pull his injured hand away. But the old woman's grip was firm and she held his forearm with both her small hands, keeping it in the alcohol.

"Tell me about your home, Peter," Josef ordered. Elsie lifted the hand out of the alcohol and Josef threaded the needle through the skin. "What does your house look like?"

"Like any house," Peter said, grimacing. "Walls, roof, windows."

"And why do you miss it?"

Peter felt the thread slide through his skin, pulling it tight. But the pain wasn't nearly as bad as the alcohol dip. He looked away, unable to watch.

"I miss my bed," he said. "My soft, warm bed. It's been years since I slept in a real bed. And my mother is there."

"And what do you hate about it?"

Peter looked sharply at Josef, wondering how the old man could have guessed he had always hated that house. Was he still so bad at disguising his feelings?

"The low roof. My father always banged his head on the doorways and took it out on me or my mother. And when he was in the same room, it felt like the walls were closing in."

Josef pulled the thread tight and Peter felt the skin being drawn across the front and back of his hand, closing the gap.

"Were you happy to leave it?"

Peter didn't answer and simply stared at Josef, searching the old man's eyes and his expression for some deeper meaning. He saw pain there, something lost, words left unsaid. The old man stopped his needlework. Peter looked down and saw the bent and bloodied needle wedged into the side of his hand. Josef told Elsie to let go of Peter's forearm and Peter brought his hand close to his face and inspected it.

"He demanded perfection," he said at last, looking inside his hand, fascinated by the intricacies of its inner workings. "Always looked for mistakes. And he was hardly perfect himself."

"We none of us are," Josef said. "Fathers normally demand of their sons what they themselves lack."

Peter held out his arm and the needlework continued in silence. He occasionally winced with pain, but did his best to keep his hand steady. He thought of home, of how much he had wanted to get away and now how much he wanted to get back. Would there be anyone or anything left? Did they already consider him long dead? He was a deserter now, a traitor, and would not be well received. Perhaps it would be better if there was no one and his shame would belong only to him.

"There," Josef said, wiping his hands. "It's not perfect but it'll hold your soul inside."

Peter inspected the needlework and the shape of his new hand. The skin was drawn tight across the back of his hand and the remains of the palm, so that all the bones and ligaments underneath showed clearly. He could not move the hand without pulling the stitches and causing pain.

"We'll make you a splint so you don't move your hand," Josef said. "It will take a few weeks before we can remove the stitches. Are you by chance left-handed?"

Peter smiled and shook his head.

"Well, this will be an excellent chance for you to learn. Perhaps it will encourage your brain to unlearn all that nonsense they taught you."

Elsie hauled Peter from the cold bath and started roughly towelling him down. She seemed unperturbed by his nakedness and he was too tired and hungry to be embarrassed. Josef left the room and came back with some clothes. Elsie frowned when she saw them and started cleaning up the floor that was wet with water and blood.

"Our son was about the same size as you," Josef said, holding out the clothes. "I think the shoes might be a bit too small, though."

"What about my boots?"

"I'm sorry. I had to burn everything." Josef offered him a coy smile. "Besides, it might look unusual for a refugee to be walking around in army issued boots, don't you think?"

Peter nodded and dressed himself. The clothes were musty from having been packed away and the material was coarse, itching at his now clean skin. As he adapted to this new outfit, he thought about the previous wearer; he guessed he had died defending his country against Peter's comrades when they had first swept across the land.

Seeming to read Peter's thoughts, Josef said, "It's okay. We don't blame you or anyone else from your country. Elsie might think differently, but she doesn't know war like I do. Wars are fought by strangers who are forced to kill and die for the prejudices and grudges of their leaders. Perhaps in different times, the two of you would've been great friends."

"I'm sorry," Peter offered. "I never thought it would be how it was. You have to understand. I'm not a killer."

"And neither was he, but you both got caught in the middle of it. I comfort myself with the idea that it might be better to die in a battle than to live a lifetime with the memories of war."

Peter nodded. "Thank you, Josef, for everything." He reached into the canvas bag that held his possessions and offered Josef a few of the rings he had stolen. Josef held up his hands.

"You may need those on your journey home."

"You could come with me. Life will be terrible when the enemy comes. If they don't kill you, they'll take everything away."

Josef smiled. "They drummed that into you to make you fight without mercy, to stop you from retreating. Your enemy is your enemy, not mine. They have no argument with me."

"They'll take your farm."

"That is the way of their system," Josef admitted. "But we're old and we can't do the work here anyway. This war has taken a lot from us, and if the farm goes too, then so be it."

Peter sighed, disappointed with the old man's willingness to accept his fate, but greatly touched by the charity he had shown him despite their respective roles in the war. "I'd like to stay here and work, for as long as my army holds the line and as long as I'm welcome. But if the enemy breaks through, I'll have to leave."

Josef nodded, accepting this agreement. "I suggest you burn all your papers and identification, and claim you're a wandering refugee. There seems to be plenty of them moving about at the moment."

Peter went to the kitchen fire and threw his papers on it one by one. He thought about burning the diary as well, but decided to keep it.

"I thought you folks liked burning books?" Josef said.

With his head down, Peter said, "I never supported any of that."

Peter put the book into his canvas bag and then looked up defiantly at Josef, waiting to be handed the responsibility for the actions of his nation. He wondered if it would be like this for the rest of his life, with him the token devil everyone could heap blame on.

Josef offered a thin-lipped and cunning smile. "Hide it well then," he said, giving the book a final glance.

***

They started out together at dusk. Peter thought the going would be slow, what with the old man's stump, but Josef was surprisingly nimble and it was Peter who struggled to keep up. They walked in silence until they were deep in the forest, the skeletal trees shrouding them in an embrace of a thousand bony arms. Josef knew a quick way through and they soon found themselves looking at the hill Peter had climbed two days earlier. Was it really just two days ago? he wondered.

The hill was steeper than he remembered, rockier too, with many small rocks hidden under bushes. Peter tripped several times and when he fell, he tried not to break his fall with his injured right hand. Josef stayed close by, always ready to help Peter back up, and seemed to quietly enjoy his physical dominance.

At the top of the hill, they crouched behind some rocks and looked down on the scorched plain. The front line was easily discerned by the smoke rising from assorted fires. In the waning light, Peter could just make out slithers of smoke coming from the enemy's line far in the distance. Nothing had changed. He smiled to himself, quietly proud of his comrades. No wonder my small nation nearly conquered the world, he thought. We're strong and determined; it's the elements and the ambition of our leader that have defeated us, not the enemy.

"Doesn't look like much of a line," Josef said. He had an old pair of scratched field glasses and focused them on the collection of vehicles, motorbikes and tents gathered behind the line. "They're not even bothering to bury their dead."

They were numerous grey lumps scattered between the base of the hill and the front line. Peter was surprised to see just how far he had run in the darkness, more surprised still that he hadn't been shot from behind like the others. Their corpses lay in twisted heaps, with crows dancing on and around them, cawing, feasting, celebrating.

"They can't bury them because that's when the snipers shoot," Peter said. He could see Josef frowning in the darkness.

"Wasn't like that in my day. We stopped fighting to bury our dead, often helped the enemy with theirs too. I guess that was the last noble and honourable war."

"The snipers shoot even when we try to use the latrine. They're cold-blooded and merciless."

"And you're not?"

"We don't shoot people when they're taking a shit," Peter said, offended.

"No, just take them from their homes and send them some place where it can be done more efficiently."

Peter looked down at the ground. He swallowed hard, recalling his early years in the war. "You know about that?"

"Only rumours, and from what the doctor told me." He turned to Peter and his eyes were shiny white in the darkness. "Are they true?"

Peter shook his head, not wanting to believe them himself. "Take those rumours and multiply them by a hundred. It's much worse than people know, so bad people may not believe it unless they see it for themselves."

Josef changed the subject. "How many men are down there?"

Peter shrugged, recalling the solemn march he had seen yesterday. "More just arrived, but it's hard to say how many. I saw about a thousand marching to the front yesterday."

"Just more to bury."

"They may be tired and defeated but they're resilient," Peter said without thinking. "They'll hold to the last man and the last bullet."

Already the words sounded foreign. It was the kind of talk the officers loved, and the soldiers played their roles in the hope of preferential treatment, but it was boardroom talk; tubby generals in tight fitting uniforms dealing in numbers and square kilometres and not in harsh realities, leaving encircled armies for dead and others like this one, forced to die slowly holding a meagre piece of land nobody wanted.

"Splendid," Josef said. "I'm sure their fathers will be proud." The old man sighed and shook his withered and wrinkled head. The conversation seemed to age him, and Peter wondered if seeing the battlefield brought back a lot of horrific memories.

"Such senseless waste," Josef continued. "I tell you, the human race will never change, not even after the horrors of this war are discovered. They'll still find reasons to march their sons off to die. The Bible's full of it. There's bloodshed on every page, and this is what our religion is based on."

The battlefield was quiet, one of the many lulls in which both sides waited for supplies and equipment, or waited for the other to move first. Peter guessed the enemy, with plenty of time on its hands and millions of soldiers, was building up reserves for one final all out attack. They would send wave after wave of soldiers until his comrades had no more bullets to fire. Similar stalemates were taking place at all the front lines. His comrades had taken their oath and planned to uphold it. He had already broken his and he knew his father would never forgive him for it. Perhaps it was better just to stay on the farm with Josef and Elsie, pretend to be a local, maybe even their son, and blend in when the enemy came.

Suddenly, Josef stood up and started clambering back down the hill. Peter took a last look at the battlefield and followed, stumbling in the darkness.

When they were back in the forest, picking their way between the leafless trees, Josef asked, "You got a girl, Peter?"

"Yeah. But I haven't seen her for a while. She's a nurse."

"Where is she now?"

"Last I heard she was in Paris, but that was a few years ago. We planned to get married after the war. But we didn't think it would last this long."

"Your arrogance is your people's greatest weakness, always has been. You always underestimate your opponents."

"I wonder if it isn't that we overestimate ourselves."

Josef stopped and turned to Peter. "Think you'll see her again?"

"I'm a deserter, a traitor. She won't have anything to do with me. Nobody will, and they won't understand what I've been through. I've changed too much."

"War does that to you. Kind of takes the warmth out of your chest, leaves you cold inside."

The small shoes hurt Peter's feet, but he didn't complain. Josef talked about the forest, about how it had been before the war. There had been deer and hare, he said, and lots of birds. He didn't know where they had gone but was convinced they would come back once the fighting was over.

"Nature suffers almost as much as people in war," he said.

Peter thought of all the tarnished and destroyed fields and plains he had seen, those stale patches of land where it looked like nothing would ever grow again. The lifeless and raped plains, the promised living space they had headed east to fight for.

They were soon back at the house where Elsie had a hot soup on the fire. It was tasty, but looked a little too much like the bath water from the morning. Peter was too hungry to care. That night he went to bed early and slept a dreamless twelve hours.

***

Peter soon fell into the routine of the farm, though his injured hand hindered his work and his ambition; he wanted to earn his keep and prove to the two farmers what a hard worker he was. Every second day, late in the afternoon, he walked with Josef through the forest to the top of the hill to check the battle positions. Nothing changed, but they both noticed that no more reinforcements had arrived. The number of men was slowly dwindling and those who lived maintained the vigil.

When soldiers came to the farm, Peter hid in the cellar. He fumed when he heard Josef or Elsie being abused or beaten and it was difficult not to want to rush out and protect them. But that would risk exposure and then they would all be killed. One day, Wilhelmina, the thin sow who followed Peter around like a dog, was taken at gunpoint. Her squeals of protest brought tears to his eyes. He nursed the two farmers after these visits, and they held no grudge against him.

The weeks passed. The winter was cold and bitter, but Elsie kept the house warm and they had enough to eat. Peter, never wanting to touch a gun again, devised a primitive bow and arrow and went hunting in the forest. It reminded him of his youth, when he had hunted rabbits and deer, hoping to please his mother with a prized score only to have his father find some fault with it; the deer would be too thin or the rabbit diseased and mangy.

With the cleverly crafted arrows that he shaped with gentle care during their quiet evenings together, Peter managed one day to bring down a large deer he had found on the other side of the forest. He knew the land well now and had filled in most of the burrows, marking each one with a small cross. The deer kept them in meat for a week. Elsie tailored a pair of gloves from the pelt that perfectly fitted Peter's mangled hand and made a matching hat in the local style.

"She'll be teaching you the dialect next," Josef remarked.

Peter smiled and tried to speak the dialect: "I picked up some already."

Elsie laughed at his attempt. They were happy times and Peter felt himself smiling again. Except for the treks to the hill, he almost forgot about the war that was raging all over the continent.

That was until his last walk up the hill when he saw the smouldering ruins of the trenches, the burning wrecks of vehicles and the enemy marching forward in the distance.

Four

The images floated around him, the frilly lace brushing his skin, the shapely forms always drawing near then drifting away before any physical contact. There was music playing, muffled like it was being played on the other side of a closed door. He picked up the rhythm of the bass and drums, tapping his feet, nodding his head. There was something carnal about the music, the rhythm of porn. It was a party, in a house that looked familiar yet he couldn't place. There were lots of girls: famous actresses he recognised, girls from his old school and girls he had only seen in his classes or sashaying down the long walkway of the new school. They were all scantily dressed and drifted past him like wafts of perfume, parading, winking, licking their lips. It was just a question of which one to choose.

The music stopped. From outside the house came the calling of a woman, the voice getting louder with each call. The girls all looked at him, disappointed and somewhat embarrassed, hastily covering their nakedness.

"Time for school, Ricky," said his mother. "Your father's got a meeting in Perth and he can drop you off on the way. But you better hurry."

Eric opened his eyes to see his mother draped in the mess of orange that was her breakfast apron. She threw the bedclothes from him, forcing him onto his side to hide his morning manhood; it had plagued him all year and he wondered if men suffered from it their whole lives. Though too embarrassed to ask his father, he was, however, quietly proud. What had been barely bigger than a thimble was suddenly in competition with the length of his forearm. He hustled quickly to the bathroom after his mother had left and concentrated fiercely on brushing his teeth. His member finally retreated.

In the garage, his father waited in the big Ford, drumming the steering wheel with his fingers. The engine whined loudly. His father kept the air conditioner going permanently, as if the cold air reminded him of his progression up the real estate ladder. Like the lifeless house, the new car had come with the job.

"Eric, I've told you a thousand times. Put your bag on the floor, not on the back seat. Otherwise, it'll be you cleaning the car on Sunday, not me."

Eric lowered his head and did as he was told. Another empty threat; he had never washed a car in his life. His father controlled the cars. Eric's mother was never allowed to drive them, and any talk of a second car had always led to a heated argument with his father storming out of the house. He also cleaned the car himself, lovingly, as if this pile of polluting metal was a prized horse. Eric felt like asking if he should sit on the back seat as well, perhaps in a plastic bag so he wouldn't make any mess, nor breathe on the windows and make them misty, but did not want to encourage him. His father had a way of talking that sounded jovial, but had just enough spite under the surface to rankle.

Eric heard it again: "Hurry up or you'll be late."

It was a warm morning, with the December sun high and bright. The glare reflected off windows and pavements damp from excessive watering, making Eric squint no matter which direction he looked. But the car was like an icebox. He toyed with the electric window switch, hoping to sneak the window open a few inches and let in a blast of warm air, but feared his father's wrath.

"How's the new school?" his father asked. He seemed to drive precariously close to the curb, so that every few seconds there would be a loud thump as he hit one of the metal grated drains. When Eric closed his eyes, he likened it to the rhythm of a train.

They passed through one of the gates and out of Crescent Bay. His father gave the guard a familiar wave.

"All right," Eric murmured at last. As he waited for the next question in the ensuing silence, he wondered which was worse: being tormented on the school bus or having to answer his father's annoying and pointless questions in the freezing car. He smiled to himself, unable to decide.

"Have they got a cricket team?" his father asked, clearly uneasy with the silence. He had his left hand positioned close to the radio, ready to switch it on if Eric chose not to answer.

"I guess."

Eric turned and looked out the window at his new town, waking up for another workday. There was a lot of cleaning going on, with the salt and sand being washed away from store front windows and outdoor café tables. Suited men were rushing to work holding shiny briefcases and sipping coffee from small paper cups. A dry easterly wind was blowing, ruffling their suit coats and blowing the odd piece of litter against their pants. Eric promised himself he would never wear a suit, no matter what job he had. His father, and all these other suited men, looked like robots churned out of an office employee factory: black pants, matching coats, white shirts, white undershirts, perhaps a novelty tie to make them seem like humorous types. Millions of suited automatons completely interchangeable. Eric would rather become a baker with flour in his hair.

The usual morning reports about the crisis in the Middle East came over the radio. His father made it louder, feigning interest. Again there was talk of war. Eric listened to the reports, but looked out the window at the fresh morning, avoiding eye contact with his father and praying the old man wouldn't ask any more of his stupid questions. The reporter prattled on about Saddam Hussein and his evil regime, and about some place called Kuwait. Eric wondered who this guy Hussein was and what he had done. Already there was talk of Australian soldiers being sent to the Gulf. He didn't understand why. What reason did his country have to fight an obscure enemy nobody knew about in a country which posed no threat whatsoever to Australia? His mother had rather scathingly said at the beginning of the crisis that since the fall of communism, the Americans had been left without an enemy. They no longer had a cause to fight for which would prove their superiority, reinforce their place as rulers of the world and show just how fervently they fought for democracy and, she laughed, peace. But for Eric, it was a complicated answer, and in the end, it was easier just to think about cricket and girls than to know who Hussein was and why Iraq had to be attacked. Or was it that Kuwait had to be defended? He couldn't remember, but oil was always mentioned.

"Can you walk from here, sport?" his father asked as he pulled off the main road, just before the turn-off to the school. "Your dad's running a bit late."

Eric nodded. There it was again. The masked joviality. Just enough of a dig to make him feel responsible for making his father late: the lilting voice and suppressed anger, the way he said it so off-hand and carelessly, but the menace was there, lurking just below the surface, desperate to blame. Eric closed the door gently but didn't wave as the car took off with a spray of gravel. He turned and walked toward the school, and smiled as the car made a loud thump when it hit the first drain.

"Idiot," he said.

It was twenty minutes before classes began and Eric, not knowing how to kill the time, walked as slowly as he could towards the school. But once there, he didn't know where to walk or look. He saw some of Drew's friends lounging on the steps near the gym, their brown faces pointed to the sun; one or two still had wet hair from a morning surf. There were girls too, and Eric picked out the long flowing blond hair of Pepper, the girl who sat next to Drew's girlfriend in maths. Through the branches of a wilting tree, he watched her talk animatedly with the other girls until one of them tapped her on the shoulder and pointed in his direction. They all turned to look and he heard their laughter as he ran for the safety of the library.

Despite his lack of interest in books, the library had been his sanctuary during the terminal morning and lunch breaks, when he had no group to sit with, no friends to feel secure with. The library was small and sparsely populated with boys, bookish and academic and also alone, who sometimes asked Eric to play chess or Scrabble. Sensing their unpopularity and thinking they might infect him with it and make his situation worse, he turned them down. They soon stopped asking and he became just another unpopular library nomad.

It was the second last day of school and few students had bothered to bring their books and files, let alone pens and paper. In maths, they played board games, with Eric sneaking glances at Pepper as she rolled the dice. He thought she had the most beautiful neck he had ever seen, long, thin and delicate, and her head seem to balance on it weightlessly. She was a pretty girl, even though her face was rather elongated, and she had bright blue eyes. When she flicked back her hair, which she rarely did, he was surprised to see that she had rather large and unattractive ears which were pink and peeling from too much sun. But her hair covered them most of the time and when he couldn't see them, he forgot about them. The school had prettier girls, but there was something intangible about Pepper, something beyond skin, muscle and bone, and it made him stare at her for long periods, searching her face, trying to figure out what it was.

In biology, they watched a boring nature video, while in woodwork they made pathetic Christmas tree decorations worthy of unloved and seldom seen aunts and uncles. After lunch, Eric enjoyed showing off his sporting abilities during a softball game, forcing the rest of his team to take an interest in him, but made more enemies on the opposition team, which included some of Josh's group. Eric took some quiet satisfaction from catching their hits and throwing them out, though no doubt it would fuel their chase after school. Who cared? Pepper was on his team and impressing her was more important and worth a few extra punches. He hit several home runs and caught a few hard to reach balls. He wanted to talk to her, but she always seemed to have friends around her and he was afraid what they would say. At one point, while fielding, they ran together to retrieve the ball, almost colliding. Eric got there first and fired a throw that caught the runner out.

"Nice throw," she said.

Eric felt the blood pumping to his face and groin. He somehow managed to say "Thanks" and then ran self-consciously back to right field, feeling her eyes on his back.

In history, that last class that never seemed to end, they watched another graphic documentary about the Second World War. There were lots of shrivelled old men with floppy faces talking about battles and the friends they had lost. The film ended with a summary of fallen soldiers for each country. For the Soviet Union and Germany, the numbers were in the millions. Europe must be one big cemetery, Eric thought.

Throughout the class, Josh passed him notes hinting at what fun they would have together after school. With the class over, Eric again lingered behind with the withered historian. He was sure this time the bikers would cut him off from both sides of the walkway. There would be no escape, no chase, and they would escort him away to some quiet place where they could slowly beat him to death. He needed a miracle, and tried to delay the inevitable in the hope his saviour might surface.

"Come on, young lad," the teacher said with a haggard just-one-day-left look on her face. "You don't want to miss the bus."

Eric stood up slowly, racking his brain for a relevant history question. "Do you think there'll be war in Iraq?"

The teacher scoffed and looked at her watch. Eric was stunned to see that it was a Disney watch, which had a bright red band, a round face and Mickey Mouse's gloved hands pointing out the time.

"The Iraqis are hardly a match for the Americans," she said.

Eric considered this, furrowing his forehead thoughtfully, acting it up a bit, hoping to prolong the conversation. Through the open door, he heard the echoed shouts of joyous teenagers.

"Will Australia fight? Does Iraq want to invade us?"

45

The teacher cackled, the laughter straining in her throat, getting stuck, and making Eric think of a rooster slowly being strangled at dawn; dying, but still committed to calling out the start of the day.

"It's rather more complicated than that," she said, composing herself. "Let's just say that we stand for freedom and peace."

She pulled taut her cardigan – grey today – flattening it against her chest. Eric looked closely. There were breasts under there, he thought, but only just. They could simply be two misplaced marbles, but Eric was not going to go searching for them to prove it.

"But if we stand for peace, why do we fight?"

She sighed heavily and her already stony face turned hard, becoming another shade of grey as if a film of dust had settled on it.

"Sometimes," she began, talking through gritted teeth, "peace needs to be defended. When you're older you'll understand Australia needs allies, that we will always help America and England in order to build alliances and protect ourselves."

Eric nodded, pretending to understand. To emphasise her point, the teacher took off her glasses and let them hang from the red chain against her chest.

"Australia has fought in every war this century," she said, not without spite. "I presume this time will be no different."

Her bottom lip quivered and she lowered her head. A bony arm draped in mottled wool pointed to the door and Eric walked out. Dressed in baggy boardshorts and a muscle shirt, and with the weak sea breeze ruffling his scraggly blond hair, Drew was waiting for him. Behind him stood Pepper and Drew's girlfriend, engrossed in a secret conversation. Eric looked past them and saw Josh and his group waiting in front of a water fountain a few metres away. Eric tried to look cool, but smiled eagerly at Drew. Was this going to be his miracle?

"Hey. Pepper says you're quite a softball star," Drew said in that slow, loping way of his.

Eric blushed, and Pepper talked behind her hand to Melanie; they giggled.

"Just lucky, I guess," he said.

"Can you play cricket?"

"Of course."

"We gotta game on Saturday, but some of the guys are already on holidays. Can you help us out?"

The bikers started to edge closer, but seemed reluctant with Drew standing there. He was captain of the lower school cricket team, popular, untouchable, his group powerful.

"Absolutely," Eric exclaimed, his voice croaking and breaking.

"Cool. I'll pick you up on Saturday morning. Me mum's the scorer and she'll drive us." Drew smiled. "By the way, we wear pants, not shorts. I don't know what you guys wear in the country." Drew chuckled and added, "Better wear shoes too."

"I got all my own gear," Eric said, "including shoes. I was one of the lucky ones."

Drew smiled and held out his hand. "Bag?"

"Thanks," Eric said, handing it over. It was a nice gesture, but he would have preferred an escort.

Josh and his friends closed in. Eric saw Josh tap Pepper on the shoulder, but Melanie's barked "Go away!" made him take a few steps back. The bikers laughed at him.

Pepper gave Eric a shy smile and the three walked away, blocking the bikers and giving Eric enough time to leap over a nearby wall and start his escape. He thought about running for the demountables again, but felt they would be wise to that plan. Instead, he ran across the dried grass towards the forest trail he had run through yesterday. Drew's delay had given him enough of a break that he reached the trail with the bikers far behind. He smiled at the success of his getaway, and he thought of Pepper and her slender neck and how much he wanted to kiss it. His rising energy spurred him on and he ran faster, past the deserted buildings where the cool kids smoked during lunch and towards the low houses of the suburbs. He rounded a sharp corner and was tripped by an outstretched leg. He fell hard to the ground, scraping his knees and elbows. Two fat boys stood over him, laughing. One of them kicked him hard in the stomach and they laughed harder, teasing him for being a wimp, a cry-baby, a fag.

Josh and the rest of the group came around the corner. They all cheered when they saw Eric curled up on the ground clutching his stomach.

"Pick him up," one of them said.

The two fat boys hauled Eric to his feet. They held him firmly to the spot and the group made a tight circle around him. Josh stepped into the circle and the rest of the boys shouted "Fight, fight, fight." Their eyes met, and Eric was surprised to see Josh's betrayed a hint of fear.

Up close, he was swarthy, with a baby face that had the dirty strands of an unshaven moustache under his nose. He had an immense amount of thick, dark brown hair, the fringe of which hung past his eyes, making him always flick it to the side. He was about the same height as Eric, but thicker set and more muscular. He wore the same denim outfit – tight black jeans, a black shirt and a black denim jacket – but didn't seem to wear it as comfortably as the others. Eric decided that he was Josh's offering, the test that would bring him into the group. Josh certainly wasn't the leader.

"Hit him, Josh," the boys called out.

Two boys grabbed Eric from behind and Josh hit him in the face and stomach. But the blows didn't hurt as much as the humiliation; how weak and helpless he felt with his arms pinned, outnumbered and unable to defend himself. His cowardice would be the talk of the playground tomorrow. He wanted to fight Josh on his own, but he already understood that life often doesn't work out that way.

With the beating over, the boys let go of him and he slumped to the ground.

"That's enough for today," Josh said loudly, standing over the crumpled mess of Eric and breathing hard. He turned to the others. "Search his pockets."

Two boys rummaged through Eric's pockets, but stood up shaking their heads. One of the group, a small, mean-looking kid, edged forward. Eric had seen him earlier, lurking behind the group, with only a passing interest in the beating. After only a week at the school, Eric already knew him to have a notorious reputation for getting into trouble with teachers.

"Now," he said, blowing out cigarette smoke, "if you had some money maybe we would've left you alone. But you'll keep seeing us until you've got something to give us."

"I don't get pocket money," Eric said, his voice far too high-pitched and girlish for his liking.

The boys laughed, pointing at Eric, having a great afternoon.

"Sure you don't," the small boy said. "But that's your problem."

He started to move away and the boys followed.

"And stay away from my girlfriend," Josh added, trying to sound tough.

The boys patted Josh on the back and crowed about their success. Eric saw Josh turn around once; he looked almost apologetic. With the group gone, it was suddenly very quiet. Eric wiped the blood on his shirt and tried to stop himself from crying. It must have been the stifled sniffles that the phys ed teacher heard as he ran past.

"Are you all right?" he asked.

Eric quickly wiped away his tears and nodded. He struggled to his feet and brushed himself down.

"I'm fine, thanks," he said and started to walk away. But the phys ed teacher placed a firm hand on his shoulder, stopping him in his tracks.

"Who did this?"

When Eric just stared blankly at the ground, the teacher's attitude changed abruptly. He grabbed Eric's arm and dragged him back towards the school. All the way to admin the teacher asked questions to which Eric gave no reply, which was sure to make his situation worse. The nurse cleaned him up while the phys ed teacher spoke with the deputy principal. Ten minutes later, Eric was led into her office.

It was a big room, perhaps it had once been a classroom, and it had a wall full of windows which daydreaming kids had probably once stared out of, imagining a more exciting world outside. Chairs were lined up along one wall where children could wait for the deputy, and as Eric closed the door, he saw a thin bamboo cane leaning against the wall in the corner. He had got the cane once in primary school for throwing rocks at girls. He had been innocent, but receiving the cane had made him so popular, so admired and feared, that he had decided to withhold the truth.

There was a big desk of heavy, dark wood with a woman commanding it. She stood up to greet him, rather formally Eric thought, as she extended her big hand to shake his. She was a stout woman, yet tall, and her dress accentuated her squareness. She wore a stiffly ironed number with shoulders heavily padded that made her look like an American Football player. You could easily draw straight lines from her shoulders down her sides and, with the right formula, calculate her surface area in square centimetres to the decimal. In her physical appearance, there was little shape or curve recognisable as womanly, and she even talked like a man, barking out her words gruffly, with short, sharp intonation. She had a large face, heavily made up. Her big mouth, painted ruby red, which also streaked her front teeth, moved quickly between smiles and frowns, friendliness and hate, and encouragement and scorn as she decided what to do with him. On her desk, Eric saw a photograph of two young children standing next to an elaborate sandcastle, and he wondered if she was their mother, if at night she told them stories as she tucked them in with care and love. Or did she simply cry "lights out" in a military manner and flick the switch? Suddenly, he had great sympathy for the two kids in the picture.

She repeated the same line of questioning – straight from the teacher's interrogation manual, volume one – as the phys ed teacher, and Eric gave her the same lack of response, though he did shrug his shoulders slightly to show he didn't know who the culprit was. She stared at him, trying to read his thoughts, and then her face softened and sagged, like letting the air slowly out of a balloon, and she looked quite motherly and friendly.

"You're new here," she said softly, leaning back in her chair. The leather squeaked and she folded her meaty arms. Her tone was friendly, but she smiled with thin lips and narrow eyes. "And you need to understand that things are different at this school. Students aren't afraid to be honest, to make the school safer for everyone. So, I ask you again, who did this? Don't worry. They won't know it was you who gave me the information."

Eric looked around the room, weighing up his choice. On the walls were pennants from successful school sports teams and framed photographs of teachers and classes. There was a large photograph of the deputy, half moon glasses perched on her nose, standing at a podium and giving some kind of speech, perhaps accepting the award for Australia's most evil woman.

Of course they would know it was him, and that was a reputation he did not want.

"I didn't see who it was," he mumbled. "I tripped and fell and blacked out. I only came to when Mr Tyson found me."

She tilted her head to one side, unconvinced. "I hope they didn't have good reasons to come after you," she said with a trace of sarcasm. But then she turned serious. "There is no bullying or fighting in this school and I don't want rough country boys changing that. Is that clear?"

Eric lowered his head and nodded, marvelling once again at how oblivious teachers and principals were to the realities of the schoolyard.

"Let this be your first and only warning," she added. "You can call your parents at the reception."

She offered him a friendly, conspiratorial smile, an expression that said, "stick with me and you'll be fine." Eric wanted none of it. He stood up and left the office.

His mother had no car and his father was sure to be late home, as he always was after meetings in Perth. He had no choice but to start the long trek back to Crescent Bay. It took over an hour and he dawdled, following first the estuary and then walking along the beach. The sea breeze was blustering from the south-west and the beaches were deserted save for people walking their dogs. At the beach closest to his house, he tore off the bandages and plunged into the water. He had thought he might find Drew there. He wanted to ask him if Pepper really was Josh's girlfriend. But Eric swam alone, fighting hard against the current. The salt stung his cuts, but it felt good in a way, cleansing and refreshing. He stayed in the water until he no longer had the strength to fight the current and slowly walked home as the sun was setting.

***

"I fell on the concrete when we were playing cricket after school," he explained. His mother eyed him suspiciously. The scraped knees and elbows suggested a fall, but he knew his black eye and bruised chin would make her think he had been in a fight. And the deputy had probably called too.

"Drew said you're going to play cricket with him on Saturday," she said. "Maybe you should play with him after school and not with these other friends."

Eric looked up at her and knew that she knew. "Don't tell dad," he said. She nodded, and he hoped this time she would keep her word.

Five

The unseasonably warm rain made the ground soft. The tight shoes rubbed against his heels and burned the corn on his little right toe. But he ignored the pain and ran hard through the forest, leaping over fallen logs and dodging the crosses he had left by the burrowed graves. He sweated and his breath came in short, uneven gasps; in the grip of his fear, he fell a few times, dirtying his pants and hurting his hand.

As he neared the farm, the familiar smell of burnt dung broadened his nostrils. Through the trees, a plume of yellow smoke rose from the chimney of the farmhouse. Already he missed it. It will all be taken away, he thought, and he wondered if he would ever have a chance at happiness again, or would some higher power always intervene and prevent it, forever vengeful, intent on making him suffer.

If not for the smoke, the farm appeared deserted, which was how Josef liked to keep it. The animals stayed in the barn and Elsie almost never left the house. When Peter burst through the door, the two farmers looked up at him. He kicked off his shoes and wiggled his toes, sighing with relief.

"You're back early," Josef said. He was suffering from a bout of bronchitis and was lying on the sofa. He had explained to Peter some days earlier that every winter he suffered from severe coughing; he had been gassed during the Great War and his lungs had never fully recovered. He put down the leather bound diary and looked at Peter.

"They're coming," Peter said, breathing in short, heavy rasps. He moved quickly through the room, gathering up his things, throwing them hastily into his small canvas bag. Elsie and Josef watched him with unblinking eyes. Then Josef sighed and took up the diary to continue reading.

"Let them come," he said defiantly.

Elsie jumped up and clapped her hands loudly, theatrically. "If they're here, that means the war is over."

"I hope so," Josef said from behind the book. "But it probably just means that this line of defence has fallen. And if that's the case, then the war is far from over."

Peter threw his bag to the floor. "It doesn't matter if it's over or not. They're coming and we have to go."

Josef put down the book. "You are free to run, but that only delays the inevitable. Stay here and face them. We'll protect you."

Peter scoffed, frustrated that the old farmers didn't understand the world outside their fence line. He stalked around the room, blowing out air, disappointed, afraid for himself. They would protect him? he thought. An old woman no bigger than a mouse and a one-legged man dying from bronchitis. Perhaps it's better they stay; they would slow me down otherwise.

"They'll take your farm," he said. He pulled on his coat, eager to get started. "Your land and your freedom. Elsie will be raped and you'll probably be killed for harbouring me. I've got to go, for no reason than to save you."

Josef got up from the sofa. He coughed loudly. "You people always twist the truth to make it suit you, make cowardly retreats sound noble and brave. You don't need to save us. We don't fear what you have been taught to fear."

"Damn it, Josef," Peter shouted. But his rage quickly turned to sorrow, and he tried to suppress his sobs, swallowing them down. The old man was right. It was learned fear. But still, in deciding to stay at the farm, Josef was disappointing him. Peter had assumed all along that, when the time came, the two farmers would go with him.

"Josef, please. You've both given me so much. Let me help you." He turned to Elsie when Josef went to the window. Peter wondered if the old man expected to see the victors marching towards the farmhouse. "You can't stay," Peter said to her. "They'll take everything away from you. They'll ship you out to labour camps. I know. I've seen such places."

"Peter," she said, "this is not our war. We survived your lot and we'll survive the next, and the next after that. The victors change, but we still have to plough our fields."

"This is everyone's war. And the enemy will bring it to your doorstep."

"It was you who brought the war to us. You made our son go off and fight." Her head fell into her hands and her shoulders bounced with sobs. There was a muffled wail from behind her hands and she started to run for the kitchen, but Peter caught her. He pulled her wet hands from her withered, cracked face and embraced her. She seemed so small and frail wrapped in his long arms, that if he pressed too hard, she might crumble to the floor, a mess of brittle bones and wrinkled skin.

"I'm sorry, but I've got to get home and tell them the truth."

"You'll be needing this," Josef said, handing Peter the book. "Get this home and keep it locked away until the time is right."

The old man opened his arms and embraced Peter, but had to withdraw quickly to cover his coughing.

"I don't want to go," Peter said. "But I can't stay here."

"Be careful," Josef said. "From what I read in that book of yours, your army doesn't think highly of people like you."

"I'm not the only deserter. And when the fighting's over, the whole army will desert. They would have sooner if not for their oath. Only the true zealots will keep fighting and there aren't many of them left."

Josef nodded, coughing, trying to keep himself from doubling over.

"Now you get yourself back into bed, Jo," Elsie said. "Let the boy go. His life is ahead of him and ours is behind us."

Josef smiled at Peter and shuffled back to the sofa. "You heard the woman."

Elsie put a bag of food together while Peter scrawled down a map, with Josef detailing the best route to take. Peter wrote unsteadily with his left hand; he wondered if it would take a lifetime to perfect it. When he was ready to go, he wrote down an address.

"This person will know where I am," he said. "Write to me. Let me know if you're in danger and I'll do what I can to help."

He picked up his bag and headed for the door. He squeezed his feet into the tight shoes, intimidated by the long journey that lay ahead.

"Don't forget us," Elsie said. "Memories are important, good and bad."

Peter nodded.

Josef raised a hand from the sofa. "If there is a God, may he go with you."

***

The carts were close to bursting, their contents roped down and swaying from side to side: suitcases, trunks, furniture, photo albums, shoes, books, anything that could be carried. Old women sat on the backs of the carts as the men and children pushed and pulled them along. They were a ragged lot, with dirty, hollow faces that had the green tinge of the malnourished and the blank stare of the homeless.

They shuffled forward, in no real hurry to get to where they were going, for they had no real destination, and just walked in the opposite direction of the advancing enemy.

The line snaked through the scorched plain and rolled over the hills in shades of black, grey and brown. The refugees were doing their best to look insignificant and harmless, dull specks drifting through the winter landscape. With his farmer's clothing, handmade bow and arrow, deer gloves and local hat, Peter fit right in, joining the long column as it moved west. People saw his injured hand but asked no questions. There were a few other men his age, walking quietly at the sides of the column, heads down, collars turned up, and he wondered if they too were deserters.

Nobody seemed to know where they were going. When Peter asked anyone, they simply answered "west". The word alone seemed to give them hope, even if he knew this west was hardly going to be the promised land. But he walked with them, helped them push their carts when the mud was heavy, and sometimes carried children on his back when they were too tired to walk.

Soldiers occasionally milled around, looking for strong men to drag into the ranks, and conscripts looking for some food and some action. They grabbed at the women, hauling them away from the column as if this was their right, amid the shouts and protests of friends and family. Peter wanted to help these girls, but in the madness of it all, he ignored their screams and kept walking. He had his own preservation to think of. The soldiers sometimes stopped him, to order him to join the ranks, but Peter just had to show them his mutilated hand and speak the dialect he had learned from Elsie and they would leave him alone. The bow and arrow added to his mystique as the backward woodsman, and he became more and more confident that they would not pull him back into the army. As long as he stayed obscure and unwanted, he would make it back home where his mother could hide him until the war was over.

But as it did in the trenches, events often transpire to bring kindred spirits together and Peter soon made friends with a young man and his sister. This came about after Peter had seen the man fighting with an older man over a jacket, with both pulling hard on it, trying to win possession but almost ripping it apart. Peter intervened and saw the sparkle in the young man's eyes. He knew he was attracted to people with charm, because he had none of it himself. The youth had jet black hair and brown eyes. A straggly beard grew only in patches, betraying his youth, and his body stooped over slightly, like he had just been badly beaten or was suffering from long term exposure to cold. Without thinking, Peter reached into his bag and offered the older man one of his wedding rings. The sliver of gold lit up the man's eyes and he let go of the jacket. The younger took his prize and threw it over himself, getting lost inside.

"Do you have any boots?" Peter asked the older man, who was biting the ring to be sure it was pure gold. "I think that ring is worth more than just a jacket."

Peter smiled as he walked with the young man, able to wiggle his toes inside the new boots, his blisters no longer being brutally rubbed. It was such a small difference that amounted to so much relief. He knew he could walk all the way back home in these boots.

"Thanks," the youth said, showing his stained teeth.

"Forget it." Peter shrugged, acting like he did such good deeds every day. "What's your name?"

The youth hesitated. He pulled the stiff collar over his ears, hiding most of his face from a sideways view. The jacket was far too big for him, with the cuffs well over his hands and the bottom already caked in mud.

"Remo," he said at last. "What about you?" He looked at the bow slung over Peter's shoulder. "Robin Hood?"

Peter laughed, his face muscles straining with the forgotten movement. Even the laugh sounded foreign. "Are you the poor I should give to or the rich I should steal from?"

"You just proved that. You stopped that rich fool who was trying to rob me of my jacket."

Peter raised his eyebrows, enjoying the banter. "Your jacket?"

"Well it is now, thanks to you, Mr Hood."

Their laughter was cut short by the girl who sidled up next to Remo. She had a pretty, round face, dark like Remo's. On her head was a thick woollen hat which struggled to keep her long black hair under it. She kept having to tuck her hair back in, as if the hat was for a child and too small for her head. She wore a thick coat and men's clothing; only up close could Peter see that she was a girl. She had a voluptuous mouth, with full lips, but her eyes were hard and Peter was so struck by her cold stare that he had to look away.

"Who's he?" she asked Remo. The confidence in her voice made her sound fearless.

"This is Mr Hood," Remo said. "He just helped me get my jacket back."

"I was wondering where you got that," she said, curling her sensual mouth into a smile of reproach. Peter noticed then that her lips were cracked by the harsh winter wind. She licked them, making them worse.

"My name's Peter," he said. It had been so long since he had spoken to a girl. As always, he wanted to be charming and witty, but didn't seem to have the knack.

She looked at the bow slung over his shoulder and the deerskin hat perched on his head. "Are you some kind of hunter?"

Peter laughed, so hard that his guffaws made him stop walking and double over. The girl took offence.

"What's so funny?" she demanded. She put her hands defiantly on her hips – a little girl's gesture – but in doing so, showed the curves of her body, the roundness of her femininity hidden under the big coat.

"Nothing. Yes, I'm a kind of hunter. The worse kind."

"Maybe you can catch us something to eat," she said, clutching her stomach. "I'm so hungry."

"Don't give her anything," Remo said. "I need her thin so I can sell her, trade her, or marry her off. The best situation would be all three."

She gave him a hard punch on the shoulder. Even with the heavy material of the jacket, he yelped with pain.

"You'll do no such thing," she said, pointing a finger at him. "You don't own me."

Rubbing his shoulder, Remo said, "This little devil's Michaela, my sister, but everyone calls her Izzy."

"I hate that name," she said, pouting.

But she smiled just as quickly and Peter enjoyed the rapport the siblings had, the way they laughed and joked despite their situation. The three of them walked together for the rest of the day. Peter shared some of the food he had, but was reluctant to because his provisions were almost at an end. Remo and Michaela divulged snippets of their story, often exchanging looks before anything was said.

They were from Vienna and had been young teenagers when they had hidden in the cellar while their parents were taken away. They had spent much of the war roaming from one safe house to the next, finding safety neither in the cities of Austria nor in the villages. The nation-wide witch hunt left no stone unturned, and few people were willing to risk their lives to save two teenagers from transportation. Rather, there were plenty who were more than willing to turn them in to improve their own situations. They had drifted across Europe, through Czechoslovakia and the eastern lands, working sometimes, but mostly hiding and foraging for food, always hungry, always afraid. They had joined the line of refugees in the hope it would swallow them up. Adept at hiding themselves and able to lie convincingly, they had managed several times to avoid capture and now, as seasoned refugees, blended in well with the others, knowing the right things to say and the right way to behave.

As Peter became friends with them over the days and weeks of walking, he did well to obscure his own past. Remo and Michaela asked prying questions, and Peter told them about his farm and his grandparents Josef and Elsie. Old and frail, they had sent him away to escape the coming enemy. Yes, it had been very hard to leave, he explained, turning his sad eyes on Michaela who knitted her bushy eyebrows together sympathetically, but it had been the right decision. A bear attack had injured his hand, taking two fingers and a chunk of his hand, but he had brought the beast down with his trusty bow and arrow. Sitting around the campfire in the evenings, the two siblings from Vienna loved hearing the bear story, and after Remo had played his songs on a borrowed guitar and Michaela had sung and danced, they would turn to Peter and beg for the story, like children wanting a tale before bedtime. Other refugees sitting around the fire were gripped too, and the story was translated into other languages as Peter told it. The children would sit close to their parents and with big eyes watch Peter as he acted out his fight with the bear. With each telling, the story got more fantastic and exciting, the bear bigger and fiercer.

They were happy times, huddling around the camp-fire at night. They were tired from the day's walk and gathered close together for warmth and comfort. There was often music, with the gypsies singing and dancing the nights away. Peter liked watching Michaela dance around the fire, her long hair flowing, but was always too shy to dance with her. And he was as equally repulsed by her as he was attracted, but couldn't explain why.

Even in this fast friendship, there was a clear absence of trust. Peter knew that Remo and Michaela were forever lying, contradicting each other and their story, trying to make themselves sound more than they were, and other times less. They also had their secrets. Peter could only guess what they were – deported parents, gassed probably – and he wondered if they had been a family of note in Vienna. Remo sometimes hinted that there was something to go back to, something to claim after the war. He talked incessantly about the future, the plans he had to restore his family's position. The young Viennese was balding prematurely and Peter wondered if he pulled his hair out in chunks during his sleep when his nightmares raged.

Lying and deceit aside, they did help each other and that was something, sharing what food they had and their blankets. Peter bartered his watches and rings for the benefit of all three while Remo was adept at the art of thievery, though the refugees hardly had anything worth stealing. Michaela often reproached her brother for robbing people who were already poor and suffering. But even she went quiet if Remo offered her a stolen morsel of food.

They were desperate times.

Peter went hunting, normally at dusk, but there were so few animals about, he rarely had success. When he did catch something, the other refugees, children and women mostly, surged towards him hoping he would share his bounty or catch them something too. He often had to hide dead rabbits and rats under his jacket until he was sure he was alone with Remo and Michaela and they could cook their feast over a small fire away from the others.

They walked all day, depending on the weather, overtaking others because they carried so few possessions. When they eventually arrived at the next city, they joined the masses camped in the park. It was a stinking, seething horde of humanity, cramped, hungry, cold and with very little hope. The families sat on their belongings, staring blankly into space, waiting for someone to come along and tell them what to do, to give them a purpose. The only solace for all these nomads was that in this place, they might be safe. They had all come for security, because this was one of the few places that was almost never bombed.

Each day, Remo and Peter went around looking for work. They might get half a day here, a few hours there, but there were so many others who had come here, trying to start a new life, that they had little chance, and Peter wouldn't accept a job without Remo. Potential employers welcomed the tall, blond haired farmer, but soured at the sight of the swarthy Viennese. Peter knew he would be better off without Remo, safer too, but he decided to stay with the two siblings until the end of the war, convinced that work was sure to present itself.

He couldn't face the idea of Remo and Michaela being shipped away. He had to protect them somehow.

When they had a bit of money, they went into the city in the evenings. The old town was still mostly intact, and it was a delight just to stroll the streets, enjoy a festive evening and forget, at least for a while. Remo would steal some food and they would have picnic dinners outside restaurants and dance to the music they could hear. If there was no music, Remo and Peter would clap their hands and Michaela would sing and dance around, kicking up the dust with her feet. In those evenings, her dark eyes would focus on Peter, looking at him with such strength and intent that he could not hold her stare, as much as he wanted to. And Remo was always a distraction, keeping them from coming together, always making sure they were never alone.

On one particular night, there was a festival in the old town. Remo and Peter had worked that day. Their pockets jingled with coins and they were in the mood to celebrate. Peter asked locals if the war was over, but they said it was a religious festival. Children were dressed in colourful costumes and everyone danced in the streets. Having suffered for so long under the depression of a country deep in the throes of war, the locals were keen to let their hair down. There was almost a collective urgency to have fun and make the most of the occasion. Men got drunk fast, throwing down beers and collapsing in the streets. The music was loud and the three youngsters moved amongst the crowd, dancing and rejoicing. Peter laughed and drank. He had made it back to his homeland and things would be all right in the end. In the throng, people swapped partners, linking arms and spinning around and around. The colourful lights shone on the smiling faces of locals and on the faces of refugees from all over Europe. Everyone danced together. The alcohol gave Peter the courage to put his arms around Michaela's waist and dance with her. He held her tight and got lost in the blackness of her eyes.

They didn't hear the air raid sirens – no one did – and kept dancing like everyone else. Even when the police came out to hustle people into bomb shelters and cellars, they only moved along reluctantly, scoffing, like everyone else, that it was just another warning. Peter and Michaela did not move, and people brushed them as they hurried past. Her warm tongue tickled his furry teeth, and her mouth was warm and soft. She was much shorter than he, and he had to lift her up to kiss her. They spun around, kissing and forgetting, Peter drugged by her musty smell.

The first bombs hit with a thunderous crash, quietly whistling through the air and then throwing bodies in all directions with a deafening roar. Peter and Michaela fell to the ground together. Instinctively, he put his body on top off hers to protect her and he was happy when she didn't struggle. The air was quickly full of dust and heat, and all the lights had gone out. Through the haze, Peter saw people panicking and running in all directions. The light from burgeoning fires let him see more. The street was littered with corpses and body parts, some people with legs missing trying to crawl away. With the explosions, the roar of the fires, and the screams of people, Peter thought his head would explode just from the noise.

He waited for a break in the bombing and thought back to his army training. Michaela still hadn't moved from under him and he thought it was good she wasn't panicking like the others. Fires, bombs, no water, he thought; got to get out of the city, buildings will fall. Get to the river.

He got to his knees, expecting Michaela to pop up too.

"Come on, Izzy," he said giving her an aggressive shake. His throat was already dry and hoarse and he lifted his undershirt over his mouth and nose. When Michaela didn't move, he bent over to pick up her up. In the firelight, he saw the piece of shrapnel wedged in her neck, the wound already caked in dust. The black eyes stared up at him and her lips were still slightly puckered, frozen in the joy of their kiss. He looked up at the sky, at the planes droning overhead, but the heat of the fires made him drop her and run. He joined the mobs of confused people. A couple of drunks were still arm in arm and singing, thinking all the lights and noise were part of the festival. Peter tried to get into the cellars of buildings, but they were already full and he was forced out, sometimes at gunpoint. People were screaming, calling for help, scrambling about blindly, coughing dust and smoke, and struck deaf and dumb by shell shock. Some just gave up and collapsed on the ground, unable to breathe the smoke anymore and resigned to a death by cremation. Others crawled around, legless or armless, pleading for help. They grabbed at Peter as he ran past. Streets were blocked by fire, and already walls were peeling away from buildings. He found his way back to the park, but was met by wave after wave of refugees running in the opposite direction. Behind them, Peter saw the park ablaze, the fire leaping athletically from tree to tree, inhaling the meagre belongings of Europe's forgotten people and scorching those too frail to run where they stood. That smell; it took him right back to his time at the camp, where the wind blew the ashes onto his uniform and into his hair and itched his skin like a thousand hands tickling him. He turned and ran with the others rushing towards the river. On the bridge, he held onto the rail and watched the crimson and violet fires envelop the old town. People were next to him and then they were gone. He heard a short yelp as they were sucked into the fire by the fierce wind. The planes buzzed overhead, the fire crackled and breathed, tearing the city to pieces, and the falling bombs made a banshee scream as they plunged to earth. Houses and buildings disappeared as if by magic. Peter fought against the strong wind that sought to suck him into the fire and somehow got to the other side of the bridge. Sitting on the banks of the river with thousands of others, wet clothing wrapped around their heads, he watched hypnotised as the flames licked at the buildings of the old town, swallowing everything in their path, burning people alive and cremating those already dead. The church spires burned and buildings fell soundlessly to the ground. The stench of burning flesh lingered. Michaela was in there, Remo as well, two more people he had got close to who the war had taken away. He sat and watched the burning city. The planes dropped more and more bombs, destroying the rubble. There was no way anyone in the city would survive, he thought. He tried to cry, but the heat was too intense and he was too dehydrated. Dry sobs were all he could manage and he thought himself heartless and pathetic.

***

The dawn was devastating. Peter couldn't tell where the red of the flames ended and where the pink and yellow of the sunrise began. It melted together, creating a striking sky illuminated and shining with the thousands of souls floating up to it. He got to his feet and staggered across the bridge with the others, into the ruined old town. Charred corpses littered the street, many of them naked. The old town, which only last night had looked like something from a fairytale, was now a smoking, stinking ruin. People shuffled around, avoiding the falling beams and pieces of burning debris, looking stunned and confused, and calling out names with vague hope. Some carried dead bodies in their arms and asked for help, for something to drink, for an explanation. A group of policemen stood staring at the door to a cellar, afraid to open it and see what was inside. Could it really be worse than what they saw on the street? Peter wondered. Everywhere were the bodies of women, children and the elderly. Soldiers at the front were meant to die, but to murder these civilians in cold blood? It was surely an act of mercilessness from an evil enemy. The British always claimed themselves to be so noble and honourable. Could they really be responsible for such a cowardly and inhumane act?

He tied a handkerchief around his face to ward off the smoke and the smell, and continued to walk through the town. If he'd had a camera, he would have taken pictures, but he thought no photographs would aptly capture the reality of what he was seeing.

He found Michaela where he had left her, eyes open and the piece of metal still stuck in her neck. Her hair had been burned away, as had her clothes. Her skin was blackened and her legs and arms were slightly flexed from the heat. He was surprised to see how young her body really was, that she could not have been older than sixteen. Just a girl.

Had he loved her? He had seen too much horror to be able to love anything again. It was probably just desire, and for a Jewess no less. It hurt to see her lying there, not because he might have loved her, but because she was just a poor soul born at the wrong time, one who had suffered at the hands of others and been powerless to stop them. Pursued for years by Nazis, she had finally died from bombs dropped by British planes.

Remo lay next to her. Somehow, in the madness, brother had found sister and they had died together. Peter bent over Remo and saw that the young Viennese held a gun in his scorched hand, and had a bullet hole in the side of his head. Peter stared at their charred bodies, but couldn't make himself cry. They had been victims throughout the whole war. How many more Remos and Michaelas were there? How many stories of suffering and survival? How many fatal demises?

With a gloved hand, Peter bent over and removed the piece of shrapnel that was stuck in Michaela's neck. He felt the heat of the metal in his hand as he walked away. People urged him to stop and help, but he just looked at them blankly, not breaking his stride. He shrugged off the ones who grabbed at him. His people had done many terrible things, and in his twisted logic, he felt they deserved to suffer as a result. They had gone out into the world armed with guns and ideology, and wiped out millions of innocent people. He felt sorry for those lying on the ground and the families who cried and clutched at the dead loved ones, but his remorse was short lived. We deserve it, he thought. Not Michaela and Remo, but us, the soldiers, the followers. The wrong people are being punished. I should be dead, strung up by the British in person, and not these poor refugees and civilians.

He fought against the crowd and walked out of the smoking devastation of Dresden. He walked in a daze, almost without stopping, across the plains of his Fatherland. He stole what he could, though the people had nothing and most were starving. In Magdeburg, he traded the last of his rings and bought a train ticket home to Hamburg.

Six

"Have you thought about what you want for Christmas?"

Always questions, he thought. Such pathetic attempts to maintain communication. And why ask about Christmas presents? he wondered. Wasn't it supposed to be the season of giving, sharing and surprise? No, tell me what you want and I'll buy it for you. Some spirit.

His mother sipped her coffee expectantly, waiting for an answer. She had dispensed with her breakfast apron and now sat in front of the morning paper, left in a folded mess by his father. The smell of fried eggs and bacon hung in the air.

"Surfboard," he muttered, face buried in his bowl of cereal.

"But you don't even know how to surf. Who put that silly idea in your head?"

Eric shrugged. "You asked me what I want and that's what I want."

"Don't take that tone with me," she snapped back, pointing a finger at him. "Keep talking like that and you'll get nothing."

Eric stood up angrily, his cereal half finished, and threw his bag over his shoulder. They had argued earlier about him going to school this last day, but his mother was in no mood for leniency.

The early school bus was nearly empty – all the bikers staying away as he had guessed – with mostly year eights and nines who didn't have the courage to play truant or whose parents believed they learned something even on the last day. It was more likely that the parents just wanted them out of the house; one final day of peace before the madness of summer holidays. Eric recognised a few faces, but took a seat at the front of the bus, feeling self-conscious because of his bruises and convinced everyone knew of the beating. He thought he could hear them whispering behind him and felt his face turn red as a result. Drew wasn't there, neither was Pepper, who also lived in the neighbourhood. Eric had seen her once or twice walking slowly through the park with a big-haired old lady.

Eric looked sombrely out the window as the bus lurched and rolled towards the school. He saw the same dull town, the same suits trudging to work with such self-proclaimed importance, the same sunburned streets and mirror-image housing. It was supposed to be the coastal ideal. But to Eric, it seemed there was little happiness in this paradise; all the locals walked through life as if struggling against a stiff wind, head down, restricted, frustrated, making no progress. If it was punishing to be a teenager, then it looked downright depressing to be an adult.

The argument about going to school had been in vain for none of the bikers showed up. Classes were merged together and these groups collected in large classrooms to watch videos, none of them educational. It was a complete waste of a day, with most kids leaving after lunch break. The few that remained looked at Eric and talked behind their hands, pointing at him. Everyone knew about the beating, but not about Eric's visit to the deputy's office. The kids spoke about Josh with awe and fear. With no friends and no money in his pocket, Eric sat and watched the movies, trying to ignore the kids pointing at him and snickering, until the day was over and an extremely relieved teacher dismissed him.

He was almost alone on the bus as it took him back to Crescent Bay. From the school to his neighbourhood, the bus drove through the entire social spectrum; from the lower class areas further east of the shopping mall, to the middle class banality of the town centre, to the expansive double-storey houses of Crescent Bay. The suburb got its name from the large bay that curved along the coastline. Surfers liked to ride the waves at both ends of the bay, where the breakers curled around the points of the crescent and smashed against the rocks. The residents were a mix of families and seniors, who all no doubt felt secure behind the high wall that surrounded the suburb. At the two entry roads, the gates brightly lit and guarded at night, "Welcome to Crescent Bay" was written on the wall in blue and green. Eric jumped off the bus at one of the gates, preferring to walk the rest of the way home.

There were giant billboards advertising new real estate developments in the area and depicted smiling, white-toothed and well-adjusted families having barbecues on verandas overlooking the ocean. One billboard in front of the wall, facing the highway, advertised a large house on the beach, with ocean views and a dream lifestyle. In the bottom corner, Eric saw the trustworthy, friendly, yet slightly arrogant face of his father. The comb-over was well organised and the photographer had taken his better side. Eric was surprised to see how good the old man looked. He had a strong face, big and square, and a Hollywood jaw line made even more prominent because he thrust it out. Eric stared at the face that was also a part of his own, and both wondered and dreaded if he would grow up looking the same.

He passed through the gate. The guard came out, a young guy who seemed to like the uniform, the importance it lent him, and all the gadgets and weapons that came with it. He looked at Eric and then at the billboard.

"Hey, are you Roger's son?" He chewed gum, moving his jaw sideways like a horse munching on hay. "You're a dead ringer for ya old man."

Eric nodded and continued walking down the road. He casually entered the supermarket and stole a chocolate bar and a flavoured milk. It was easy to steal here. His routine was to walk in and pretend to be looking for his mother, even asking people who worked there if they had seen her, to the point of describing how she looked; last week, they had even made an announcement over the PA. He would tour the shop, searching earnestly and asking around, swiftly steal the things he wanted, and then pretend to see her walking from the checkout to the car park. He would rush after her, claiming to the workers that he saw her pushing her trolley away, and waltz through the checkout with the stolen items in his bag. It was easy here because people didn't know him or his mother yet. That would soon change, so he had to make the most of his anonymity.

He crossed the street to the park, sat in the shade of a big tree and devoured his booty. He watched the scattered dogs chasing each other, their careless owners chatting in a small group. A light wind blew from the ocean, the sea breeze coming in later than usual. It would be nice down the beach, he thought. But he was comfortable under the tree and thought he could sit there the whole afternoon; the last place he wanted to be was at the house his father's company owned. It was too much like living in someone else's house. He was scared to touch things, to mark the walls or make too much noise.

"I reckon this nerd went to school," a voice said behind him, snapping him out of his reverie. "Teacher's pet right up to the last day."

Eric sprang to his feet. Josh and a few of the bikers stood in front of him, arms folded, dressed in their denim uniforms despite the heat, and trying to look tough and intimidating. One of the fat boys at the back was demolishing a hamburger, getting red sauce on his chin. It looked like he was biting the head off a large rat.

Josh held out his hand, palm up. It shook a little. Eric stared back at him defiantly. In a gesture that might have been comedic in other circumstances, he reached into his pockets and turned them inside out. Josh looked down at the chocolate wrapper and the empty milk carton.

"Now why did you buy that after what we told you yesterday?" Josh asked.

"I stole it."

"Yeah, right."

Eric clenched his fists, ready to attack his tormentor. He didn't care if he was outnumbered. He just wanted to get one or two good punches in and shut Josh up. Fighting back sometimes proved your worth; at least that was how it was in the country.

The bikers laughed and Josh turned around to laugh with them, ingratiating himself with the group. Eric spied the leader standing between two larger boys, like they were his bodyguards, and was again struck by how mean he looked, despite his lack of height and stature. Eric knew he was the driving force behind this mob. When he was gone, they were probably all the nicest boys, who kissed their grandmothers' cheeks, watched silly cartoons and ate their vegetables in the hope of having seconds for dessert.

When Josh turned around again, Eric slammed his fist into Josh's left eye, knocking him to the ground. He sprawled on the grass, clutching his face. Eric had put everything into the punch and had even surprised himself at how damaging it was. It certainly felt good.

The leader looked down at Josh and frowned. He balanced on one leg, and seemed almost about to give him a kick in the stomach, but decided against it.

"What do we do, Robbie?" one biker asked the leader.

"Get him up," Robbie said. Two boys stepped into the circle and followed the order.

Josh brushed the dried grass from his shirt. A trickle of blood curved down the side of his round face and fell in small drops to the ground. Taking advantage of this diversion, Eric turned and sprinted across the park. The big flavoured milk wobbled and gurgled in his stomach, bouncing around like a mound of jelly, quickly giving him a painful stitch. The bikers ran after him. Eric was nimble enough to evade their grabs, but he was soon brought down by a hard tackle. The bikers circled around him, waiting for Josh and Robbie to arrive.

"You boys there," a voice called. "Stop that."

Through the gaps between the bikers' legs, Eric watched an old man limp towards them. The bikers started to back away as the man raised his walking stick in the air, using his left hand to swing it around like a sword.

"Leave that kid alone," he shouted.

Robbie snickered and had the gumption to take his time over lighting a cigarette. He blew smoke in the old man's face.

"We're finished here anyway," Josh said. "Come on, boys."

He started to walk away and a few of the bikers followed him, but most stood by Robbie who was still staring at the old man and blowing smoke at him. It seemed to Eric like a ridiculous standoff.

"Your dad know you do that?" the old man asked. He was breathing heavily from the run. Eric wondered why he kept his right hand in his trouser pocket.

Robbie smiled. "He smokes the same brand. Gives me packets when I see him."

With that one sentence, Eric thought he knew everything about Robbie: divorced parents, with him swinging between a mother who couldn't handle him alone and a father who tried to win him over with presents, giving him everything he wanted; bad at school because he had no borders or discipline at home; being mean a cry for help; starved of attention, so being a bully and getting into trouble got him all the attention he needed, but not the actual attention he craved. The old man seemed to know it too, and he frowned sympathetically at the small boy. But Robbie didn't want this old man's sympathy. He stubbed out his cigarette, turned his back on the old man and then gave Eric a hard kick in the stomach. Eric was caught unaware, his body unprepared. All the chocolate and milk came up in a brown and pink mess. The bikers pointed and laughed, and then Robbie led them away, walking slowly and confidently across the park.

When they were near the road, Josh shouted, "Drop dead, you old Nazi."

Surprisingly, the old man smiled, but Eric saw something bitter in the smile. It disguised a silent sadness, a kind of pity, perhaps not for himself, but for the boy who had insulted him. Sighing, he bent over and reached out his gloved left hand to Eric who took it and allowed himself to be hauled to his feet. Eric wiped his mouth, tasting the acidic bile of his stomach.

"All right?" the old man asked. In contrast to his aged and lined face, his voice was strong. Eric detected the hint of an accent, a bit like his mother's accent.

He dusted himself off. "I'll live," he mumbled, embarrassed by it all.

Eric looked at the old man, trying to place him. Had he seen him in the supermarket earlier? He was tall but hunched over, his round shoulders inverted as if trying to make himself smaller, and his upper body seemed to lean to one side. The nose, flat and perhaps many times broken and bulging in the middle, was the centrepiece of an unremarkable face that had a timid mouth held firm by a protruding chin. The cheeks sagged and were marked by the lines of time and assorted scars, which up close gave him a sinister look. The gloved hands also made Eric wary. And why did he keep his right hand in his pocket? There was a twinkle in his blue eyes, though, a shine, a friendliness and warmth that could easily be misconstrued. Eric found himself suspicious of it. The old man's small mouth worked itself into a thin smile as he watched the bikers swagger across the street, in search of more entertainment.

"Some things never change," he muttered.

Eric wondered if the old man was referring to the old Nazi comment or to boys in general, that they roamed in packs and preyed on lone targets.

"Thanks for your help," Eric said. "But I'm not allowed to talk to strangers."

Eric thought back to primary school, to the man in the white van driving around the country town. The warnings of his parents and teachers, the fear it put in him, "don't take sweets from strangers," like every old man was a possible child molester.

"Now that's something that has changed."

Eric heard the accent again, something pronounced with a Z.

"My name's Peter Fischer," the old man said. He lifted his right hand from his pocket and extended it. Reluctantly, Eric shook it, briefly shocked by how small the hand was in his, and stopping to see that two fingers and part of the hand were missing.

Fischer smiled. "Now we're not strangers. You new around here?"

"We moved here two weeks ago."

"What's your name?"

"Eric."

The old man nodded. A trickle of sweat slid down the side of his withered and gnarled face. He tried to catch it with a handkerchief, but was too slow and missed it. He wiped his forehead instead. With long pants, long shirt and gloves, he was overdressed for the summer's day, but Eric wondered if Fischer was sweating because he was nervous; it sure looked that way. Again, the fear. He took a couple of short steps backwards.

"And that's why the boys come after you, because you're new?"

Eric shrugged and looked at the ground. "I guess."

"Better get used to that. It's human to fear what we don't know."

"Look, I gotta get home." He turned to walk away. "Thanks again, Mr Finger."

There was a pause. Eric could only hear the wind rushing past his ears. The sea breeze was stronger now, blowing pieces of litter across the grass. The old man laughed.

"It's all right," Fischer said, holding up his gloved right hand with the ring finger and pinkie missing. "The body falls apart. Just keep your soul together."

Eric forced a smile, but was too ashamed to speak, lest something else stupid find its way out of his mouth. He turned and walked back to the tree where only ten minutes ago he had sat so peacefully. He picked up his school bag and walked across the park. He looked back at Fischer. The old man waved to him, moving the handicapped hand from side to side. Eric reluctantly waved back and walked as fast as he could across the park and down his street. He looked behind him to see if the old man was following him, but he was alone. His stomach hurt, but nothing seemed to be broken. He would still make it onto the cricket field tomorrow. Fischer had rescued him just in time.

His mother was asleep on the couch. Eric spied her wine glass, with the clear remains of the melted ice cube which she laced her wine with in summer. The glossy characters of an afternoon soap opera moved across the television screen, pouting and accusing. Eric turned them off and left a short note on the table, saying he was off to the beach and would be back before dinner.

The afternoon sea breeze was blowing the tops off the waves and creating a mess of white caps and spray. In the hotel parking lot opposite his favourite beach, he saw the blue license plate of the company Ford; his father was probably showing some clients a house. The trustworthy and friendly face of his billboard father was clear in his mind, the face of a seller: aggressive, pushy, selfish and shallow. He continued around the bay to the next beach. Despite the wind, he somewhat childishly built an elaborate dam near the water's edge that included a long canal that helped the water flow into the dam. Proud of his structure he fell into the water and washed the sand from his knees and from under his fingernails. The salt water felt good and the weightlessness of the ocean made him forget his aches and pains. Only the humiliation remained. He thought of old Fischer with the missing fingers. He seemed nice, but at the same time a little strange, and Eric felt afraid of him. Something made him think Fischer lurked in the night, emerging from the shadows with his gloved hands, shiny cane and sparkling eyes, offering sweets or money or whatever. Even Robbie had seemed scared of him, and had tried to hide his fear behind mockery. Eric's thoughts were interrupted by the wave that dumped him and spun him around. Gasping for air at the surface, he scanned the beach to see if anyone had witnessed his dumping. Fortunately, when the wind was like this, nobody came to the beach except for die-hard surfers and dog walkers.

The company Ford was still in the hotel lot when he walked past. He thought about trying to find his father, but had been told off enough times for disturbing his work. He followed the already familiar streets back home. Watering systems were blasting in front gardens and lawns were glistening wet. Sometimes, he was forced to walk on the road because the footpaths were dotted with puddles.

At home, his mother stood at the stove, draped in her white dinner apron. All the windows were open and the breeze was blowing through the house, but the only smell was steak frying in the pan. She greeted him brightly as he closed the door to the garage. He always came in that way; the house had a front door that was hidden behind trees and seldom used. It opened into the special living room, used for entertaining. That room had a short bar in one corner and furniture from another era: a beige leather sofa worn smooth by time, two matching armchairs and a wooden coffee table with a glass cover you could slide magazines underneath. Even the magazines were decades out of date. To Eric, the room felt cold and foreign, like a room in a museum depicting life from the early seventies.

"Have a nice swim?"

Here come the questions, he thought, rolling his eyes.

"Bit windy," he mumbled, barely louder than a whisper.

"Your father called. He's going to be late again. So it's just you and me for dinner tonight."

Eric thought about the company Ford parked in front of the hotel, but decided not to mention it. His father was probably entertaining some clients – he often did that – and if Eric did say something, then his mother would just ask more questions.

They watched the news during dinner. There was more talk about the crisis in the Middle East, with reporters wearing special protective vests and standing alongside sand-coloured tanks. They looked earnestly at the camera, knitting their eyebrows together and emphasising words like war, blood and oil. To Eric, they looked like the glossy characters from the afternoon soap operas his mother watched.

"Mum, do you know an old man called Fischer?"

His mother slowly drew herself away from the television. "Hmm. He's sometimes at the golf club."

Crescent Bay had its own golf course. His mother had joined in the hope of meeting some local women, and maybe make a connection to a new job. But the fact she spent so much time at home meant she had so far been less than successful.

Eric pictured the gloved right hand. "Does he play?"

"Oh yes, given his age and disability. He's quite good. Still has a handicap in the mid-twenties." She laughed. "He has one of those buggies you sit on, you know, with a motor. A lot of the seniors here have them."

"I met him in the park today. He's weird."

His mother looked up from her dinner. "You're not the only one who thinks that. They talk about him at the club. Robert, the club pro, he told me he damaged his hand in the war. He's from Germany, you know."

"You mean he really is a Nazi?" Eric asked, eager for more information. He leaned forward in his plastic chair. But his mother retreated.

"They were all Nazis," she said flatly, and then she turned the volume up, ending the conversation.

They watched television together until his mother's third glass of wine drove her to bed. Eric stayed up, listening for the noise of a car so he would be ready to jump up and dash for bed. But when the key turned in the garage door, he was too slow to react. He turned and there his father was leaning on the kitchen counter. The tie was gone and his shirt tails were hanging out. He wasn't a tall man, but seemed to take up more space than necessary: always moving quickly, standing too close, talking too loudly, forcing you to listen to his demanding voice. It was the same man from the billboard, minus the finishing touches that covered up the blemishes and the putty that filled the gaps. No doubt he had been a good-looking young man. Eric knew he kept a picture of himself in his private school uniform rather vainly on his desk.

"Evenin', sport," he slurred, staggering about the room, moving things around, picking things up and putting them down again. "Was celebratin' a big contract with the boss."

He put his briefcase on the plastic dinner table and dropped his keys on top. He had an inordinate number of keys, as if each pertained to his level of importance; all those doors he could open.

"I'm glad you're still up," he said slowly, carefully pronouncing each word and trying hard not to slur them together. His blue eyes were vague and glazed, and he swayed a little. "We need to have a talk."

Inside Eric's head, alarm bells were ringing. Danger, run, another talk, get out quick. But Eric was stuck on the sofa. He took the cue and turned the television off. He sat up straight, knowing what was coming, but trying hard to keep his face blank and innocent. His parents were such disappointments. What had happened these last few years? It had always been that his parents were able to do everything, knew everything, and were tall, strong and smart. Now they looked old and used, saying the same old lines, with nothing left to offer, and leaving him to fend for himself. Why didn't they understand what he was going through in this torturous new town?

"Now, you never got into much trouble before," his father began. He ran a hand diagonally across his hair, to hide some of the baldness, but actually bringing more attention to it and the pathetic way he tried to hide it. "And when you did, you always fell in line pretty quick."

Because you hit me, Eric thought. Don't forget to mention that I stole from you. Don't lose the chance to rub salt into that wound one more time.

"That's why in this new town we gotta set up some new rules."

Eric lowered his head, making a pact with himself never to trust his mother again. His father came over to the sofa and stood towering over him. He tucked in his white business shirt and tried to look intimidating. Quite ridiculously, his fly was open, and as he tucked in his shirt, part of it popped through the open fly.

"You think this is funny? You think pickin' fights is funny?"

Eric opened his mouth to explain, but his father raised a hand.

"I don't wanna hear your excuses. No fighting, that's the rule. The way you behave, you're gonna need a lot more rules. So, to make you understand that, you're grounded for the weekend."

"But I'm playing cricket for the school tomorrow," Eric said, immediately regretting it.

His father gave him an arrogant smirk. "Well, you shoulda thoughta that before you went out pickin' fights."

Eric jumped up from the sofa. "Maybe you should cut off my pocket money too. Oh wait, I don't get any."

His father stepped closer. Eric wondered if he was about to get hit again. It had been years since the last beating, when his father had discovered that Eric had been systematically stealing from him. Eric thought that was about to change; alcohol had been involved the last time too. But Eric was almost as tall as his father now, and though outweighed, was at least able to look him in the eyes. His father was no longer the towering man he had grown up worshipping. Or was it that his father had taught him to worship, building himself up as a small time god? There was something pathetic and old about him now, drunk and balding, his shirt hanging out of his fly. He ruled this house and went out into the world snivelling at the feet of his customers, begging them to buy. Eric again saw the face on the billboard: trustworthy, sincere and downright fake.

The hit didn't come. His father just smiled and shook his head. "You have got so much to learn. If you'd listen to me once in a while, you'd learn a lot."

Eric looked down at the worn carpet. There were stains near the sofa that had perhaps been there for years – coffee, red wine, semen, who knew what it was – and they showed that this was someone else's house. He thought then about packing up and leaving it. He was fifteen, old enough to leave school, go back to the country and learn a trade. But he wanted more than that simple life. He wanted a university education, a chance to travel. Just a few more years, he told himself.

"Eric," his father continued, this time more tenderly, or at least attempting tenderness. "We're trying to help you."

"By keeping me prisoner," Eric replied, fighting to keep himself from crying. "But even prisoners get some money."

His father sighed and rubbed his eyes, looking at Eric like he was another problem that had landed in his in-tray: a cancelled contract, a tenant wanting new windows, a bankrupt company unable to pay its lease, a renegade son who couldn't be controlled.

"You want money so much, get a job."

"Okay. I'll go out looking tomorrow. Oh, I can't. I'm grounded."

"You're too much like your mother," his father said, shaking his head. He turned and walked slowly to the refrigerator, steadying himself on different pieces of furniture as he went. He took a fresh can of beer from the fridge and Eric took the chance to escape to his room.

He didn't turn the light on and just got into bed and waited. The stars on the ceiling were dull. In the silent darkness, he heard the familiar sound of pressure hissing from a can of beer. His father moved heavily through the house, pissing loudly in the laundry toilet, singing snippets of old songs, until finally he went to bed. Eric got up and carefully rummaged through the boxes in the spare room. He found his cricket gear and packed a bag with his pads, gloves, protector and his beloved Slazenger bat. His grandfather had bought him the bat two years ago as a present, but had died before Christmas that year. Eric had been unable to thank him for it, though he was glad for the memory. In the kitchen, he filled a bottle with water and made some simple sandwiches, and put those in his bag too. He slid the bag under his bed and went to sleep.

***

His father slept late on Saturday morning, like always, and when Drew knocked on the garage door, Eric, lying on his bed in his cricket whites, hauled his bag from under his bed and ran for it. His mother grabbed his arm as he passed.

"But you're grounded," she said, struggling to hold him. He broke her grasp and ran for the car just as it was pulling away from the curb. It stopped just as suddenly and Eric jumped in.

"Hey, you made it," Drew said, turning around in the front seat. His hair was shining gold against the white of his cricket shirt. "Your mum said you were sick."

"Yeah, well, here I am."

"Hello, Eric," said the leather-faced driver. "I'm Mrs Collins, Drew's mum."

"Nice to meet you. Thanks for taking me today."

Mrs Collins smiled broadly, cracking her deeply tanned faced into a road map of squiggles and lines. "No problem at all."

Drew turned around again. Eric saw the faint outline of pimple cream not fully rubbed away. Up close, Drew's face was awash with acne. When he flicked back his hair, he unveiled a scabbed and spotted forehead. Eric was thankful acne only hit him in patches.

"Survive the last day of school?"

"Yeah, but I'm gonna get Josh."

Drew smiled. "Can't say he doesn't deserve it. He won't leave Pepper alone."

Eric sat back in his seat and grinned. It was the best news he had heard in weeks.

Even though he batted almost last, he made a quick forty runs, took a couple of catches while fielding and the team won the match. He made friends on the team simply because he was a good player. When he got home, even after his father hit him once with his belt and declared there would be no Christmas presents, Eric's good mood still did not evaporate. He didn't care about Christmas. Since his grandfather had died, he never got many presents anyway. Hopefully, he would be able to spend Christmas, which had become a painful experience the last few years in his grandfather's absence, alone in his bedroom. He smiled as he fell to sleep that night. He was now a member of the cricket team, Pepper was available and Drew had agreed to teach him how to surf.

Seven

The ruin of war spread through the countryside. The fields were dotted with bomb craters. The land smoked and ached. The trees were twisted and burned, or cut down as firewood. In the villages and cities, buildings were left with only one or two walls standing, and there was rubble and detritus everywhere. It looked like a land should after it has been ravaged and raped. Despite the propaganda, it all looked hopeless. Why were the people fighting to the end? he wondered. Old men were still lining up to join the Volkssturm, the boys of the Hitler Youth too, thinking battle would make men of them. And they wanted to defend this mess, probably because they knew the country had no future and it might be better to die in battle than live in defeat and ruin.

Through the window of the packed train, he saw hunched over old women rummaging through the ruins of buildings in search of food and valuables, trying to piece together some sort of life from this destruction, or simply trying, like good Germans, to look busy. Young children hopped around the rubble too, using their small hands to fish out treasures buried under wood and bricks. They will survive, he thought. They will rebuild Germany, probably better than before, but he didn't want to be a part of it.

He waited for hours in Hannover for the connection north, huddling with the mass of humanity that had squeezed into the train from Magdeburg and no doubt wanted to force themselves onto the train for Hamburg. He would have to stand all the way, and he was thankful for the comfortable boots he had traded a wedding ring for back in Poland. He smiled as he remembered the circumstances in which he had met Remo and Michaela; two people, like so many others, he had briefly shared experiences with, enjoyed their company, only for them to be swept away by the tide of war. Now, they were random deaths that would be mere statistics for years to come and not individual people who had lived, survived, suffered and died. When he closed his eyes and concentrated hard, he could still feel Michaela's soft lips brushing against his, her lustrous scent wafting up his nose. He had kissed a Jewess, almost fallen in love with her, but what of that? She was hardly the poison they had been made out to be, yet he couldn't help feeling disgusted with himself. In the camps, the SS men had often hand-picked the more fruity and flouncy of the Jewesses who stumbled out of the cattle cars; it was no secret. And since Heydrich had died, everyone had talked about his Jewish descent. He had even heard quiet talk that the Führer himself had Jewish blood. With his black hair and pasty skin, he was far from the Aryan ideal he preached so fervently.

He wondered if it was guilt that had brought him close to Michaela, some part of his brain convincing him that maybe by loving a Jewess, protecting her and saving her, he would absolve his own guilt and shame. He felt the shard of shrapnel in his pocket. How small and light it was, just a piece of metal, yet so damaging.

He sighed.

There would be no Jewish love, no absolution or forgiveness, no one to confess his sins to. He was once more alone with his past. It was only a few weeks since he was happy on the farm. What had become of Josef and Elsie? And what about all the comrades he had fought alongside, the ones he had abandoned? And the others he had marched victoriously east with, only to watch them die on the frozen battlefields of Russia, cast in a lasting pose of anguish by General Winter. So many had died and he had survived. He mocked this thought for it went against the grain; surely there were many others more worthy and stronger who should have taken his place. Why should he, wounded, emaciated, weak of heart and cowardly, be naturally selected? Who was calling the shots, anyway, a business-like God sitting in a bunkered meeting room surrounded by advisers and deciding who would live and who would die? War had made Josef question his faith, with his only belief now that you should show kindness to people and accept your fate, whatever that may be. Josef's fate was to be overrun by the Red Army. He was a good man, yet Peter knew he would meet a horrid end, and no amount of goodness and kindness would save him from that. Where was the logic, the superior races coming to the fore? Hitler had been wrong about everything, and after so many had died for him and because of him, that it had all been in vain was hard to accept.

But through it all, Peter lived on. He had survived the battlefields, four eastern winters, and stepped over the bodies of his countrymen which littered Russia. The supposedly barbaric Asian hordes were going to be victorious. Hitler had led Germany in a devilish dance, spinning the people around and around. The allies were advancing from all directions, surrounding the fatherland, bombing the hell out of it, ready to put it to the sword and take the spoils of victory. It could have been over last year had the one-armed count succeeded with his bomb. It all came back to the Hitler. The soldiers had taken their oath to him and that would be annulled if Hitler died. Peter had taken it with the other soldiers of his regiment, screaming out the words with pride and force.

"I swear by God this holy oath, that I will render unconditional obedience to the leader of the German Reich, Adolf Hitler, Supreme Commander of the armed forces, and that as a brave soldier, I will be ready at any time to stake my life for this oath."

In other words, go forth into the world and kill people you have never met, who have never harmed you in any way, for the cause of some little man who fell far short of the perfection he demanded; and when victory is no longer attainable, die before accepting defeat. Hitler had succeeded in rearing an army of sons who fought with blind obedience for the approval and respect of their fathers, those men who had supposedly proven their worth by honourably losing the First World War and then suffering under the brutal terms of the Versailles Treaty. So their version went. It was Hitler who had restored the greatness and power of Germany that the older generation remembered, and it was the sons who went out and died for it, knowing that in death, they had failed their fathers who had demanded victory at all costs.

As the train rumbled north to Hamburg, Peter again stared out the window, the cold wind harsh against his weathered face. The train was so full of people that all the windows were open to let in fresh air. He recalled the cattle wagons swaying eastward, where the skeletal remains of Jews had to be scraped out when the train arrived at its destination. At the station in Hannover, there had been a mad fight for seats and then a frenzied push as hundreds tried to force their way onto the train. Luggage had been thrown out the windows to make more room for people, and as the train had pulled out of the station, squalid refugees had emerged from the shadows, scampering towards the platform to pilfer the stray bags. They fought over possessions like seagulls fighting over a morsel of mouldy bread, snapping at each other and cawing. Those who hadn't squeezed onto the train ran after it, making one last desperate dash to get on, swearing at those already on board who sought to keep them from getting on.

Nobody had a ticket, and there was no chance for the conductor, if there was one, to move through the carriages to check. The train stopped at every station, but few got out and even more tried to get on. Local officials, old men in makeshift uniforms with hastily sewn on badges, had to hold people back. Families forced their children onto the train, thinking they may have a better chance in the big city of Hamburg than in the desolate wasteland of the ravaged countryside. Mothers quickly scanned the carriages, looking for kind souls who would mind their children, but no one was putting up their hands; not another mouth to feed.

The carriage stank of urine because it was impossible to get to the toilet compartment. Children openly cried and women stoically wept. All the swastika badges and pins that everyone had worn in the early days of the war were gone. No one was willing to admit their allegiance any more, and the few soldiers on the train were looked at with disdain, sometimes with hate. It's all your fault, the faces of the people said. The soldiers were battle weary and handicapped for life, and nobody gave up their seats for them. They had the ghostly pallor from seeing the horrors of war, a darkness in the eyes and the habit of staring blankly for long periods as their memories played over and over in their heads. Despite his refugee façade, Peter knew he had the same stare, the same wounded look, the same soulless face. Those tired, sad eyes scanned the battered and rotting land of Lower Saxony as the train swayed north. He saw animal skeletons picked clean by birds, the bones shiny like sticks of polished ivory. Few villages were left untouched by bombings. The people stood around, sitting against the ruined buildings, sombrely following the train with their eyes. They waited for the war to be over, for the next person to come along and tell them what to do. Death and destruction had marched out of his country but had come back tenfold. They would pay for their sins for generations. They had destroyed lands, tried to eradicate a race, cast the shadow of the devil across Europe, and Peter wondered how he had got involved in it all.

***

They had gone to Hamburg with high hopes. From their small village near Eckernförde, Ernst and Peter had been star struck by the lights of the big city and drawn to the decadence of the Reeperbahn.

They were young, free from their oppressive rural households and the limits of the countryside, and into their first year of university. Both of their fathers were party members, so it had been easy to get a place. Ernst was studying to become a teacher while Peter was attempting to follow in his father's footsteps by studying medicine, thinking perhaps then he would finally win his father's approval.

They lived in the same dormitory and spent many late nights in the bars of St. Pauli. They were real country hicks but the tough harbour city soon hardened them. Those were great days: their time in the Hitler Youth was over, the university was full of patriotic and easy girls – one simply had to express his support and admiration for Hitler and the girls swooned – and every night they celebrated the early victories of the war. The fall of France had resulted in two straight days of drinking, when they had moved through the city with large groups of men, toasting the success of the Wehrmacht and singing gaudy songs. They had all thought then that the war would be over quickly. Peter was floundering at university, medicine way out of his depth, and call up saved him from the embarrassment of having to inform his father he would soon be thrown out of the course. Ernst was not so keen on going to war. A multitude of soldiers was called to active service for the east campaign. It started out as a spirited march, and they breezed through against limited resistance, winning a succession of decisive and – so they were told – historically significant battles. Ernst lost an arm and part of his face to a mortar shell when they were still marching forward and was sent home a hero. It had been a sad goodbye for the two friends, with Peter promising to stay alive and make it back to Hamburg where they could continue their interrupted lives.

Now, he had made it, but there was no way just to pick up where they had left off.

It was late in the evening when the familiar spires of Hamburg emerged like pointy witches' hats against the black backdrop of night. There had been interminable delays, with the train stopped for hours while the track was repaired. The passengers fought for positions at the window to see the skyline of the city they perhaps thought they would never see again. But debris was piled high on the streets, with most of the buildings gutted by fires. Large chunks of houses and buildings were missing and windows were taped up with newspaper.

Off the train, Peter walked through the wreckage in a daze, down the shattered shopping stretch of Mönckebergstrasse. It wasn't as bad as Dresden, but that was a city foreign to him; this was his town, a mess of half-ruined buildings and piles of bricks. In the dark and almost deserted streets, he tripped over stray bricks and pieces of wood, and at one point stumbled into a police officer.

"Watch yourself," the officer grumbled.

Peter apologised, slipping easily back into the local slang. The officer stared at him.

"What you doing on the street so late?"

Peter caught himself and spoke with the accent of a refugee from the east. "I just got in by train," he explained, his voice tired and dry.

"Show me your papers."

Peter shrugged. "Don't have any. I'm from the east."

The officer eyed him suspiciously. He was old, with a long handlebar moustache like the men wore in the time of the Kaiser. The face was lined and hard, the eyes narrow slits of white, but rubbed red because of the dust that blew into them while he walked his beat.

"I think you better come with me," he said, withdrawing his club. "We can't have refugees roaming the streets. There's been too much looting by your lot."

The old policeman reached out to grab Peter by the arm, but Peter was faster and he dodged the officer, who swung the club towards Peter's head, missing by millimetres. With the policeman off-balance, Peter gave him a hard shove and the officer went sprawling to the ground. There was a dull thud as skull connected with brick, but Peter didn't stop to inspect the damage or help. He ran under the train tracks at Dammtor and across the university to the student house where he hoped Ernst still lived.

He remembered his friend as the smiling, gangly, stooped-over youth who had excelled at being a goalkeeper. When Peter had visited him in the field hospital, Ernst had cried, like a small boy, that he would never be able to keep goal again. Peter had tried to lift his friend's spirits, saying that he would have to become a striker and score goals instead. How brightly Ernst had smiled then, his dirty teeth, long and crooked, like broken black piano keys against the cream of his bandaged face.

The man who opened the door had the same stoop but the angularity was gone. The cheeks had a rosy glow, perhaps from alcohol, and the stomach bulged a little, despite the rationing. The left side of his face was a confused tangle of scars and pockmarks, and in the darkness of the doorway, he looked like a figure from a horror film. Only the crooked grin showed him as the Ernst of old, his buck-toothed front teeth pulling at his bottom lip.

"What the hell are you doing here?" Ernst exclaimed, trying to keep his voice down. "I thought I'd lost you."

They hugged each other hard, like old comrades. Peter withdrew, slightly embarrassed, and then held up his mutilated hand. Ernst grabbed it and brought it closer to his face for inspection.

"I've lost more than you," he said at last, releasing the hand. "Thankfully, it's not a competition." He smiled again, but this time more broadly, and his front teeth stuck out freakishly.

"My soul's out there somewhere too," Peter said, his voice echoing in the hallway.

Ernst nodded solemnly. "Yours and about a million others. Mine too."

They stared at each other.

"You look like hell," Ernst said, stepping out of the doorway. "Better come in and warm yourself up with a drink."

Peter stepped into the small, cluttered room. It was the same size as what he had had, but his had been much neater and orderly. But then, Ernst had always been a messy person. The single bed had a thin mattress and several layers of blankets. There was a smell, alcoholic and sour, which Peter couldn't quite place; perhaps empty bottles left open, their contents fermenting further and giving the room a rich fug like an old bar. Dog-eared books lay open on the small desk, pressed flat because Ernst couldn't hold the pages open and take notes at the same time, and other books were stacked on the single bookshelf. It was a decrepit room, seedy, but it took Peter back to his university days, when he was young and had yet to see a hundred Jews smouldering in a pit they themselves had dug.

"Are those my books?"

Ernst hastily tidied up the table – not an easy thing to do with only one arm – marking pages and putting books on the shelf. The shelf became so full Peter wondered if it might come out from the wall and crash to the floor.

"I've changed to medicine," Ernst explained. "My father organised it. I was going to tell you, but when there was no word…I thought you were dead. I mean look at me, I couldn't be a teacher with a face like this."

Peter forced himself to smile, reminding himself to expect a lot of things to be different. If Ernst had given him up for dead, then it was highly likely that everyone else had too.

"Probably not, but the kids would have no trouble coming up with nicknames."

"Scarface, Funkenstein, Funk the freak." Ernst said, laughing.

"It's good to see you, Ernst. You've got no idea how it's been."

Ernst frowned, his teeth making him look like a sad rabbit. "Probably best not to talk about it. At least not until you get your life back to normal."

Peter nodded, wondering what that normal would be. He wasn't interested in university, and just wanted to go back to his village and crawl into bed. His mother would be there and she would take care of him.

Ernst draped his one arm over Peter's shoulder, a serious look on his scarred face.

"But I've got to ask you one thing," he said, whispering. "How much do you know?"

"About what? The camps? The war? What's not to know?"

Ernst shook his head. "That's all over. I mean about your family."

"What is it?"

Ernst paused. He ran his front teeth over his bottom lip, a nervous gesture, and he seemed to be choosing his words carefully.

"Didn't you hear anything?"

Peter knitted his eyebrows together, wondering what news would break the last of his spirit. "I haven't heard anything in months."

Ernst lowered his head. "Maybe it should wait until morning, when you've had a good sleep."

"You can't start like that and not finish. How can I sleep when you leave me hanging like this?"

Ernst held up his hand in apology. "Okay. Don't shout. You know we're not allowed to have visitors. I don't want Herr Müller knowing I've got someone in here again. He spies on me, on everyone. I reckon he's with the Gestapo."

"You can't tell anyone I'm here." It was Peter's turn to look down at the floor. "I...I...deserted."

And it was Ernst's turn to get angry and shout. "You what? If they find out you're here, we'll both be dead."

"I know. That's why I came tonight. I'm going back to Thöby in the morning. I'll be in touch, but I'll stay away."

"You don't know what they've been doing to traitors these last few months," Ernst said. "And you can't go back to Thöby."

"Why not?"

"Because there's nothing there."

Peter's voice cracked. "What do you mean?"

Ernst offered his one, battered chair and Peter took it, bracing himself. But once seated, he felt incredibly tired, as if the fatigue had built up over the years and all he wanted now was to sleep.

"Your mother's dead."

Peter felt sick to his stomach. If he had eaten anything that day, he would have thrown it up at Ernst's feet. Instead, he swallowed down his dry-retches and grabbed at the old wound in the side of his stomach.

"Someone heard her talking bad about Hitler," Ernst explained. "It was probably Frau Henkel in the bakery. She's always gossiping and blabbing to her husband, the Gauleiter."

"But what did she say? I mean, she's a party man's wife for goodness sake." Peter slumped in the chair.

"I don't know. I only heard it from my mother. Something about Germany surrendering and that all the Nazis should be rounded up and shot. Nobody disagreed with her, it's what everyone thinks these days, what with the Brits just down the road, but nobody supported her either. People in Thöby said the Gestapo took her to a labour camp. You know how they talk. But your father said it was a car accident, on the way to Hamburg."

"You've spoken to him?"

"He came up from the camp to give a lecture about his research a few months ago. He recognised me in the crowd and we spoke about home, about you, about all the people we'd lost."

"What did he say about me, and about my mother, and what bloody camp are you talking about?" Peter was shouting, restless in his chair and fighting back tears.

"Neuengamme. The camp south of Bergedorf. The one nobody admits is there. Your father works there, doing some research with miracle drugs. It's all pretty top secret, but it could be revolutionary."

"He never said anything about that to me. How long's he been there?"

"He didn't say. Couple of years, I guess, judging from the amount of research he's done."

"And what did he say about my mother?"

"Not much, just that she was a traitor and it was probably good that she had died before word had got out. He trumpeted some nonsense about these being tough times and that those who were loyal had to stand up and show their worth. But still, she was his wife, and I thought he should've shown more heart."

Peter scowled. "The bastard has no heart. Probably had her arrested himself. Anything for the party."

Ernst sighed and sat down on the unmade bed. It creaked under his weight and one bundled blanket fell to the floor.

"I fear he might be more than just a party member," he said. "He had a horde of SS guards with him, and a few other high rankers sat in the front row of the lecture theatre. If you ask me, I'd say he's up to no good at Neuengamme, experimenting on humans or something. There have been rumours of stuff like that going on in the camps."

Peter sat in silence, remembering how his father had vehemently pushed him to join the Schutzstaffel. Peter had wanted to go to university with Ernst, to the exciting harbour city and not to another military camp; five years in the Hitler Youth had been more than enough. But war changes everything. And when he got called up, it was more glamorous to be an SS recruit than a Wehrmacht conscript.

"Don't get me wrong," Ernst added hastily. "I know he's your father and everything, but if he's involved in some bad stuff, he'll get it when the war's over, especially if he's in with Himmler's mob."

Peter was silent for a moment. "Is he at Neuengamme now?"

Ernst nodded. "I guess so. He said he sold the house in Thöby and bought a villa in Bergedorf." He cocked his scarred head sideways, a gruesome gesture which made Peter only see the damaged side of his face. "You're not thinking of going out there, are you?"

"I've got to know the truth. If he turned my mother in, I'll kill him with my bare hands."

Ernst struck his mattress with frustration. "What good will that do? Then they'll know you've deserted and you'll be strung up like the others."

Peter shrugged. "I'm not sure it matters anymore. Haven't you seen our fatherland? Don't you know what we've done? There's nothing left to live for."

Ernst opened his mouth to reply, but the knock on the door made him freeze.

"Funk," a voice barked from behind the door.

Ernst and Peter both jumped to their feet and looked around the room: no space under the bed, desk too small, the closet. Ernst shoved

87

Peter inside and then opened the door. Peter peered through a crack in the wood.

"I heard voices, Funk," Müller said. He had the droopy face of an overweight Rottweiler and the voice to match. When he spoke, his cheeks and neck flapped.

"Oh, I was just talking to myself," Ernst said, rubbing his eyes. "I do that sometimes to get the facts to stick in my head, when I'm studying."

Müller tried to look past Ernst and into the room. He sniffed at the air, moving his nose and nostrils, a dog on the prowl.

"You know the rules, Funk. No visitors."

Ernst nodded and closed the door. "That was close," he whispered.

Peter climbed out of the closet. "What happened to Jensson?" he asked, copying the whisper, aware of the danger he had put Ernst in. "He was harmless."

"They took him away. He was harbouring Jews, from the university. Listen. I know some people who can hide you, but you've got to promise me you won't go to Neuengamme."

Peter stared at the floor. Ernst had laid an extravagant Oriental rug to cover the worn wooden floor; more artistic brilliance from the Asian hordes.

"Promise me," Ernst said.

Peter smiled, recalling how often Ernst had changed him with the force of his will, and all the promises Peter had in turn broken. "Anything else to tell me?"

Ernst reached under his bed and pulled out a battered shoebox. "There's quite a lot of mail," he said, putting the box on his lap. "I confess I read some of it in the hope there might be news about you I didn't know. But there was nothing. I'm sorry."

He reached out and handed the dust-covered box to Peter. It was full to the brim with letters, including some he had written to Ernst. He thumbed through one such letter, amazed by his brash and positive tone, the words of another person.

"What's this?" Ernst asked as Peter handed him the leather book bound by the short belt.

"Got anything to eat or drink? I think we both have a bit of reading to do."

***

The bicycle creaked and groaned as he pedalled through the fields of Allermöhe. Most of the fields were deserted, and the houses seemed that way too, with the curtains pulled tight and only a few chimneys smoking. They were hiding from the war: old men who didn't want to join the Volkssturm and farmers' wives who wanted to stay as far away from Speer's munitions works as possible. Hitler had called for "total war or total destruction", so Ernst had said, but the people didn't want to be part of either anymore. They hid themselves in their houses and waited for the British to arrive. It was a far cry from the early days of the war, when Allermöhe had been the place to be, especially in summer. Peter and Ernst had often gone to the lakes for a swim and to look at the girls. Now, it was almost deserted, and only the thinly smoking chimneys gave away the people behind their doors. Eichbaum Lake was a layer of ice, but no children were venturing out on it on skates.

It was a long way to Neuengamme, but the road, leading to a camp of importance, was in good condition. He was thankful for the extra jacket Ernst had given him last night as a blanket. He had slept fitfully on the Oriental rug, dreaming of his mother, whose image was already fading in his sub-conscious. He had a photograph, bent and wrinkled from being carried across so many battlefields and from being unfolded and looked at in all weather conditions, and she was even fading from that.

When he saw the first observation tower in the distance, he stopped and hid himself and the bicycle behind a clump of trees. There was the smell again, that sickly smouldering that had burned his nostrils in Dresden and at other places during the war. He looked through the trees at the tower, and could just make out a helmeted SS man standing on top, a machine gun clutched to his chest.

He had woken early that morning, taking Ernst's field glasses and commandeering his bicycle while his friend was still snoring. So much for that promise. He would bring everything back and then they could have a good talk about the diary and all the other photographs and documents stashed inside it. As Ernst seemed to no longer support the war, maybe he would know what to do with all of it.

He settled down to wait, like he had spent so many days during the war, waiting, freezing, his stomach burning with hunger. He took out some of the letters he had been unable to finish last night and skimmed through them to pass the time, though he had little desire to keep reading about his destroyed life. Even the smallest reference to mothers or family nearly brought him to tears. Also painful were the letters from Gisela. She had fallen for an American soldier during the liberation of Paris and wrote scathingly about Hitler and the Nazis, and the German people as a whole. Indeed, she made no attempt to separate German and Nazi except to say that she herself had always been opposed to Hitler. She could never return, she claimed, not since she had learned what hideous atrocities the Nazis had committed. Peter was sure she didn't know the half of it.

A large truck rumbled down the road. He took up the field glasses and scanned the cab, knowing he would not see his father who he knew would much prefer to ride in a car. The truck pulled into the camp and the gate closed behind it. More prisoners or a truckload of week-old bread?

He went back to his letters and sighed, thinking of Gisela and what hard work it had been to seduce her. In the end, it was the SS uniform that had finally made her lead him to the barn at the back of her house. How disappointing that was, and quick too, he thought, like Gisela was doing him, and her country, some great service. Still, he had marched off to war the next day with a story for his comrades which his imagination – and short experiences with the Reeperbahn – made more colourful and erotic. They had promised each other to stay true and get married after the war, with Gisela a proud Aryan keen to breed a litter of the master race for her Führer.

But even without the American or her change of allegiance, he knew they could hardly be together again, not after what he had seen and done. It made sense that she, like many others, would quickly side with the victors, denounce Hitler and claim that they were all part of the resistance. It was a good plan except that almost every known resistor had been killed, so by claiming yourself a resistor and a survivor would immediately mean that you were lying. Gisela had been an active member of the Bund Deutscher Mädel, the female version of the Hitler Youth, and had always been a fervent supporter of Hitler. Peter recalled that she was unable to talk of anything else. She had left for Paris amid great excitement, judging by her letters, thankful that she finally had the chance to serve her Führer. Now, with defeat at hand, she had got into bed with the victor, and Peter thought that made her nothing but a prostitute whose payment was lifelong absolution of her guilt. She would return with Doug to Atlanta when the war was over and they would be married there. She was sorry, she wrote, but claimed repeatedly that she could never marry a German soldier, nor live in a country that had punished the world with such violence and severity. It was over, and she had done the right thing by only ever following Hitler on the surface; deep down, she had always been against him.

Peter scoffed and put the letters away. Her change of attitude was typical of how everyone would act when the war was over. He had already heard it from Ernst: the denouncement, the removal of guilt, the shifting of blame, the admission of resistance. That's how it would go, and they would claim they had simply done what they were told, had only followed orders and were not to blame. He realised then that that was what had made the Nazis so successful, the Führerprinzip, a clear hierarchy of power, delegating orders at each level so that the further it went down the chain, the person who gave the order had less responsibility, and that all involved, except the one at the top, could claim they were simply following orders. It also meant that even the lowest in the chain could taste power; that while they were subject to the ones above, they ruled the ones below. That power drug, coupled with the return of Germany's greatness, had cemented the Nazis in power and given Hitler the place at the top of the hierarchy, and he had proven his predictions with crushing and glamorous victories in the early years of the war. But was it really that simple, he wondered, or was there something innately violent about his people? How could we, and he had to admit he had been one of them, have swallowed that rubbish about us being the master race? This small group of people crammed into an even smaller country were the world's dominant force?

With his last address being the student house in Hamburg, all undelivered mail had come back there and Ernst had collected it and read it. Ernst had suggested that he escape the country and make a new life somewhere else, with a new passport and identity.

"The post-war world is going to be a bad place to be a German," Ernst had said solemnly before dropping the diary and falling asleep.

As Peter huddled himself in his coats, thankful for the deerskin gloves and hat Elsie had made – his time with the Polish farmers already felt like a lifetime ago – he thought about what kind of life he could make for himself and where he might go. He had only a high school education and a failed year of university. He knew he wasn't cut out to be an academic. He would have to work, but what could he do with a crippled hand? He frowned, trying to picture himself working in a mine or on a ship, the other workers staring at his hand and talking in whispers about the German who wouldn't speak of his past, nor work with such efficiency and skill as they could. Perhaps it would be better to claim Polish heritage, farmer stock, just another misplaced person caught in the middle of the war; a victim who deserved sympathy and a few breaks.

The rumble of a car engine snapped him from his thoughts, like the bombs used to when he waited behind the machine gunners for the next wave of charging Russians. The car came down the road, driving away from the camp. He took up the field glasses and watched it pass. The back seat was empty and he followed the car until it was around the first corner and on the way to Bergedorf.

I can't keep up with a car on this pile of rust, he thought, looking at the unloved bicycle.

This was the only access road and his father was not the kind of man to take detours. Back on the creaky bicycle, he was happy to be pedalling away from the camp and its sickly stench.

On the outskirts of Bergedorf, he set himself up behind a mound of rubble, dropping the bicycle on the ground and positioning himself so that he could watch the road to the south and not be seen. It was like playing soldier again, like they had done all through his years in the Hitler Youth, when every exercise, sport or otherwise, had had a military twist to it. He moved some bricks and dug a small crevice that he could lie in and be more comfortable. When the cars drove up, he scanned the windows using the old field glasses. He knew his father would have no beard or moustache, and guessed he would probably look just the same as before: the towering figure with the pale gold hair so wavy it looked styled, and the large, round, pompously held head set off by equally round and pompous glasses. He had flirted with a monocle in the early days, but had done away with it because the Gauleiter of Eckernförde had advised him to look more working class.

Peter was sure to monitor the cars driving towards the camp even though he was certain his father would not be inside. His father was a methodical man who liked routine and set hours, a day worker who demanded eight hours sleep and ate big breakfasts and dinners, normally at the same set times each day.

The sky was a light grey, typical for Hamburg in February. He wondered if spring could burst this wasteland to life, cover the trees with buds and bring the farmers out of hiding to plant their crops. He nestled himself in the rubble and frowned, thinking that not even nature could relieve his suffering nation. Just to look around, especially in the eyes of the people, was to lose all hope.

The afternoon passed slowly. He burned the letters from Gisela, one by one, the small fire warming his hands and face. He wanted to destroy all traces of his past and start again. The war years – and when he was honest, they had started as early as the Berlin Olympics – held too much pain and suffering. They had all known war was coming. The fathers wanted redemption and prepared their sons, who were themselves eager to prove their own worth in battle, to go out and get it.

The car came as darkness was falling, just after six. It shimmered along the road like a liquid shadow, driving without headlights. Through the field glasses, Peter just made out the circular face of his father; there was a glint in the round spectacles in the fading light. The car, a Mercedes, had SS plates, and the driver was dressed in the black uniform of the Schutzstaffel. Peter could see the twin lightning strikes on the collar. He quickly gathered up his things and started after the car. His heart was racing and though he pedalled vigorously, he was no match for the Mercedes. But there were so few cars on the road, he had no trouble following it. The damaged streets also inhibited the car's progress, causing the odd detour. He wondered if his father would be annoyed by that, or maybe he was used to it by now, the daily detour around fallen buildings and bomb craters.

The black shadow twisted and turned into the old part of Bergedorf. Most of the village was destroyed, bomb weary or damaged by fire. Many buildings were gutted or piles of rubble, but the Mercedes stopped in front of an untouched villa in the Jugendstil style that most Nazis, following Hitler's penchant for concrete monoliths, had chosen to hate. But Peter knew his father to be a cultured man of taste, crafty too, and a tight man who was aware of the value of things. If the villa survived the war, it would be a prized and valuable property.

From the end of the street, he watched the driver open the back door. His father climbed out. He was heavier than Peter remembered, although it could have been the bulk of the fur-lined coat. He climbed the stairs with that familiar heavy stomp that made you think he was trying to pound the earth with his feet, happily crushing ants and spiders as he walked. The driver waited to see that he was safely inside the house, then got back into the car and drove away. Probably to ferry the next SS big shot in his fur-lined coat to his villa, Peter thought.

With the Mercedes gone, driving again without lights, the street was quiet. Peter stood staring at the house as one by one the windows were lit by the flickering light of candles. A beautiful villa but no electricity, like everyone else. He thought about getting on the bicycle and riding away. But he had to know the truth, and it didn't matter if he exposed himself. Maybe his father would help him, give him some money and a place to hide; there had been no car accident, and all the stories about the Gestapo taking away his mother were just rumours.

He left the bicycle against the leaf-less hedge and walked up the stairs to the front door. His heart thumped against his chest. He tried to swallow, but his mouth was too dry. He wondered how he must have looked. Ernst had gawked at him last night, but that could simply have been shock, setting eyes on the living dead. Still, he must have looked a sight: thin, dirty, pained and soulless.

When the doorbell made no audible sound, he rapped loudly on the heavy wooden door. The knock echoed through the house. He heard footsteps coming towards the door, and then the hinges creaking as the door cracked open. A young maid, dressed in a blue and white Dirndl, stood in the doorway. She was not pretty, but had a long plait of shining blond hair and her body held the freshness and brightness of youth which older men seemed to find so appealing, as if it made them younger too. Her nose was small and soft, and was made smaller by a large, moist mouth that seemed crowded with teeth. With her full lips painted blood red, she looked slightly grotesque. An admirer of Frau Goebbels, he decided. She showed a smudge of lipstick on her front teeth as she smiled carefully at him, inquiring his business.

"My name is Jäger. I'd like to speak to the Herr Doktor, please. My father."

The maid brought a hand to her mouth in shock, as if she, like Ernst, had seen a ghost. Behind her, Peter saw his father's round head emerge from a side room to peer down the hall towards the doorway.

"Son?" he asked, squinting at the darkness.

"It's me, father." Peter's voice was an adolescent croak. There was something still there, that undying love which, despite all the let downs and lies, remained unconditional.

His father moved forward, stumbling a little, his slippered feet thumping the floorboards.

"Come in, come in," he ordered, gesturing with his hands. "Quickly now. You're letting all the cold air in. And take your boots off."

And just as suddenly, it was gone. Why had he thought this time might be different, that his father would open his arms, comfort him, treat him as an equal, sit down and really listen? No, it was the same old divide, that cold medical distance that had always made him feel like he was his father's patient, the one who could never be cured.

Peter stepped into the light of the hallway, took off his hat and gloves, and slipped out of his boots. The maid grimaced slightly, wrinkling her tiny nose at the smell; another who had no idea of the reality of the war, he observed. She stepped back as his father reached out his hand. Peter shook it, feeling the big hand envelop his own. His father withdrew quickly, badly hiding his repulsion, but recovered himself and grabbed Peter's wrist, examining the hand so close to a candle that Peter felt the heat of the flame.

"I wasn't informed that you were wounded again," he said, inspecting the mutilated hand. "The needlework was appalling. You'll have scars for life."

"I'd rather have scars than no hand at all."

His father snorted and then smiled, showing the gap in his front teeth. When Peter was a boy, it had been his father's great trick to wedge coins between his teeth. But now, the gap looked sinister, that Peter could see through it into the darkness of his soul.

"Go on, Gretl. Fix him something to eat," his father said to the maid. His face turned sour, taking in Peter from head to toe, clearly thinking that his appearance was Peter's own fault. "He looks like he hasn't eaten in weeks."

The maid scurried towards the kitchen. Peter noted the way his father spied the bounce of the Dirndl, and how he called his servant by her first name and not Fräulein.

"Where's your uniform?" his father asked, turning back to him. "And why did you get sent home with only an injured hand? The soldiers of the SS continue fighting even with such minor injuries."

Peter swallowed hard, wanting to talk, to tell of how the war really was, how everything hurt, how the bloody images spun around in his brain.

"I was shell-shocked as well. I couldn't see for a few weeks."

His father nodded slowly. "Your eyes look okay to me. A bit vacant, but you always looked like that." He laughed his peculiar short guffaw, that deep, mocking laugh that brought attention to himself in crowded rooms. "Now, come into the study and we'll see if we can get the truth out of you."

Bootless, Peter followed his father silently into the study. In the old house in Thöby, the cramped workroom, with its beakers and unfinished experiments, had been off limits. This room, like the hallway and no doubt the whole villa, was opulent and luxurious, a room the war had yet to touch. His father sat in a high-backed leather chair behind a broad desk of heavy, gleaming wood. The shelves were lined with books and a set of deer antlers hung above the door. The gold of the candlesticks sparkled in the soft, flickering light, and the candles made the shadows dance on the wood-panelled walls. On the wall behind the desk was his father's prized possession: the Führer had his arms folded, with the red, black and white swastika armband positioned in the centre of the picture. He wore full dress uniform with his Iron Cross pinned to his thin chest. His drooping face was set in a pose of grim determination; he would fight for their cause with all his strength until the bitter end. Under the dead cockroach moustache was the faintest of arrogant smiles, and the blue-grey eyes had a coldness and clarity so striking it made Peter wonder if he was actually looking at him from behind the picture, peering through holes cut out for eyes. Under the picture was the quote: "The German people is a young and strong people, a people with its future before it."

Peter took a seat in front of the desk, facing the two men who had controlled his life. He felt the old fear inside him, the relic from the intimidation tactics which had started as early as he could remember: the unexpected clips over the ears, the soft beatings when his father had whispered insults throughout, and the hard beatings when the big man had hit him with all his strength. Across the desk, his father looked fit and healthy, despite the war. His skin was pale and his cheeks were slowly turning into jowls from good living. Ten more years and he would have the jolly, round, fleshy face of Peter's grandfather; though there was little that was jovial about his father and the puffy cheeks hid a cruel streak Peter knew only too well. He had been a young father, just out of medical school when Peter was born, and was now in his early forties, in the prime of his life, and living in luxury while millions of his countrymen suffered, starved and died.

They sat in silence, like they had often done. It was up to Peter to talk first. He stared at the floor, not knowing where to start. His father absently took off his round glasses, pulled a white cloth from his pocket and cleaned them; a brisk, practised gesture which showed his patience, or his disinterest.

"Where's mother?"

His father's face did not change, but there was a pause enough for Peter to suspect something, a flash across the eyes, the unexpected trump card dropped rashly on the table by the novice player.

"Didn't you get my letter?" his father asked, tilting his head slightly sideways.

The letter had found its way into Ernst's shoebox and described the events of the car accident that had killed his mother. The letter had been cold and objective, like a newspaper article. No, like a doctor's report.

Peter shook his head, trying to play dumb. "What letter?"

"There was an accident," his father started, frowning and inspecting his fingernails. "The car ran over an unexploded bomb."

Peter raised his eyebrows. There had been no mention of a bomb in the letter. He wondered if the story was evolving with time, that others had asked for more information and his father had been forced to lie further.

"I can't believe it," he said, burying his head in his hands. But his attempt at sorrow was pathetic, and Hitler stared down at him, judging, watching his every move.

"It was a shock to all of us." His father picked up an ivory handled letter opener and started toying with it. "I'm sure you know she had not been well, and I for one was very worried about her health."

Something else that hadn't been in the letter. "What was wrong with her?"

His father began pressing the sharp end of the letter opener into the tips of his fingers; a conscious gesture, Peter thought, to show his hands were whole, his body superior.

"One might say she had given herself over to moments of delirium, saying things she didn't mean and later regretted."

"Traitorous things?" Peter said, unable to meet his father's eyes.

"Sometimes, yes. We had to keep her locked up for a while, just as a precaution. What she said was quite damaging, especially for me."

Peter was certain he saw the smile on Hitler's lips broaden ever so slightly. He took a deep breath, but his mouth was dry and he still couldn't swallow. All the words he wanted to say were stuck in his throat.

"You might want to look a little sadder than that," his father said. "She was your mother."

Peter looked his father in the eyes. "Did you have her killed?"

His father leaned forward. The leather chair squeaked and his round face turned hard. He drove the letter opener violently into the desk.

"How dare you talk to me like that. You come in here a pathetic cripple too weak to fight, and not a single medal or promotion after four years, I might add, and then accuse me of killing my wife."

Peter shrank in his seat. The truth ate at his insides, gnawing like a dog on a bare bone, and he felt the bile sting his throat. His father stared at him, blowing the air through his now red cheeks, his wavy hair slightly ruffled. Peter could not meet his or Hitler's gaze.

"Where's your uniform?" his father demanded, standing up quickly.

Peter continued to stare at the wooden floor, so polished and shiny, so clean. His father came around the desk, moving swiftly for such a big and heavy man. He took a handful of Peter's hair, lifting the head to look him in the eye. He studied Peter, searching his face, smiling slightly when he saw the truth. He threw the head away roughly, took out a handkerchief and wiped his hands. He went back to the desk and picked up the phone, turning his back to Peter, his eyes fixed on the Führer. Casually, he slid his free hand into the pocket of his pants.

"Send some guards," he said, his voice steady and controlled. "Immediately...Yes, to the villa."

He replaced the receiver gently, the soft click like a gun shot in the room, and continued staring wistfully at Hitler. He rocked slightly back and forth in his slippers.

"You're too much like your mother. Weak and narrow-minded. You don't see the big picture, only think of yourself. We made Germany great again, had the world at its knees, but it was people like you who ruined it, who weren't strong and ruthless enough to deliver the final, crushing blow."

He turned to face Peter and seemed surprised to see him standing. Peter landed the first blow low in the stomach, where the flesh was soft and flabby. His father doubled over, seemingly more from shock than pain. The second punch got him on the side of the head and he fell hard to the floor. Peter stood over him, unable to hit him again, fighting with himself whether to help his father up and apologise or to kick him.

"You don't know what it's like," he shouted. "You talk of honour and blood from behind a desk. You order others to go out and fight for you, and complain when they don't succeed, claim they're not worthy and too weak. Pick up a gun yourself and go freeze to death in Poland."

His father gripped the desk with a meaty hand and hauled himself to his feet. A trickle of blood curved around the side of his face, a perfect semi-circle, and dripped onto the floor. He opened his mouth, snarling, showing the gap in his front teeth and the abyss beyond it.

"You started too early, my Führer. You should've waited until this Weimar filth had been filtered out, dispersed to labour camps where they belong."

"You'd send your own family to a camp? And what do you know about camps? Have you seen what we've done?"

"We've exterminated the vermin of Europe, to secure your future."

"My future? Look what you've done to our fatherland."

"Nobody was complaining a few years ago, when we ruled the world."

"No, only when we started killing our wives and mothers and shipping children to labour camps."

His father's eyes went cold and the ivory handled letter opener slid easily into his hands. He lunged at Peter, missing with the first strike, but landing the second. Peter reared against the wall, the letter opener sticking out of his left shoulder. He ducked quickly around the desk, and the two of them circled it, both in search of a weapon. The doctor went for the candlestick on the window ledge. Peter reached up behind him and pulled the portrait of Hitler from the wall. As his father lunged at him with the candlestick, Peter brought the picture down hard over his head. There was a sickening thump as the thin wooden backing cracked against his skull, followed by a loud rip as the canvas split. His father tumbled to the floor with the picture looped around his neck. Peter looked down at his unconscious father and saw that the picture had cut through the face of Hitler, so that the head on top of the uniform with the Iron Cross and swastika armband was now his father's. He stood up and started to leave the room, but was stopped by the unmarked envelope that lay on the floor. It must have been attached to the back of the picture, he thought. As he bent over to pick it up, blood ran down his left arm, leaving dark circles on the wooden floor. Grimacing, he pulled the letter opener from his shoulder and slid it under the flap of the envelope, staining it with streaks of blood. He put the bundle of Swiss Francs into his pocket, wiped the letter opener on his pants and pocketed that too. His father groaned and stirred on the floor. Peter picked up the gold candlestick, hit his father on the head with it, and then put it in the pocket which now bulged with riches. For good measure, he rifled through his father's pockets, taking the money from his wallet and his Neuengamme identification card for good measure.

"I hope they get you."

Gretl jumped backwards as the study door was thrown open. Peter pushed her aside and ran for the front door. As he put his boots on, he saw her slowly enter the study.

"Darling," she exclaimed.

There was a pot of goulash steaming on the hall table. Peter picked it up, pocketed the silver spoon, and slammed the door behind him. He jumped on the bicycle and pedalled with the pot precariously cradled under his injured arm. As he rounded the first corner, he saw the same black Mercedes come roaring down the road. It paid no attention to the struggling cyclist and turned the corner towards the villa. Peter pedalled out of Bergedorf and hunkered down behind a clump of bushes to eat the still warm goulash.

***

"They'll come after you," Ernst said solemnly. With Peter's help, he threaded through the stitches, washing away the blood with strawberry Schnapps, the only alcohol he had. "It was a fool thing to do. You've got to get away."

"Where can I go?" Peter asked, wincing as Ernst pulled the thread tight with his teeth.

"Good question. I know some people who can hide you until the war's over."

"It'll never be over. And I'll hide myself up north."

Ernst smiled, his buckteeth pulling at his bottom lip. "Sure it will. When we've got no more bullets to fire, no more stones to throw, no more kids and grandpas to send to the front. Hitler and his gangsters will do themselves in and it will all be finished. The Nazis will be a footnote in history."

"You don't seriously believe that? Didn't you read the diary? Come on, Ernst, you were there, too."

"Settle down. This is hard enough with only one arm without you thrashing about, and we can't have Müller sniffing around again."

Peter slumped into the chair again and let Ernst do the work. He took greedy swigs of the sweet Schnapps to dull the pain, to dull everything.

"Yes, I read the diary," Ernst went on. "Most of us know it anyway, though no one will admit that. They may not know all of it, but they can't plead complete ignorance. All the Jews simply didn't just move away. And look at the times before the war. Don't tell me you're shocked by what's happened. All the signs were there leading up to it."

"Yes, shocked, and guilty, and the world will never let us forget."

"You have to stop talking like that. This is a national problem. Remember, Hitler was voted in. He didn't take power by force."

"And what about the Jews?"

"We went to school with Jews, remember? Played with them, were friends with them. And we looked in the other direction when they were singled out, and asked no questions when they suddenly were gone. They were just like us. It was the Nazis who told us they were the reason the country was in the toilet. We were too young to understand and question, and just followed everyone else. Our parents have a lot to answer for, but that doesn't remove our guilt. When I finish university, I'm getting the hell out of this country, before another Hitler comes along."

"There won't be another Hitler," Peter said.

"Oh yes there will, because like it or not, we're a bloodthirsty lot. Our racist hate will hide in our forests and fester in the villages and factories, all the nationalists waiting for the next Hitler to offer us the place in the sun we think we deserve."

"Maybe, but I'll be damned if I fight for him."

Ernst smiled sarcastically, and with his scarred and marked face, the smile made him look sinister and comic at the same time, like an actor on the stage, showing the audience for the first time that he was the villain of the play.

"You say that now. Probably say that, given the time over, you wouldn't have fought for Hitler. But you'd fight. Everyone would."

"You're so sure of that?"

"Yes, because we're sheep. Majority rules, like it does everywhere. We follow orders, love our groups and sports clubs, and worship the leaders who stand up and tell us what to do. It'll happen again. It might take a few decades, but it'll happen again."

Peter was in no mood for discussion and didn't reply. People like his father were surely in the minority – the whole country couldn't be Nazi – yet those in the minority held all the positions of power. But who would be held accountable when the war was over? Would the world stop and listen to individual stories, to decide who were good Germans and who were not? Or would they just bundle them all together under the Nazi banner, all guilty?

Peter helped tie the stitches when Ernst was finished. They were much neater than the ones Josef had made. He wondered if Ernst had managed to hold his soul inside; maybe it had leaked out on the ride back from Bergedorf, what was left of it.

"Good job, but how will you be a doctor with only one arm?"

Peter pulled on his shirt and coat, feeling the weight of the Swiss Francs, the letter opener and the gold candlestick in his pocket. He wondered if Ernst noticed the bulge.

Ernst wiped his hand on a matted towel. "The professors say I've got a real aptitude for it. They say I should think about going into administration, for hospitals and what not."

Peter nodded. "You'd be good at that. You always liked ordering people around."

Ernst smiled at the compliment, but seemed to miss the rather grim joke Peter had made at his expense.

Eight

With the sun bright and hot, and with most of Crescent Bay still asleep, Eric followed Drew down to the beach. Both of them had surfboards tucked under their arms. They kept their sandals on until they got to the cooler, damp sand by the water's edge. A dry desert wind was blowing from the east and it reminded Eric of the dusty country of his previous life. His new life shimmered before him, an ocean of crystal blue ebbing and flowing and crushing into white foam as it collided with the land. The days of picking dry snot from his nose and smelling like sheep shit were over. Now, it was about blond hair, golden tans, salty skin, girls in bikinis and riding the waves. But even here on the coast he couldn't escape the desert winds which blew in the mornings until the sea breeze kicked in after lunch.

Drew had a new six-foot board, with three fins and a red foot strap. The board was covered in outlandish splashes of blue and green and wild streaks of red, the mess coming together to form a hungry shark chasing a trail of blood. His brother Adam, who Drew said was at university in Perth, had an old single-fin board. Eric dropped this heavy plank on the sand, took the piece of wax handed to him and copied Drew's motion of rubbing it on the board.

"The ocean is alive," Drew began sagely, but ruining the act by picking small flecks of wax from under his fingernails with his teeth and spitting them onto the sand. "It breathes and flows. Surfing is about finding that rhythm and going with it."

Eric nodded. His only concern was not to make a complete fool of himself. The whole mystical side could wait until he was able to stand up on the board. Fortunately, nobody was at the beach this early, so only Drew would witness his embarrassment.

He had waited out his grounding impatiently, brooding around the house, not talking to either of his parents, wanting to get started with surfing and to pursue his friendship with Drew. More than anything, he hoped to have the chance to meet Pepper in a situation where he could talk to her without having all her friends around.

On the sand, Eric followed Drew's instructions and practised how to paddle and stand up. After a few tries, he was able to jump to his feet and have his balance.

"You're a natural," Drew said, though he could have been referring to himself. He ran a hand slowly through his hair, letting the wind run through it, and then picked up his board. "Come on. Let's hit the waves."

It wasn't a big swell, but the half metre waves were just high enough to ride and good for learning. Eric paddled hard when Drew told him to, riding the waves lying down at first to get the feel of the timing and motion as Drew had instructed.

"You're doing great," Drew said as they waited for the next set to roll in. "Let the wave take you, but once you have it, then you take the wave."

"That makes sense," Eric said. The surfer mysticism was a little lost on him, but he tried not to let Drew see this.

"Has Josh been after you lately?"

Eric shook his head. He squinted at the sun to guess the time. He had promised to go shopping with his mother, to help her carry the heavy bags home from the supermarket.

"Not since school finished," he said, looking down at his board, slightly embarrassed. Why did Drew have to ask about that? "His mates got me in the park, but I managed to land one good punch, cut his eyebrow open."

Drew smiled. "Cool. Don't worry. You'll get your revenge."

"I think he's gone away or something. I haven't seen him around."

"Probably gone somewhere for Christmas. His family's loaded. They live in that mansion near the south end of the bay. You know the one, with three storeys and windows for walls."

Eric looked at the water thoughtfully. He had mastered the technique of sitting on his board while waiting for a wave, keeping his balance by making small circles with his feet. He tried not to think about the sharks possibly circling below. Josh acted like he was working class and his friends did the same. They were probably all rich, he thought, and the working class disguise was just to make them seem tough and hard.

"Look out," Drew shouted, turning his board and paddling to where the waves were rolling in. "This one's got your name on it. Get up on that board. Go, go."

Eric felt the wave suck up water from behind him. He was scared he was too far forward and the wave would crash on top of him. But the heavy board was steady, and he pointed it at the beach and paddled hard, driving his arms through the water. He felt the pull from behind as the wave took hold of the board, thrusting him forward like being fired from a slingshot. He kept his weight at the back of the board, making sure the nose was above the water. As the wave reached its zenith, he stopped paddling, gripped the side of the board with both hands and pushed himself up. His feet landed on the board and he threw out his arms to balance himself. The force of the wave powered him on, the wind whistling past his ears. He went dead straight, afraid to move his feet or turn lest he fell off. The wave crashed behind him and white foam slithered across the surface of the board. But just as quickly as it had gained power, the wave petered out and the board sank under his weight, or its own. Eric fell from the board and sat in the shallows breathing heavily and grinning. He saw Drew far out readying himself for the next wave. He must have watched me, Eric thought, beaming at his own success. He marvelled at how far the wave had taken him, almost to the shoreline, and he had stood the whole way. He watched Drew jump to his feet and take control of the wave, turning sharply and spraying water, even trying to ride the small tube, gripping the board with his hands when he crouched down low.

"I'll be doing that soon," Eric said to himself. He pulled his board back and started paddling out past the low breakers. Drew joined him halfway, having given up on his wave before it turned to mush. He held out his hand for a high five and Eric met it with a slap.

"Awesome, man. You rode that sucker the whole way. You'll be rockin once you get a real board." Drew slapped his bloodthirsty shark. "These things turn themselves. Ask your folks for one for Christmas."

Eric nodded, but thought of his father's threat that he would get no presents this year. He hoped that it, like many others, had been an empty threat, mere words. Because it was not just a matter of being friends with Drew, meeting Pepper and being safe in their group; he was now hooked on surfing. He wanted that weightless feeling of gliding along the crest of a wave, feeling its force and tasting the salt as the spray went into his mouth. All his years in the country and he had been missing this.

They rode a few more waves until Eric explained he had to go home. It was okay. They seemed to have little to say to each other beyond Drew giving instructions and Eric responding. Drew stayed in the water, saying that Eric could take the board home with him and leave it behind the backyard gate. As Eric staggered from the water – he couldn't remember when he had felt this exhausted – some of

Drew's friends came down the path to the beach. They had surfboards under their arms and big backpacks, as if they were going to make a day of it. There were girls as well, and when Eric saw Pepper carrying a pink surfboard and a matching backpack, he felt sick. She wore a bikini top with tight shorts. He used his free hand to flatten his salt-matted hair.

"Hey," said one of the boys cautiously. He was tall and lean, with sculptured arms and shoulders from years of paddling a board. Across his nose and lower lip, he had luminous zinc cream that looked like modern war paint. "How's the surf?"

"Uh, real nice," Eric said. "They're coming in sets of four," he added trying to sound knowledgeable and win their approval.

The boy smiled, but Eric wasn't sure if the smile was friendly or mocking. "You met Drew here?"

Eric paused before answering, weighing his options. Best not to jump too quickly, he decided. "Just by accident."

Pepper and Melanie stood next to the boy. They looked like twins with their flowing blond hair and matching outfits, though Melanie was slightly heavier, with folds of skin hanging just enough over the side of her shorts to look unsightly. Pepper's tanned and slender neck was on full display and her small breasts were crammed into the tight bikini top, pushing them together, and making a small crevice that Eric longed to run his finger down. His mouth went dry and he could think of nothing more to say. He fumbled with the foot-strap, trying hard to look cool and relaxed, but his hands were shaking and he felt their eyes on him.

"Isn't that Adam's board?" Melanie asked, her voice a patronising squeal. She snarled a bit, and Eric recalled the wrath of teenage girls, how with their pouting, abuse and rumour circulation, they could do much more damage than the fists of teenage boys.

"Drew lent it to me," Eric said, putting more spite into his tone than he wanted. "So I could learn. There's not much water where I'm from."

Melanie pouted and turned away. She waved to Drew and he beckoned her to come in. She picked up her yellow and red board and ran for the water, the folds of skin bouncing on the waistline of her shorts. The boy went too, but slower, giving Drew and Melanie the chance to have a quick kiss before joining them out past the breakers.

"Where are you from?"

It was Pepper. She was talking to him and she was alone. The others had picked up their boards and gone out. A friend called to her, but she stayed where she was, rubbing sunscreen onto her slender arms and shoulders. She struggled to get some cream on her back too. Eric wanted to offer to do it, but couldn't get the words out. She would probably laugh at him and then everyone would know that he liked her.

"Merredin."

He couldn't make eye contact and racked his brain for something clever and witty to say, but the inside of his head was as dry and barren as the land near Merredin. He tried to look relaxed with the board under his arm, but his hand was sweaty and the board slipped and fell to the sand with a dull thud. Pepper smiled.

"That's on the way to Kalgoorlie, isn't it? I've got cousins there. I think we stopped for petrol in Merredin."

"That's probably the only thing the place is good for."

Pepper laughed slightly, covering her small mouth, her grey eyes shining.

"My name's Eric."

"Come on. I know your name." She gave him a sarcastic snarl, like Melanie's, but without the spite. "You stickin around?"

"Well, we just moved here."

"I mean at the beach, stupid."

"Oh. I'd love to, but I gotta get home and help my mum. You know, with Christmas shopping and everything."

Eric felt himself blush, the red blotches creeping up his neck and onto his cheeks, burning his ears. He had used the words love and mum in the same sentence. What a fool Pepper would think he was.

She bent over and picked up her hot pink board. "Will you be here tomorrow?"

"Absolutely. Same time as today."

Pepper shrugged nonchalantly. "Well, maybe I'll see ya."

And with that leading sentence, she turned and ran to the water. She had long, thin legs and danced across the sand. But she didn't hit the water landing on her board with one smooth motion like the others had done; she threw her board to the side and dived in like a swimmer, getting her hair wet and then arranging it so that it covered her ears. Eric watched her tanned and wet body glistening in the morning sun, and followed her with his eyes as she paddled past the breakers, hoping she might turn around and wave. She duck-dived expertly under the whitewash and joined her friends. Eric saw them talking and pointing at him on the beach; they were teasing her for talking to him. Pepper splashed water at them in response, but a set of waves came in and this took their interest. Eric picked up the heavy board and walked up the path to the road, the hot sun shining in his eyes, thinking he may have a glimmer of hope.

***

Eric watched with one eye as the television shouted the news about the crisis brewing in the Middle East. War was mentioned in almost every sentence; it seemed the media demanded it. Hussein was deemed a madman and there were constant references to Hitler, with the Iraqi regime supposedly like Nazi Germany. Slow talking generals were dusted off and propped in front of cameras to give their expert opinions, the hardware pinned to their lapels tilting them sideways. They made references to the Second World War, Korea and Vietnam, and crowed about the success of the American Army.

Eric toyed with his food, using his fork to carve the crude outline of a surfboard in his mashed potatoes. His parents fixed their eyes on the television screen between mouthfuls, commenting blandly on the events, his father praising the Americans and reaffirming his opinion that Australia should support the allies when the war came. His mother was more pensive, frowning at the screen and at the arrogant American soldiers who predicted a swift victory with no casualties, on their side that is.

"Dad," Eric started tentatively. His father murmured a response, but didn't break eye contact with the television. "You know what you said about Christmas, is that really true?"

His father chewed his steak and looked at him, scowling a little, hating to be interrupted. "What did I say about Christmas?"

"You know," Eric said, scraping his fork across his plate, tracing the cracks. "About the presents."

"You went out when you were grounded," his father said softly, his voice composed and even, almost gentle. "You broke the rules and you have to pay the price for it."

"Come on, Roger," his mother pleaded. "It's Christmas, after all."

His father glared at her. "I don't want my son to grow up into some kind of hooligan. Boys need rules. It was like that with my father and look how I turned out."

Eric snickered.

"What was that?"

"Nothing."

His father cocked his head sideways. He was a bully, but Eric knew he was far from stupid.

"What is it you want? That's it, isn't it? You're always nice when you want something, just like your mother. You've got no idea how good you've got it. I had nothing when I was a kid, not nearly as much as you have now. So? What is it?"

Eric looked up from his plate and stared at his father defiantly. He knew from his grandfather that all those stories of suffering and hardship were lies.

"A surfboard."

His father threw back his balding head and laughed heartily. His face turned red and he had to put down his knife and fork, dropping them on his empty plate with a clang. He ran a hand across his head, organising his comb-over that his laughter had left askew.

"You want a surfboard? You wouldn't know what to do with it. You'd probably try to eat it. I mean, that's all you do around here, eat and watch television."

"It's not fair," Eric shouted. "All the other kids get pocket money and big presents and I get nothing. And it's only because you want to save money and not because of rules and shit."

His father hit the plastic table with his fist. Cutlery clattered against dishes and his mother's almost empty wine glass tipped over.

"No swearing in my house," his father said, pointing a finger at him. "That's one rule you definitely need. Now go to your room."

Eric stormed from the living room, knocking the table with his legs and spilling some of his father's beer. He didn't look behind him and slammed the living room door.

"You want money so badly, get a job and earn it like the rest of us," he heard his father shout. "We give you food and shelter and clothing, but you want the world. Go out and earn it."

Eric closed the door to his bedroom, finally blocking out the booming voice of his father. He picked up a ceramic dog and hurled it against the wall. It shattered and the pieces rained on the carpet.

He fell onto the bed with his head on the pillow and cried, thumping the mattress with his fists the way he wanted to thump his father's face.

***

The sky was overcast the next morning, the surf low and mushy. Eric stood on the deserted beach with the heavy surfboard under his arm, trying to decide if it was worth going in. Some seaweed had washed in overnight and much of it lay stewing and stinking on the sand. As he paddled past the pathetic breakers, more seaweed grabbed at his arms, making him wince with disgust. He did his best on the small waves, but they didn't have enough power to propel the heavy board. He spent most of his time pulling seaweed from his arms and scanning the beach for Pepper or Drew. But no one came. After a lonely hour of failure, he got out and slumped home.

His mother was stationed at the sink, washing the old frying pan with the electrical connection that had to be kept out of the water. His father demanded a cooked breakfast every morning, claiming it gave him the strength to make the big deals. She turned as Eric staggered through the garage door.

"You're up early again," she said brightly. The kitchen window faced east and the morning sun, which had finally broken through the early clouds, bathed her face in shining light. But he thought she looked sad and old, her long face drooping, her big mouth limp, and no amount of forced gaiety could hide her sadness.

"Beendownthebeach."

He stood in the kitchen at a loss what to do next. He was hungry, but that meant staying there and answering all his mother's questions. And how was he supposed to kill the whole day?

His mother wiped her hands on her orange breakfast apron. "I'm sorry about last night, but you have to understand, he only wants what's best for you."

Eric sniffed, catching a hint of fried bacon and instant coffee. The only thing dad wants is what's best for himself, he thought.

"I know it's hard changing cities," his mother continued, her speech sounding rehearsed, as if she had been waiting all morning to deliver it. "But we're suffering just as much as you. We left our friends just like you left yours, and I left my job behind too. It's not easy making friends here. The people are so cliquey."

Eric went to the fridge and took out a carton of the cheap orange juice his mother always bought in bulk when it was on special. It was sickly sweet and he filled half the glass with water and the other half with juice. His mother often praised him for his economy, but he just preferred it that way.

"But maybe there is something in what your father said," his mother went on, following her script, "about the job, I mean. There are lots of retired people around here. Maybe you could do some work for them, like gardening and housework."

Eric gulped his juice and grimaced, picturing himself slaving for bitter old wrecks who barked orders at him and were never satisfied. He saw himself vacuuming musty living rooms and weeding jungle-like gardens and then being rewarded with ginger sweets and a few out of circulation coins.

"I can ask at the golf club," his mother said, unabated, taking Eric's silence as agreement. "I'm going up there today."

Eric thought of the bloodthirsty shark on Drew's board, of Pepper's round breasts wedged into her tight bikini, and Josh chasing him around the neighbourhood.

"All right. But I only wanna work in the afternoons, when it's too windy down the beach."

His mother smiled brightly, her face lifting. She turned back to the scratched and beaten frying pan and cleaned it with renewed vigour.

***

Mrs Canter lived in a small duplex at the top of the hill near the golf clubhouse. The house was modest and had the red brick Eric knew was used in the sixties and seventies. In front of the house was a low brick wall, the same red, and the white gate had flecks of paint peeling off it, showing the orange rust underneath. It squeaked as Eric pushed it open. He looked at the garden, the grass high, the trees growing out of control, and saw only work. On the roof, the gutters were jammed to overflowing with dried leaves and sticks.

The screen door was locked, the fly wire lifting at the bottom. In the gap, a spider had spun an intricate web. A fly was caught in it and beat its wings intermittently, knowing it was stuck but not willing to give up. Eric wondered where the spider was; perhaps on holiday with its rich family.

Mrs Canter had a shock of blue hair coiffed and whipped into a ball of fluff, sticky and stringy like fairy-floss. The house was warm, with Eric getting a blast of warm air when the door opened. He thought she looked familiar. Maybe he had seen her in the supermarket or somewhere in the neighbourhood. Her head was small, her face sagging. He tried to erase the lines, lift the sunken skin and see the beautiful woman she perhaps had once been, but could see only a lonely old woman who perhaps spent too much time at the hairdresser reading women's magazines. Her expression was dour, and even when she smiled, there was more than a hint of bitterness so that the smile came across as a sneer. She seemed to have spent her lifetime stopping herself from having fun, as if laughter was a sign of weakness, and there was work to do, a husband to care for, children to breed and raise, all those middle class values to uphold.

"Are you Eric?" she asked cautiously, reaching out to unlock the screen door, but waiting first for confirmation. He nodded and the lock turned with a resounding click. He looked quickly at the windows and saw thick security screens in front of them. Mrs Canter was taking no chances, even in this affluent part of town.

"Well, you're right on time. Most boys your age are always late. Can't trust any of you. So, I guess we should put you to work, but come in first and have a sweet."

Eric followed Mrs Canter into the house, down a short hallway, and then took a seat on an old sofa in the living room. The sofa had a garish floral design in pink and yellow and was worn in the middle. The room was cluttered with knick-knacks and numerous vases filled with flowers in various stages of decay. She had two cabinets jammed with framed photographs, cookbooks and photo albums. On a shelf next to a reclining armchair, there was an extensive collection of dog-eared Mills & Boon novels. He was surprised to see she had no television, and the room felt empty and lifeless for it. Perhaps she has one in her bedroom, he thought, and he pictured her lying in bed surrounded by tissue boxes as she watched yet another romantic mini-series.

She came into the room carrying a tray of sweets and a pot of tea which she put down on the low coffee table. In doing so, she bent over right in front of him, pointing her rather broad behind in his face. He saw a flash of white, wrinkled skin, unloved flesh that hadn't seen the sun perhaps since the house was built.

"I don't suppose you drink tea," she said, taking a seat next to him

112

on the sofa. Eric shook his head. She poured out a cup for herself and took a sip, leaving a film of red lipstick on the rim of the cup, and then picked up a tray of boiled sweets, offering them to Eric. He couldn't believe they made them anymore, those hard candies of white and red or white and black. He took a white and green one; it was sticky. He put it in his mouth. All he could do was suck on it and wonder if the candy was older than him. But having the candy in his mouth meant he was now breathing through his nose. Fragrances attacked him from all sides: the potpourri on the coffee table, the withering flowers in the vases, and Mrs Canter herself, whose sweet, musty smell he couldn't quite place, like lavender perfume way past its used-by date.

"So, your mother tells me you're interested in doing some work. I must say, the garden is a disaster. No one's touched it since my Gerald, bless his soul."

Her bottom lip quivered slightly and she took a quick sip of tea. Eric looked down at the carpet, worn plush still thick near the walls. He saw then there was a somewhat overweight orange cat sleeping in the far corner under the window.

"Just say what you'd like me to do and I'll do my best," he offered, uneasy with the silence. Mrs Canter turned to him and smiled, or sneered. She reached out a withered hand and gave his bare knee a pat.

"Well, it sounds to me that you're a fine young man, like Angela said. Come. I'll show you where Gerald kept his tools." She stood up, rather too quickly so that the cat rose with a start as well. It then stretched lazily and waddled across the room towards the kitchen. "That's Beatrice," Mrs Canter explained. She bent over and swept up the heavy cat which meowed in protest. She bundled the cat in her arms and led Eric outside. Once in the garden, she dropped the cat and it swiftly went around to the back of the house to where Eric guessed there was a cat flap in the back door.

"Independent, just like me," Mrs Canter said as the orange tail disappeared around the side of the house. She unlocked the garden shed, being sure not to let the rusty lock dirty her hands, holding it in her fingertips like it was a soiled pair of underpants, and stepped back to let Eric pull the door open. He frowned when he looked inside. There were old garden tools that would only make the work harder, and perhaps a few thousand spiders lurking inside the handles of shovels and saws.

"So, cut the grass, prune the trees, but not too much mind, and pull out all of the weeds," she ordered firmly, morphing from a kind old lady into a vicious school matron. "I know Gerald kept some garden bags in there somewhere. Rummage around and you'll find one. Put all the weeds and branches in it and the curator from the golf club will collect it."

And with that, she pivoted on her heels and went back into the house, perhaps late for a date with Mills & Boon. Eric looked inside the abyss of the shed, scared to enter, wondering if the ghost of Gerald was lurking in the shadows, deliberately hiding those elusive garden bags. The lawnmower was in easy reach so he grabbed that and threw it onto the grass. A few black spiders ran from it, scampering quickly back into the shed. Eric took a hose and watered down the old lawnmower, drowning a few spiders and washing away the cobwebs. He wondered if his mother had already negotiated the rate for his afternoon work, and that he would be grossly underpaid.

It was an old push mower, the bearings rusted stiff and the blades blunt. He stuck his head into the shed and found an old can of oil. Lubricated, the mower was soon running easily across the grass, but cutting it unevenly, making him do the same spot several times. He raked together the clippings and then set about weeding.

The hours passed. It was hot.

Mrs Canter came out onto the porch when he started pruning the trees. She offered him a glass of a cold and very bitter lemonade which he drank in thirsty gulps, trying not to let the liquid hit his tongue. She brought a chair out onto the porch and gossiped with him, talking in a bouncing, flighty voice about the people in the neighbourhood and the members of the golf club. This was an outrage, that was embarrassing, and something should be done about him or her, banned from the club at the very least, and the young members and teenagers, don't get her started. Eric thought she sounded smitten with a man named Baum. She talked about how good he was at golf and how he often asked her to dance at club functions. She pined for more such events, claiming the golf club should have them every week. Eric worked as she talked, and she talked incessantly, seemingly unaware that he was barely listening. She knew everyone in the area and felt no shame in sharing rather intimate information with him.

Towards the end of the afternoon, Eric inquired after the man named Baum, if he lived in Crescent Bay and if perhaps Eric might be able to do some work for him too. Mrs Canter beamed and went inside to use the telephone. Her cheeks were flushed when she came back out and she smoothed the creases of her ancient dress.

"He's on his way," she said, giving her blue rinse a fluff. "He'll take tea with me and then drive you over to his house. You're almost finished, aren't you?"

Eric wiped the sweat from his brow and nodded. His hands were blistered and cracked. He hated the idea of more garden work and the thought that it would bring him closer to his goal was of little motivation. Tired and dehydrated, he went into the shed. Having delayed the inevitable the whole afternoon, he now needed a few of Gerald's garden bags. He found a light, tried the switch and jumped when the light came on. He saw shapes scurrying for the dark corners and gingerly took a few steps inside. With the light on, he could see the whole shed. It gave him a rather intimate insight into Gerald and the life he had led. There was a dusty set of golf clubs in one corner and a miniature train set built on a table in the other. All the carriages were covered in dust and this small world that Gerald had built was now a thriving colony for spiders. There was a dartboard, a few half-finished carpentry projects, and even an old fifties style refrigerator. He edged the door open and saw beer cans, steel ones with tongue shaped pull-rings. This shed had been Gerald's hideaway. He wondered how long Gerald had been dead. Mrs Canter talked like it had happened only yesterday.

He found the garden bags under a stack of old newspapers. He grabbed the bags in his fingertips and then flung them out onto the grass. An issue of Playboy, withered and yellow and the pages somewhat disgustingly stuck together, slipped out and landed on the grass. A large huntsman spider, hairy and confused, crawled onto the magazine, uncertain in which direction to go. Eric attacked the spider with the hose, covering the nozzle with his thumb to make the water spray more powerful. The spider rolled itself into a ball and Eric brought the shovel down on top of it, squashing it against a pair of naked breasts. He cleaned the bags of spiders, small and more dangerous redbacks, and then got to work filling them. The Playboy was the first to go in.

It was as he was gathering up the branches and weeds that a cream coloured Mercedes with tinted windows drifted next to the curb, coming to a stop just in front of the rusted white gate. Eric watched a tall, elegant figure climb out from the left side of the car and wondered who was driving. The man wore yellow pants with a light pink sweater and leather loafers that squeaked slightly as he walked. Eric noticed the man wore no socks. The face was long and tanned, the age hidden under the shadow of a broad summer hat, which had a rather feminine floral band around it. But the man had the elegance to carry it off and maintain his masculinity; indeed, there was something daring about it. He looked like an ageing aristocrat on a summer holiday, replete with fancy car and handsome smile. He swept off his hat as he approached the porch. Eric saw him better with the hat off. Baum had a high forehead with neatly parted, thin white hair, still dark in patches. Through the gaps of hair, Eric saw the small brown sunspots that plagued the seniors of Australia.

Mrs Canter had timed her entrance perfectly, and now came onto the porch to greet Baum. "Christian," she said, drawing every syllable from the name, perhaps one too many. Her lips were freshly painted and both cheeks were red with rouge. "So wonderful that you could come at such short notice."

"Oh, I need little excuse to partake of your company and your cakes," Baum said.

Mrs Canter laughed. Eric felt she almost giggled like a girl, and she raised a withered and arthritic hand to cover her mouth as a girl would.

"This is the young lad I told you about on the phone," she said, gesturing to Eric with a sweeping and theatrical movement of her arm. "He's an excellent worker and a charming young man."

Eric blushed slightly, unused to such grand and glowing introductions.

"Nice to meet you, Eric," Baum said. He held out a thin hand that had long, tapered fingers. Eric quickly wiped his hand on his shorts and gripped the old man's; it was surprisingly cool and smooth. Baum made no attempt to grip Eric's hand. His breath smelt of mint and his freshly shaven faced glistened with moisturiser.

"We'll talk later," Baum continued, leaning closer to Eric and talking conspiratorially. "She makes the most delicious lamingtons. I'll nab a few extra for you." To fix their pact, he wiggled his grey eyebrows up and down, and his pale blue eyes sparkled with the enjoyment of secrecy.

Eric watched the screen door close behind the yellow pants and pink sweater, and heard the resounding click of the lock. He turned and admired the Mercedes. It was a sleek two-door number, long and luxurious like a yacht. It spoke of wealth, and he already started counting the money he would earn from Baum.

He cleaned up the last of the mess and put all the tools back in the shed, making sure they went in the same place as they were before, just in case Gerald was still puttering around in there in some form. He washed his face and hands under the tap at the side of the house and then sat in the cool shade of the porch to wait for Baum. His head throbbed and he felt slightly dizzy. He really should have worn a hat. Or was he just hungry? He longed for one of the lamingtons.

Cars drove past noisily. In the lull between cars he could hear the sounds of golf coming from the nearby course. He heard the cheers of a long putt, the shouts of fore and the cursing of mistakes. He looked at the garden and admired his work. Perhaps Mrs Canter will pay me extra for doing such a good job, he thought.

Baum gave Mrs Canter a peck on the cheek in the doorway and thanked her for the tea and cakes. In his hand he held a plastic container loaded with the chocolate and coconut covered lamingtons. Eric stood up, hungry for the cakes and the money he had earned.

"Thank you for your help today, Eric," Mrs Canter announced grandly. "I'll be sure to give your mother a cheque the next time I see her at the club."

Eric was slightly taken aback. He felt Baum's eyes, watching, judging, waiting for his response. The blue eyes bore at him, unblinking and inquisitive.

"Uh, thank you. Please tell my mother if you need more help."

"I most certainly will do that."

Baum tipped his hat to the old dame and led the way down the short path to the front gate.

"Come along, Eric," he said. "I can only hope you will work as hard for me as you have for this grand lady."

"Oh, Christian. You make me feel twenty years younger."

"But that would make you far too young for me," Baum said, buttering the old lady with a warm smile.

Eric, feeling slightly uneasy with their behaviour, closed the gate behind him and followed Baum around to the passenger side door.

"I'm afraid your seat is on the other side," Baum explained, pointing at the left-hand drive steering wheel.

Eric looked at it briefly in wonder before running around to the other side.

"It's an import from Germany," Baum said, waving to Mrs Canter through his lowered window as he pulled away from the curb. "I brought it back from Europe a few years ago."

The upholstery was blood red and the interior, like the exterior, was impeccably clean. Eric toyed with the container of lamingtons Baum had handed him, afraid to eat one and get small flecks of coconut all over the seats and floor, but hungry just the same. It was strange to sit on this side of the car and he still felt dizzy from his afternoon's labour in the hot sun.

They manoeuvred down narrow streets, taking the back way to the main road, Bayside Drive, which curved around the length of the bay. They pulled into the driveway of a smart, two-storey house at the north end of the bay. Eric breathed a sigh of relief when he saw the groomed and manicured front garden, the grass cut low like a putting green. The garage door opened automatically and Baum edged the Mercedes inside. There was a work bench in the far left corner, with tools orderly arranged on the wall next to it. There were no half-finished projects lying around and Eric wondered if the bench was just for show. A set of skis, old fashioned and made of thick wood with rusted metal bindings, was fixed to the wall and a newer set, bright yellow with matching poles, was leaning in the corner behind Baum's golf bag.

The inside of the house was air-conditioned and sparsely furnished, with a large open area that included the living room, dining room and kitchen. It was spacious and bright and hinted quietly at wealth. Large windows faced the ocean and the afternoon sun was streaming through the yellow curtains. The floor was made of large pink tiles, clean enough to eat off. Paintings hung from the walls and what furniture there was matched the colours of Baum's clothing: there was a lemon sofa, a pink easy chair, and a cream rug almost identical in colour to the Mercedes. Through the broad windows, Eric could see the ocean awash with white caps. He had to squint to make out the coloured specks surfing the waves at the north end of the bay. He joined Baum in the kitchen and handed him the container of lamingtons. He wondered if he should take his shoes off, but didn't want to pollute the air with his foul feet. He noticed Baum had already slipped into a pair of rather ridiculous house clogs.

"Let me get you a plate and a fork," Baum said, floating behind the long counter that separated the kitchen from the dining room. "Sit yourself down at the table."

The chair scraped loudly across the tiled floor, echoing in the open room. Eric sat down quite a distance from the table because he was reluctant to pull the chair in and make the same scraping noise again. Baum set down a plate with two lamingtons on it and formally placed a small fork next it.

"Something to drink? Maybe a glass of milk?"

Eric nodded. It had been years since he had drunk cold milk, but he was too scared to refuse. Baum sat down at the table and poured the milk. It was in an old-fashioned bottle like the ones Eric remembered the milkman delivering to the door in Merredin when he was very young. Baum watched him as he ate.

"A healthy young man should have a healthy appetite," he commented, smiling and showing his small, even teeth, which were a bit too small for his long, elegant head and seemed out of proportion in an ugly way.

"Will I be working in your garden?" Eric asked, his voice echoing in the open room.

Baum eyed him curiously. "Do you think it needs it?"

Eric smiled and shook his head.

"Are you new around here, Eric? I only ask because not many local boys are interested in working, least of all my grandson."

"We moved here a few weeks ago, from the country."

Baum smiled knowingly. "That might explain it, but it could also be in your genes." The grin turned sly, as if Baum might know something about Eric that he himself did not know.

"My father's a real estate agent," Eric said, feeling a little uncomfortable with Baum's twinkling eyes on him. "He works hard, but not with his hands."

"Would that be Roger Messer, by chance?"

"You know him?"

"I own a few properties that his office looks after. I met him last week." He paused, inspecting his fingernails, choosing his words. "A competent man."

Eric nodded, thinking it an unusual thing to say, as if Baum had wanted to say something nice and complimentary, but competent was the best he could come up with; and because it went against the normal trend of people saying something nice regardless of their true opinion, it came out negatively.

"But I wonder though," Baum said, stroking his smooth chin and narrowing his eyes. "Is your family from Australia?"

"Sure. I mean, I was born here. My mother's Dutch and my great grandfather came from Germany after the First World War. My grandfather said there were lots of problems at that time in Europe. The war had left Germany in ruins."

"It was a bitter defeat," Baum said softly, with the kind of regret and pain that made Eric think he had suffered through it. "And the Weimar Republic was a disaster."

"Are you German?"

Baum's eyes were cold, but he forced a smile. "Oh, heavens no. I was born in Innsbruck, in Austria." He sighed wistfully. "But now I'm Australian like you."

Eric looked at the table, wondering what that meant, to be born in one country and now claim the nationality of another. If the two countries played sport against each other, who would he support?

"When did you come here?" he asked, uncomfortable with the silence.

"Not unlike your great grandfather, I left when my country had been left shattered by war. The Second World War. The bombing killed my family. There was nothing left for me."

"I'm sorry."

Baum waved off the apology, as if swatting at an imaginary fly.

"It's not that bad. It brought me here, and I've been lucky to have lived in this country of hope than to have suffered in a country of defeat. You can't imagine what it was like after the war. The bombs had wiped out whole cities. The Allies were merciless, didn't care if they killed civilians."

Eric thought about the documentaries he had watched in the last weeks of school: the destroyed or gutted buildings, the piles of bricks and rubble, the open graves with naked and twisted bodies piled one on top of the other, the American soldiers riding on tanks and winning children and women over with chocolate and cigarettes.

"May I ask what the name of your great grandfather was? Also a Messer?"

Eric nodded. "George Messer."

Baum stared at Eric briefly. Eric looked down at the table again, uncomfortable with Baum's eyes boring into him.

"It could be that it's your genes after all," Baum said, the hint of a smile on his face and in his eyes. Abruptly, he stood up, his chair scraping loudly on the floor. "Come on, then. We can't sit around talking all day. Let me show you what I want to do and then you can go home for a well-earned dinner."

***

Eric walked along the beach, tracing wide arcs with his toes, as he had done on summer holidays when he was younger, copying his father. Their relationship had been great then, he thought. How could it have gone bad so quickly? The sky was awash with reds and pinks. The sun, glowing like a neon orange ball, was slowly being swallowed by the Indian Ocean. The wind had died, as it often did in the evenings when the next day promised to be blistering hot. A few people ran past him, red-faced and panting, still wearing the look of stress and doubt that they had brought home from work. He marvelled at the way they forced themselves forward, heads down, pumping their arms spasmodically, somehow propelling themselves down the beach at a speed their bodies seemed ill-equipped to handle. The adults always rushed, he thought, as if they had so many important things to do but not the time. Or did they just want to show the world how busy they were? For him, his childhood days couldn't pass quickly enough, when he would be seventeen, finished with school, and he could leave the house forever. But he had two more years of school left and the time dragged.

A small campfire was burning at the beach. He saw the shadowed outlines of people crowded around it and felt afraid. Someone was plucking at the strings of an out-of-tune guitar and singing intermittently in a croaking voice. He kept his head down and walked quickly towards the path up to the road. A waft of cigarette smoke blew up his nose as he passed, causing him to cough rather loudly.

"Hey, Rick," a voice called out. It was Drew, standing next to the fire and beckoning to Eric with his free hand. Eric, feeling all eyes on him, stumbled in the sand, his legs suddenly heavy and immobile, and slowly found his way to the fire.

"Hey," he said.

The guitar stopped and there was a chorus of greetings, some friendly, some cold. The kids were trying to act as cool and relaxed as possible, blowing big clouds of cigarette smoke in the air and gulping beer from cans. Pepper was there, sitting with Melanie and a few other girls whose faces Eric recognised but whose names escaped him. The boy playing the guitar was the same bronzed, zinc painted beach warrior who had spoken to him yesterday.

"Wanna beer?" Drew asked. He flipped open a small cooler bag. Eric had tasted beer a few times and didn't like it much; he found it too bitter. But as he glanced around and saw the other boys and most of the girls with beers in their hands, he nodded his head, reaching out his hand as Drew gave him a cold can. He popped it, took a large gulp, swallowed hard and let out a refreshing "Aaaahh," like the men in the commercials. It was just contrived and self-conscious enough for a few of the kids to find it funny and laugh.

"Didn't see ya at the beach today," Drew said, his speech slower than normal. "Don't tell me you've given up already."

"I was here in the morning. But there wasn't much swell."

"It picked up around lunchtime. When the tide came in, it went off."

Eric took a seat in the tight circle around the fire, sitting down too quickly so that some sand went down the back of his shorts. He tried to get comfortable, to feel included. Drew kept him in the conversation, mainly by making jokes at his expense. Eric smiled through the jokes, sneaking looks at Pepper and wishing he could have another chance to talk to her alone. She giggled with Melanie and the other girls. They talked behind their hands and smoked cigarettes which they stubbed out in the sand. Eric was sure he was the topic of their conversation, that they were laughing at him. He drank his beers, tried to look relaxed and stared into the fire. The guitar, which at first had sounded like a cat slowly being strangled, sounded better with each beer he drank, and Drew's jokes died away as he turned his attention to Melanie. Drew tried to pull her away from the girls group, but she wasn't interested.

After a while, they toasted marshmallows. Their sticky sweetness was in stark contrast to the bitter beers they drank, but no one complained. With the afternoon's work in the sun, the very lemony lemonade, the lamingtons and milk, and now the beer and marshmallows, Eric was longing for a baked potato and a few litres of water.

Having given up on enticing Melanie away, Drew went back to taunting Eric, making jokes about people from the country: something about sex and sheep, or sex and kangaroos, or sex and siblings. Eric forced a smile. He was suddenly aware that it was dark and knew he had to get home. If his father found out he had come home after dark, he was sure to be grounded again, and he couldn't afford to spend his days inside. He got to his feet, swaying slightly.

"Hey, I gotta go. Some of my cousins are coming to dinner tonight."

Drew made a loud joke about sex and cousins and there was muffled, almost forced laughter.

"You comin down tomorrow mornin?" Drew asked. "If you do, we might be surfin down at South Corner." He pointed with his beer can in the direction of the break.

"Okay. Same time?"

"We'll be here, won't we guys?"

There was a loud chorus of agreement. In the firelight, Eric saw a pile of sleeping bags and a few tents still rolled up. He would have liked to stay at the beach and camp with the others, but he was living under a tyrant and had to get home.

"See ya," Eric said, stumbling towards the path. He tripped in the sand and fell. The group's laughter came out of the darkness and slapped him sober. He got up to his elbows and then saw Pepper standing over him. She reached out a hand and helped him up. He brushed the sand from his arms and knees, and tried hard to maintain his balance.

"Thanks," he mumbled.

"It's all right," she said, her eyes bright in the darkness. "I gotta go home too."

Eric waited, but it was clear she didn't want to be seen leaving with him. So he started alone up the path. When he got to the top, he waited in the darkness, thinking Pepper might be just behind him, but she wasn't. It was really dark now and he started for home at a run. But he only got to the first corner before he had to duck behind a clump of bushes to vomit. When he got back on the road, he saw Pepper silhouetted in the street light at the top of the beach path. She waved to him and was then enveloped by the darkness.

***

123

His mouth felt like the inside of an old vacuum cleaner, dry and furry. Blood throbbed at his temples. The sunlight streamed through the curtains, overly bright, making him squint his eyelids shut. He tried to piece together yesterday evening: lamingtons with Baum, beer on the beach, the twang of the guitar, Drew's jokes, Pepper helping him up from the sand and then waving to him from under the beam of a streetlight, vomiting next to someone's letterbox, his mother's harsh words, his father at a Christmas function in Perth – saved.

He tried to sit up in bed. His head hung limp against his chest, seemingly heavier than his whole body. And when he moved his head, it seemed something moved inside too, a sharp rock bouncing off the walls of his skull, echoing and vibrating. It was only his full bladder that got him standing, and he managed to stagger into the bathroom. But what a great feeling that was, the dam breaking, the piss gushing out of him like oil struck from the ground.

His mother was sitting at the table reading the morning paper, surrounded by the dirty dishes of breakfast, abandoned when his father had finished.

"Hungry?"

Just the thought of eating made him sick, yet his stomach rumbled. He took the sweet juice from the fridge and drank it straight, emptying the carton.

"You must've worked hard yesterday. You were asleep when you came in the door. Didn't even have any dinner."

"Sorry I was late. Mrs Canter called Mr Baum and I went with him to his house to talk about more work. I'm going there this afternoon."

She put the paper down, straightening the pages and folding it away. Eric saw that some of the corners were stained with grease and butter, and the front page had a dark coffee circle. His father getting first read.

"I'm really proud of you, Ricky, not just for taking responsibility for your own money, but for helping the seniors. They're a pretty lonely bunch. Mrs Canter is always complaining that she has no one." She laughed. "I hope you won't be like that when we're retired."

Eric tried to picture his parents as dithering seniors, puttering around the house with nothing left to say to each other, struggling to fill their days: his mother withered and dried out, her spirit crushed, reaching for the wine bottle before breakfast; and his father bitter and mean, yelling at the plumber who can't fix the pipe, shouting at the mechanic who can't repair his car, and screaming at the world he can't bend to his will.

"I'll be around," he mumbled. "Gotta be ready to grab my inheritance." Such as it would be, he thought.

"I've heard of this Mr Baum," his mother said. "He sounds like quite the charmer."

"I think Mrs Canter's in love with him."

His mother let out a shriek of laughter that could have shattered a thin window. The sound grated inside his head and made him wince. He crunched up the carton and threw it in the bin.

"What a pair they would make," she said.

"By the way, if you see her, she said she would give you a cheque. I don't know why she didn't just give me the money."

"She's from a different generation, Ricky, when they wrote cheques for everything. I guess she hangs on to the old ways like everyone does."

Eric frowned, wanting to hold the money in his hands so he could see the results of his toil.

"What will you do for Mr Baum?" his mother asked. "More garden work?"

Here come the questions. Quick, he thought, run while you have the chance.

"He collects stuff," he said, making to leave the kitchen.

"What kind of stuff?"

"Dunno. Photos, pictures, all kinds of weird things."

"And what does he want to do with it?"

Eric edged around the kitchen counter and headed towards his bedroom. "I think he wants to make some kind of museum, in his house. His place is huge."

"Sounds interesting," she said, keeping him in the room. "Not as hard as labouring in the sun. You got a nice sunburn yesterday. Why didn't you wear a hat?"

Eric shrugged. "Forgot."

"Well, remember next time. You only get one skin."

He looked down at the worn carpet. How he hated to be told what to do, how to act; as if the adults knew everything better and never made mistakes. What a joke, he thought. He promised himself that if he ever had children he would let them run riot, not give them any rules or borders, and throw all the money he had at them.

"What kind of things does Mr Baum collect?" The reproachful tone had been quickly replaced by that slightly disinterested line of inquiry which Eric was tormented by, the endless questions that he felt obliged to answer.

"I dunno. Stuff from Europe, from the wars. I guess it's his hobby."

His mother nodded, suddenly solemn and quiet. Eric took the chance to duck back to his room. He slipped into his coolest swimming shorts, smeared on some sunscreen, banged a cap on his head and then dashed for the garage door, hoping to escape another interrogation.

"Don't forget your sunscreen," he heard his mother say, but he was already out the door. He retrieved the heavy board from behind Drew's gate and tucked it under his arm.

It was a beautiful day, the blue sky sparkling and the sun glistening like pale gold, but he headed towards the beach without energy. His steps were languid, slow and uninspired, the sun too bright and reflecting into his eyes off pavements still wet from early watering. It was a hot morning and a heat haze shimmered above the road. One car had been pushed to the side of the road, a steam cloud drifting from under the bonnet. Few people were outside and there weren't even any kids out playing. The roofs of houses were decorated with Santas and snowmen and reindeer, and Eric imagined these plastic figures, monuments to a kind of Christmas never experienced in Australia, melting under the broiling sun, dripping red and white down the sides of roofs and clogging the gutters when the plastic hardened again.

He was sweating when he arrived at the beach. He saw the charcoal remains of last night's fire, the scattered beer cans, numerous cigarette butts and other rubbish. There were condom wrappers too, lying near flattened stretches of sand where some kids had slept together. But the group was gone. He took a quick swim to cool off and then began the long walk around the bay to South Corner. It was something he had yet to do in his short time in Crescent Bay, and despite the heat, the heavy board and his hangover, he found it very relaxing, and walked in the shallows when he could stand the hot sand no longer.

It was a long way to the south end. He could see the rocks, but they never seemed to come any closer. The beaches were peppered with families already enjoying their Christmas holidays. He recognised the familiar look and manner of country kids, the way brothers and sisters stayed so close together, the elders protective and the younger ones obedient. Dads were hairy-chested and strong, still wearing their broad brimmed farming hats, their skin a light reddish-brown as if the dried soil of the country had formed a film on top that could never be scrubbed away. They had radios and tried to pick up the stations they normally listened to. Mums were small and wiry, with hands that looked decades older than the rest of their bodies; they were no strangers to hard work. They were watchful of their children and any word from a mum was taken as the rule.

At South Corner, he looked with fear at the sharp rocks which jutted out of the water. He saw Drew's group huddled together far out past the breakers and wondered how long it would take him to paddle out that far. The waves were big too, curling around the point and slamming against the rocks. The surfers riding them could only take the waves left – any move right would be dangerous – and had to give up on the waves early before they broke against the rocks. Eric started to walk away, but Drew waved and he was forced to wave back.

The whitewash was strong and he paddled out slowly, fighting the current that tried to suck him towards the rocks. It seemed to take forever, and he would get over the top of one wave only for the next to drive him back. The heavy board felt like a small ship and his arms were tired, not strong enough to fight the current or the whitewash. Finally, and tentatively, he paddled towards the group. They were waiting for the next set of waves and watched him draw closer. They even gave him a cheer when he made it and that heartened him somewhat. Perhaps he was in the group after all. They were all there, tanned and happy and popular.

"You look like shit," Drew said as he paddled up next to Eric. "Got a hangover?"

"I had more beer with my cousins after dinner. We played cricket down the park, made a drinking game of it."

"Cool," Drew said, nodding admiringly.

"Hey, Drew," one of the boys called out. It was the guitar player from last night, and he had fresh zinc cream across his nose and bottom lip. "Let's ride the next one together. Play chicken with the rocks."

"You're on, Brad."

The set rolled in and Eric let the others catch waves first. He went for the last one, which grew like a mountain as it sucked up more and more water. He paddled half-heartedly and was thankful when he fell off the back. He turned and paddled back out. Pepper waited alone. She wore a different bikini top today, green with white flowers, but the result was the same; there was the crevice that Eric found so inviting, and the neck he wanted so badly to kiss. She sat rather forlornly on her pink board, running her hands lightly through the water. Eric paddled up to her, as casually as possible, and then tried to sit on his board in the same way, but slipped and fell into the water with an undignified splash. She laughed as he struggled to get back on the board, slipping a couple of times before finally getting into the sitting position.

"You can do it easily," she said, cocking her head and putting her hands on her hips. "You're just trying to make me laugh."

"Is it that obvious?"

She looked down at the thick plank wedged between his knees. "You really need to get a new board."

"Yeah, I know." Again he looked down at the water, wondering if sharks were circling beneath. An awkward silence fell between them. Here's my chance, he thought, and all I can do is worry about sharks.

"Um, do you know maybe where I can get one?"

Pepper watched her hand trace figure eights in the water. "There's a good shop out at the mall," she said, tentative, cool. "You know where that is?"

"I think so." He was struggling to keep his voice steady, and was happy that Pepper was doing most of the talking. "Is it where the pool is?"

"That's the other mall, stupid."

Eric swallowed hard, his body shivering in the cold water. Was the water always this cold? A rash of gooseflesh sprouted on his arms and shoulders.

"Maybe you can show me where it is."

Pepper giggled. "Sure. Today?"

Eric shook his head. "I can't. What about tomorrow?"

"That's Christmas Eve."

"If you don't have time, it's all right. You can just tell me where it is." He felt her slipping away. He had come so close and now he was making a complete fool of himself.

"If you don't want to go with me then just say so," Pepper responded snidely.

"No, wait. I want to go with you, really. I didn't know if you had family stuff or not, that's all."

Pepper smiled and he breathed a sigh of relief. He relaxed just enough to lose his concentration. The board slipped out from under him and he fell into the water again. When he popped his head out of the water, Pepper was laughing at him, so he reached out and up-ended her board, sending her into the water as well. Then she started splashing water at him. After a brief splashing fight, Eric shouted that Pepper was the winner and they both climbed back onto their boards.

"I'd hate to see you riding a horse," she said. The water had slicked her hair back and her rather large pink ears stuck out from the side of her head. She saw Eric looking and quickly arranged her hair.

"My board's about as heavy as a horse," Eric said, undeterred by the unsightly ears. Everything else about her overshadowed them.

"My grandma's going shopping at the mall tomorrow," Pepper said. "We can go with her."

"Great."

How warm the water suddenly was, and how empty his head became, and how thankful he was that other members of the group joined them, ending their embarrassing silence. When the next set rolled in, his confidence was soaring. He went after a big wave, driving his arms through the water to get over the lip. He slid down the face and jumped to his feet. He had his balance briefly and thought what a hero he was, a real surfer. He tried to turn the board left but the nose tipped too far forward and caught the water. He went in head first, the wave following through and spinning him around and around. Arms flailing, he waited for a sharp rock to split his head open. When it didn't, he opened his eyes. It was only the leg rope that told him which way was up. He climbed it and broke through the surface, gasping for air. He looked up at a wall of water. A surfer was heading straight for him.

"Out of the way, sheep lover," Brad shouted.

Eric quickly ducked under, the fins narrowly missing his head. The wave crashed and he broke the surface again gasping for air and coughing. He managed to get back on his board before the next wave came and paddled over the lip just before it peaked. When he got out past the breakers, Brad was already there again, with Melanie.

"Classy," Brad said, his zinc-green lip curling into a mocking grin.

"You don't belong out here, country boy," Melanie snapped.

"Yeah, better off riding sheep than waves."

The two laughed loudly and Eric stared down at his board, unable to think of a comeback.

"You all right, Rick?" Drew asked when he joined them. "You got onto a real dumper. You got watch out for them, especially here with the rocks and all."

"I'm okay."

He wanted to say that the board had failed him, that they all had it easy because they had flash boards, but he said nothing. For the rest of the morning, he felt too scared to catch a wave, making pathetic attempts to get onto one, always just falling off the back and making a show of being disappointed, slapping at the water and cursing. It was a miserable morning and the group singled him out and made jokes at his expense because he was such a bad surfer. He was happy when it was time to go in and he caught a small wave, lying on the board the whole way. Not even the date with Pepper could lift his spirits.

At the beach, he kept his back to the water, not wanting to see the group pointing at him and laughing. Josh's three-storey mansion loomed over the beach. It was at the southern point of the crescent and looked out over the ocean. The windows glimmered in the sunlight, reflecting it in all directions, blinding him if he tried to look directly at the house. Eric walked up the path to get a closer look, hoping to confirm that Josh was not there. The garden was like Mr Baum's: pristine, immaculate, cared for by a professional. But the house was lifeless, the driveway empty, and a blue light flashed intermittently near the top of the roof. Hopefully, he thought, Josh will stay away for the whole summer.

**

A tall glass of milk was waiting for him on the table. It stood like a lighthouse, the lone beacon in the aqua sea that was the table surface. Baum was dressed in white shorts and a tennis shirt in red, green and yellow, the stiff collar turned up. With the blue canvas shoes, he looked like a retired yachtsman, or an old tennis pro. He smiled and led the way into the locked room that Eric had seen yesterday. Baum reached out to turn the lock but was interrupted by a woman standing in the hall. Eric's view was blocked by the old man and he leaned back to get a look at her. She was of Asian descent, but Eric was not worldly enough to say from where exactly. In his limited view, he had to admit, they seemed to all look the same. In her thin arms she carried a bundle of white sheets. She stared at Baum, waiting for him to talk first.

"Yes, Annie?" Baum inquired, a hint of frustration in his voice, as if she was always coming to him with problems. "What is it?"

"You want brue sheets or yerrow?" she asked.

Baum rubbed his eyes, as if such trivial decisions belonged to people much less important than him. "I think blue," he said, emphasising the L.

Annie nodded and scurried past, smiling at Eric as she went, showing her small and "yerrow" teeth. He hadn't seen many Asian people before – there were none in Merredin – and he marvelled at her slanted eyes, tea coloured complexion and tiny stature. Short, thick legs stuck out the bottom of her simple blue dress, and her feet were so small, Eric wondered if she had to buy children's shoes. She disappeared quickly around the corner and went towards the garage.

Baum clicked the lock and slithered inside the room. "Four generations and she still can't speak the language fluently," he muttered. "How can those people possibly produce the best students every year?"

The room was slightly more organised than yesterday. Eric assumed Baum had tidied up after he had left. There were still full boxes stacked on the floor, and the large paintings depicting soldiers and battles were leaning against the walls. Other paintings, unframed and their corners curling inwards, were piled on the floor one on top of the other, with empty frames scattered nearby, some in pieces tied together with old string. There were two cabinets and the walls had empty shelves at about head height. There was a single desk and a chair, both antique, but in excellent condition. The desk was surprisingly empty, nothing on top and the drawers missing, as if it had only just been moved in. Eric tried to picture old Baum and his miniature cleaning woman shifting the desk into the room. There was still a lingering smell of fresh paint, but Baum didn't open the window.

"I know it looks like a lot of work," Baum said, looking around the room and placing his hands rather girlishly on his hips, "but I want to get some order from this chaos before I go on holiday tomorrow. And I'm expecting a few more boxes next week."

Eric nodded, but was still unsure of where he stood with Baum, whether he was his slave or co-worker. "Where do we start?" he asked.

Baum moved into the room, keen to begin and keen to lead. "First, we need to clean these cabinets so we have somewhere to put the delicate objects. The big stuff in the boxes can wait. I want to get the important pieces inside the cabinets and set in place."

The cabinets were of a dark, reddish wood, finished with blood-coloured varnish. Each had four glass doors, with two narrow shelves behind each door. Baum handed Eric a bucket of tepid water and a brand new sponge and he set to work mopping the shelves of dust, which was also red and led him to believe that the cabinets were freshly made. For some reason, he thought they also smelled fresh, as if the cut wood was still dripping with sap.

They worked in silence, side by side. Eric cleaned the shelves, while Baum wiped the shelves dry with a dishcloth, also new, and then placed his items delicately on the shelves. They stood so close, Eric could feel Baum's breath on his bare left forearm; it was cold and made his hairs stand up, like soldiers called to attention with each breath. He hated the closeness, and tried to edge away, but Baum stayed close. It was only because Baum's work took longer that Eric started to get some distance from the old man. Eric watched him from the corners of his eyes, unsure what to think. Annie was still in the house somewhere. If Baum tried anything, he decided, he would just have to shout for her.

Baum's important, delicate items were figurines, toy soldiers wearing pointy helmets and clutching rifles with bayonets on the end. There were others dressed elegantly, sitting with straight backs on horses, with long swords dangling from their sides and small coloured circles of medals painted on their chests. Baum handled them with care, placing them carefully on the shelf and putting them in striking positions.

"These are cavalrymen from the Great War," he said, not taking his eyes from his work. He placed one mounted soldier after another on the shelf, forming a long line that seemed ready to charge off the shelf and into battle. "They were the great men of Prussia, the elite who fought more for their own honour and glory than for that of their Kaiser." Baum paused and looked sideways at Eric who had stopped mopping the shelf to listen. "I think your great grandfather might have been one of them."

"Really?"

"There once was a great German named Georg Messer," Baum explained, pronouncing the name Ge-org, with hard Gs. He reached out his long fingers to move the figurines slightly and get them perfectly in line, squinting as he did so. "He was a famous cavalryman who disappeared after the war."

Eric looked at the line of riders in disbelief, trying to imagine his great grandfather, a man he had only seen in pictures as old and frail, as a young and proud member of the Prussian cavalry.

"He became quite famous during the war," Baum continued, "for his bravery and ruthlessness. He was an example for the men who followed, men who believed in the greatness of Germany and who would do everything they could for victory."

Eric looked at the soldiers again, Baum's words almost bringing them to life. The horses seemed to snort steam and stamp on the spot, sensing the coming battle, ready to break into a fast gallop. His grandfather had told him stories about George, how he had immigrated to Australia and built a life from nothing. He had been a successful farmer, even during the depression, and had hold sold the farm before the Second World War and moved to the city. A smart move, his grandfather had said, because during the war, nobody wanted to do business with German immigrants, and sometimes chased them from towns or threw them in special camps.

"I'm not surprised your family didn't tell you about him," Baum said. "It's not fashionable to talk of German heroes anymore. The world doesn't want to know about them and the world doesn't want to hear Germans speaking proudly about themselves and their history."

"Was he a hero?" Eric asked. He dabbed the sponge half-heartedly at the shelf, but wasn't watching what he was doing and some water dripped onto the floor.

"But of course," Baum said. He came close to Eric and bent down to mop up the water with another new dishcloth. Eric mumbled an apology, but Baum waved it off, seemingly happy to be standing close to Eric again.

"The Kaiser himself pinned the Iron Cross to his chest. And that was only in the first year of the war. After that, and this is what made him legendary, he refused all medals and promotions so that he could stay at the front line." Baum sighed heavily, his grin crooked and wistful with admiration. "He was a true fighter, one of the many brave Prussians driven out by the Weimar villains, and by that ridiculous treaty which imprisoned many of them behind the Polish border. He was handsome too, tall and muscular, and Hitler himself was known to have been a great admirer. He represented many of the things Hitler stood for."

Eric's burgeoning pride turned quickly to shame.

Baum looked down at Eric, his blue eyes shining. "Would you like to see a photo?"

Eric followed Baum to the empty desk in the corner of the room. He saw then that the desk wasn't empty after all. There was a fraying photo album on top that had a similar colour to the surface of the desk. Baum turned the cover gently.

"I had a look last night and that's when I was convinced."

Baum carefully turned the withered pages. Eric got glimpses of soldiers standing in proud repose, some in scuffed uniforms, others with dashing outfits. The men had long handlebar moustaches, hats pressed firmly on their heads and held their faces grimly, nobody smiling. Baum stopped and pointed at a photograph that filled the page. Eric leaned closer, almost burying his head in the photo album.

It was black and white photograph. The man was dressed like the cavalrymen lined up on Baum's shelf; the long sword hanging from his belt almost touched the ground. Eric wondered how a man could walk with such a sword and not trip over it. He had a pale, handsome face, his cheekbones sticking out and making his cheeks hollow, like he didn't eat enough. But the face was strong, and the eyes were hard. He had seen blood and death and was ready for more. Eric saw a glimmer of the man he had seen in his grandfather's photographs. Baum leaned closer so that their two heads hovered over the photo. Eric smelled the sweet cologne and tried to edge away from the old man, leaning a little to the side, but keeping his head over the picture. He wondered why the old man always had to stand so close.

"You see that long dagger in his belt?" Baum asked, extending his tapered index finger to point it out but careful not to touch the page. "He was famous for that knife. It had been passed through his family for generations. Messer is German for knife. Georg and his family were famous for their knife-work."

Eric looked at the knife hooked under the belt, but went back to the face, searching for something that would convince him that he was looking at a part of himself.

"He had beautiful blond hair and startling blue eyes," Baum said. "Just like you. The picture's black and white but the resemblance is clear, don't you think?"

Eric nodded dumbly, wanting it to be true, wanting to have a hero's blood running through his veins. He studied the hard face, tracing the high forehead and protruding cheekbones down to the sharp points of the Iron Cross, then to the glistening sheath of the sword and landing on the dagger hooked in the belt; trying to join those dots to make a picture of his heritage, the man he might have become had history turned out differently.

Abruptly, Baum snapped the book shut, causing Eric to pull his head back. Baum lifted the album and put it in a box filled with similarly brown and fraying albums. Eric peered into the box and knew he would never be able to find the photograph without Baum's help.

"Well, we can't spend the whole day looking at photos," Baum said.

They resumed their respective positions and worked in silence until Eric, brimming with questions and unknowns, asked, "If he was such a hero, why would he leave Germany?"

"It was not such a good place to be after the Great War," Baum said, his words directed at the toy soldiers in front of him like some kind of morale-lifting speech. "The treaty took away the army, and the aristocracy lost a lot of properties and titles. And there were new borders too that left Prussia in tatters. I'd say Georg lost his place in society. His identity." Baum's voice was low and sad, full of pity. "The world he had known and identified with was gone. And the Weimar Republic was no place for men of his ilk." Then the old man's voice turned hard and brittle, and he spat his words. "The money-handlers took control of everything. It was the same in Austria. I was just a boy in the twenties, but I remember how it was. There was nothing to eat and prices went up and up. You can't imagine it. Georg was probably one of the many great men driven out of their homeland by those money-grubbing thieves."

Baum continued placing soldiers on the lower shelf. He bent down and put his head almost inside the cabinet, to be sure he got the soldiers in the positions he wanted. Eric noticed the soldiers had dull grey uniforms, making the black and red swastikas stand out clearly. From his vantage point, now standing on a chair to reach the top shelf, he saw Baum give the soldiers a thin smile.

"But then Hitler came along and turned everything around. Gave back to Germany everything the treaty had taken away, and got rid of the greedy thieves, but unfortunately not for good." He laughed, a snorting, mocking chuckle. "History makes him out to be a monster. How conveniently they forget he took a country from the gutter and made it a world power in four years. Incredible. Of course, it had a lot to do with the character of the German people, so hard-working and obedient." He looked up at Eric and smiled. "They have a remarkable work ethic."

Eric dabbed the sponge on the top shelf, breathing in the dry smell of freshly cut wood. Baum was scaring him. He had never heard someone talk so warmly of Hitler and Germany. Then he remembered: Austria had been part of Germany too, during the war and before, but he couldn't remember what the connection had been exactly.

"Were you in the war?" he asked tentatively. He had wanted to ask if Baum was a Nazi, because he sure sounded like one. His sympathy and admiration of Hitler went against everything Eric had been taught at school and had seen on television.

Baum laughed. "I wish I had been, and it's nice of you to think I would make a good soldier, but no I wasn't. I had polio when I was a child. The army turned me back." He chuckled again, but Eric thought there was something sad about it. Baum stood up slowly and stretched to his full height. With Eric on the chair, they were almost at eye level, Eric slightly higher. "I admired the soldiers greatly, more so because I couldn't fight alongside them. But a war is more than just bullets and tanks and men. There's a lot of work to do in the background, to keep the economy going and to maintain the production of arms and that's what I did. I worked in the Reich Economic Administration Office. I was more suited to numbers than to battle. The only blood I saw was from the civilians when the British bombed our cities. But I was never a Nazi. And the rumours I heard about the Jews at the end of the war caught me by complete surprise. I was so shocked by it, I left Austria, ashamed that my country had been part of it. Still, you can't help but admire the German people. They nearly took over the world."

"My grandfather used to say that Germans need goals," Eric said, trying to sound informed and mature. "Something to fight for and work towards. He also said they needed someone to tell them what to do, to set them goals and give them a reason to keep going. When that reason is gone, they don't know what to do."

Baum smiled, nodding his head slightly, agreeing. "And the Weimar Republic showed that. But it's not that simple. I'm guessing your grandfather never lived among the Germans. They're more complicated than he thinks, and not all of them have the same goals. You should tell him I said that."

"He's dead."

Baum's shoulders drooped, his sadness so genuine it made Eric feel sad. "I'm sorry."

"It's okay," Eric said, trying to make light of it and prove to Baum he was a strong and hard-working German, destined for heroism like his ancestor. He rubbed hard at the last shelf, determined not to leave a speck of sawdust on it. "Do you think there'll be another war?"

"You mean in the Middle East? Those Arabs have been killing each other for centuries. But because of Israel, and oil, America will go after the Iraqis. Try to keep an open mind, Eric. It's difficult because of the propaganda that comes from America, and from here too. The Yanks are not the heroes they make themselves out to be. Remember, the one who writes the history paints himself as the hero."

Eric nodded, not really understanding. His knowledge of world events was limited. The news always claimed Israel was the victim, that Hussein was like Hitler and that the good guys from America would save the world. He kept cleaning the shelves, going back over the ones he had done earlier with the new-found pride of his heritage, but was unsure what to say. Baum closed the first cabinet and stood back to admire it. The toy soldiers were neatly arranged, and not just German soldiers. Baum pointed out the Americans, British, French and Italians, talking about each in turn, the avid collector. To Eric, they seemed to all be the same man, but with a different uniform painted on.

"When you've finished with the cabinets," Baum said, "move on to those other shelves."

"I think I should change the water," Eric said, looking down at the murky red coloured contents of his bucket.

"Good idea. You know where the kitchen is."

Eric went out of the room and carried the heavy bucket to the kitchen, careful not to slosh the contents onto the floor. Annie turned around as he entered, nodding her head several times, up and down like a chicken pecking at seeds, and then went back to cleaning the kitchen.

"I just need some water," Eric said slowly, not wanting to interrupt her.

"I never see you before," Annie said. "You another grandchild?"

Eric shook his head. He emptied the bucket in the sink, rinsing it to get the muck from the bottom and then started filling it with warm water.

"Mister Baum good man," Annie said loudly, but then leaned close and lowered her voice, "but not so good grandfather."

Eric lifted the bucket from the sink and then saw the red ring he had left. He started to clean it, but Annie placed a small hand on his forearm. The hand was cold and the intimacy shocked him a little.

"It's okay," she said, looking Eric in the eyes. He found her brown eyes almost hypnotic. "I'll clean it."

"Uh, thanks." He lifted the bucket and carried it with two hands back to the room.

Baum looked up as Eric came back in. The old man's eyes were shining. He was filling the second cabinet with model planes, tanks, cars and guns, placing them side by side in long rows. He cleaned each item carefully before placing it on the shelf. Eric asked the occasional question, but soon stopped because Baum gave him long-winded and complicated answers and descriptions, sometimes so technical, the words flew right over his head. The afternoon passed and the work was soon finished. At the end, they stood and admired the two cabinets. Baum lightly placed an arm around Eric's shoulder. He froze, feeling the lean fingers gripping his shoulder, squeezing it slightly. He was unsure what to do; he had still to be paid.

"It's good that you're interested in your roots, Eric. You can't ignore the blood that flows in your veins, or what your ancestors have done. It's the same with Australians. They've persecuted the Aborigines for two centuries, almost completely wiped them out, a Holocaust if you will, and now they try to ignore their past." He laughed sarcastically. "And they give the Asians a hard time. I'm sure Annie could tell you some stories. And they go out into the world proclaiming their multiculturalism. What a double standard."

With his arm still around Eric's shoulder, Baum led them out of the room and into the kitchen. Annie wasn't there. Eric hoped she was still in the house somewhere. Baum freed him and went to the refrigerator. Eric dashed for the table and took a seat to prevent further close contact. Baum took out a milk bottle and poured two glasses. Eric gulped at his, the cold milk hurting his teeth.

"You know a lot of Germans came here after the war," Baum said, beginning what sounded like another long monologue. Eric was tired of hearing the old man's drone, and wanted to leave this lifeless room in favour of the warm afternoon outside. "Nazis too. It's not so well known, but the Australian government even brought a few of them here, scientists and doctors and professors. This convict colony was hardly a breeding ground for geniuses. And others came in under false identities." He looked at Eric and winked. "There are even some in this town."

Eric was listening now. He sat straight up and shivered in the air-conditioned room, the cold milk leaving a trace of gooseflesh on his arms.

"Really?"

Baum wiggled his eyebrows up and down. "Keep a look out for an old man named Fischer. He has a crippled hand and always wears gloves to cover it. No one knows how he lost his fingers, but there are plenty of stories going around."

Eric studied the milky film left on the side of his empty glass and thought about the man he had mistakenly called Mr Finger, the old Nazi who Josh had told to drop dead. But his thoughts were interrupted by Annie scurrying quickly into the room.

"Annie?" Baum said, looking up in surprise. "Why are you still here?"

"I cleaned rooms on top floor too," she said, pointing at the ceiling. "I ready now. Can give boy ride home."

Baum looked back at Eric, clearly disappointed that their intimate afternoon together was about to be interrupted. Eric looked at his watch.

"I better be going," he said standing up, his chair scraping loudly on the floor. "But I can walk. It's not far."

"Yes, it is rather late," Baum conceded, reluctantly. He stood up, paid his two workers, then opened the front door for them both.

Eric and Annie walked to her car in silence, but both breathed in deep gulps of the warm afternoon air. Eric was surprised when Annie stopped next to a relatively new car and whipped out her keys. The alarm system beeped, the indicators flashing once, and she got in.

"My son's a dentist," she explained, speaking clearly as she climbed into the car. The front seat was as far forward as it would go. She even had thick sheepskin covers, but Eric thought she would still have to lean forward to reach the pedals. "You sure you don't need a ride?"

Eric shook his head and smiled, wondering if her name was really Annie.

"No thanks." He looked towards the beach. "I think I'll take a swim."

Annie smiled. "You do that, and be careful of Baum. I can't be there every day."

The engine started easily and then purred. Eric watched the car disappear around the first corner.

Nine

The horns sounded and the engine powered up, churning the brown water as the big ferry edged away from the dock. People leaned over the railings, waving handkerchiefs and yelling last minute promises they would never keep. The people on the ferry felt like film stars bidding their adoring public farewell, blowing kisses, some even throwing flowers and pathetic paper streamers which could have simply been cut up tissue paper. Those remaining on the dock cheered and cried, the men standing stoically and waving, and the women burying their faces behind old kerchiefs, perhaps the same ones they had worn over their mouths and noses just after the war, cleaning out the destroyed buildings, when the dust and smell had been at its worst.

Peter stood at the very back of the ferry, leaning on the railing. People pushed against him, trying to get to the railing, then bumped him with their elbows as they waved several last goodbyes. He looked down at Ernst standing solemnly on the dock, one sleeve of his coat hanging limp, his only hand stuffed into his trouser pocket, and wished his friend would wave just once; some form of recognition of the time they had spent together, the quality friendship they had once enjoyed. But Ernst didn't wave and so neither did Peter, and both were quietly content they might never see the other again. The war had ended their friendship like it had many others, but it was the occupation that was making former friends bitter enemies as people chose allegiances which would help them the most and sought to erase their pasts.

Denial was the fashion of the season, ignorance the old trend. With the British in Hamburg, the Americans in the south and the Russians encroaching further from the east, many Germans were reassessing their pasts, switching sides whenever it best suited them, altering their histories, and working hard to drop dangerous contacts – be they friends or family members – in order to save face in what was now an occupied land. The occupying armies needed Germans they could trust, but to them, all Germans were Nazis and few worth saving. Peter thought that there were no good Germans in the minds of the allies. A new era was beckoning, and the quick, sly and adaptable would profit in this new Germany once they had won the trust of the victors. Peter wanted nothing of it.

The horns sounded again. The gangway was released and several young men, barely teenagers, grappled with it to bring it back to the dock, almost dropping it over the side. Peter watched Ernst step forward to help them, using his one arm to steady the gangway while many able-bodied men watched. There was the new Germany, Peter thought: the hell with you, what's in it for me? There was no way Ernst would survive. He had become far too kind-hearted during their time together in the POW camp.

After Dönitz had announced Germany's surrender, Peter and Ernst had served their two years in camp. The Führer was dead, the Nuremberg Trials were over, with most of the leaders executed and the others having escaped. Everyone wanted to forget the Nazi era. Their opinions changed to suit every audience and situation. Peter felt that Germany had no future, that the past would always be called up, never forgotten, and Germans, innocent or guilty, would forever be held responsible for what had happened. The Jews had made him understand that. This was the biggest crime in history, murder on a seven figure scale, the concentration camps clear evidence of the killing machine the Nazis produced. It was the benchmark of horror to which every war and crime would be weighed against for centuries to come. His solution was to run and start afresh in a land of promise. What vehement arguments he had had with Ernst over the future of Germany, over accountability and guilt. Ernst now believed that all Germans had the responsibility to remain in the country, to rebuild it and face their collective guilt. The Nazi witch-hunts were a waste of time, he claimed; the country was on its knees and people needed to eat. The future was survival, helping each other and proving to the world through their actions that they were good people who had just been mislead by a tyrant who came along amid a set of circumstances that would never come to pass again.

The rift was finalised by Ernst refusing to vouch for Peter when they entered the camp. Peter wanted a new name, and because he had no documents, he only needed some others to say he was who he said he was. It meant that three or four soldiers could all vouch for each other and come away with new identities, their pasts erased. Soldiers who were SS men could say they were only Wehrmacht conscripts, and the proof of this was the stolen uniforms they wore and the other soldiers who vouched for them. Ernst refused to help. Peter claimed he would need a new name regardless of whether he left Germany or not because his father was a wanted war criminal. But it made no difference, and in the last months of their term, they worked hard to avoid each other.

Peter had no trouble finding other soldiers to vouch for and who would vouch for him. Indeed, it was better to have total strangers who knew nothing of your past. There were not many who had returned from the east campaign, having been killed or taken prisoner by the Russians, so he was seldom recognised by anybody in the camp. When released, he had a new name written on a formal piece of paper with which he could then organise all his important documents. The only time he saw Ernst was to visit the student residence to retrieve his meagre possessions from the cellar. Luckily, the cellar had not been ransacked. He pocketed the diary, the bundle of Swiss Francs, the ivory-handled letter opener and the gold candlestick, and was thankful that Ernst asked no questions. Peter explained he had stolen it all from his father and Ernst had nodded his head, his eyes giving away his disbelief and mistrust. But he then surprised Peter by saying he would come to the dock to see him off. Peter's last image of Ernst was of the one-armed man struggling with the heavy gangway while all around him men, strong and vital, watched. Ernst was then surrounded by the young dock workers, and he patted them on their backs and tussled their hair. The new Germany, Peter thought, with the elders caring for their own future; but it was the children, innocent yet hardened by the times, who would rebuild the country.

The tower of Landungsbrücken faded into the haze of the early morning fog, and the spires of Hamburg, the few that had not been destroyed, slowly lost their sharpness until Peter could no longer define their outline through the fog. The ferry chugged along the Elbe, the murky brown water slapping the side and sometimes spraying onto the deck, depending on the wind. Peter looked down at the water, polluted and poisoned from the bodies dumped into it, by the hundreds who had killed themselves on the river beaches just before the war's end; the zealots who would rather die a Nazi than live in an occupied land.

Most of the passengers, still wary of the cold after several punishing post-war winters when coal had been as prized as nuggets of gold, retired to the warm, stuffy confines inside the ferry, but Peter stayed on deck. He heard the faint strains of music and feet stamping on the floorboards as people danced, celebrating their great and final escape from this land of misery. He turned his back on the music, trying to let the wind block it out, and looked at the riverside villages destroyed by the air raids. The British and the Americans had bombed everything, nothing strategic about it; just break the people's morale by killing babies and destroying houses so families would freeze in winter. The villages were scarred and ruined, but already his plucky people were putting the pieces back together, forever industrious and spirited, desperate to be busy. He feared his country would rise again, become a force that craved power. The people had it in them. He had it in him, and so did Ernst. It might take a few years, but it could happen again and he did not want to be a part of it.

His new life was before him. He was heading for England, then on to Australia to start with a clean slate. He had a new name, money in his pocket, and a willingness to leave his German identity behind. He would need a new history, though, and could not go around the world proclaiming his nationality and his role in the war. He would have to play it down, that he was wounded early in the war, an unwilling conscript dragged from university, then a fervent anti-Nazi who had deserted and spent most of the war hiding on a farm in occupied Poland.

In the POW camp, all the men had talked about immigrating, to America, Canada, Australia, and even to Argentina and Spain where they were apparently being well-received. Peter even heard talk of organisations which helped men escape, and the secret route south to Innsbruck and towards the safety of the Vatican City where new passports could be arranged and safe passage from Europe provided. It was the SS men who talked of this route. They wore peasant clothing or Wehrmacht uniforms, but Peter knew the SS type, and those who talked of escape were probably officers. They gathered together in the camp, young, tall, blond and arrogant, a powerful group still feared by all.

Some soldiers talked about the village of Hahndorf and the Barossa Valley near Adelaide, Australia's German enclave. Some of the men thought they would be safe there. But Peter wanted to get as far away from Germans as possible. He decided to go to Perth, to the most isolated city in the world, and make his new life there.

The arduous journey took him to the other side of the world. He boarded a much bigger ship in England, crowded with hopeful immigrants from all over Europe. The ship pulled into port towns along the way, towns completely untouched by war. Europe was a smoking, stinking ruin, but it seemed the rest of the world was intact and this was heartening.

He was a loner on board. There were other Germans on the ship, all heading south to start a new life and eager to put as much distance between themselves and their homeland as possible, but they didn't gather in groups like the other nationalities did. The Greeks, Italians, Serbs and Slavs all formed big, boisterous groups, passing the time drinking at the bar and playing cards. Sometimes there were fights, as old differences boiled to the surface, with the occasional full-scale rumble erupting over the smallest triviality. The British soldiers sometimes intervened and other times just let them fight. Peter, like the other German loners, kept his distance, not wanting to announce his nationality and be held responsible for lost friends and families and the destruction of home towns.

But he had an aptitude for sports and games, and he succumbed to his boredom and tried to join the games of soccer the men played on the deck in the afternoon sun. He knew that being good at sport often meant quick acceptance regardless of your background or beliefs, and he was soon drafted into the Italian team after an injury gave him a chance to show his skills. They played short, aggressive matches against the other nationalities and tempers often ran hot. It was only the presence of a few British soldiers, refereeing and sometimes playing, which kept things from turning violent. For Peter, it was good, competitive fun, and he released a lot of his anger and energy chasing the round ball. He was also a social animal who did not like being alone or outside of a group. It felt good being in with the Italians who were often singing and having fun. Peter was also relishing the power and fitness of his body, once more strong and healthy after two years in the luxurious British camp. He bounded around the deck, tall and lanky, yet surprisingly quick and nimble. All those years in the Hitler Youth, with its emphasis on physical supremacy and competition, had sharpened his reflexes and honed his skills. He couldn't deny it. He quickly became one of the star players on the ship, and a rumour spread that he had perhaps been a member of the German national team before the war. Other teams on the ship tried to lure him away from the Italians, pushing their hatred for all things German conveniently aside in favour of short-term glory. But when he refused to change teams, staying instead with the countrymen who had been his former allies in the war, they cursed and insulted him, calling him Adolf behind his back and raising their right arms in the fascist salute any time he entered the room. Peter did his best to ignore it, and was glad for the support of the Italians. But he wondered if it would be like this for the rest of his life, regardless of where he lived.

Salvatore was the striker for the Italian team, and he often scored his goals from Peter's leading work in the midfield as he cut the defences open with his dribbling and accurate passes. United by their sporting prowess and successful combination, the two men struck up a fast friendship. The Italian spoke heavily accented English which Peter, whose schoolboy English was by no means fluent, found impossible to decipher. But they found a way to communicate and were often seen together doing laps of the deck and drawing football strategies in the bar.

Salvo was from Padua near Venice. He often talked about the town's glorious cathedral and the restaurants that piled out onto the streets in summer and where every night there had been a festival. The early days of Il Duce had been reason to celebrate; how great it was then to be Italian. Salvo told many stories about the pre-war days, when he was a teenager in love with a different girl every week. Peter listened to the stories and laughed, trying to picture the small, swarthy Italian as Padua's Don Juan. He was hardly good looking, especially when the sun caught his face and his scars were clear. Peter hoped they had come from too many dangerous intrigues with young Paduan girls rather than from the war. But Salvo was the right age. Peter was convinced he had worn a uniform and wondered what the bright Italian had seen and done. Their countries had started out as brothers in arms, but had ended as bitter enemies, each blaming the other for their defeat. Peter asked no questions about Salvo's past, as was the norm on the ship, while Salvo could only talk of the future.

He had relatives in Australia, banana growers in Carnarvon. He was headed there to work, learn the trade and eventually start his own plantation. He couldn't wait to get started and suggested Peter come with him. There was bound to be enough work for both of them and then they could start a plantation together. Peter was unsure and made no commitment. He wondered if anyone would accept him as a worker with his crippled hand. Why would they take a cripple when the ship was full of young, strong and able-bodied men? And surely they wouldn't take a German?

The ship docked on a bright, sunny morning in Fremantle. There were men leaning against large trucks waiting on the dock, and the passengers on the ship fought each to be the first down the gangway. They crowded around the trucks, pushing against the men in grubby suits who pointed at the ones they wanted. The selected workers then climbed into the back of the truck. Peter, still on board and waiting to get off, watched this slave trade and frowned. There was no way he would be selected. The young Europeans shouted the few words of English they knew, pushing smaller men out of the way to get themselves in front of the suited selectors. The trucks were soon full and they drove away from the dock, leaving those who remained smoking cigarettes and trying not to look disappointed. Maybe some other trucks would arrive, with more people looking for cheap workers. They waited in line at the makeshift customs area, their papers clutched in their hands.

"Like Roma," Salvo said, walking next to Peter down the gangway, "but in time of Empire."

Peter nodded. What an introduction to a country: slave traders and selection based on size and strength, with the smaller and thinner left on the dock. Some of these men, after it was clear no more trucks were coming, began walking towards the centre of Fremantle, that maybe they would find work there. But Peter could see in their body language, in the way they trudged forward with their small bedrolls on their backs, that this opening disappointment might be an introduction of what to expect.

Salvo jumped onto the dock. He stamped his feet and took in lustrous gulps of air.

"Land," he said, showing Peter his white teeth and then looking around.

The harbour was quite large and reminded Peter of Hamburg. But the first thing he saw was the barrel of a large gun protruding from a bunker perched on top of the hill. He could almost hear the boom and groan of the Russian guns, the incredible sounds they had made in the close confines of the street fighting in Stalingrad that left his ears ringing for days. His comrades hadn't been able even to talk to each other, shout warnings, or tell each other to duck.

"Hey," Salvo said, slapping him on the back. "You come or not?"

Peter nodded. The fascist stigma had followed him onto the boat and the images of war now bombarded him in Australia. Would he ever forget, or be allowed to?

"How do we get there?" he asked, not even sure which direction Carnarvon was.

Salvo held up his small hands. "Someone give us ride," he said smiling.

After a lengthy goodbye with the remaining Italians, the two men slung their rucksacks over their shoulders and started walking towards Perth.

It was a brave new world here, a young city carving itself into the harsh land. But they were deceived by the coast as they followed the beach road, sweating in the sun as they walked; they thought the land would be bountiful and green all over and slapped each other on the back, thinking they had found paradise. It was late autumn in this part of the world and still warm. After a few hours of walking, they stopped at a beach, stripped down to their underwear and plunged into the water. Peter let the waves dump on him and sat splashing in the shallows like he had in the Baltic Sea in his youth. He then sprawled on the sand and let the sun burn his back. He felt a peace he thought he had lost; those moments when he was so still and relaxed that he ceased to feel or hear anything, and in the deepest lull, he thought he could feel the earth slowly turning beneath him.

After Peter bought them lunch at a beach-side restaurant in Cottesloe, they continued north. Much of the coastline was undeveloped and often they had to walk through low scrubland, with the harsh branches scratching their legs and ripping their pants. The dirt was very dry, and when the wind picked up in the afternoon, it blew that gritty earth up their noses and into their eyes.

They slept the first night on the beach. Peter lay awake staring at the millions of stars in the sky, not wanting to fall asleep and have someone steal his bag. It was a moonless night, but the stars gave enough light for him to see the dark shapes which came down to the beach. They looked in his direction, spoke together in a musical, bouncy language, and then went about their business, collecting mussels and crabs left behind by the tide. Some of the men waded into the water with long spears and caught big fish. The women collected everything in the bottoms of their dresses and then the dark shapes disappeared back over the dunes.

They walked further north the next day, following an inland road after asking for directions. A milk truck stopped and took them to Lancelin. The driver spoke with a nasal drawl that was hard to decipher over the roar of the engine. Peter caught snippets of what he said. He had had trouble with some of his workers; blacks, he called them. He complained about how useless they were, how none of them wanted to work and couldn't be trusted if you gave them a job. And the women, don't get him started.

"They start all free and easy, but then you try to make somethin and they run away," he shouted, grinding through the gears. His face was deeply tanned and lined, like worn leather, and he looked much older than he was. "I reckon they like it when you take em by force."

Peter listened and tried to offer his agreement, not wanting to get on the man's bad side. He thought of the blacks he had seen the night before, quietly fishing and gathering mussels. They seemed peaceful enough. Peter had been outnumbered, but hadn't felt in any danger. Perhaps this man had just had a few bad experiences.

In Lancelin, Salvo and Peter helped the man unload the truck. He repaid them by buying dinner and drinks at the local pub. He became quite hearty and offered them both jobs.

"You maybe a noodle and you a Nazi," he said, putting his arms around the two men, "but you'd be better than any a them blacks."

When they turned him down, the man quickly became bitter, like he was insulted, and he turned his force on Salvo, whose skin had already turned a few shades darker from the sun.

"They should keep you darkies outta my country," he said, raising his voice and making people in the bar turn and look. "And knock off the blacks while they're at it. Australia's for whites."

A few people in the bar cheered and raised their glasses to the truck driver. Salvo was about to punch the man, but Peter stepped in front of him, and backed him towards the door.

"Yeah, get outta here, you bloody useless migrants," the man slurred, pointing to the door. "We don't want you here. This's our country."

A glass was thrown at Salvo and he ducked just in time. It smashed against the wall, and as they quickly ran through the door other glasses were thrown. Peter started to run, thinking they would all come pounding out of the bar, but the door stayed closed. Salvo stopped, fished around in his backpack, and pulled out a long and shiny knife.

"No, Salvo, it's not worth it," Peter said, trying to hold back his friend. But Salvo turned away from the bar and walked towards the milk truck. He dug the knife into the two front tyres and the released air blew the dust around him.

"You all immigrants," he said spitefully, spitting on the truck. He walked into the night and Peter rushed to catch up with him.

***

Two days later, further north in Geraldton, they were again offered work, this time on a fishing boat. The Greek man promised good money, accommodation and board, and Peter especially was reluctant to turn him down. It seemed there was work everywhere, that the land was untamed, unpopulated and alive with opportunity. It was a harsh land though, and it got harsher the further north they went.

Salvo was a good travelling companion. He made friends easily with his big smile and musical laugh, and as long as nobody insulted him or his heritage, he was passive enough. After Lancelin, Peter only saw the knife when Salvo killed an animal for their dinner. They became close, this new land a welcoming respite from their respective histories and wartime roles. Peter had never felt so free, so awake to the broad scope of life, that it could take many forms. He knew he would make it even with his crippled hand, a nightmarish past and a damning nationality. Nobody seemed to care too much that he was German and Salvo Italian. As long as you were able to work and weren't Asian or black, for the most part, you were in. They turned down quite a few offers during their trek: farm work, construction, even basic office work in the small towns on the main highway north. They passed through a land that was dry and cracked, populated with animals that hopped and with blacks who hid behind bushes and stared at them as they passed.

In Carnarvon, the land was fresh and green, the wind salty and brisk. Salvo's relatives gave them a hearty welcome, even though none of them had met Salvo before and only knew him from photographs. They had a big feast that first evening, then went out early in the morning to work. The days turned into weeks and the weeks into months. Peter and Salvo shared a small room annexed from the main homestead and spent their free evenings going to the pub in the town. Salvo even tried to get some people together for a regular soccer game, but the locals were more interested in their own sport which they called football. It was a violent game where they chased, kicked and caught a red, egg-shaped ball. Just for something to do, Peter started to play, learning slowly at first, somewhat reluctant for the hard, physical clashes. But he liked running around and chasing the ball, even if he could never seem to get his hands on it. The other players admired him for trying.

Sometimes there were girls. Salvo always found them, rustling up a second so they could all go out as four. Peter, still awkward and shy, had little success. He still thought of Michaela, who sometimes came to him in his dreams, and they danced together in the burning streets of Dresden before she was dropped into an open grave, thrown into a cattle car or that same piece of shrapnel flew into her neck. In his dreams, she died a million deaths with himself always powerless to stop it. Sometimes he was part of it: pulling the trigger himself, dumping her into a mass grave or slamming the crematorium door shut and later sweeping out the ashes.

When on dates with girls, Peter was sure to keep himself distant, even if he liked the girl. He felt he would somehow be let down, that if he got too close, it would hurt even more. The war had taken away everything and everyone, and he thought, as some form of punishment and redemption, he would be forever denied happiness.

After three months of working the fields, sharing the room and enjoying plenty of laughs, Salvo found the diary. Peter had got up early to go into town on an errand for Uncle Roberto. Despite his hand, he was a good driver and often did such errands for the plantation owner.

Peter came boisterously into the room they shared. "Come on, Salvo. You still sleeping?"

"I'm awake to you now, Reinhard," Salvo hissed, the book open in his hands, resting there like a prayer book.

"Why are you reading that?" Peter asked. His heart thumped in his chest. It was happening again. He had let himself have some happiness and now it was about to be swiftly ripped away. "And why did you call me Reinhard?"

Salvo loudly drew the spittle from his throat and spat on Peter's boots.

"That's not my diary," Peter said, holding out his hands, pleading. "It was given to me on the eastern front by a dying SS soldier. I was only in the Wehrmacht, a lousy conscript, you know that."

Salvo laughed. He pulled his lips back and Peter could see the big white molars that filled the Italian's mouth. Then Salvo gritted them together and snarled like a dog. Peter wondered about the knife.

"You all say that," Salvo shouted. "You will always say that. You bastards murdered my brothers, hanged them from their necks in front of their mothers when they would no longer fight for you."

"That wasn't me. I was an ordinary soldier. I was wounded, deserted my unit, dressed myself as a refugee and walked back to Hamburg. I was never a Nazi. I hated them from the start."

Peter couldn't stop the sob that got caught in his throat, but he somehow managed to hold back his tears.

"You cowards," Salvo said with disgust. He threw the diary to the floor, the loose contents spilling out, and spat on the cover. He pointed to the door. "Pack up. You're not welcome here anymore."

The Italian pushed past Peter and slammed the door behind him. Peter quickly gathered his gear together, fearing that Salvo might tell the other Italians and they would come after him. He thought about leaving the diary behind, but scooped it up and the loose photographs and papers and threw it in his bag like the curse it was. He took one last, sad look at the room and knew that, even in this land of promise and opportunity, he would forever come up against people who would hold him responsible for the past. He closed the door and started walking south down the highway, the sun beating down on his hatless head.

***

Peter stood in the small and stuffy church, the sweat trickling down his sides. The tie was choking him. He hadn't worn a tie since he had arrived in Australia. This was a country where one didn't have to wear a tie, and he had argued playfully with Betty that he would walk down the aisle tie-less because that was how things were done here. But he had relented to the noose and now kept his hands tightly clenched together to stop himself from yanking at it. The priest droned on, prattling about sickness and health, having and holding. How pretty Betty looked in her cream dress, Peter observed, and what about all the friends who had come to the wedding. Most of the football team was there and his mates from the fishing boats. Betty knew everyone in Geraldton; their wedding was a big event.

Later, at the reception at the football club, Peter sat next to his wife, listened to the speeches, looked at the tanned, lined and smiling faces gathered around him and marvelled at the course his life had taken.

He had drifted down to Geraldton, taken work from the Greek man he had met earlier in the year and, despite his disability, had become a star of the local football team. The locals admired him for his hard but fair play and for playing with a handicapped hand. How they loved a battler. That was the true Australian spirit, succeeding despite limitations, getting it done when the whole world was against you. Of course, it helped that he was a good athlete and a player who helped the team win. He wasn't complaining. Being one of the best players and a hard worker on the fishing boat had won him a lot of friends and the prized scalp of Elizabeth Warner, now Betty Fischer. As a result, many of the locals conveniently forgot he was from Germany. He wasn't surprised that these people valued achievements in sport and labour above intellect and culture. Australia was a childish land, he thought, populated by children, with easy answers given to easy questions; the my-dad's-bigger-than-your-dad country. He missed the culture and diversity of Europe, but fell in love with the relaxed simplicity of his adopted home. Australia was bounding forward while Europe was still rebuilding, and all the cultural and intellectual prowess of the Europeans simply amounted to one utterly destructive war after another, their petty squabbles magnified by the technological innovations of their warfare.

With his marriage he took Australian citizenship. It was both a proud and sad day when he went behind his garden shed and burned his German passport and papers. No one could hurt him with the past. He was now as Australian as the millions of other immigrants and sons of immigrants who called Australia home. His German accent faded with time and he relished the slang of the locals, even if he knew it sometimes sounded contrived when he tried to copy their peculiar speech. But he had mastered their sport, wooed one of their local darlings, bought one of their houses and now had one of their passports. He'd made it.

During the fifties, Peter dug out the battered and well-travelled Swiss Francs and started his own fishing business. He bought a fleet of boats, expanded into cray fishing and eventually into wreck diving during the scuba boom of the seventies. Geraldton's coast had many wrecked ships from colonial times and earlier, and people came from all over the world to drop down and look at them.

Peter's life, which had started out so promisingly and turned so nasty, became a success. He was well known around town, employed lots of local people and took to coaching several junior football teams when he could no longer play. Unable to have children of his own, he became a father figure to many young boys whose fathers worked long hours, drank too much in the bars, or who were disinterested in their sons' sporting endeavours. Peter and Betty seldom talked about their inability to have children and rumours spread around town that their marriage wasn't a success because of it. Betty blamed herself, but Peter knew his lack of offspring was one more punishment for the misdeeds of his youth.

They lived a quiet life, with Betty involved in her charity projects and with the local Girl Guides. When she was older, she took to lawn bowls and spent many days at the club.

Only the letters disturbed his peace. His father had escaped after the war and was living in Buenos Aires. The letters started arriving after Peter's wedding, after he had taken Australian citizenship. His father wrote that some friends in Australia had tracked him down and they offered help if he needed it, financing too, and protection and legal assistance if necessary. He wrote long letters, making broad statements about the past and the mistakes he had made. He had married again and had three more children. Didn't Peter want to visit Argentina and meet his three sisters? Peter never replied to the letters – the sender's address was in Nuremberg – and he kept them hidden in an old shoebox in the garden shed. Also in the box was the diary and the piece of shrapnel which had killed Michaela. But his lack of response didn't stop the letters from coming, one at Christmas and one for his birthday in May. His father was a wanted Nazi criminal. It was Peter's secret hobby to collect information and newspaper clippings about the search for such criminals. There wasn't much to collect however, and none of it mentioned his father. The world wanted to forget the war and to get on with living in the prosperous present. Doubtless, thousands of Nazis, criminals every one of them, had walked, and Peter was convinced most of them still lived in Germany, perhaps carrying on similar lives to what they had led before the war.

After Adolf Eichmann was kidnapped from Argentina by Israeli agents in 1960 and later tried and executed, Peter's father moved to Madrid where, despite his age, he continued to work as a doctor. But he still gave no address and all mail came via the same Nuremberg address. Peter wondered if his father was actually living there and had been the whole time. The letters were written in German, in the beautiful Sütterlin script that Peter remembered, and were signed Josep Cazador. When he had received the first letter, Peter had visited the local library and looked up Cazador in a Spanish dictionary. The name was a direct translation from Josef Jäger. He hated getting these letters, but there was still something there, an unspoken, unaccountable love and loyalty, and though he never wrote back, he never turned his father in either.

Betty's battle with cancer ended in 1985, and she died knowing as little about him then as the day they first met. Shattered, Peter sold his business to Japanese investors and retired to the coastal hamlet of Crescent Bay. His life was quiet, and he played at least nine holes of golf everyday for exercise and entertainment. But the letters still found him. Age had turned his father meaner and more bitter, and the long letters revelled in the glories of the past, when the Nazis had brought the world to its knees, and they had successfully driven the unworthy from their lands. They were nasty letters, and Peter, now an old man himself and haunted by his own past, tasted bile when he read them. Why couldn't the old bugger just die and be done with it, he wondered. There was no reason to track him down and prosecute him or any other criminals. Time would take them and their crimes to the grave.

Then one afternoon, when he was relaxed and watching the Boxing Day cricket test, a young boy knocked on his door.

Ten

The cream Mercedes lounged in the sun, shining from its wash, some beads of water still glistening. The expensive wax glowed as Eric rubbed it in. When he was finished, he stood back and admired his labour. Baum came out of the house, the handle of a leather suitcase in each hand. He lifted them into the boot and put them next to his set of golf clubs.

"The car looks magnificent, Eric," Baum said, sliding his sunglasses onto his face. "You've done your family proud."

Eric pulled his shoulders back. "It doesn't take much to make this car look good. It looks great even when it's dirty."

Baum smiled, but because his eyes were hidden behind the glasses, Eric couldn't tell if the old man was happy or maybe just a bit more interested in him than usual. Baum kept smiling as he reached into his pocket and pulled out a thick roll of notes folded over a gold money clip. He snapped off a crisp fifty and handed it to Eric.

"Thank you, Mr Baum," Eric beamed, holding the note in his hands. "But it's too much and I don't have any change."

"I believe in paying people what they're worth," Baum said grandly. "You deserve that. I'll be back in a week and then we can continue in the war room."

Eric nodded, wishing Baum would stay over Christmas so he could earn more money and have an excuse to get out of the house. His two uncles were coming with their families for Christmas Day and just the thought of it made him groan.

"Where are you going, if I can ask?"

"I'm joining my daughter and her family down in Dunsborough," Baum said, seeming none too excited about it. "They have a holiday house there and it is Christmas. They've been down there a couple of days already."

Eric listened with his right hand in his pocket, sliding the fifty around his wax-sticky fingers and pressing his fingertips into the note's stiff corners. Baum stared out over the ocean, the wind blowing back his fine grey hair. Again Eric was reminded of an aristocratic yachtsman. Baum seemed reluctant to leave and lingered like he had more to say, that he needed to explain himself further.

"My grandson's about your age," he said, looking down at Eric expectantly. "I believe he's in the same class as you."

"What's his name?"

"Joshua." Baum chewed the words like they were something distasteful he was forced to eat. He turned to Eric for confirmation, a sour look on his face. Eric snickered.

"Something amusing?"

Eric caught himself, not wanting to insult the old man and get on his bad side. "It's just that, yeah, I know Josh. We've already spent some quality time together."

"Are you friends?"

Eric heard something in the lilting tone of Baum's voice, as if the old man was somewhat appalled that Eric could be friends with Josh.

"I wouldn't say that. I'm not sure that's what he wants."

"He's a bad kid," Baum said. "Too much like his father and far too spoiled, like those people have always been to their children. Just give them everything. I've argued with Heidi about it for years, but the money-handler commands that castle. I told her not to marry him, but I think she did it just to spite me."

Eric stared over the ocean, not sure what to say and wondering again what a money-handler was. A banker perhaps? He remembered the word from Scripture classes in Merredin, but couldn't think of the context. He wanted to ask Baum, but didn't want the old man to think him stupid and uninformed. So he stared at the water, wondering if he would have time for a quick surf before his date with Pepper. Probably not. He needed to go home and shower and put on some decent clothes. Should he shave? he wondered, absently stroking his smooth chin.

"By the way," Baum said brightly. "I ran into our friend Mr Fischer at the golf club yesterday evening. He takes most of his meals there, you know. Anyway, I told him a bit about you and he'd like you to pay him a visit."

Eric thought about the sinister old man who had rescued him in the park. It was Josh who had called Fischer a Nazi.

"Is it safe?"

Baum chuckled. "I don't think old Fischer can do you any harm now. His best days are a long way behind him. He lives around the corner from Mrs Canter. The poor woman despises him, thinks he's the devil himself, and turns white when she sees him at the club." He laughed more heartily and leaned closer to Eric, keen to confide a secret. Eric felt that Baum loved secrets, those quiet confidences which bound them together in conspiracy. "She keeps her funeral dress in pristine condition," he whispered, "ready for the day when she can pull it on for Fischer's funeral."

Eric offered a lame, manufactured chuckle that hardly complimented Baum's boisterous guffaws.

"Don't worry," Baum said, reaching out his arm and taking Eric roughly by the shoulder, shaking him a little. It was the first time Eric had felt the strength of the old man and he was surprised by it. "You're safe, my boy. I think you might be a good influence on him. Ask him about the war. You've got blond hair and blue eyes, so there's no chance he'll turn you away." Baum wiggled his eyebrows up and down, his face shining with pleasure. "Maybe he'll even teach you a few secret Nazi handshakes. Go and see him after Christmas, and greet the old warrior for me."

"Okay," Eric said softly, feeling uncomfortable with Baum's hand gripping his shoulder.

"He may not be able to pay you much," Baum said. "I don't think he got any of that loot the Jews claim the Nazis stole from them."

Baum released Eric and then moved around to the left side of the car. He inspected the roof, flicked away a few small flecks of dirt and sand, and then eased himself behind the wheel.

"I'll be back after New Year," he said, roaring the car to life. It purred impatiently, eager for the open road. "Come and visit me and we'll continue. There's lots more to tell you and I want to know how you go with Fischer."

"Have a nice trip," Eric said, raising a hand as the Mercedes reversed down the driveway. "And merry Christmas."

Eric watched the Mercedes roll smoothly down the road, cruising like a mast-less yacht. He began to walk home, rushing because two hours may not be time enough to get ready for his date. He tried to remember what Fischer looked like, but couldn't get a clear picture of his face. All he could see was the crippled and gloved hand. His fear was matched in equal amounts by his curiosity, and despite a childhood of hearing endless warnings about dangerous old men, Eric knew he would pay a visit to Fischer. If he really was a Nazi, then what stories could he tell?

***

"I'm glad you're finally home, Ricky," his mother said as he came in through the garage door. She stood in the kitchen, red-faced and flustered. The counter was covered in food, some things peeled and cut and other things still in bags and cans. On the stove, a pot was boiling over, spilling a milky white liquid that sizzled and burned on the hotplate.

"I really need your help to get the house ready for Christmas." She followed his eyes to the stove and rescued the pot, grabbing at it with her bare hands and shifting it to the side. She swore loudly and ran her fingers under the tap.

"But I told you I was going shopping this afternoon. I'll help you later. Besides, no one's coming till tomorrow. There's plenty of time."

"Why are you so selfish?" his mother shouted, and she slapped her palm on the counter. Her anger and stress twisted her horsey face into a mess of lines and indentations. She dropped her head and wiped her hands sub-consciously on her apron.

"Go on," she said coldly, waving him away. "You're just like your father. You make promises and then break them, never do what you say."

"But I never promised…"

She held up her hand, the palm facing Eric. "I don't want to hear any more of your excuses. If Christmas turns into a disaster, we'll know who to blame."

Eric's anger rose. Christmas will be a disaster whether I help or not, he thought, like it always is. Every year his mother tried desperately to impress her in-laws who were never satisfied with her, who pounced on her every mistake like snakes on a limping mouse. She could have been a master chef; his aunts and uncles would still find something wrong with the food. But Eric thought his mother was also at fault because she took their quiet, understated insults and never fought back. Worse, she invited them every year hoping that she might finally have a win against them or at least be brought into their tight circle.

"I don't see why I should do anything," he said. "I'm not even getting any presents. I'm surprised I haven't been sent to military school."

She turned on him, her hands now covered with white, bubbly detergent suds. "I'm starting to think you deserve to get nothing, and right now I'm not sure even military school could pull you in line."

Eric stormed from the room. He showered quickly, scrubbing at his arms and legs furiously, hoping to wash away all traces of his family. He thought his parents were losing their minds. They seemed to think he was out of control, a vagrant, a hoodlum, a law unto himself. But here he was working, coming home before dark and just trying to survive in this new town. Is someone spreading rumours about me? he wondered. His mother's harsh words were particularly hurtful, because she was often on his side when his father was disciplining him. Now, even she had turned against him. But none of it would matter in the end.

"A couple more years and I'm outta here," he said as he pulled on some fresh clothes. He ran through the living room and slammed the garage door behind him. He heard his mother call out his name, and he could hear remorse and apology in her voice, but he ignored her and walked through the garage. He sat down on the hot curb to wait for Pepper. He had Baum's money in his wallet and he knew exactly what he would do with it. The surfboard could wait; he didn't have enough for it anyway.

***

Mrs Canter drove an old Beetle. Eric saw the familiar quaff of hair through the narrow windscreen. The car was bright orange and Eric guessed that it seldom ventured beyond the walled enclosure of Crescent Bay. Pepper climbed out of the front seat and pulled it forward so Eric could fold himself into the back. She wore a floral dress, red with white flowers, cut just above the knee. Eric took note of the Quicksilver label. Where did she get her money? he asked himself.

"Well, isn't a small world," Mrs Canter exclaimed. She turned to look at Eric squashed in the back seat, but still gripped the steering wheel with both hands. She wore thin leather driving gloves that had small silver buttons at the wrist.

"Hello, Mrs Canter," he said.

"You two know each other?" Pepper asked, slightly embarrassed, but still with that aloof coolness Eric found so appealing. She climbed into the front seat and fastened her seatbelt. Eric fished around in the back for a belt as well, but there wasn't one.

"Eric is that wonderful boy I was telling you about," Mrs Canter explained. She turned the key in the ignition and the engine made an awful grinding sound; it was still running. "He's managed to restore a smidgen of my faith in the youth of today."

160

She manhandled the gear-stick, reversed a couple of metres by mistake, then managed to lurch away from the curb. She looked uncomfortable and uncertain behind the wheel, like a motorist from the twenties, still grappling with this new technology, unsure how to harness it. She bunny-hopped through the first two gears, working the clutch like pumping the pedal of a spinning wheel. She drove too slowly for the gear the car was in and the steering wheel shuddered in her hands, making her question whether there was something wrong with the car. When she eventually got to third gear, the car went more smoothly and her confidence grew.

"He was the one who beautified my garden," she added, drawing a few extra syllables from beautified.

Pepper turned in her seat and raised her eyebrows at Eric, a curious and questioning yet playful look. She seemed to know what he was up to, but he couldn't guess what she thought about it. Perhaps she thought he had taken a roundabout way to win her approval? He decided he would tell her the truth later, that he was getting money together for a surfboard. It was just coincidence that his first client was her grandmother. Would she hate him for being poor or admire his independence and work ethic?

It took quite a while to get to the mall. Mrs Canter drove achingly slow, braking when the traffic lights were green and screeching the car to a stop when they turned amber. She seemed unable to make a right turn because she couldn't judge the traffic when it was coming from both directions; but then, even a left turn was a challenge. Eric found himself willing the car forward, praying for traffic lights to stay green, urging the car to start again when it stalled, and gritting his teeth when she put the car in the wrong gear.

It was a long journey and nobody spoke. Mrs Canter became very stressed, even shaking a gloved fist at other drivers. Horns sounded around the car, and one man even shouted through his open window, "Get off the road, you old bag." Pepper seemed to think this rather funny because Mrs Canter mused in response, "Now, that's no way to talk to a lady," convinced the man was addressing another motorist and not her.

Once at the mall, Mrs Canter parked diagonally in a disabled parking space close to the entrance. Eric unfolded himself from the back seat, stretching when he got out. The car park was very full and people were pouring through the mall entrance, rushing to finish the Christmas shopping they had put off all December.

"Don't worry about us, grandma," Pepper said as they passed through the revolving door, the mall receiving them with a blast of cold, air-conditioned air. "We'll take the bus back home. I want to take Eric to some other shops in town."

Mrs Canter cocked a painted-on eyebrow suspiciously, but quickly relented. "Just be back before dark," she declared. And with that, she strolled, without a hint of disability, into the hairdresser and took a seat in front of a wall of mirrors. Pepper grabbed Eric's hand and pulled him away.

"Let's get as far away from her as possible," she said.

Eric let himself be pulled, a smile on his face; they were already holding hands. But once they were walking, Pepper let go of his hand. They walked together through the throng, sneaking glances at each other, wanting the other to start talking first.

He could think of nothing to say, and every sentence he thought about starting just sounded stupid, so he said nothing. He looked around the mall for inspiration. Stressed mothers pushed full shopping carts and screamed at their screaming kids. There was a lot of shouting and pushing and not much friendliness and cheer. The people shoved each other and fought for items, complaining when they had to wait in the long lines and sighing loudly. Children begged for things they weren't allowed to have, picking items from the shelves and looking at their parents expectantly or putting them in the shopping carts when mum wasn't looking; arguments ensued and more than one child got a swift clip over the head.

"The season to be jolly," Eric murmured, frowning at the scene. He wasn't aware that he had spoken and now Pepper looked at him. "I mean, Christmas, it's lost its meaning a bit, don't you think?" he added, his voice croaking. "Not much goodwill in here."

Pepper looked around and nodded. "Is it like this in Merredin?"

"Worse. There's only one shop. They have fights to the death over Barbies."

Pepper laughed. Eric loved it when she laughed. He couldn't quite explain it, but there seemed to be something sad about her, that when she wasn't putting on airs and enjoying herself, she stared glumly into space, lost in her own private sorrow. Eric decided he would try to make her laugh as often as possible; it was awful to see her sad.

"Come on," she said, taking his hand again easily. "There's the surf shop."

It was almost empty. Most people were food shopping today, stocking up on beer and meat for Christmas Day and Boxing Day. In the shop, colourful clothing hung on circular racks and, along one wall, jeans were stacked on a high shelf that went to the ceiling. A ladder was leaning against the shelf and a shop assistant was perched halfway up it. His boardshorts hung too low and Eric could see a rather disgusting and hairy wedge of bum-crack poking out the top. The word sale was written on all the walls in bright red and there were banners too with only the percent symbol. But when Eric sneaked looks at the price tags, he frowned. It seemed nothing was on sale. Baum's money wouldn't go very far in here.

Pepper moved gracefully through the shop, weaving between the racks, stopping sometimes to pull off a shirt or a bikini and hold it up to Eric. His token response, "It would look great on you," sounded more and more lame each time he said it. His voice had lost its usual steady tone and was now an uncontrollable croak, sometimes loud and high-pitched and other times soft and low, barely audible. He was afraid to open his mouth lest strange noises come out.

The surfboards were lined up along the back wall behind the cash register. Pepper knew the cashier and he let them come around the counter to have a closer look. He smiled knowingly at Eric, urging him on to success. Or just wanting a sale?

He saw the prices first – $200, $299, $450 – and tried to hide his disappointment. He had budgeted $100 for a board, $150 at the most, and he frowned as Pepper showed him the boards she thought would be good for him. He looked at each one closely, pretending to be interested, running his hands over the smooth fibreglass and admiring the design. He wanted something simple, and cheap, something more subtle than Pepper's hot pink number or Drew's bloodthirsty shark. At the end of the rack, Pepper took hold of a light blue board covered with dolphins swimming along the crest of a wave. Eric knew then that was the board he wanted. The price tag said $399 and that it was on sale. Pepper handed the board to Eric. He wondered if she expected him to buy it then and there, slam $400 down on the counter and impress the pants off her. He took the board lovingly into his hands, caressing it, trying to look like an expert, and then tucked it under his arm as if ready to walk down the beach with it. It was so light it made his learning plank seem like a slab of concrete.

"Hey," said a loud voice behind him. "Watch it with that thing."

Eric turned quickly around, standing the board upright so he wouldn't hit anyone else with it. He fumbled a bit and was lucky to catch the board before it fell to the floor.

"Sorry."

Brad's long hair was pressed underneath a backwards baseball cap and he had fresh pink marks on his face from where he had squeezed his pimples that morning. Eric only saw the marks up close; from a distance, Brad was a good looking boy. His snarl turned into a surprised smile when he saw Pepper emerge from behind the dolphin board.

"Go away, Brad," she said snidely.

"What are you doing here?"

Eric looked briefly between Pepper and Brad, wondering if Brad was talking to him or not. He opened his mouth to answer but Pepper jumped in.

"Looking at boards, moron," she said, putting her hands defiantly on her narrow hips. "What's it look like?"

"I mean with this sheep lover." Brad pointed at Eric, then edged towards Pepper, invading their space.

Eric breathed loudly through his nose, but couldn't think of a comeback. Brad was several centimetres taller than he was, and had broad shoulders and a deep, strong voice. Pepper grabbed Eric's board and slid it back onto the rack.

"I'm not a leep shover," Eric managed to say. Brad looked at him and laughed. Eric blushed at his mistake. Brad moved closer, his chin at Eric's eye level. Eric saw the black strands of the goatee beard Brad was trying to grow. It didn't match the blond hair and he wondered if Brad bleached it.

"Come on, Pepper," Brad said, reaching out for her arm. "I'll save you from this tongue-tied loser."

But Pepper was quicker and she struck Brad's extended arm with her small fist, making him recoil in pain. He rubbed at his forearm. Behind him, the cashier laughed.

"Leave em alone, Brad," the cashier said, stepping between Brad and Pepper. Eric looked him over, impressed by the definition of the man's arm muscles, by the strength rippling underneath the tight t-shirt.

Pepper took this chance to grab Eric by the arm, pulling him away from the boards.

"You're such a dickhead, Brad," Pepper said as she walked past.

Despite being guarded by the cashier, Brad managed to extend his leg and tripped Eric as he went past. Eric stumbled forward and caught his balance on a rack of clothing. He turned to retaliate, but the cashier intervened again.

"No fighting in the shop," he said, pointing a finger at Eric. But he smiled and winked at him, enjoying the situation and showing he was no threat. "Pepper's right about Brad, but he's still my brother and I have the unfortunate duty of protecting him."

"I don't need your protection," Brad said, trying to push past the cashier. But the elder was stronger and shoved him back with such force that Brad struck the rack of boards, with some of them crashing to the floor.

"Now look what you've done," he said to Brad, exasperated.

Pepper grabbed Eric's arm again and pulled him from the shop. She darted through the mall, yanking at his arm to make him keep up. They burst through the entrance and walked across the car park, getting lost amongst the people and moving vehicles.

"That guy's such an arsehole," she said. "I don't know why Drew's friends with him."

"He doesn't seem to like me much," Eric said, wondering again what he was doing to make the whole school hate him.

They crossed the big car park. Horns sounded and people wound down windows to shout at others to hurry up or to hurl insults at each other. The muffled sounds of Christmas carols came from the cars, sometimes with kids on the backseats trying to sing along.

"He's scared of anyone who's a threat to his world," Pepper said, folding her arms angrily. "You should see him when other surfers try to ride his waves, even older guys. He just goes after them and picks fights, carries a knife and everything. He's lucky his brother's one of the best surfers in town. You see the way he sticks up for him."

"His brother seems all right," Eric said, smiling as he remembered the wink the cashier had given him.

"I'm glad he was there." Pepper looked Eric up and down and her eyes were sympathetic. She clearly thought Brad would have beaten him up otherwise and this made Eric bristle.

"I'm not scared of him," he said.

"Fighting doesn't solve anything." She cocked her head towards a small café across the road. "Come on. Let's get something to drink."

Eric spent the first of Baum's money, buying two milkshakes – they both liked strawberry the most – and they slurped these as they walked into town. They followed the main road, with the cars preventing conversation but loud enough not to leave them caught in awkward silence. There were quite a few kids around, riding skateboards and bicycles, and others who gathered in groups and sat under trees, eager for something to do, some adventure which such a small town could never offer. Eric looked at these groups to be sure there were no bikers around, but it seemed they were all away on holidays. During a lull in the traffic, Pepper explained there were other surf shops in the centre of town. Once they got there, Eric followed her into these shops but looked half-heartedly at the boards on offer; he had seen the one he wanted.

As the date wore on, he relaxed more and more. Pepper wasn't going to run away, nor was she embarrassed if people saw them together. With that security, his voice settled down. In a video shop, he bought a collection of westerns for his father, while in another shop, Pepper helped him pick out a nice perfume for his mother. She was impressed with these gifts, that Eric cared enough to spend money on his parents and not on himself.

"You must have great parents," she said, her pretty face dropping and her bright eyes turning dull.

Eric laughed sarcastically. "They're all right." He hoped he sounded convincing enough to stop Pepper from prying further into his home life.

Inspired by Eric, Pepper also bought some presents for her family; small trinkets that were more for show, and other funny gifts the humour value of which wouldn't make it past New Year. They walked back to Crescent Bay with shopping bags swinging from their hands. Eric wanted to reach out and take Pepper's free hand, but didn't have the courage. He would start to do it, slowly extending his hand, but could never quite finish the job. It felt good, though, to walk through the town with this pretty girl, to know that other kids had seen them together. He may yet be popular by the time school started again.

They detoured to the fishing pier and licked at ice creams while watching old men pull in the small fish that liked to feed near the rocks of the man-made groyne. Relishing some common ground and anxious for conversation, they talked about Brad, with Pepper telling some embarrassing stories which Eric enjoyed immensely. They were so funny, he wondered if she was making them up. Eric forgot about the incident in the surf shop, and the image of his mother standing in the kitchen and yelling at him was a far distant memory. Pepper even allowed him to walk her home. She lived a few doors down from Baum in a modest, two-storey house which had a small front yard, mostly paved. There were several cars parked in front of the house; one had the red and white P plates of a first year driver taped to the front and back windows.

"Oh shit," Pepper groaned. "That's my sister's car. I hope she didn't bring her loser boyfriend." She turned to Eric, her small mouth screwed up in disappointment. "Do you have any loser sisters or brothers?"

"I'm a lone loser," he said. Pepper laughed and slapped him lightly on the shoulder. She seemed reluctant to go inside the house and the two of them stood on the driveway with nothing much left to say to each other.

"Well," Eric started, uncomfortable with the silence, "thanks for showing me the shops today. I'm going to buy that dolphin board with the money I get for Christmas."

"When you goin surfing again?" Pepper asked. She sneaked looks at her house, perhaps checking to see if any family members were peeking through the curtains.

"I reckon on Boxing Day. But not at South Corner." Butterflies fluttered like mad in his stomach. "Wanna meet me?"

Pepper looked at her sister's battered and dented car. "I don't know what's happening on Boxing Day. I might have to go to Perth to visit relatives. But if I'm here, then I'll meet you at the beach in the middle of the bay, where we had the camp fire. If I'm not, then I'll be there the next day."

Eric beamed. "Great. See you then."

Pepper smiled. "Have a nice Christmas." She turned and started for her front door.

"Hey, Pepper," Eric called out, chasing after her. He reached inside his bag and pulled out a small pink box. "Merry Christmas."

She blushed when she took it in her hands and started to open it.

"Hey, not until tomorrow."

She smiled at him and then leaned close to give him a kiss on the cheek. Her lips felt cool against his hot face and his ears burned with embarrassment and desire.

"You're really sweet," she said, almost as if she didn't deserve such attention. "Are they all like you in Merredin?"

"Well, like Brad said, the sheep love us."

She laughed and gave him a playful push, coming close to him again and hinting, he hoped, at her own desire for more physical contact.

"See ya on Boxing Day," she said. And she pivoted on her right foot and sashayed down the driveway. Eric watched her narrow hips swaying under the red and white floral dress. She turned to smile and wave before slipping through the unlocked front door.

He ran home, his legs pounding the pavement, the videos and perfume bouncing in the plastic bag. He felt a burst of energy he had never felt in his life and he thought seriously about dumping the shopping bag and running clear across the country.

***

The long table was brought in from the garage. Eric was forced to help his father, but only listened with one ear to the instructions the old man constantly gave. Together, they unfolded the table, brushed away and killed a few spiders, and then set it up in the living room. There had been talk of eating outside, but his father had declared, cutting Eric's mother down to size for even suggesting such a thing, that there would be too many flies. It was too hot anyway and the living room was air-conditioned.

The plastic Christmas tree, with the same tacky decorations as every year, stood rather desolately in the corner of the living room, with only a few scattered presents for uncles, aunts and cousins under it. When the other families arrived and saw the tree, his father proudly explained that, due to his rampant disobedience and vagrancy, Eric would be getting no presents this year, hence the empty tree. There followed a long and earnest discussion about kids today, how they went against everything their parents told them and needed more discipline, like they themselves had had when they were young. There was a chorus of agreement that teachers should punish students more severely, and it was Eric's father, already working on his second can of beer, who suggested that the cane be brought back into the schoolroom. They all agreed the schools and teachers were to blame, not the parents. Eric slumped on the sofa, the sole representative of teenagers everywhere, unable to fight back against this nasty, ignorant group that was his extended family. How mean and negative they all were, he thought, so ready to point fingers but never at themselves, and always criticising, as if by being critical they showed how intelligent they were.

There was Uncle Frank, an assistant manager of a branch of the Commonwealth Bank somewhere in Perth; Eric could never remember where. Frank was the spitting image of Eric's grandfather, but while he resembled him physically, he had none of his joviality, charisma and spirit. And so, whenever Eric saw Uncle Frank now, he thought of his grandfather and the gaping hole he had left in the family; that is, a member who was kind, patient, tolerant, giving and fun to be around. Eric's father and two uncles, Frank and Matthew, were sombre men, hard working and boring, men who laughed heartily at their own jokes and seemed to need copious amounts of beer to relax. Their only form of conversation was complaining about work, about the stupidity of the bosses above them and the incompetence of the employees beneath them.

Uncle Frank had two sons. Simon was at university while the younger, Mark, was in the army, having been forced into the ranks after being caught by the police driving under the influence. Neither came for Christmas dinner. For Eric, it was the one bright spot of that horrendous day. His two cousins hated each other, but had always united in tormenting him. He had tried hard to win their approval, but four years is a big difference when you are young.

Uncle Matthew had three girls now aged four, six and nine, and each frustrated Eric's mother because of their peculiar eating habits, which changed every year. The girls battled hard for the attention of their parents, especially for their father's attention of which all three seemed particularly starved, and shouted loudly and tried to make jokes and do cute tricks. The competition was intense between the girls, as it also was between Eric's father and his brothers, but it was the three women who were the most competitive, fighting bitterly for housewife supremacy. Eric watched his two aunts crowd his mother in her own kitchen, helping out busily, adding extra ingredients when she had her back turned, giving snide suggestions and sour, understated insults. His aunts were so inconsequential Eric often failed to remember their names or worse, got them mixed up. He just called them auntie and gave up trying to remember. He only saw them at Christmas anyway.

They all sat at the long table, Eric relegated down to the kids' end despite taking a seat between his mother and father. The three girls stared at him as he sat down. He scowled, trying to show who was boss, but these three were used to ruling houses and were not intimidated by his show of viciousness. Jodie, the oldest, lauded with compliments about what a stellar student she was – which gave Eric's father a reason to call attention to his reduced scholastic achievements – sat next to Eric, staring at him and kicking his leg under the table. He tried to move his chair away from her, but she matched his every move, and continued kicking him until he gave up resisting. Realising it no longer annoyed him, Jodie stopped kicking him and then took to copying his actions: drinking when he drank, eating when he ate, mirroring his positions. He found it extremely annoying, but the adults thought it cute and laughed that Eric was perhaps enamoured with Jodie. It was Eric's father who had suggested this, pointing at him with his can of beer and laughing when Eric blushed, claiming that his embarrassment made it true. Eric did his best to ignore it all and tried to concentrate on his food, but his family was loud and the men especially continued to bring attention to themselves by shouting or laughing heartily. He wondered, like he did every year, if he was adopted, but then thought about the great cavalryman, Georg Messer, his possible ancestor. As he looked around the room, the possibility that these three men were direct descendants of that brave soldier seemed very remote.

Uncle Frank, when he got the chance because Eric's father monopolised the conversation, talked about a new colleague at his bank, a stuck up and prim man from Frankfurt who apparently had no sense of humour. Frank laughed as he explained the mistakes the German made, the jokes he didn't get, the subtle memos and office cartoons which he didn't understand, and then made broad, sweeping and stereotypical statements about Germans in general and how he hated the lot of them.

"But we're German," Eric said. He had said nothing the whole day and now the sound of his voice was strange even to him. But while he hadn't spoken, he had listened carefully, noting down new prejudices, altered allegiances and old contradictions. Now, the whole table turned to him. They had stopped eating and held their gravy-stained knives and forks expectantly. One of his aunts had a large mouthful of food and chewed this thoughtfully as she stared at him.

170

His father chuckled, but his insecurity was not lost on Eric. "What are you talking about? We're as Australian as Vegemite."

Eric swallowed hard, hating having all eyes on him. "But, but your granddad...he came from Germany," he mumbled, and again he saw the picture of Georg Messer in his head. He tried to look up at his father, but couldn't meet his eyes. He knew he was out of line and would probably pay for it later, but they were all against him anyway, so what did it matter?

The atmosphere became unbearable. The room was so silent, Eric could hear the asthmatic whistle and wheeze of Matthew's middle daughter Brianna. It sounded like someone was vacuuming in the next room.

"I was born here," his father declared loudly. He hit the table with his fist, perhaps with more power than he intended for glasses rattled and serving dishes clattered. "My father was born here. I don't speak a word of German. Why, our Uncle Marcus even fought for Australia in the Second World War."

Frank pounced on Eric. "Don't tell me you want to be German," he said snidely, saying the word German with disgust, like it was some foul disease. "They're all Nazis. Give em another excuse and they'll try to take over the world again. Our granddad did the right thing by leaving and becoming an Australian."

"They're all pagans," Uncle Frank's wife added, buttoning her mouth together like she had swallowed a lemon. "I read about it in *Women's Weekly.*"

Uncle Matthew's wife nodded knowingly, as if she had read the same article, which she probably had, and the two women edged closer together, the corners of their shoulder pads touching.

"That poor woman," Uncle Frank's wife said sorrowfully, as if they had been the closest of friends. "To marry a German man and leave Australia for him only to be thrown into a world of pagan ceremonies and sacrifices."

"What's a pagan?" asked Kylie, the youngest. She seemed to like the sound of the word and repeated it again and again until her mother yelled at her, rather viciously, to stop. Kylie then pouted and looked at her father who smiled and whispered a few secret words and Kylie went back to fighting with her peas, struggling to get them on the fork that was too big for her hands. Her mother had questioned Eric's mother earlier as to why there was no child-sized cutlery and had subtly suggested that she would be held responsible if Kylie was hurt in anyway.

"Someone who worships the devil," Eric's father said. Eric looked up to see his father staring directly at him, pointing the pagan out in the crowd. "Hitler was a pagan, but really it's just another word for someone who breaks the rules, the pagan who goes against God's commandments."

Eric's family had never been religious. They had sometimes gone to church at Christmas, but that was because many of his father's colleagues and customers had gone and it was a good way of networking. His father often claimed he lived by "God's Ten" but went against them so often, Eric hated it when any reference was made to them. It was another of the old man's many contradictions. But now, uttering these pious words and sitting at the head of the family table, Eric thought his father looked a little like a village pastor, ready to listen and advise, but just as ready to cast one into the fiery pits of hell.

Coming to her son's rescue, his mother said, "I think what Eric's trying to say is that it's not so clear what it means to be Australian. Almost everyone here is an immigrant, or the descendant of an immigrant. I guess only the Aborigines can claim to be true Australians."

"The lazy Abs?" Eric's father mocked, his voice loud and high-pitched. "All they do is sit around under trees sniffing petrol and getting high. Can't give em a job cause they'll go walkabout and never show up."

Eric looked down at his plate. He'd heard his parents arguing this point before. In Merredin, his mother had been a teacher at the kindergarten and had often come home complaining that other parents didn't want their children playing or mixing with Aboriginal kids. She had sometimes sarcastically observed that perhaps it was good there were no Asian families for they would be prejudiced against as well.

"It's precisely that racist stereotype which ruins everything," his mother said. "How would you feel if your children have been taken, your land confiscated, and your culture packaged and sold as a tourist product? And no one even gives them the chance."

Eric smiled at his plate. His mother's spirit and character often surprised him. He wondered where it came from, because all the other women in the family seldom expressed an opinion that was contrary to that of their husbands, or indeed, an opinion that was their own.

"What chance would that be?" Uncle Matthew asked. "The government throws money at them and they drink it way." He grew incredulous. "And then they have the nerve to hold us responsible for the past. They're racist too, but you can't say that to them. They're the ones who don't give us a chance."

"There are no blacks where we live," his wife said. "I'm quietly glad about it. I don't want my girls going to school with them."

The room went silent. Eric's mother seethed. He watched her tanned and wrinkled chest heave up and down, but she said no more, knowing she was powerless arguing against the whole table. And what was the point? Their prejudices ran so deep, there was no chance to make them see the other side. Still, Eric hadn't missed the rather stark contradiction. They considered all Germans Nazis, held them responsible for the past, but refused to be held responsible themselves for the Aborigines.

Eric's father, clearly uncomfortable with his brothers witnessing this family argument, swiftly changed the topic to New Year and asked Matthew and Frank what plans they had. Both replied there were parties organised through their respective offices and this was cause for more talk about work. Eric stopped listening and thought again about Georg. He couldn't believe that his father and two uncles, these soft-fleshed, spineless, cowardly office workers, carried the same genes as the great Prussian cavalryman with the dagger hooked into his belt. There had to be some mistake. He heard his father mention that they would be going to Geraldton for New Year and he groaned silently and slumped in his chair.

They ate roast chicken with boiled potatoes and steamed vegetables. Uncle Frank's wife made cutting remarks during the meal, that she would never serve hot food at Christmas because of the weather. She would serve cold meats with salads and dips. But this comment was a chance for Eric's father to boast about the house's air-conditioning. His mother said nothing, but Eric could see that the insults hurt. Uncle Matthew's wife held her criticism for dessert, the traditional plum pudding with hot custard, musing that it no longer suited the modern Australian Christmas, again because of the weather and because it was so old-fashioned. Eric watched his mother again take these comments in silence, chasing down her anger with chilled wine, but even the wine had been criticised by that pillar of support, her husband. All that work and not single compliment.

"That meal was fantastic," Eric offered at the meal's conclusion, but his mother was still angry with him for yesterday.

"There's still the dishes to do," she responded, pursing her lips together, her work never done.

After lunch, they sat around the living room struggling to make conversation except to criticise things. Eric's cousins opened their presents and played with them on the floor. All the adults watched and the three girls thrived on the attention, crying loudly when they thought they weren't getting enough. There was a minor drama when Kylie broke her plastic doll, but her father managed to get the arms back on and Kylie stopped crying just as quickly. Eric heard his aunts murmuring together that the gifts were cheap and of the lowest quality. He thought about helping his mother with the washing up, but his aunts beat him to it. The three women crowded the kitchen again, bumping into each other and doing the dishes in record time. The aunts didn't ask any questions about where things went and put pots, pans and cutlery in places they thought best. His mother would never find anything again.

The afternoon dragged. Eric sat around, wondering how much longer he had to wait before being able to excuse himself. With the dishes washed, he took the chance to give his presents to his parents.

"I think you might finally be learning, sport," his father slurred, making it seem he had expected the present all along and had not a trace of guilt. But there was quick look exchanged and Eric was sure his father knew his true intentions.

"Thank you, Eric," his mother said softly, lifting the top off the bottle and smelling the perfume. "But where did you get the money?" She leaned closer to him, already smelling of the perfume. "You're not stealing again, are you?"

"I worked a few days for Mr Baum, remember?"

Her eyes went blank and she stared at the floor, the alcohol and stress preventing the connection. Finally, it clicked and her face showed how sorry she was for accusing her son.

"Oh, Ricky. It slipped my mind. Thanks for the perfume." She reached out a dish-pan hand and stroked his cheek. It was a nice gesture, he knew, but he withdrew, not wanting her to embarrass him in front of the others. He complimented the meal one last time. Then, thinking his obligations were over, he slipped from the living room to hide in his own domain.

He sighed heavily as he opened the door, hoping at last he might find some peace. Jodie looked up as he entered. She was rummaging through his chest of drawers, having already emptied out three and was now working on the last one. His stuff was scattered all over the floor.

"Get outta here," he shouted. The young girl darted from the room crying. Eric bent over and started cleaning away the mess. He folded his shirts and shorts again, liking them orderly, and put them back in the drawers. It took about two minutes for his father to appear in the doorway. Uncle Matthew lurked behind him. The two of them, paunchy, both lilting from alcohol but determined to prove their sobriety, crowded the narrow doorway.

"Why did you hit Jodie?" his father demanded.

"Yeah," Uncle Matthew added. "Why don't you pick on someone your own size?"

"I didn't hit her," Eric said, sensing already that he was arguing a mute point. Their judgements had been made, but he went on nonetheless. "She was messing in my room and I told her to get out."

"Jodie told me you hit her," Uncle Matthew said. He had a high-pitched, grating voice that made Eric think of a whining child or a deep voice on helium. "She said you dragged her in here and hit her."

Eric watched the satisfied smile curl on his father's lips. "I didn't touch her."

"But you have to ask yourself," his father said, "in light of recent events, with you lying and fighting and sneaking out and all, if you were in my situation, who would you believe?"

Eric sighed heavily and gritted his teeth. He wanted to say that he would believe his son at all costs, back him up at every point in his life, support him whenever he needed it, even when he was wrong. The last thing he would ever do would be to cut him down, destroy his confidence and use him as a means for making himself bigger.

"If I were you," Eric said, "I'd think my son was a liar and hit him for it, and never let him go outside again."

"Right, that's it." His father came into the room and slammed the door. "I'm sick of your antics. You think you can win us over with presents, but you've got a lot to learn about treating people the right way."

He slapped Eric hard on the face. Eric fell to the floor, clutching his burning cheek, somewhat surprised he had been slapped.

"That's for hitting Jodie," his father shouted, trying to maintain his violent air of dominance and control.

Eric got to his feet, keen to prove his strength to the old man. He stared defiantly, raising his eyebrows, questioning if that was the best his father had. He felt the tears coming and tried to swallow them down. His fear and hate made him pull his shoulders back. This show of bravado seemed to motivate his father further and he raised a hand to strike Eric again, this time with the back of his right hand. Eric saw it coming and could have moved, but decided to take the hit, knowing that with it, his relationship with his father would move into a different phase. The thick wedding ring caught him high on the cheekbone, splitting the skin on impact. He fell to the floor, holding his hands over his face.

"And that's for trying to make us feel bad by giving us presents," his father said, but the edge was gone from his voice. He turned and opened the door. Uncle Matthew still stood in the doorway and through the gap in Eric's fingers, he saw his uncle smile at the bundled up mess on the floor. The door was slammed shut again and Eric was finally alone.

With one hand hard against his bleeding cheek, he got up and checked his face in the mirror. He took one of his handkerchiefs, which Jodie had tossed to the floor, and tried to stop the bleeding. He saw his mangled and bruised face and promised himself he would not say another word to his father for the rest of his life.

***

Eric surfed alone on Boxing Day, and while he was disappointed Pepper didn't join him, he was happy to have avoided explaining his bruised and bloodied face. He wheeled the old plank over the waves, starting to get some simple turns going. It was an effort with the heavy board, but his motivation was fed by his progress. When he got himself a real board, how much easier it would be then.

When he took the board back home, he found Drew zigzagging up and down the pavement on a skateboard.

"Check it out," he said. "Got it for Christmas."

"Cool." Eric also observed, from the brightness of the colours, that Drew had got some new surf clothes too. A profitable day.

"Hey, what happened to your face?" Drew got close to Eric to inspect the cuts and bruises, close enough for Eric to see the scabbed and pimpled mess just visible under a layer of cream that was Drew's own face. "Take a spill or something?"

"Yeah, something like that." Eric lowered his head, aware his blushing was probably turning his bruises a darker purple, making them more prominent. "By the way, thanks for letting me use the board."

"Pepper said you found a good one out at the mall."

Eric nodded, wondering if it would still be there when he had enough money to buy it. He had got nothing for Christmas, as expected. He had held a glimmer of hope for the usual $20 each from his uncles, but his father had prevented that. Probably pocketed the money himself, he thought bitterly.

"She called this morning," Drew said. "She went to Perth. Couldn't come to the beach today."

"That explains it," Eric said, somewhat downcast.

Drew smiled, clearly privy to all the details of Eric's burgeoning relationship with Pepper. No doubt he knew about the date, the pathetic bracelet Eric had bought her and the kiss on the cheek.

"But she said she'll be back tomorrow," Drew added. "You around then?"

"We're going to Geraldton in three days, for New Year."

"Cool. Good surf up there. Bit windy though. Wanna take the board?"

Eric frowned, imagining how his father would mock him for wanting to bring a surfboard along.

"I don't think so. But thanks anyway." He started to walk away.

"Hey, Rick." Drew idly spun the wheels of his skateboard. "You might wanna watch out for Brad. He's always had a thing for Pepper."

Eric nodded. "Thanks. See ya." As he walked towards his house, he heard the tic-tac of the skateboard as Drew continued playing with his new toy.

In the living room, his hungover father, who seldom took a day off from work, was spread-eagled on the sofa and watching the cricket. He looked up expectantly as Eric came in.

"Come on, sport," he said jovially, sitting up to make room on the sofa. "The test is on."

Eric ignored him and made himself a snack of yesterday's leftovers. He walked quickly past his father towards his room. His mother was in there, changing his sheets, probably looking for something to do that involved being anywhere than in the living room. She looked up as he came in and took his face in her hands when she saw the bruises. She removed the still wet plaster and inspected the cut. Aggravated, it started bleeding again. Eric pushed her hands away and attended to his cut. He taped it up again, his mother watching him the whole time.

"I'm sorry, Ricky," she said, almost whispering. "But you shouldn't have hit Jodie. You know how protective Matthew is."

"I didn't hit her," Eric moaned, but it was clear his mother didn't believe him either. "Oh, forget it," he added, waving her away. "You don't care what I think."

"What's the matter with you, Eric? You used to be such a nice boy."

He lowered his head, avoiding his mother's inquiring eyes. He thought that they were the ones who had changed, not him. He was just doing his best to survive in this brutal new place they had dragged him to, and they weren't making things any easier.

"Go and sit with your father and apologise, there's a good boy," she said, giving the sheets her full attention. "You always loved to watch the cricket."

Eric thought of all the time they had spent in front of the television together, the improvised games of backyard cricket, watching his father play in Merredin, and hoping one day they would walk onto the field together, members of the same eleven.

"I'm not doing anything with him ever again," Eric said.

"Come on, Ricky. Don't be stubborn like your father. Accept your mistakes and apologise."

Eric thought that maybe she was right. It would be easier to walk into the living room, sit down, watch the cricket and pretend yesterday had never happened. It had worked out like that before, as long as he was the one who conceded the error. But he was so sick of their behaviour. He felt it was time to make a stand. He went out of the room and, again ignoring his father's invitations, ducked outside into the garden. He quietly ate his snack and then sat in the sun until it was time to go to work.

"And where do you think you're going?" his father demanded from the sofa.

Eric took a piece of paper and wrote a note that he was going to work the afternoon for Mr Fischer. He thought about adding "the Nazi" or "the German", but decided against it. He dropped the note on the counter and left through the garage door. His father called out for him to come back, but Eric gritted his teeth and walked down the driveway.

It was a bright afternoon. He followed the fence of the golf course, walking along a worn track that was littered intermittently with dog shit. There were kids everywhere, playing in their driveways and front gardens, testing new toys, showing them off to their neighbours, sometimes breaking them and then running inside to their parents. He walked past Mrs Canter's house and admired the job he had done on her garden. He liked working with his hands, that he could make something, shape it and mould it, and see the results of his labour.

Mr Fischer lived a few doors down from Mrs Canter in a house similarly frozen in time. The front garden was a mess, with vines crawling out of control all over the veranda and tangling in the eaves. Bushes and small trees grew over and through the side mesh fences and over the front wall, which was low and made of bricks, like Mrs Canter's. The gate was similar too, the green paint chipped and the rust showing underneath. It creaked loudly as he pushed it open. Slowly, he walked down the short, weed-covered path to the front door. He stepped lightly up the three low steps and across the short veranda, his feet creaking on the old wood. To one side there was a battered porch swing, the seat covered with dirt and old leaves. Next to the door was an old leather armchair with a footstool in front of it. The leather was shiny from use and the seat indented in the middle. Next to the chair was a small coffee table with dirty circular rings where the dust and grime had clung to water circles left by cold glasses. From behind the door, he heard the muffled sounds of the cricket test.

He knocked. When there came no response, he started down the stairs, but stopped when the door creaked open. He turned to see a tall, hunched-over figure silhouetted in the shadows of the doorway.

Eleven

It was an effort to draw the rusty saw through the wood. The blunt teeth kept getting caught, frustrating him and quickly making his arms tired. There was the added pleasure, however, of expressing his frustration with the curses and swear words he was not allowed to use at home. Many of the tree branches were green, having grown in the early spring, and he had to twist them around and around until they came away from the tree leaving long, whitish strands. He then drove the saw through these stringy bits and the branch came free. He threw the branches on the grass, making a high pile that would have to be taken to the dump. He knew he couldn't build a fire at this time of year and the branches were too big for any canvas garden bag.

Through the open front door he could hear the television: the cheers of the crowd, the crack of the leather ball on the wooden bat, the nasal overtones of the commentators, and the raised volume of commercials. There was also the occasional sound from Fischer, a cheer or a grunt, even laughter. Eric looked at the door when he heard the laughter. His father watched the cricket seriously, in silence, often with the sound turned down so he could offer his own expert commentary. But Fischer watched the test like a child watching a cartoon, laughing and sometimes echoing the words he heard.

After he finished the pruning, Eric went tentatively into the house, his steps creaking on the wooden floor. Fischer didn't have any deep shag-pile like Mrs Canter. Eric found the old man in the living room, slouched in a battered armchair – a recliner that had a handle to extend a footstool – and knocked softly on the open door. Fischer turned quickly, almost jumping in his chair.

"You'll be the death of me if you sneak up like that," Fischer said, his rubbery mouth forming into a smile. "Why don't you make a lot of noise like a regular kid?"

Eric shrugged.

"Strict parents, eh? Well, that's not your fault. Are you done already?"

"Yep. Can I have something to drink?" he asked, hoping he might get water and not the ice-cold milk of Baum or the harsh lemonade of Mrs Canter.

"Where are you manners, boy?" Fischer snapped. "Can't you say,

'Please give me a glass of water right now?"'

It took a few seconds and for the broad smile on Fischer's face to make the joke stick, but Eric laughed. Fischer pulled the handle, retracting the footstool, and with considerable effort, hauled himself from the depths of his chair. He led Eric into the small, narrow kitchen. It had built-in cabinets along one wall, with the oven next to the sink. The dishwasher was murmuring quietly, with the occasional sound of water gushing or draining. There was a round plastic table with two fold-out chairs pushed to the edges of the table. Eric was surprised to see a bouquet of bright pink roses in a vase in the middle of the table, giving the dull kitchen, the colours of which had long ago faded from so much afternoon sunlight, a splash of colour it sorely needed.

"You should probably be drinking milk at your age," Fischer said, "gulping it by the gallon like they say on television. But I never had any milk when I was young so why should you?"

He smiled again. In the kitchen light, the room bright because the window faced west, letting in all the afternoon sun, Eric got a good look at the old man. The smile was friendly and it seemed to fit his face, as if he smiled a lot, or had done in the past, but Eric couldn't helping seeing something sinister in it: the way the lips pursed together, the cheeks pulling the corners of his mouth up; the way he showed no teeth in his smile, as if he was hiding something and restraining himself; maybe trying too hard to smile and that was the best he could do. Eric concentrated on the old man's face to keep from staring at the gnarled and disfigured hand.

"Water's fine," Eric said. He stood in the doorway. With such a small kitchen and Fischer a bulky man, there seemed not enough space for the two of them.

"I'll make us the best thing for a summer's day," Fischer said. "Any day for that matter."

He opened the refrigerator. Eric was surprised to see it was nearly full to the brim with drinks and fresh fruit and vegetables. Hadn't Baum said Fischer took all his meals at the golf club? Fischer took out a carton of apple juice and a bottle of mineral water. He half-filled two tall glasses with juice and then topped them up with mineral water. Eric took his glass and downed it in one gulp. It was refreshing and just sweet enough not to be boring, like mineral water normally was. He put the glass back on the counter and asked for another. Fischer smiled and obliged. He wore no gloves today. Eric was doing everything he could not to look at the gnarled mess of the right hand. But as he watched the old man lifting bottles and flipping the tops off cartons, he stared at the hand in motion, following it. He wanted desperately to know how it had happened. Had the fingers been shot off? Or maybe hacked off with a knife during some twisted kind of torture? If Fischer had been a Nazi soldier, who knew how it could have happened? Eric's imagination ran wild with the possibilities.

"They call it Apfelschorle," Fischer explained. "It's a popular drink in Germany."

Eric pounced on the opening, far too eagerly, and his voice was loud in the small kitchen. "Is that where you're from?"

Fischer raised an eyebrow at Eric. A smile flashed through the old man's eyes, but the rest of his face remained blank.

"That was a long time ago. I've lived here over forty years and I've only been back a couple of times. It's much better here."

Eric sipped his second drink, hoping to prolong his time in the kitchen. He had so many questions, but was too shy to ask them. He tried to see the Nazi inside this friendly old man, tried to imagine him doing all those vicious things he had learned about in history class and had seen on television. He recalled what Baum had said about the Nazis being the ones you least suspected. Surely evil was obvious, he thought, that the Nazi evil was so vile that it couldn't be hidden or disguised.

"Did you always live here?" Eric asked, pushing his other questions aside but keen to hear more from Fischer, to keep him talking.

Fischer pulled out one of the folding chairs and sat on it. The chair creaked under his weight, the legs sliding across the floor slightly.

"You're quite the interrogator." He looked again at Eric, a quizzical expression on his face, but still with a playful, cheeky smile. "Did Baum send you over here to get some information out of me? He's been at me since I moved here. Spreads rumours and tries to make my life a misery."

Eric shook his head. "I'm just curious, that's all. My family's originally from Germany. My great grandfather moved here in the twenties."

Fischer smiled grimly, like he was chewing a thought that tasted both good and bad. "He did the right thing. Got out before the little corporal jumped on his soapbox and ordered everybody to hate."

Eric fell silent, amazed at how quickly Fischer moved through his emotions and how those emotions changed the air around them both.

When he smiled and spoke playfully, the kitchen became bright and warm; when he spoke sourly, it became a depressing, lifeless place, and the roses become ominous rather than colourful. Eric wondered if this switching of emotions was the classic mentality of Nazis; that they could kill with smiles on their faces, make jokes about it, but then cry over a fallen comrade.

"Mr Baum said that Hitler did some great things," Eric said, his voice echoing just enough to make him speak softer, "things people overlook."

Fischer looked up sharply, snarling a little. "His greatest achievement was casting a spell on the youth of Germany, convincing them that they were perfect and all those Jews and Gypsies were imperfect, not to mention the cause of all their problems. And they gobbled it all up." He let out a sarcastic laugh, but it had more than just a trace of anger. "You shouldn't believe everything that Baum tells you. His version of history varies greatly from the truth."

But Eric, surprising himself, came to the defence of his moneyed employer. "He said that Hitler took Germany from the gutter and made it an economic power again, and during the depression too."

Fischer nodded. "Sure, by getting everyone employed in armaments and tank building. Put everyone in the army and no one's unemployed anymore. The people suddenly have a purpose, they become more confident, they spend more, money moves around, the economy grows. But that comes back to the German people. Hitler just gave them something to do. He can't take full credit for the economic turnaround."

But Eric wasn't giving up on Baum just yet. "He also said that Hitler assembled the greatest army in history, outnumbered, under-equipped and they beat everyone."

Fischer sighed heavily, so much so that two rose petals fell to the surface of the table, loosened by the unexpected gust. Absently, he picked them up and stroked them with his fingers.

"Well, he's right about that, and in some sick way, I guess it's something to be proud of. But again, Hitler only convinced everyone to fight. The ability and success of the army was due to the army itself and the men involved, not Hitler. He was a second rate general at best. And the army was never really Nazi."

"Were you in the army?" Eric asked, looking at the floor, his voice barely a whisper.

Fischer looked down at the two rose petals cupped in his hand. He took one petal and started running it along the side of his crippled right hand, tracing the long scars and stroking the stumped ends where the last two fingers had been.

"For someone who came to work," he said at last, "you seem more interested in history. So I have a question for you. What do you need the money for, or are you just here to confirm the rumours?"

Eric frowned. It was his turn to be cagey. "My father says I should learn the value of money by earning it myself."

Fischer shouted with laughter, throwing back his head and opening his mouth wide like a lion roaring. His face quickly turned red and he coughed out his last chuckles.

"That means he doesn't want to give you any himself." He laughed again, great guffaws that this time shook his shoulders and torso. "Twists the meaning to make his thrift sound like a character building exercise. Ha!"

Embarrassed, Eric stared down at the linoleum squares of the kitchen floor. They were worn at the centre, but near the walls he could make out the patterns of the coloured fish which had once covered the whole floor.

"It's all right, Eric," Fischer said. "That's what fathers do. They twist the truth to make themselves sound better than they are. We spend our childhood worshipping them, trying so hard to be what they want, but we fall so far short and can never satisfy them. Maybe it's because they turn themselves into gods in our eyes, rulers of the little world they call family." He dropped the rose petals on the table, like pouring water from his cupped hand. "Oh, leave it to the psychologists. Shall we get back to work?"

Eric nodded and drained the last of his drink, which had warmed in his sweaty hands. He followed the hunched-over figure through the front door and back out into the garden.

"Boy, you really gave the trees a haircut," Fischer commented from the veranda, his eyes squinting at the afternoon sun. "I'll call a friend of mine and he'll come and take all these branches away. If you're still here, you can help load the trailer."

"What'll I do till then?"

Fischer sighed, laughing slightly. "Well, I've got some bad news for you, Eric," he began, solemnly but in a joking way. The conversation of the kitchen, which had jumped so quickly between sorrow and laughter, already seemed like it was forgotten. Fischer was once more the friendly old man with the shining eyes and slightly sinister smile. In the harsh afternoon light, he looked older, and squinting his eyes made the lines on his face squiggle and curve, causing deep furrows Eric thought he could almost press his fingers inside. "I'm afraid these weeds have got to go. You want some gloves?"

Eric shook his head, eager to prove his masculinity. He had perfected the art of weeding in Mrs Canter's garden and, from her reproaches, knew how to distinguish weeds from plants.

"Don't worry if you pull out some plants," Fischer said as Eric started. "They're all weeds. Throw them on the pile and Barry'll take them away."

Fischer turned and stumbled back into the house. He whistled an old-fashioned tune which Eric didn't recognise, but its brightness was not lost on him and he set to work with a smile on his face. The old man intrigued him no end and he knew he would have to be clever if he wanted to get the information he so desperately wanted.

Barry turned out to be the golf course gardener. He arrived with a beat up, rusted trailer, and Eric helped him load the branches and weeds into it. Fischer came out and made jokes with Barry, the two men chuckling together like great mates. Barry was stringy and over-tanned, with leathery skin and an evil grin that made Eric keep his distance. Eric imagined him spending lonely nights in his dirty one-room flat watching porn films and then roaming around the neighbourhood looking for young girls he could kidnap.

"This lad's got quite a work ethic," Barry said as Eric loaded the trailer. "I didn't think boys worked anymore. I could use him down the club."

"Well, he's for sale," Fischer said. "What's your best offer?"

"I'll give ya ten camels." Barry reached into his pocket, took out his packet of Camel cigarettes and counted out ten. The two men laughed boisterously and Fischer slapped Barry on the back. Even Eric smiled at their joviality.

"Where'd you find this scamp anyway?" Eric heard Barry ask. He was smoking one of the Camels now, making a deliberate and obvious effort to blow the smoke away from Fischer.

"I believe he's one of Baum's elite," Fischer said. Eric looked up from his work to see Fischer staring at him. Their eyes locked briefly before Fischer turned back to Barry. "His mother recently joined the club."

Barry was thoughtful for a moment. "Angela Messer, perhaps?"

"Eric," Fischer called out, "is your last name Messer?"

"Yeah."

Fischer turned back to Barry. "Then I guess that's her."

Barry shook his head and leaned close to Fischer, but Eric still heard. "Starting with the highest handicap. Been taking a few private lessons from the pro, too." Eric saw Barry give Fischer a wink.

"Nothing wrong with that. If she's learning, a few lessons will no doubt help."

"Quite right." Barry stubbed out his cigarette and helped Eric with the last of the branches. He tied them down with an elastic net that hooked to the railings of the trailer and then drove away with a toot of his horn.

Eric joined Fischer in the shade of the veranda. With the mess gone and the trees pruned, the garden looked somewhat respectable again. Eric was proud of his work.

"What'll he do with it all?" he asked. "Take it to the dump?"

"I think he'll shred it and add it to his compost heap. He's very proud of his compost heap, you know. Treats it like a child, even talks to it. You know you're friends with Barry when he shows it to you, like you're entering his private domain."

Eric chuckled, trying to picture stringy, leather-faced Barry engaged in tender conversation with a stinking mound of garden waste.

"What's next?" he asked.

"I'd say that's enough for today." Fischer looked at his watch. It was one of those old explorer watches with a leather cover that he lifted to see the watch face underneath. Eric looked at it with awe, wanting one just like it. "I'm due at the club for dinner with a few people there. Can you come back tomorrow?"

Eric nodded. "In the afternoon, like today."

Fischer narrowed his eyes, acting the perfect comic book villain. "You make me curious as to how you spend your mornings, Mr Messer." And then he smiled, talking lightly: "I guess you've got the world to save, bombs to diffuse and what not, but when you're finished, you can slave away in my garden for a pittance." He reached for his back pocket. "That reminds me. I don't want you telling Baum I'm a slave driver, despite the ten camels." He handed Eric two $20 notes.

"Thank you very much, Mr Fischer," Eric exclaimed, trying hard to adequately express his gratitude, but sounding too much like he was putting it on. He was happy to be dealing in cash. The cheque from Mrs Canter still hadn't surfaced and his belief that there would be one diminished with each passing day. Bitterly, he wondered if his mother had kept the cheque, squirreling it away to pay for next year's school books or for some such thing. He pushed the notes into his pocket. They felt good there, and he played with them, rustling them with his dirty fingers.

"At least you're getting my name right. See you tomorrow."

There came from inside the house the shrill sound of the telephone. Fischer turned abruptly and went inside, closing the front door behind him.

***

The plank was like a length of wood pirates used to force people to walk off, plunging them down to the hungry sharks circling below. What an effort it was to move the board across the waves. It took all his strength just to make the slightest turn. Because of the weight, he was forced to make long sweeping turns, like the board was ten feet long, using his ankles and the balls of his feet to manoeuvre the board. But his confidence grew as the plank, despite its weight, responded to his will. He felt the thrill of the wave gathering power behind him and then thrusting him forward. There was a connection he couldn't explain, an emptiness, a short term void that he stepped into and the rest of the world disappeared; there remained only him and the wave, until the wave ran its course and the connection was lost.

In the lull between sets, he sat on his board, paddling a little with his hands to maintain his balance and making small circles with his feet. His thoughts drifted to his new employer. It had been a strange afternoon with Fischer, and he couldn't help comparing the two old men who were now in his life. If Baum was the friendly, cunning wolf, patiently waiting to strike, then Fischer was the peaceful, sleeping lion, ready to play as much as prepared to turn vicious and attack. Both men scared him a little, especially Baum with his feminine airs and the way he looked at him with such admiring eyes. But Fischer, with his mood swings and possible Nazi past, also made Eric wary. He hadn't decided yet if Fischer was a Nazi, but this only made him more curious about him, and he still had lots of questions for the old man.

Baum was not cagey like Fischer, and happily answered all of Eric's questions, sometimes with such long-winded speeches that the words got lost in a jumble and Eric couldn't even remember the question he had asked. Still, though they both scared him, they both interested him. Both were hiding their true selves, and both were not what they appeared to be.

His thoughts were interrupted by the pink blur coming down the path to the beach. Eric turned his back on the coming waves and saw Pepper walking towards the water. He grinned, but then a wave sucked up behind him and threw him unglamorously from the board, his legs and arms flailing, his cool destroyed. He got quickly to the surface, praying Pepper hadn't seen him. Why was he always making such a fool of himself when she was around? He climbed back on his board and worked hard to catch the next wave. He just managed to stand up and then executed a few neat turns, spraying some water, knowing Pepper was watching him. They met in the shallows with Eric trying hard not to look too happy and eager.

"Hi," he said, almost shouting.

"Hey."

Pepper was clearly not as ecstatic as Eric, but he wouldn't let that stop him. Girls always like to play it cool, he reminded himself.

"I missed you yesterday," he said, again almost shouting. "The surf was pretty good."

She wore a wetsuit top today, hiding her chest and the narrow valley between her breasts. Eric wondered if she was afraid to show herself in the bikini again and did his best to hide his disappointment. He missed the tanned skin of her chest and shoulders, and the flagrant display of the neck he thought was so attractive. She had just put sunscreen on her face and still had white streaks of it down both cheeks, like an actress's make up, painted on sadness. Eric thought she looked miserable. He tried not to show that he noticed, staying upbeat and smiling, hoping to turn her around.

"We went to Perth to visit my cousins," she said, tracing the water with her fingers and not looking at him.

"More relatives mean more presents, right?" he tried, desperate to lift her spirits.

"What about you?" She gave the old plank a slap. "Where're the dolphins?"

Eric hesitated. It was his turn to look down at the water and be miserable. He wanted to tell her the truth, but was too embarrassed. How uncool was it working in the gardens of old people, for Pepper's grandmother no less?

"I'm still waiting on more money," he lied, and the unsteadiness of his voice surely gave him away. "In the post, I mean."

Pepper forced a smile. He wondered if she had guessed the truth already, because she knew he had worked for her grandmother. But she was here and that meant she wasn't completely put off by knowing he was working.

"Um," Eric started, reaching his hand towards Pepper's face; the hand shook a little. "You've still got some sunscreen on your face." He tried to wipe it away, but was too scared, barely touching her face, which was fine in the end because he almost poked her in the eye. She pulled away and rubbed at the sunscreen herself. She blushed slightly, or had she just rubbed too hard? Then, she splashed water at him and dived in before he could splash her back. She jumped onto her board and crested the breakers. Her board moved sleekly, skimming across the water, and Eric had to paddle as hard as he could to keep up with her, straining his arms against the weight of the plank and being thrown back by the whitewash.

Surfing gave them something to talk about and Pepper offered Eric some good advice; more, she gave him the strategy for getting past the breakers. She showed him how to duck-dive under waves, pushing the board below the surface with his arms so that the wave didn't throw him back. It was difficult with the heavy board, but with Pepper's help, he soon mastered it.

They surfed alone for a few hours, but as lunchtime grew closer, other kids came down to the beach, younger ones with boogie boards and other inflatable paraphernalia, and teenagers with surfboards. Everything looked new; kids putting their presents to the test. Families arrived and soon the beach was crowded. The increased number of kids in the shallows made it difficult to surf, and Eric and Pepper were now fighting for waves with other surfers. When they surfed too far into the beach, adults yelled at them, ordering them to be careful of the kids who played with reckless abandon in the shallows, unaware of the rocks hidden just below the water and the stonefish that lurked beneath them. But this gave Eric and Pepper something to talk about, and they complained to each other about the dumb tourists. Pepper said they would all go home after New Year.

They gave up surfing and walked north along the beach in the direction of Pepper's house, carrying their boards under their arms. She asked about his Christmas and Eric was evasive, explaining how his relatives had visited and that it had all been pretty boring and normal. He still had the plaster on his cheek; he had told her earlier that he had run into a glass door. She asked about presents and he lied about that too, saying he got some clothes and other small things, but nothing special. These answers seemed to satisfy her and something in his voice kept her from prying further.

At the rocky part of the north end of the bay they stopped and had a quick swim to cool off. In a swift, sexy movement, Pepper whipped off her wet suit top and threw it onto the rocks to dry. There was her chest and neck on display. Eric was happy the water was so cold, saving him from an embarrassing situation as blood tried in vain to pump to his groin.

After swimming, they sat on the rocks and let the sun dry them. It didn't take long. The sun was high and hot, the sky its usual boring, hazy blue. Once more, Eric was tongue-tied, second-guessing everything he was about to say. Pepper's wet hair ran down her back and over her shoulders, in some places stuck in clumps to her tanned skin. A speck of pink ear poked out of her hair, but Eric was even starting to find those ears attractive. He thought she looked so beautiful sitting on the rocks, the water glistening on her skin, and wished he could say something witty and amusing that would stop her from looking so miserable.

He stared at her profile as she looked over the ocean. The first breath of the sea breeze blew her hair from her face. She turned to Eric and smiled, knowing he was staring at her. He looked away quickly, towards the horizon, at the white caps which would move progressively closer to the beach as the breeze picked up. He jumped a little when he felt Pepper's lips on his cheek. When she slid a warm hand into his, his whole body went rigid and stiff. She giggled, aware of this change. He tried to breathe, tried to act cool, like he did this every day. They held hands for a few minutes, with Eric working up the confidence to kiss Pepper back, guessing that was the game. He made feeble attempts to lean close to her, but couldn't go all the way. Finally, he made it, but as his lips reached her cheek she turned her head slightly and their lips met. It was like riding a wave, entering the void. He closed his eyes, tasted the salt on Pepper's lips, felt her tongue playing with his and running along the inside of his teeth, and rode the wave, hoping it would never peter out.

They stayed kissing on the rocks until the sea breeze was so strong it was whipping the sand against their legs. Eric walked Pepper home, with both sneaking sly smiles and glances at the other. It was second nature for them to kiss now, and they had one last passionate exchange before they reached Pepper's house. Eric thought she was an excellent kisser and hoped she thought the same of him, though he had little experience. Girls had only entered his life in the last few years, but the few girls in Merredin had never really caught his eye or attracted him like Pepper. They made a date to meet at the beach on the morning he was back after New Year. It felt like years away.

***

The strategy was a good one. He would thank Fischer for helping him in the park and that would give him an opening to ask about what Josh had said. Was it true? How would Josh know? And then, with the truth out, he could ask all the questions he had wanted to ask yesterday.

He walked quickly to Fischer's house, his thoughts switching between his upcoming conversations with the old man and remembering his kisses with Pepper sitting on the rocks. Just the thought of it made him walk faster. He couldn't imagine not seeing her tomorrow, or the next day. He would have to wait almost a week and sit through a torturous time in Geraldton with his parents.

Fischer was sitting on the veranda in the old leather armchair. Opera music was playing inside the house, with a speaker positioned close to the door. Eric, even though he recognised it as opera, was surprised by how bright and upbeat the melody was. The lifting piano, and his thoughts of Pepper, made him want to dance. Fischer put down his book when he saw Eric standing at the base of the stairs and stared at him.

"Mit deinem goldenen Haar und blauen Augen bist du Hitlers Traumkind."

Eric screwed up his face. "What?"

"Nothing." Fischer held up his book, showing the title. "I read in German. I sometimes miss my language. German has more subtleties than English. It's more literary as well, and there's no better language for getting angry." He gave Eric a twisted smile, trying hard to look mean and let fly with a few sentences of German that were supposed to aptly show his anger. But with his floppy face and put-on expression, he looked anything but threatening. Eric laughed.

"See what I mean?"

"I'd like to learn German," Eric said. "But we never had languages at school in Merredin."

"Ah, so that's where you're from," Fischer said, raising his eyebrows in surprise. "I was wondering about that. You don't have the…how do you say? The detached, vacant stare of local youths who have too much wax in their heads and water on their brains."

"But you can make all the sheep jokes you want," Eric said, enjoying the conversation. So much for his Nazi interrogation.

Fischer licked his lips, a rather gruesome and unattractive gesture. Then he set his jaw firmly, his face grim. "You'll get no sheep jokes from me. I have great respect for the country people of Australia, those provincial nationalists. The world needs more people like them, to run out with their pitchforks and drive the blacks from the town."

Eric looked down at his feet, unsure if Fischer was being serious or not. "It's not like that," he muttered.

Fischer's warm smile returned. "Well, perhaps not in such an extreme way anymore, but it was like that when I got here."

"Did you live in Merredin?" Tired of standing in the hot sun, Eric hopped up the steps into the shade of the veranda and sat on the top step, turning to face the old man, who loomed above him like a king on a throne.

"Geraldton, but that was bad enough. Let me tell you something, as an outsider, it was shocking for me to see the way the Aborigines were treated then, and this was coming just after all the incredible crimes my country had committed." He let out a sarcastic laugh, as if the irony was as funny as it was mortifying. "If Hitler made one mistake, it was that he made racism government policy, made it too orderly and thorough. It's easier if it's done secretly, with guys pulling on white coats or wearing masks, disguising yourself, with no one caught or condemned. Then again, the White Australia Policy was from the government."

"Most of the Aborigines in Merredin just sit around drinking," Eric said. "If they'd only get up and make something of their lives."

Fischer frowned and looked at Eric sharply, a teacher dressing down an ignorant schoolboy. "Sounds like your father's words," he said harshly. But then his voice turned soft and inquisitive. "What do you really think, Eric? Be honest."

Eric turned and stared down at the garden path at the base of the steps. Ants had dug into the cracks in the concrete slabs and had no doubt developed an intricate system of tunnels underneath, a massive inter-connected community with housing and workplaces, a distinct hierarchy where the trials and tribulations of human life were played out in minute form. He turned back to Fischer. The old man was leaning forward in his chair, his left hand tapping the armrest in time with the music.

"They looked like they didn't have any hope," Eric said, picturing in his head the Aborigines lying on the grass in the parks of Merredin, brown paper bags clutched in their hands, cheap liquor inside. All the adults in his life had warned him not to go near them, that they were all dangerous drunks. "Pissing away my tax dollars," his father had said. But everyone in town had loved Lionel, the star Aboriginal football player in the seniors' team who had won them three straight premierships.

"I don't know," Eric continued, "they did just sit around drinking, but they looked like they'd given up."

Fischer raised the index finger of his gnarled right hand. Eric stared at it, hypnotised. "But you have to ask yourself what you would do in the same position," Fischer said. "Your heritage has been stolen, your land mined and destroyed, and no white person wants to work with you or give you a job. To be a success, you are expected to turn your back on your culture and do everything the white way. I'd say you'd give up and turn to drink as well if the whole society tried to ruin you, always excluded you."

Eric had no response. There were no Aboriginals in Crescent Bay, none at the high school either. He had heard talk that there was a community inland which residents spoke of with spite, because sometimes the older kids came into Crescent Bay looking for houses to break into and cars to steal. That was why the area had a wall and two guarded gates. Eric felt Fischer's questioning eyes, the old man eager for a response. But Eric looked down at the concrete path again, focussing hard on the cracks and trying to picture the ants busily scurrying underneath.

"It makes me angry," Fischer went on, his voice louder now and echoing on the veranda. "And it still does, because when I lived in

Geraldton, I tried so hard to get the local Aborigines to play football. Not just because they would have a chance at life through sport, but because it gave them the discipline they needed, and they mixed with the other kids from an early age. People aren't born racist. They learn it from their parents and from the world around them. I thought I could change that, but I got nowhere."

"Why not?"

"Because the folks up there didn't really want that. Sure, all Australians say they do, talk and talk about multiculturalism, but the reality is that a true Australian is white. And it's a joke to think that people would look at me and think that I'm more Australian than people who have been here for thousands of years. I tell you, I never would have made it here if I wasn't white."

Eric looked at the old man. His face was slightly red from his anger. Eric wondered if Fischer would have been more comfortable giving the diatribe in German. How red would his face get then? But Eric was surprised to see how small Fischer looked in the armchair, no longer the king on the throne, but an old man whose body was folded up on itself. His bottom lip quivered and he had faraway eyes, lost in his own memories and thoughts, perhaps recalling the ideals he had held and the people he had tried to change but to no avail, and perhaps others who had hurt him. Eric hoped the old man wouldn't cry. How embarrassing would that be? He attempted to change the subject and lift Fischer's spirits.

"By the way, thanks for saving me in the park the other day. You know, when the kids were kicking me."

Fischer recovered himself, the left hand tapping time with the music again. "What was that about? Those brats were laying into you. What did you do to them?"

"Nothing," Eric said, and he held up his hands to protest his innocence. Why did everyone think it was his fault? "They chased me after school."

"Why? You look like the poster boy for this town."

Eric shrugged. "Guess it's because I'm new here, and they wanted to show who's boss."

"I'd say it's more they preyed on a weaker target, with you alone and everything." He sighed. "It's the Australian way. No, that's not right. It's the human way, also proves that we're essentially animals and all that religious creation stuff is nonsense."

"Probably."

Fischer gave him a quizzical look. "Is that why you need the money, to pay them off like they're some local mafia?"

"No." Eric laughed. "I've made some other friends and I'm hoping that when I'm in that group, I'll be safe."

Fischer nodded his head firmly. "That's right. Always safe in the group. What do you need to join them?"

Eric hesitated. The conversation wasn't going as he had planned. "A surfboard," and he regretted it the minute he said it.

"Excellent. Splendid. I guess it's better than a knife or a gun or something like that. Well, if you think that this surfboard could be the means to your security and happiness, then we better put you to work to add a few more coins to your surfboard fund." He pointed at the lawn. "Today, I want you to tame this grass of mine, cut it down to size."

Eric sensed his opportunity slipping away. Fischer was making movements to get out of the armchair, gripping the armrests with both hands, gathering the strength to haul himself out.

"Okay, but I have one question first." Eric paused, looking down at the grass he was about to tame. "You remember in the park? Why did Josh call you an old Nazi?"

Fischer grunted and lifted himself out of the armchair. His slippers slid on the old wood of the veranda and he almost fell. But he gathered his balance and straightened to his full height. He was a tall man, even now hunched-over and old. He towered over Eric who still sat on the step. Eric was impressed by this show of physical size and stature. The old man stood on the veranda, his face set in stone, like a statesman about to address the masses.

"There are two possibilities," he said, holding up the two remaining fingers of his crippled hand. "One, because I'm from Germany and most people still equate that with being a Nazi. Or two, his grandfather has been filling his head with ghost stories."

"So, you are a Nazi?" Eric ventured, his voice barely audible. He knew he was pushing his luck and was suddenly overcome with nerves. The rash of gooseflesh that appeared on his arms looked like a mountain range.

Fischer ran his right hand through the remains of his hair, patting it down and trying to cover the baldness; a practised gesture. He wore no gloves and it was still a shock for Eric to see the exposed hand.

"That depends on what you call a Nazi," Fischer began. "I lived through the time of Hitler, I fought in the war, and my father was even a member of the party. Most people would put those things together and say yes, Fischer is a Nazi. But if you take Nazis for what they really are, national zealots who know only their country and ideology and are prepared to die for it and commit hideous crimes for it, then I'm certainly not a Nazi. The Americans call it patriotism, and the Aussies immerse themselves in the Anzac myth, but it's basically the same thing. Having pride in your country and being prepared to kill and die for it can be dangerous no matter what country you come from. But then again, I'm from Germany, and most people in the world still make no difference between German and Nazi. For many, they mean the same."

Eric digested this complicated answer, the words turning around and around in his head.

"But like my former countrymen," Fischer went on, "I don't want to face my past, much in the same way the Australians try to ignore what they did to the Aborigines, and the Chinese, and any other immigrants with dark skin. Like other countries, the Australians try to sweep their bad, bloody history under the rug, and never teach it in school."

Eric looked again at the concrete, saw the black specks scurrying around and wished he was an ant, one part of a long and connected chain in which his role was clear and his life uncomplicated. All the ants had one colour, full equality, and each ant had an important role. He heard the distant cry of "Fore" from the golf club and it snapped him from his thoughts.

"I think I understand," he offered, even though he didn't.

"That's good, because I don't, and I can't imagine that I ever will. But I will say this. Nationalism in any form can be dangerous. Hitler's Germany was just a well-organised boys' club operating under a nationalistic banner, and they followed each other because they were too scared to stand out from the group. History is full of such similar situations, with everyone just following each other, absorbed by the power of the group, brainwashed by the promise of glory."

Fischer looked down at Eric and raised his eyebrows, making his point stick. Eric wanted to know more, to hear Fischer describe how life was at that time and what his father had done as a member of the Nazi Party. He had so many questions, about the war and what it had been like at the front line. Why had they all fought for one man? But Fischer cut him off. He looked suddenly tired, an orator with his wind spent, and he squinted at the afternoon sun as if it was an effort to keep his eyes open.

"The lawnmower's in the garage," he said absent-mindedly. But then he snapped from his reverie, held up his mangled hand and smiled. "Be careful."

Twelve

It's a long, lonely highway north of Perth. To Eric, it looked a lot like the highway east, which he had been subjected to more. Heading north, the road is inland, hot, flat and dry. Crows balance themselves on the roadside carcasses of sun-dried kangaroos, picking the bones clean, and are not deterred by the passing cars. It's a boring highway, straight, with nothing but desert shrubs and orange dirt on either side. Eric thought the stretch from Perth to Geraldton would have to be the longest five hundred kilometres in the world.

He sat in the back of the company Ford, his legs up on the seat. It was roomier than their previous car and the air-conditioning made him forget the heat outside. But while the car had improved, the journey was as painful as he remembered; look out the window once and it looks the same the whole way. He had campaigned to his mother that he was old enough to stay at home on his own, but she had disagreed, and not even the fact that he was working could win her over. Eric knew his father had made that decision, the old man perhaps thinking rather cunningly that confinement in the car and house arrest in Geraldton would be the kind of disciplining he needed.

Eric hadn't said a word to his father since Christmas. In response to this lack of communication – while Eric did not speak he did not ignore the man entirely, for that was almost impossible, because this attention-seeker employed all manner of cunning means to draw attention to himself – Eric's father was now giving him the silent treatment in return. This stalemate left Eric's mother in a trying position as the intermediary between to the two. They directed their questions and comments at her, having conversations and arguments through her until she complained that it was enough and they should just talk to each other. Silence would follow, and the silence bothered her enough to make her resume her role just to keep a semblance of family communication going.

Geraldton was the last place Eric wanted to be. They would stay in the company flats at White's Beach, those mouldy relics from the sixties with their brown and tan furniture, sticky linoleum floors, and thin, hard mattresses. Their distance from the town centre was a forced imprisonment for any child. And Geraldton was no place for a child to be walking around alone. There was only the beach, and this was either covered with seaweed or so windblown by midday that it wasn't possible to walk along it without getting a mouthful of sand. As every summer, there would be other families in the flats, but they would keep to themselves, and Eric would have to find some way to amuse himself. The worst thing was that he was finally making some progress in Crescent Bay. He feared that with every day he was away, that gain was bound to be reduced somewhat.

The car crawled along, staying just a tad above the speed limit, the engine pumping in cool, dry and stale air. The heat shimmered above the tarmac, with the approaching cars and trucks thrown out of focus by the heat waves, their grills becoming metallic distortions so not even the brand names could be read. Eric sighed heavily and wondered how he would kill the time. The week seemed terminal, trapped in a flat with a father he wasn't speaking to and a forever questioning mother who was very stressed and unhappy. And no television to fill the void either. He missed Pepper and hoped she wouldn't hook up with another boy in his absence. What about Brad? Would he take his chance to make a move? Would Eric come back to find out, probably from Drew, that Pepper and Brad were a couple? He shuddered just thinking about it. He wished he was back in Crescent Bay, surfing with Pepper and then working for Fischer in the afternoons.

An amazing turnaround, he thought to himself. I hated being in Crescent Bay and now want to be there and nowhere else.

He would lose a week of work, pushing the dolphin board further into the future. The only positive was that he had some money in his pocket that he could spend at will. This time, he would not have to ask his parents for money or for snacks. He knew he would save the money as best he could, but just the thought of having it, the freedom it gave him, was comforting and liberating.

The cricket was on the radio, his father sometimes turning the volume up when something exciting happened. He would then share his thoughts with Eric's mother, but the words were meant for Eric, and he made sure he spoke loud enough for him to hear. Eric's mother would respond dutifully, agreeing or simply echoing the words. Every time Eric heard his father's nasal whine, he shrank deeper in his seat, getting his head out of view of the mirror. His father kept looking in the mirror, searching the back seat, probably to make sure Eric hadn't jumped out.

They passed through a few desperate and desolate towns where the weather-beaten buildings looked like the pathetic shacks of a makeshift ghetto. A strong wind would blow them all over and then the locals would crawl out and put them back together again, their faces grim set and hiding deep disappointments, all those things they had wanted from life only to end up in an inconsequential town halfway between Perth and Geraldton.

There were lonely roadhouses too, where the petrol was exorbitantly expensive and the food heated by light globe ovens. Often, these roadhouses had the low buildings of a ramshackle motel attached. Eric wondered who would spend the night there. Long road trains were parked out the front, the trailers coated with dust and their cargo, sheep or cattle, piled on top of each other and stinking. The drivers were burly characters with tattoos and thick moustaches. They wore small shorts and dirty singlets which showed the world how hairy they were, as if all that hair was a sign of masculinity and virility.

There were always other families on the road, especially at this time of year. The Christmas-New Year period when the news broadcast every evening the number of driving fatalities like it was a telethon count. When his father stopped for petrol, Eric watched these families interact. They were coming and going from summer holidays, the country folks heading for the city and the city folks heading for the country; both thinking they were leaving something bad for something good, but, unfortunately, only temporarily. The big family sedans and wagons were full to the brim, with suitcases, beach equipment and bicycles piled high on roof racks. Some even had trailers, and it looked like they were moving house and not simply heading for the beach for two weeks. And then there were the kids, loud and complaining, always wanting what they were not allowed, expressing their frustration and boredom through tantrums and tears. These were the postcard holidays of Australian nuclear families, the dog left behind in the care of an uncle or neighbour, who perhaps also had the watering and post duties. How desperately the fathers tried to make everyone have fun; the stressed breadwinner with his one week growth, comb-over and faded floral shirt urging his family on like some demented tour guide. "Look, we're going to the beach and we're gonna have fun whether you like it or not," the two week beachcomber and shell collector would shout, imploring his charges to enjoy their one holiday of the year.

What fun those summer holidays were, Eric thought sarcastically. He hoped this would be his last. He would be sixteen in February. Surely by then his parents would let him stay home and not subject him to the horrors of the company flats in Geraldton and the boredom of the Brand Highway, or as he called it, the Bland Highway.

Finally, in the late afternoon, the dismal outer suburbs of Geraldton started to spread out from the highway. Deeper into this industrial wasteland of factories and single-brick houses, they turned off the main road and parked in the narrow slot reserved for company flat number three. The wind was howling, blowing the tops off the nearby dunes and sending slithers of sand across the parking lot. His father leapt from the car, eager to show his great spirits, to enjoy their one holiday of the year. He took lusty gulps of ocean air, holding his arms wide to let the wind blow through his floral shirt. Eric snickered and would have liked to remind his father that they now lived in a beach-side community, one much nicer than this. But he maintained his silence, lowered his head and dragged his bag into the kids' room. It had two rickety bunks, both made of metal painted dark brown. In places the paint was chipped, and some kids had even carved their initials onto the bunks or written on them; prisoners counting the days by scratching lines in the metal. He dropped his bag on one of the lower bunks and sat down, the springs creaking underneath him and the whole bunk threatening to collapse. He stared at the faded patterns of the stained linoleum floor, thinking he could still smell the vomit from the last child who had slept in there.

***

How the days dragged. Eric found it difficult sleeping in the kids' room and often slept on the sofa in the living room, sneaking in there after his parents had gone to bed. In the mornings, he got up early and walked over the dunes to the beach before the breeze picked up. He waded through the seaweed to swim in the stinky water and was stung a couple of times by the blue-bottle jellyfish that got entwined in the weed. In the afternoons, he walked into the centre with his mother to help her with the shopping while his father played golf. He dragged his feet up and down the supermarket aisles, a bored, sullen look on his face, his mother trying desperately to cheer him up. When he gave her no response, he heard her muttering to herself about puberty blues. He spent some of his money in a second hand bookshop, bypassing the comics that he loved and opting instead for novels about the Nazis and the Second World War. They turned out to be fantastic stories about brave American soldiers who fought courageously against ruthless and evil Germans. The Americans were forever outnumbered, always under-supplied, with all the odds against them and trying to pull off an operation which would save thousands, destroy a bridge of great importance, or maybe even bring the war to the end. As ridiculous and formulaic as the stories were – why did the Americans always have to be the heroes? – he read the books from cover to cover, fascinated by the Nazis, by the gruesome men of the SS, the villainous Gestapo, and by the imagery of a time and place that he just could not picture as being real.

And so Eric passed the days. It was the evenings which were interminable. His father and mother seemed to have little to say to each other that wasn't connected with the mundane talk of everyday life. Eric lay on the sofa with his back turned to them and concentrated on his books. The evening silence was filled by the nasal strains of country radio: falling wheat prices, rainfall statistics, racist call-in shows, cricket scores and bad country music. Eric and his father said not one word to each other and sought never to be alone together, with Eric's mother the gel that just held the family intact. His father spent his days on the golf course and Eric read, happy to be alone and not to have to answer any of his mother's questions. The war was much more interesting than his family's life, and he wished he had been born at a time when the world was at stake and things were worth fighting and dying for.

***

Eric remembered Steven Tomicich from when he had worked with Eric's father at the branch in Merredin. He was now working in Geraldton, and that was why Eric was dragged along to the New Year's Eve party at the clubhouse of the football club where Steven had played. It was a spacious clubhouse, with a long bar, a couple of billiard tables, some dart boards and plenty of round tables which were all occupied. People played the jukebox, filling the air with a strange assortment of music that crossed four decades and every genre. From each table, which smelled of old beer that had, over the years, seeped into the cracks of the wood, Eric could see the dried grass of the football field. The goalposts had been taken down and the field was now used for cricket. Eric sat quietly at the table, drinking one glass of soda after another and looking towards the far end of the field where a group of kids were playing cricket in the nets. He would have liked to join them, but it was almost dark.

Steven Tomicich had dark brown hair, receding on top, and he compensated for this hair loss by covering his dark face with a heavy beard, which was now flecked with grey, making him look older than he was. He had a toothy smile, which Eric thought was too broad and fake, a big, fleshy nose, and the glassy eyes that seem to be the prerequisite for salesmen the world over. The dumb stare disguising the cunning seller, Eric called it. His wife – Eric couldn't remember her name – was a bulbous woman, more rotund than round, and squeezed into clothing several sizes too small so that large rolls of unsightly fat bulged when she sat down. She was heavily made up and did her best to make conversation with Eric's mother, but it was clear to Eric that the two women did not like each other and probably hated their husbands for once more thrusting them together like this.

In the course of that dull evening they were joined by Ivan Tomicich. Steven's father was tall, with wide, round shoulders and shanks of hams for hands. In his youth, Eric thought he must have been a towering, imposing figure, but as an old man, he looked slow and heavy, burdened by the extra weight his broad frame had to carry. He lowered himself into the empty seat next to Eric.

"I heard a lot about you," Ivan said, his voice deep but croaky. His large mouth wedged itself on the top of his beer glass and he swallowed down half of it in a gulp. "Kevin used to tell me all the time about how bad you were at footy."

"I'm better at cricket," Eric said. "I'm already on the school team in Crescent Bay. Ask him when you see him. I always got him out."

"What's that?" Ivan asked, cupping a hand around his big, floppy ear. He moved his head closer and Eric could see the dark hair that grew in long, curly strands from deep inside the old man's ear, like they had their roots in the centre of his head.

"I'm better at cricket," Eric said, louder this time. From the corners of his eyes, he saw his father look in his direction. Eric turned his head slightly, making sure their eyes couldn't meet. "I'm too small for football."

"Nah, you're not," Ivan said. "Footy's that great game that has a position for everybody, big or small."

Eric disagreed, but decided not to shout this at Ivan. The old man seemed pretty set in his ways and looked like he was used to getting agreement from people. Perhaps his size had always intimidated people enough to make them agree with him, regardless of what he said.

"I played when I was younger," Ivan went on. Though he was hard of hearing, he seemed to like the sound of his own voice. Eric wondered if it was the only voice he heard clearly. "I took up the game after I arrived. Played for this club." He pointed to the boards hanging above the bar. "I was the best goalkicker the club ever had. Coulda played in Perth, but I had my work here."

Eric looked at the board and saw Ivan Tomicich's name listed as the leading goalkicker from 1949 to 1959. On the other side of the board was the list of Best & Fairests. Eric saw P. Fischer listed either as the winner or the runner up during the same period. He stared at the name, especially at the C in Fischer. The old German said he had lived in Geraldton and that he had been involved in football, but he had never said anything about playing.

"Mr Tomicich," Eric started, trying to talk loudly but not to shout, "do you know if that P. Fischer is Peter Fischer?"

Ivan raised his glass to his wide mouth – clearly able to swallow the thing whole – and paused to look quizzically at Eric before draining the white foam from the bottom, tilting the glass almost vertical. He slammed it down on the table and eyed Eric suspiciously.

"You know Handy Fischer?"

"He lives in Crescent Bay, around the corner from us. That is, if it's the same guy." But Eric knew the nickname had already given Fischer away.

"I heard he retired down south after Betty died," Ivan said. "That was tragic."

Eric looked back at the boards above the bar, marvelling at seeing Fischer's name. "Was he really such a great player?"

Ivan nodded. "A fantastic ruckman, even with only half a hand. The club won four premierships when he was here."

"Wow," Eric exclaimed, expressing himself animatedly for the first time this week.

Ivan nodded again, the nod following through and flapping the loose skin around his neck. "Great player and a good man, but we were never friends."

"Why not?"

Ivan sucked air through his teeth. "Because of the war, my lad." He raised his empty glass to the bartender. "He's German, you know. Of course, he has an Aussie passport, but that doesn't change anything. He's German and I'm from Yugoslavia. The Krauts were brutal to us Slavs. I'm pretty sure it wasn't Handy, because he doesn't have a mean bone in his body. The opposition always tried to fight with him. The league was brutal in those days. But he just walked away. Sometimes guys hit him, but he never hit them back." He leaned close again and Eric squirmed at the sight of those hairy ears. "Bit weak if you ask me. But anyway, there was too much between us, and even Handy admitted that. It's hard to forgive when most of your friends and family have been murdered by Germans." He said the word Germans with a quiet hate, lowering his voice. "But he'd be the first guy I'd have on me team," he added brightly, raising his fresh glass of beer and draining off the top. "How'd you meet him anyway? Is he coaching down south?"

"I work for him sometimes," Eric explained. He was enjoying the conversation immensely; finally someone interesting to talk to. "In his garden."

Ivan smiled thinly. "Yeah, I guess he might like you."

Eric looked down at the table and felt himself blushing. Ivan's eyes were boring into him.

"What did he do in Geraldton?" Eric asked, trying to take the subject away from himself. "For work, I mean."

"He started on the fishing boats about the same time as me. But then he got some money together and bought his own fleet. Nobody knew where he got the money. One day he was a regular worker and the next day he was his own boss."

Eric shrugged. "Maybe he won it."

Ivan raised a bushy grey eyebrow. "Handy wasn't a betting man," he said, shaking his head. "I don't like to think about it, but there were a lot of rumours going around at the time, that maybe he got it during the war or something. Nazi gold, stolen money, Swiss bank account, who knows? He was definitely no fool and was out of place on the fishing boats despite his work ethic. Too smart and cunning for us, and that made it harder for him to make friends. Helped that he was good at footy."

Eric leaned forward, resting his elbows on the table. He felt his parents watching him and smiled to himself. That's right, if you were more interesting and dealt with me as an equal, I might be talking to you like this.

"Do you think he was a Nazi?"

"What?"

"A Nazi," Eric shouted, and a few people turned to him. "Was he a Nazi?"

Ivan rubbed his rubbery face. It looked like a nervous gesture and his face seemed well rubbed. "Maybe. He certainly looked the part. Tall, blond, blue-eyed. But the Nazis were cold-blooded murderers and that was hardly the way Handy was. He was probably a soldier, like everyone was at that time. The whole bloody country was one big military camp back then." He sighed heavily and slumped in his chair. Remembering seemed to wear him out. "To be honest, I don't know, but people used to talk about it around here, even tried to keep their kids away from the football teams he coached, and that was years after the war."

"He told me he tried to get Aboriginal kids to play."

Ivan laughed. "That probably didn't help his cause much either." He quickly glanced around the bar and his voice became a whisper. "Not a lotta folks round here want their kids playing with blacks. Bad influence, they reckon."

Eric drank his soda thoughtfully. He looked quickly around the bar and saw only white faces. "How was he able to play with his hand like that? And how did he even know how to play? I thought footy's only played here."

"How did he play? He learned the game, like I did, like a lot of Europeans did," Ivan said proudly, his eyes sparkling with memories. "Check the players of the top teams in the country and see how many of them have European names. We were young and full of life, in a new country and eager to make friends and blend in. Footy gave us the chance to be in a club and to let out our aggression. And you could win over the locals if you were good at it. I tried cricket too, but I was never any good. Bizarre game."

Eric listened intently, enjoying the story. A question formed itself in his head and as he opened his mouth, a man shouted very loudly from the other side of the clubhouse.

"Hey, Ive. You up for some darts?"

Ivan turned to Eric, his rubbery face bending into a smile. "I reckon I am. Nice chatting with you, Eric," he said, standing up. "Give my regards to Handy. Tell him to write to me. I think there's enough water under the bridge. I'm still living at me old address."

Eric, disappointed his conversation partner was leaving, watched Ivan move his heavy bulk between the tables, greeting people along the way, before joining the old men by the dartboard. There was much laughter as they started their game. Ivan seemed to be the glue that brought all the others together, the jovial one who made everyone else funny as well. Eric reluctantly receded into his silence and went back to staring out the window. It was dark now. The kids in the nets had long gone home, and the windows reflected the action happening inside the clubhouse. He didn't know where to look anymore. He wished Ivan would come back and kept glancing at the dartboards, but the game was still animated and lively, with Ivan the centre of attention.

They eventually counted down to midnight and people blew small trumpets and threw confetti in the air. Eric kissed his mother's cheek and shook Steven Tomicich's hand. When his father came close to shake hands, Eric turned away and walked over to the dartboard to shake hands with Ivan. It was a new year, 1991, and Eric knew he would have to formulate a new plan, one that would relieve him from the tyranny he lived under. He wanted to earn more money and maybe get a part time job at the supermarket in Crescent Bay. He thought again about dropping out of school to learn a trade – it seemed the quickest solution for escaping the house – but he wanted to go to university, even if he had no idea what to study, what he wanted to be.

They stayed a little while longer and then drove back to the flats. Despite being quite drunk, his father drove. It was a hairy drive and Eric had to brace himself more than once. When the car went briefly onto the curb, he almost shouted "Look out", but didn't want to break his vow of silence.

***

The next day, the blessed last of their holiday – Eric was now counting down the hours and not the days, and wasn't even intimidated by the long drive back down the Bland Highway – they had a barbecue with Steven and his wife. The Tomicichs lived in a company house on the hill in Mount Tarcoola. From the patio, they had a view of the ocean and the drab expanse of Geraldton. Eric was disappointed by Ivan's absence, but not by Kevin's. Steven explained his son was still sleeping, having come back late from a big party. Eric ate his sausages quietly, brushing away the flies and holding his glass so the wind wouldn't knock it over. Soon the lunch would be over and then they would be on the road back to Crescent Bay where he could resume his life. The time ran slowly, but he knew they would start soon because his father didn't want to be on the road at dusk in fear of hitting a kangaroo and damaging the precious company Ford.

Thirteen

"I think it's time you grew up, don't you?"

Eric kept his head lowered and continued giving his dinner his full attention, hoping, almost praying, the voice would stop bombarding him with insults and questions.

"Your behaviour is just childish. You want us to treat you like an adult, but you act like a child." And to emphasise the point, his father repeated himself, shouting out each word: "Why don't you grow up?"

Eric raised his head slightly and stared into the eyes of his father. He really wanted to respond, but held his tongue and looked at the television instead. The crisis in the Middle East was still top news, with each reporter confirming that war was imminent. There was more talk about Hussein's atrocities, with the murdered Kurds mentioned again and again, making Eric think they were dying by the millions. There was also debate as to whether this evil leader might use the nuclear weapons he supposedly had at his disposal. Each reporter and expert came to the same conclusion: Hussein had to be brought down. But with the way the reporters wrinkled their foreheads so earnestly, and with the generals so beefy and battle-scarred, and with the enemy such a clear and unambiguous evil, Eric thought it was all too much like a Hollywood movie. And anyway, the Crescent Bay crisis brewing in the house the company owned was much more pressing and potentially dangerous.

Eric's defiance made his father angrier, and that felt good.

"What is wrong with you?" his father asked. Then he softened his tone: "Why are you so angry with us?"

Eric looked up and spoke to his mother. "I'm not angry with you, mum."

The words hung in the air. His father seethed, hating to be ignored, hating to have a problem he couldn't handle.

"Ricky," his mother began, perhaps sensing her chance and putting on a very motherly air, "what's wrong? You can tell us. Do you really miss Merredin that much? You always loved the beach. Why are you so unhappy here?"

Eric shrugged and looked at his plate.

"Don't worry, Angie," his father said. "He's just got puberty blues, that's all. Like they all have at his age. You've seen the teenagers walking around the neighbourhood like gangs of thugs. They don't care about anything or anyone except themselves." And then he added with a mean grin, chuckling as he spoke, "He's probably in love."

Eric dropped his cutlery loudly and stood up from the dinner table.

"You're not excused," his father said. But Eric was already out of the living room. He slammed his bedroom door, but he went straight to the window.

"What did you do to him at Christmas?" he heard his mother say. "Why did you hit him so hard?"

"Don't you start with me. I work all bloody day to feed this family and all the both of you do is sit around watching television. Anyway, it was just a slap. If the boy can't take a hit like that then he must be gay or something."

"I had to give up my job when we moved here. And I'm looking for another job here." Then she lowered her voice, so Eric could only just hear her: "You should give Ricky a break. We moved at exactly the wrong time. You, with your suburban upbringing, all the time the same house and your private school, you have no idea how hard it is to change schools, to start again from the very beginning with no friends. I did it when we moved over from Sydney. I know what he's going through."

"It's just so wonderful when you give people so much and they just chuck it back in your face. All the men in this country are treated the same way. It's pathetic. We should be worshipped for the work we do to raise families."

"That doesn't give you the right to hit your son."

Eric heard the scrape of plastic on tile and he guessed his father had stood up.

"I should've listened to Frank," his father said. "He was right. I never should have married a European. Australian women are much more subservient."

Eric thought about running out to protect and defend his mother, but as he moved cautiously towards the living room, he heard the loud slam of the garage door, the muffled sound of the company Ford starting and then its tires screeching as it pulled out of the garage. From the living room doorway, he saw his mother hunched over in her plastic chair, the table littered with dirty dishes and half-eaten meals. He edged forward and wrapped his thin arms around her. She responded and held him tight, crying on his chest and saying over and over, "I'm sorry."

***

Eric feared divorce, that ugly demon which, he assumed, lurked in the closet of every kid's bedroom. He'd seen it a few times in Merredin, friends of his whose parents first tormented their children with a period of separation; living with one and visiting the other, with the child spoiled by one and restricted by the other, but in an altogether worst situation than before. They never really recovered from the destruction of their families; that supposed constant in the tumultuous and changing world that is childhood. He already understood that, regardless of their economic or social situation, all kids define themselves by their family. And when that world is destroyed, what can they cling too? Where do they turn for definition, for a base?

Eric had thus far been spared that agony, though he sometimes feared it might come. His parents often fought, with his father threatening to leave, but it had not yet gone that far. And though he despised his father, now more than ever, deep down, he did not want him to leave. With his world changing rapidly, thrust into this new town and amongst all these new people, he needed his family to stay together. Otherwise, it would be one more problem to deal with, one more complication.

When Eric went for his morning surf, he saw the gaping hole the company Ford had left in the garage. He wondered if his father had gone to work early, rising with the sun to avoid any confrontations. But when he got to the beach, he was surprised to see the Ford parked in front of the same hotel as it had been a few weeks ago. He thought of Pepper, who was to meet him at the beach like yesterday. He wanted so much to kiss her again, to feel her cool lips pressing against his, like they had done just before he went to Geraldton. But something drew him to the hotel.

He stood the heavy plank against the wall outside and went into the reception office. A withered old bag with a beehive blue rinse stood behind the counter. When Eric asked after his father, she shook her wrinkled head, explaining there was nobody in the hotel by that name. Eric thanked her and went back outside. He picked up the board and pointed it towards the beach, not wanting to keep Pepper waiting. Suddenly, the door to number seventeen opened and his father came out. Smiling and squinting in the morning sun, he closed the door behind him, but stopped short of his car when he saw Eric standing in the middle of the car park.

"Eric," he said, taken aback. He glanced quickly over his shoulder at the closed door. "What are you doing here?"

Eric thought of the promise he had made at Christmas, to punish his father with silence. He wanted to turn and walk to the beach where Pepper was waiting for him. But he stood rooted to the spot.

"I stayed the night here," his father said, taking his keys out of his coat pocket, almost dropping them. He clicked off the car's alarm. "Your mum and I, we had a bit of an argument. Sometimes you need to step away from things to see them more clearly."

Eric chewed his bottom lip. His father walked towards the car, then stood facing Eric, the sun behind him so he cast a long morning shadow. Eric had to squint into the sun to see him, so he looked down at his feet, at the cracks in the bitumen. There were small mounds of sand the ants had dug out, and black specks darting around, the morning shift hard at work. He wondered if they were connected to the ants at Fischer's house.

His father spied the surfboard. "So, you have been surfing. That's quite a hunk of wood you got there. Where'd you get it, from Drew?"

Eric nodded. Then his father shocked him, almost enough to make him break his silence.

"I'm sorry I stopped you from playing cricket. I know how keen you are on it. I guess it'll start again soon now that the silly season is over."

Eric nodded again, trying to keep his mouth closed. He wondered if his head might break off from all his nodding. Why didn't he say something? His father had admitted he was wrong. Wasn't that enough? Eric sneaked looks at the door to number seventeen, hoping it would open and that he would see a scantily clad woman in the doorway, her bathrobe tied loosely around her shapely form. Or would he see a middle-aged housewife, with legs dumpy from child bearing, all stretched skin and sagging breasts? But then, he hoped the door wouldn't open at all, and his father had only spent an innocent night in a single room in order "to see things more clearly."

"Well, I gotta get to work," his father said, moving around to the driver's side of the car. "I'll be home for dinner. Tell your mum I'm sorry." And he smiled his salesman smile, his eyes glassy. "I know you're still speaking to her."

Eric nodded one last time and watched the company Ford drift out of the car park. It floated down the road and Eric heard the loud clunk as two wheels hit the first metal water drain. He turned and looked at door number seventeen. From the corner of his eye he saw the old receptionist with the beehive blue rinse standing in front of her office. She smoked a cigarette, rather indulgently, taking long, slow draws and blowing smoke from the side of her mouth. Eric looked at her. She shook her head slightly, a surprisingly sympathetic look on her heavily lined face. Then she smiled.

"Beautiful day," she said brightly. She blew a cloud of smoke at the cloudless sky. "I bet it's real nice down the beach. Probably a lotta skinny girls in little bikinis down there too."

She pointed with her cigarette towards the ocean and Eric followed it, raising a hand in farewell. He gave the door one last glance, but it stayed closed.

***

Pepper was already at the beach. She waved from the water, catching a wave in so they met in the shallows. Eric's glum expression made her come alive with questions, their roles quite interestingly reversed.

"Just family problems," Eric said, hoping that would be enough to make her not ask any more questions. "My parents had a big fight last night." He jumped on his board and they paddled out past the breakers. Once there, they sat on their boards, waiting for the next set to come in.

Pepper scrunched up her little nose. "Do you think they'll get, like, divorced?"

"I don't know. I hope not."

Pepper ran her hands through the water lightly. "My parents got divorced when I was nine. My dad lives in Sydney now. I've only seen him a couple of times since he moved."

"I'm sorry," Eric offered, taking some quiet comfort that his situation was not the worst.

Pepper looked at the water. "I wanna go to Sydney on my own and visit him, but my stupid mum says I'm not old enough." Her voice grew bitter. "She just doesn't want me to see him, and makes me spend time with Blair."

"Who's Blair?" Eric asked, but he had already guessed and regretted asking.

Pepper looked up from her board and Eric was startled by the candid sadness in her eyes. He saw something there: a glimmer of pain, a plea for help, both a desire to tell him her secrets and the strength to hold them inside.

"My step-dad," she said at last. "I'm supposed to call him dad, but I can't."

"A friend of mine in Merredin had the same problem," Eric said, happy the problems were not his, at least not yet. "He just fell apart, started running with a bad group, stealing cars and stuff like that. His father sent him to a boarding school in Perth."

"That's terrible," Pepper said, but she clearly thought her situation was worse. "Did you ever try to run away?"

"Me?"

"Yeah."

Eric thought about that one night after he had been hit for stealing from his father. He had packed his bag together, even sneaked into the kitchen to take a pot and a few cans of soup; even went as far as to pack a box of matches and some candles. And then he had sat in his room, his bag packed, with no idea where he could go.

"I tried it," Pepper began, smiling as she remembered the story. "Just after the divorce. But I didn't even have money for the bus." She laughed slightly, recalling the memory, though it probably wasn't as funny at the time. "I ran to Mel's house and that was the first place my mum called. She and Mel's mum are friends. She drove over and picked me up."

Eric offered a meagre laugh and looked down at his board. He felt the water being sucked forward by the coming waves, but was in no mood to catch one. He let the set roll over and Pepper did the same.

"I don't know why everyone thinks it's so great being a kid," Eric said, breaking the silence.

"I know what you mean. My gran says I'm so lucky being young, but I just want to be an adult and out on my own."

"No more rules, no more school, no more parents."

"No more Blairs. Complete independence."

214

They smiled at each other, sharing the secret wish for freedom. As they fell into silence again, Eric pondered the idea of him and Pepper running away together. But how would they survive? How would they finance their lives? Working for old people was hardly the stuff of a modern breadwinner.

"Pepper?" He broke out in a rash of gooseflesh so intense it almost rippled the water. "Will you…be…you know, my girlfriend?"

She blushed, but tried hard to look coy and disinterested. "You mean go round with you?"

"Uh, yeah."

"Okay."

Eric paddled his board close to Pepper's and they had an awkward kiss to celebrate their union, almost knocking their teeth together. The next set of waves came tumbling in and they continued surfing, once again with little left to say to each other.

When they were too tired to surf any more, they lay on the deserted beach. All the tourists had left after New Year and the beach was theirs once more. Eric closed his eyes and slipped his hand into Pepper's. They said nothing. It was enough to have the sound of the crashing waves, the odd squawk from the seagulls flying overhead and the splashing sounds they made as they plunged into the water after small fish. He was happy to have this blissful moment, here on the beach with a beautiful girl, his family troubles miles away.

His reverie was broken by the sound of motorbikes, the roar getting quickly louder until he was forced to open his eyes. He grimaced when he saw Josh and his group riding down the beach, making big turns and spraying sand in all directions. None of them wore helmets and all were dressed in their usual black uniforms. Josh saw Eric and the group roared in his direction.

"Oh, not these dickheads," Pepper said, jumping to her feet. She looked at Eric who was trying to put on a brave face, but his heart thumped against his chest. She grabbed his arm and tried to pull him away. "Come on. Let's go."

"This is our beach," he said. "We're staying."

The group stopped in front of them, with some of the riders trying to cover them with sand by sliding to a fast stop. Robbie gave a signal and all the engines stopped. It was strangely quiet. The crashing waves, which had sounded loud before, were now just the gentle lapping of a riverbank.

"Look at these lovebirds," Josh said loudly, pointing, laughing. "Eric's got himself a girlfriend."

The boys snickered and made obscene gestures with their hands.

"This is our beach," Robbie said. Eric was surprised by the high pitch of the leader's voice, as if it had yet to break. "And you have to pay to use it."

A couple of boys got off their bikes and stood behind Josh. To Eric, they all seemed to have grown over Christmas. They pushed Josh forward. Eric saw anxiety in his opponent's eyes, even though the face tried to look mean.

"Get lost, Josh," Pepper shouted. "This is our beach more than it is yours."

"That's the way, country boy," Josh said. "Hide behind your girlfriend."

The taunt seemed to empower Josh and he took a couple of steps forward, closer to Eric, his fists clenched.

"She's not my girlfriend," Eric said.

The group laughed, having what was probably the most fun they had had all day.

"If you wanna fight," Eric said, stepping towards Josh, "I'll fight you, but on your own."

Josh smiled, but it was a put-on grin. "Tough guy wants to impress his girlfriend. Oh, save me, Eric, save me."

Eric stepped forward and punched Josh hard in the stomach, again catching him unaware. He went to punch Josh in the face while he was doubled over, but two boys seized his arms, pinning them behind his back. He struggled, but the boys were stronger. Josh stood up, groaning and rubbing his stomach. He turned around and looked at Robbie. The leader gave a disinterested nod of his undersized head. He seemed rather bored by the whole thing, and as Josh stepped forward to lay into Eric, Eric saw Robbie sidle up next to Pepper and try to talk with her. But he was several centimetres shorter and she pushed him away. In response, he threw a handful of sand in her face. She ran to the water.

The beating began. The group laughed and cheered as Josh pummelled Eric, but once again, Eric was surprised at how little strength there was in the blows. He lay curled on the sand, trying to protect his groin and face. When it was over, Josh and a few others covered him with sand, leaving only Eric's face uncovered. Josh then picked up the heavy surfboard. Robbie signalled to bring it over to him. He laid it carefully over a small rock and started jumping up and down on it. But it was a thick board and Robbie wasn't exactly a heavyweight. He jumped and jumped until finally there was a resounding crack and the board split in half. The group cheered and Robbie held up the two pieces in triumph. Eric lay under the hot sand, his face burning with humiliation.

The motorbikes came alive and the group tore off down the beach, heading in the direction of South Corner and Josh's mansion. Eric got slowly to his feet, pushing the sand aside. He gingerly walked a few paces; nothing felt broken. He heard Pepper's voice, asking if he was all right. But he couldn't look at her, and staggered into the water to wash all the sand off. The salt stung what small cuts he had, cleaning them. He swam out past the breakers, afraid to look behind and see Pepper gone. There was no way she would be his girlfriend now. How could she possibly be with someone who had been humiliated like that? When he did finally look back, he wasn't surprised to see the beach deserted. He lay on his back floating, staring up at the pale blue sky, wondering if it was worth trying to swim to Africa.

"I think you're really brave."

Pepper lay on her pink surfboard, the roundness of her form curving on the fibreglass, her long neck glistening with water and sunscreen.

Eric trod water with effort, tired from surfing and sore from the beating. "I'm gonna get him."

"What difference will that make? He'll just come after you and then it'll be worse. You shouldn't have hit him."

"Maybe. But I gotta stand up."

"I don't believe in fighting." She rested one elbow on her board and her chin in her hand. "Nothing's worth fighting for. And there'll always be people bigger and stronger to overpower you."

Eric nodded, but inside he disagreed. "I wish you hadn't seen that," he said, still feeling the heat of the humiliation.

"Don't worry. Some people have it much worse than that. You wanna come in with me on my board?"

"I think it's too pink for me."

"Oh, shut up."

Eric lay on the board and Pepper lay on top of him. It was such fun that they tried it for several more waves, laughing as they wiped out, happily getting themselves tangled in each other. Then Pepper gave Eric the leg rope and he revelled turning the light board all over the face of the waves. The good board made him look like an expert and Pepper was impressed. Eric was glad to see he had redeemed himself a little.

"Now you have no excuse," she said. "You'll have to get yourself a new board."

"What'll I say to Drew? He'll be back from holidays next week and his brother will be here too. I'll have to buy him a new one."

Pepper laughed. "I seriously doubt that."

They kissed goodbye on the beach, with Eric adventurously sliding one hand down Pepper's back to give her buttocks a squeeze. She giggled and then pushed him away playfully. Eric, as had been his strategy every time he saw Pepper, was once again happy he had worn his tightest underwear.

***

The war room was starting to take shape. The cabinets were full of toy soldiers, model vehicles, miniature weapons and planes. Eric noticed the old man had done some tinkering with the cabinets. The row of Prussian cavalrymen was now on a higher shelf, at eye level. He wondered if Baum had done it just to spark his curiosity about his great grandfather. Or did the old man simply prize those mounted toy soldiers the most? Eric worked with his back to that cabinet, trying to keep himself from staring, knowing that Baum knew when he was looking.

He was rotating between the two old men now, with them both having agreed to his proposal of working alternate afternoons. He had worked the previous afternoon in Fischer's garden, but the old man had been in poor health and had spent most of the day inside, in no mood for talk. Eric hadn't even been able to tell him about meeting Ivan Tomicich in Geraldton.

Today, he was in the air-conditioned comfort of the war room, but Baum was equally reserved and quiet. Eric had inquired about Baum's trip to Dunsborough and the old man had given him surprisingly short answers, clearly not having enjoyed the holiday period. So Eric held his tongue and did his work as efficiently as possible. They were lining the shelves with the photographs that Baum prized the most. It was Eric's job to take the selected photos from the albums and slide them into the frames Baum had bought especially for the project. With Baum's permission, Eric cut the photos to fit the frames and these were the only words spoken between the two during the first hour.

The photographs were mostly of soldiers, group shots or individuals. There were Nazis in uniforms of brown, black or grey, looking stoically and arrogantly at the camera, as if they knew a great secret. They were in the trenches in winter, their white eyes peering through the layers of clothing wrapped round their faces, and mounted on tanks in desert locations in North Africa, with knobbly knees sticking out of khaki shorts. Baum murmured famous names, pointing people out in the photos, and they spent a good ten minutes discussing a shot of Hitler and his generals crowding over a large map-covered table. Baum knew all the men and talked about what had happened to them, if they had escaped, been put on trial or been killed, or had killed themselves. He seemed talkative again. Eric was fascinated by the dramatic stories of escape, especially the mysterious disappearance of Martin Bormann, Hitler's right hand man.

"I believe he made it out," Baum said, squinting at Bormann huddled behind Hitler at the end of the table and, surprisingly, the only one looking at the camera. "Perhaps to Argentina. Bormann was a survivor and probably would've given up his own mother to escape."

"And who's this?" Eric asked. He held a profile shot of a handsome and determined looking man who had a straight nose, a strong jaw, and a head full of thick brown hair.

Baum smiled and took the photo in his hands. "That's von Stauffenberg. He tried to assassinate Hitler." He laughed incredulously. "A bomb in a suitcase. Like something from a cheap spy novel. He thought he had killed him and went back to Berlin to try to take over the city, thinking it would be easy with Hitler dead. But old Adolf was a survivor too, even survived a gassing in the Great War, and he survived this bomb as well. Stauffenberg and the other traitors were rounded up and executed."

Eric appropriately expressed his astonishment. Baum looked up at him, a twinkle in his bright blue eyes.

"I was lucky not to be hanged with them."

"You were a member of the resistance?" Eric liked that word and tried to give it a French twinge that sounded pathetic even to him.

He had read about the French resistance in his war novels and now enjoyed being able to use the word, and prove to Baum that he also knew a little about history. But he had trouble picturing Baum as a brave and heroic fighter of the resistance.

"Not exactly," Baum admitted. "But I knew most of the men involved because of my work in the Economic Administration. And I was quite well known for being against the war, though I made sure nobody of importance knew that."

"Did you know him?" Eric asked, pointing at the picture, the man's name slipping from his mind.

"Of course. Unfortunately, he was hardly the hero history makes him out to be." Baum's bright smile turned quickly into a frown. "Nazi Germany had almost no resistance movement, and the Germans today cling to the one-armed count grimly, the one token hero from that time. That is, a hero it's politically sound to admire."

"I think I understand," Eric said, again studying the aristocratic profile of the count. "There were other heroes, but it's wrong to admire them because they were Nazis."

"Precisely. Take Rommel," Baum said, grabbing a photo from the shelf. "One of the greatest generals in history. The British held him in great admiration, von Mannstein too. In any other country, there would be statues of these men in every city. Schools would be named after them. Boys would grow up hoping to emulate them. But it's not the case."

Eric thought quickly about Australia's lone war hero, Simpson and his donkey, whose story was told every Anzac Day. No great warriors or generals in his country's history; just a lot of dead or wounded soldiers to carry, with the heroes the ones doing the carrying. Eric felt Baum's eyes on him. The old man was looking him up and down again, admiringly.

"It's amazing how German you look, Eric. Almost the spitting image of the great Georg Messer."

That photo was on the shelf already, one of the first they had put up, and Eric turned to it once more to study the face and the uniform, searching for clues, for hints that would make himself more than he was, more than just the only son of a real estate agent living in suburban banality south of Perth. He was convinced he saw his own eyes, his own face, the man he hoped he would grow up to be. The man he wanted to be right now.

"Unfortunately, there were not enough men like him," Baum said. "And a few too many like Stauffenberg, only interested in their own positions, blinded by their own hunger for power."

Baum handed Eric some more photos, pointing out the famous generals, and went on about how they were innovative and brilliant men highly respected by the British who had revolutionised the art of modern war. Eric slotted the photographs into the frames, securing the cardboard backing and then laying them face up on the shelf so Baum could later arrange them to his fancy, all the while only half listening.

"But tell me," Baum said lightly, "what does our friend Mr Fischer say about Germany? Did he admit to being a Nazi?"

"He said he was in the army," Eric said, unsure if what Fischer had told him had been in confidence. Surely Baum knew it all already. "And that maybe he was a Nazi. I don't know for sure. He gave me a pretty complicated answer when I asked him."

"You're very brave to ask him directly like that, Eric. Such directness and honesty requires courage and conviction which many men in this country lack, especially young men."

Eric bristled with pride, pulling his shoulders back a little. "He did say his father was in the party," he said, hoping for another compliment about being a young man with high potential, better than the rest.

Baum stroked his smooth chin thoughtfully. Eric had never seen a whisker on the old man's face.

"Interesting. I wonder if his father was someone important. I would assume that Peter Fischer is not his real name. You'd be surprised how many Nazis got away. A lot of them continued to live and work in West Germany like the war had never ended, and they were running the show in East Germany. In fact, you could argue that most of Germany never lost its Nazis, was never really de-Nazified as the Americans claim. They just changed their names and melted back into society. You have to remember, these were the elite of Germany. They were needed to run things, to tell others what to do and help the country recover. The economic miracle in the fifties was led by Nazis, who held most of the high positions in the economy and in powerful companies. And all those strong and industrious workers were children of the Hitler Youth."

"But I thought most of them were caught?" Eric remembered the war documentaries with the Nazi leaders crowded in the docks in

Nuremberg, big headphones on their heads like television antennas.

"The top men were. That is, those who hadn't held their oath and committed suicide rather than surrender. Although one must admire the way Goering handled himself at Nuremberg, laughing through the trial and then killing himself before they could hang him. Hitler had been wrong about him. A brilliant man. Speer too."

"Do you think Mr Fischer was in the party?"

"Well, being in the party was a family thing. The sons went with their fathers." And he followed this statement by wiggling his eyebrows up and down, using that comical gesture which was less and less funny each time he used it.

"Grandpa," a voice shouted from the living room.

Eric saw Baum grimace briefly before putting down the photo album and excusing himself. Eric went to the doorway of the war room to listen to the conversation. He heard Josh whining for money, like a small boy asking for a second helping of dessert. Baum was hesitant, explaining he had given him plenty at Christmas, and why not ask his parents.

"But they don't give me enough pocket money," Josh moaned.

"Maybe you should get a job and earn some of it on your own," Baum said. Eric, familiar now with the way his employer's voice changed with each emotion, heard the old man's anger rising.

"Working's for losers," Josh said. "Come on. Just ten, then I'll be happy."

Baum said nothing. Eric guessed money was changing hands, and he could almost hear the snap as the bill was whipped from the gold money clip.

"Thanks, grandpa."

Eric jumped, almost to the ceiling. Someone had tickled him in the side.

"Not good to listen in on other people's conversations," Annie said, a bundle of unfolded towels in her arms. She narrowed her eyes comically. "I bet you don't like it when people listen to yours."

Eric smiled, happy to see Annie and to know someone else was in the house. "Hi, Annie." He was about to ask how she was, but she interrupted him, looking past him, not over his shoulder but peering under.

"Watch out," she whispered. "Here comes Baum. Look busy." She bustled away, the big bow of her apron bouncing on her lower back and her short legs moving so quickly Eric wondered if her feet actually touched the ground.

He went back to the shelf and resumed his work. He heard an exchange between Baum and Annie outside the door and was curious to hear Annie's put on Asian accent again. Baum edged back into the war room, slightly embarrassed, his feathers ruffled. The expression on his face made Eric think the old man had drunk a litre of Mrs Canter's lemonade.

"Too much like his father," he said. He snatched up the photo album and started turning the pages roughly, not with his usual care and love. "Those people can never have enough money. They think they can rule the world with it."

Eric did his best to ignore the impasse and continued to work diligently. Every workday brought him closer to the dolphin board and he wanted to work hard to make the money come quicker. If he consistently got $30 or $40 every afternoon, he would have the board in a matter of weeks. Maybe it might even be on sale by then. He had to get out to the mall and check if it was still there, maybe take Pepper with him. Lost in his thoughts, he dropped one of the frames and it crashed to the floor.

"Oh, Eric, you clumsy boy," Baum shouted.

Eric was stunned when the old man clipped him over the head. Annie burst into the room, dustpan in hand, and swiftly cleaned up the glass.

"No ploblem," she said, sure not to leave a speck of glass on the floor. She even rescued the photograph and Baum inspected it closely. "Everyone make mistake."

"Well, there's no damage done," Baum said. To Eric's surprise, he handed the photo to him and gave him a new frame to put it in. The old man smiled, somewhat sheepishly, ashamed of his behaviour. "It's all right. You can't bake a cake without breaking some eggs. And we've got plenty of frames."

Eric went back to work, careful this time to concentrate and not let his mind wander. Annie gave him a smile as she scurried out. Baum began arranging the framed photographs on the shelf and the two worked in silence again. But Eric felt their relationship had changed, with both of them unsure what to do about it. Baum lined the German generals along the shelf. They were mostly middle-aged men, though they could simply have been younger men aged by battle, with deeply lined and sun-dried faces set grimly. Eric could see in the vacant stare of their eyes that they had both seen a lot of killing and caused it.

At length, Baum said airily, "I sometimes wonder if the world would be a better place if our Mr Fischer and his friends had finished the job properly."

Eric nodded slightly, unsure what Baum was talking about, but not wanting to look stupid nor say something contrary. If anything, he wanted to get back into the old man's good books.

"Can you do me a favour, Eric?"

Eric looked up expectantly, hoping this might be his chance to redeem himself.

"Try and find out Fischer's real name. I've often wondered about it myself. He could be a wanted war criminal, and if he is, you could become a hero by capturing him."

"But he's an old man now. He was pretty sick yesterday. My mum says he's got heart problems."

"She's right. And Mrs Canter may soon be able to put her mourning dress to the use she's dreamed about for years. But that doesn't mean he's exempt from the law. I know some people in Germany. If we had his real name, then I could contact them and see if he's on the wanted list."

"Okay. I'll try."

"You're a good lad. Georg would have been proud. You're a hard worker, brave and loyal. If you had been born in the Hitlerzeit, you would most certainly have gone to a Napola, the elite school for the gifted boys of Germany. And with your heritage, you would really have gone places."

Eric stared at the photo he had just slid into the frame. They were young officers of the SS, all with slim, strong faces, deep set and pale eyes, closely cropped blond hair pasted to their skulls, and intimidating looks of determination. But what was most striking was the arrogance. They were the best, they knew it, and they were about to conquer the world.

Fourteen

The bed was an old-fashioned rout-iron double, hastily made with the pillows still flattened and ruffled from the previous night's use. The room was dark, with the only window sheltered by a large tree growing from the neighbour's yard. The tree had grown well over the fence and was invading Fischer's garden. It reminded Eric of how his father had battled their neighbour in Merredin, almost going to court because the neighbour's tree had crossed the fence and he had refused to cut it back. But Fischer didn't seem to care about the encroachment and the room was cooler for being always cast in shade.

In front of the bed was a single wardrobe of old pine with a matching chest of drawers next to it. The wood was a dirty yellow, as if decades of dust had slowly seeped into it, discolouring it in patches and streaks. The pine wardrobe and the rout-iron bed were miss-matched furniture and their contrasts were startling.

Eric inspected the bedside table. Again it was of a dusty, dirty pine. There were books with German titles, with some of the pages marked with scraps of paper. There was also a glass with a murky liquid inside which Eric assumed housed Fischer's false teeth every evening. He resolved to start brushing his teeth twice a day, no excuses. The bedside table had one small drawer. He looked at it, thinking it was too obvious a place to hide something of value, and moved softly on the carpet back to the wardrobe.

The house was quiet. Through the open door, he could hear the murmur of cars passing on the street outside. There remained no sound from Fischer who had fallen asleep on the veranda while Eric was cleaning the gutters, his great frame bundled and crumpled into the worn armchair in front of the door. When Eric had whispered that he was going inside for a glass of water, the old man had barely stirred. And now Eric was in his bedroom, snooping around, unsure what he was looking for or where to find it, but fully aware he was doing something wrong. But it wasn't just Baum's request that had him raiding the room. He was driven by his own curiosity, his own desire to know the truth, and by his silent wish to become a hero. No one would bully him then, and how impressed would Pepper be.

The wardrobe made a loud, grinding squeak when it opened. He stood momentarily frozen to the spot, listening for sounds of movement within the house, then peered inside. There were shirts on hangers and many pairs of pants. The shoes were lined up neatly along the bottom. Eric was again impressed by how orderly and neat the old man was, and wondered if he had an Annie as well. The smell was interesting, musty and slightly sweet. It reminded him of his grandfather's clothes, how some unidentifiable sweetness, almost sickening, clung to the material, as if they had always been washed with too much powder, or simply washed too many times.

Eric moved some of the clothes aside, the metal hangers scratching along the crossbar. He was surprised to see a tennis racket behind the clothes, a wooden one secured in a press to keep its shape. Had Fischer played tennis as well as football and golf? He still had one good hand. Eric tried to picture the old man dashing around the court, forever dropping the ball when he tried to serve because he couldn't hold it in his right hand.

He closed the door slowly, with each squeak sounding like a gunshot in the silent room. He paused after each sound to listen for Fischer, and it seemed to take an eternity before the door was finally closed. He moved on to the chest of drawers. He was invading the personal world of a man he hardly knew and felt guilty for it. He remembered how he had rummaged through his father's drawers in the same way, searching for the money-box that stored his father's loose change. He hadn't felt guilty then, and how great it had been to have the jingle of the coins in his pockets, the weight of them pulling down his shorts. The world had suddenly opened up to him, things finally within reach. He could go with his friends to the shops and buy sweets, and to the arcade to play video games. No guilt; he felt he had deserved that money.

The drawers held nothing of value; only large underwear like the sails of ships, and undershirts in grey, white and blue. Eric slid his hand underneath the piles, feeling the wood of the drawer, but was somewhat put off touching the underwear. He wondered how long it had been since the old man had bought new clothes. Maybe he was hard up for money, but it didn't seem that way.

That left the drawer of the bedside table. He edged it open, careful not to pull too hard and spill the contents onto the floor; he had already done that once in his life. He took out the Australian passport, and on the inside page saw a head-shot of Fischer at a slightly younger age than today, his blonde hair fading but not yet grey, and his face friendly and soft, smiling broadly, hamming it up for the camera even though it was only a passport shot. The passport had expired several years before. Eric thumbed through the pages, seeing stamps from countries in Europe. The old man had travelled to East and West Germany, Poland, France, Austria and Italy. The exotic stamps ate at Eric's own yearning to see foreign lands, to experience first-hand what he had only seen on television and read about in books. What was it really like in Berlin? Was Paris as romantic as everyone claimed? Where had Georg Messer lived? And his mother's family in Holland? He felt a sudden urge to get on a plane and go to all of these places, hoping that by experiencing them, things would become more clear and absolute.

There was a chequebook in the drawer with the passport but little else. Some foreign coins were scattered about, small gold, silver and copper pieces, some with holes in the middle and marked with languages and symbols Eric didn't understand. He marvelled that Fischer had a box of condoms, a twelve pack with several missing. Eric tore one off and stuffed it in his pocket.

He sighed. Baum would be disappointed. If he brought nothing back, there would probably be no chance of a financial reward, no heroism. Fischer was probably just a boring old guy who happened to be from Germany. He went to the bedroom door and stopped to listen. He could just hear the muffled snoring coming from the veranda. Fearing his search was coming to a complete loss and not willing to give up, Eric bent down to peer under the bed. The carpet was thick with dust, but there was nothing. As he stood back up, a green and gold shoebox caught his eye. He went to the wardrobe and reached underneath for the box, sliding it out. There was a film of dust on top. As he lifted the lid, his fingers made long streaks in the dust. He paused again to listen for Fischer and then looked inside. There was a pile of envelopes, all addressed to Peter Fischer, with the top ones delivered to Crescent Bay and the older ones underneath, yellowed by age, to an address in Geraldton. Eric recognised the street name; the Tomicichs lived on the same street. He wondered if they had driven past Fischer's old house. Under the envelopes, which had the same handwriting on all of them, was a battered leather book bound together by a short belt, with a thin piece of jagged metal wedged underneath the rusted buckle. He inspected the book briefly, turning it over in his hands, feeling its weight, its age, and then put it back in the box. He took an envelope from the pile at random and turned it over. The sender's address was in Nuremberg. He slid the letter out. It was written in a beautiful hand, with the broad strokes and sharp lines, not to mention the unnecessary blotches, of a fountain pen. He couldn't understand the script, but did recognised that the letter was signed Josep Cazador. He put the letter back inside the envelope, laid it on the floor next to the box and then reached for the leather book.

The noise startled him. The sound of the toilet flush sprung him into action. He dropped the leather book back into the shoebox, jammed the lid on top and slid it back underneath the wardrobe. He stuffed the one envelope he had put aside into his pocket and flew from the room. In the kitchen, he poured himself a glass of water and drank quickly, swallowing down his adrenaline. He slid one hand into his pocket and felt the corners of the old, well-travelled envelope.

Fischer appeared in the doorway, bleary-eyed. "I must've dozed off," he said. Painfully, he arched his back, stretching it from having been wedged in the old armchair. He raised his arms over his head, completing the stretch. Eric got a flash of Fischer's withered and leathery belly, which was hanging rather unattractively over the tight belt. To Eric, his employer suddenly seemed very old and frail, and he had taken advantage of that frailty by snooping in his room and stealing from him. This feeling was magnified by the fact he had seen Fischer's passport photo, a healthier, younger and more energetic man than the one who stretched before him like a dying cat.

"Want something to drink?" Eric asked, wanting to make himself useful.

"Mix me an Apfelschorle, will you?" He shuffled past Eric and lowered himself gingerly onto one of the kitchen chairs, sighing heavily when he made it. He opened the orange bottle of pills and swallowed one, grimacing as he did so. Eric handed him the drink and he swallowed it in short gulps, absently spilling a little on his chin, which then dripped onto his shirt. He didn't seem to notice. Eric wondered if the old man could see the square outline the envelope made in the pocket of his shorts. Surely the conspicuous circle of the stolen condom stood out as well?

"Finished with the gutters?" The old man's chest sagged with the effort of breathing and his round shoulders fell forward, like his head was about to connect with the table. He looked like he had just woken from a deep sleep and the surroundings were new to him, so he hunched in on himself for protection.

"Just need to test them." Eric turned his body sideways, so that the pocket with the envelope was out of Fischer's view.

"You know where the hose is." Fischer took another short gulp, emptying his glass. His top teeth caught the rim of the glass and the denture clanked to the bottom. He drove his crippled hand, which fit easily, into the glass and fished his teeth out. It was a practised gesture, and he did it without embarrassment, like someone dropping a fork.

"Need my help?" Fischer asked when his teeth were back in place.

Eric shook his head, eager to get outside and work again. "I can do it."

"Good. Don't think I'm up for much today."

"Are you all right?"

Fischer sighed, exhaling the decades. "Just old." But he turned to Eric and smiled in a bright, wise and magical way. It made Eric feel incredibly guilty for having invaded the old man's bedroom and for stealing the private letter. "It happens to the best of us. You're young and strong, your life's ahead of you, but it'll happen to you too. I'm not that old, but the war aged me twenty years. You can't imagine the trouble I have at airports, setting off the metal detectors because of all the bits inside me."

Fischer wheezed a laugh, his eyes shining, but his thoughts seemed elsewhere. Eric didn't know what to say.

"I hope it doesn't turn bad in the Gulf," the old man went on. "Imagine, if a war starts, and it looks like it will, so I should say when the war starts. Anyway, when it starts, Australia will go, and if it drags on a few years and becomes another Vietnam, who knows? They might have conscription again and then you could be sent over to fight."

"Me?" Eric exclaimed, startled by this revelation.

"They had conscription for Vietnam, you know, and that was only twenty years ago. It could happen again, given the right circumstances."

"But I don't know anything about war." Eric tried to picture himself in uniform, his thin body unable to fill the big coats they would have to wear in winter. "Why should I go to the other side of the world and kill Iraqis?"

"That's a very good question. Probably because your father would make you, or because your group would go, the ones you call your friends. They'd drag you into it and you won't have the courage to say no, because otherwise they'll exclude you from their group. And then you'll be walking along one day, marching from one battlefield to another, thinking this pathetic stretch of territorial gain is of vital importance, and a bomb will come whistling from the sky and your friends will be blown to pieces."

Eric looked at the floor. "I don't want that."

Fischer caught himself and cleared his throat loudly. "I'm sorry, Eric. It's just that a lot of people don't really understand the reality of war, and they never seem to learn from it either. They make it sound noble and heroic, and necessary, dying for the cause of freedom or nationalism or whatever. The reality is that it's ugly, dirty, horrific, inhumane and for a lot of the time, very boring."

"Boring? I've never heard war called that before."

Fischer smiled at Eric. "You're a sharp lad. The Nazis would've loved you, although they might've struggled to teach you the blind obedience they preferred. But it was a different time then. You would've been obedient anyway, because that's the way it was. It was like a club. You were either in or you were out, and if you were out, that probably meant you were dead."

Fischer coughed gratingly and banged his open left hand against his chest. He held out his empty glass and Eric took it, filling it to the brim. Despite his lack of energy, and breath for that matter, the old man seemed in the mood to talk and Eric was keen to hear more stories. But he stood self-consciously in the kitchen, trying to hide the massive bulges he thought the stolen items were making in his pockets.

"War is boring because there's a lot of sitting around, waiting for the enemy to move or for your army to get into position. I remember these long marches through the wasteland of the east, our promised Lebensraum. Who'd want to live out there? And this is what we were fighting for and dying by the thousands for. And killing millions for."

Eric drained his own glass. His head felt like an overloaded computer, with too much information to process. He couldn't remember if Baum had said certain things or if Fischer had. The two old men seemed to blend into one, filling Eric's head with stories and ideas he was too far removed from and too young to understand. And though he was curious, he didn't really want to understand all of it. He just wanted to know if Fischer was a Nazi criminal or not. Given the choice, he would've preferred kissing Pepper on the rocks to hearing stories in this kitchen or in Baum's war room.

"Is that what the war was for?" he asked. "Trying to find a new land to live on?"

"It was one of the reasons, so we were told. But I think Hitler just wanted to succeed where Napoleon had failed. One inadequate and short commoner trying to outdo another," he muttered underneath his breath. Then his voice returned to normal. "My point is that it was a reason that none of the soldiers thought was worth fighting for. I mean, there we were, an army, perhaps the greatest land force ever assembled, standing in this wasteland trying to picture it as our future home."

"If the land was so bad, why did they fight?"

Fischer's old eyes twinkled, and these eyes fell on Eric admiringly. Eric turned away, feeling the old man's eyes were too prying, too watery and wistful. Baum sometimes stared at him the same way and it gave him the creeps.

"I was wrong," Fischer said. "And I apologise. They wouldn't have liked you. You question things too much, which is healthy in this day and age, but the Nazis hated people who asked questions. They thought that anyone who had a question was a traitor. They wanted obedience and subservience, and I'm happy to say they might not have got it from you. I wish I'd been as strong and inquisitive, though I would've been killed for it."

Eric took the convoluted compliment lightly. "Mr Fischer..."

"I think you can call me Peter from now on," the old man interrupted.

Eric, who had always struggled to call adults by their first names, asked, "Do you know someone called Georg Messer?" He was careful to pronounce it in the German way as Baum had done.

Fischer gave him a sceptical look. "Think you're related?"

"Well, my great grandfather's name was George Messer, and Mr Baum said there was a famous Prussian cavalryman with the same name."

Fischer laughed and followed through with a nasty coughing fit, his pale face turning bright red. He gripped the table with his left hand and held his ravaged right hand to his chest, which pumped up and down rapidly.

"I think Baum has been filling your head with fairytales," he said when he had recovered himself. "Do you have any idea how many Georg Messers there are in Germany? It is a very common name.

Sure, I know who Georg Messer is. The Nazis loved men like him, but the chance that he's your relative is extremely remote. Anyway, I heard he went back to Germany after the Nazis took power."

"Mr Baum showed me a picture of him," Eric said, wanting to hold on to this ideal. "He looks just like me."

"The eyes sometimes see what the brain wants to see. Like some of the soldiers on the eastern plain, their heads so full of the idea that this was paradise, that that's exactly what they saw. Baum's a good storyteller, but don't be drawn in by myths and legends. The Nazis used to deploy those methods well, manhandling the truth and twisting it for their own purposes. Champions of propaganda. You're a smart boy, Eric. Don't take all the information you receive as being the truth."

"But then I shouldn't believe you either," Eric said, surprised by his own clever reasoning.

Fischer blew the wind from his lungs as if there was evil inside them. "You're right. I'm no different. Much of my life is a fallacy. My opinions were tainted by the information I received which I took for the truth. I trusted what people told me when I should've questioned it. And I went with the group when I should've stood up and protested. It's not easy to live by your convictions. There are always others whose convictions seem more important and pressing."

"My father says a lot of things about himself that aren't true."

"Most fathers do. I think they learn that at fathers' school, or perhaps there's a manual."

Eric jumped on the opening. "What about your father? You said he was in the party. Did he go to prison after the war?"

Fischer turned and looked out the window. Eric saw that Fischer had lined up small pieces of old bread along the windowsill. Now, a willy-wagtail hopped around on the ledge, breaking the hardened bread with its beak and tilting its neck back to swallow it down.

"He should have," Fischer said finally. "He was a fervent Nazi, the worst kind, and he did some terrible things." He tapped a finger against the glass and the bird opened its beak wide hoping to get a grip on the finger. The beak scraped against the window, a consistent tapping that sounded like confusion and not curiosity. "He was a doctor and experimented on some inmates of the concentration camp near Hamburg. Not much is known about it because a lot of the research was destroyed when the camp was abandoned. When the war ended he escaped to Argentina, changed his name and married again. To me, he exemplifies everything bad about Nazi Germany and Germans in general."

"Why?"

"Because he was a careerist," Fischer said turning to Eric. The old man's face sagged with the bitter memories. "Like many others, he joined the party to further his own career, and then he got swept up by the power of it all. He was brilliant, ruthless and self-serving to the end, the way a lot of the Nazis were, especially at the top level. They were highly intelligent men. But true to their collective character, when the time came to take responsibility, they jumped ship and ran. Like rats. There were many like my father, one day obedient Nazis and the next day grovelling at the Americans' feet, or sneaking out of the country."

"What happened to him?"

"He lives in Spain now. He'll be ninety-three this year. The old bastard still writes to me. I don't know how he found me, but the Nazis are well connected. They may have been disbanded, but they never disappeared."

Eric frowned, thinking of the letter in his pocket. "Do you really think the war in the Middle East could mean that I'd have to fight?"

Fischer sighed again, his body deflating like a leaking balloon. "I hope not. It might just become another Vietnam, a drawn-out conflict where the Americans destroy everything, kill civilians, take home a few trophy wives, lose the war, claim victory and leave a complete mess behind for the locals to clean up. And then make films about their heroes."

"I don't want to go to war."

But Fischer didn't hear him. He took a deep breath and launched into a rant about America. His voice gathered strength and he called the USA a modern version of the Third Reich, an empire in the true historical sense of the word.

"They preach peace but go out looking for enemies, knowing they need them to solidify their place as the good guys. They use the media brilliantly to fester their own nationalistic, no, patriotic propaganda. They turn nothing countries into enemies simply to have a cause to fight for, an ideology of evil to battle against and prove their own benevolence. Their power comes from their economy, from middle-class ignorance, and they go out into the world pilfering resources from weaker economies and interfering in world affairs only when they themselves have something to gain. The Middle East crisis, Eric, it's economic, a battle for the liquid gold that America uses more of than almost the rest of the world combined."

Much of it flew over Eric's head and he watched the old man curiously. When Fischer got really angry, the rumpled skin on the back of his neck turned red. When the diatribe was over, he sat breathing heavily, his face glistening with a light sweat.

"And Australia supports them," he said, his voice dry. "This country is the Italy of the Second World War, no, the Romania, thinking themselves equal to their ally but completely subservient to their master, the first to be thrown at the enemy."

Fischer held out his glass with a shaking hand. Eric filled it and the old man gulped it down.

"I'm sorry," he said. He licked his lips, running a thick tongue over his chin as well and then wiping his lips with the back of his left hand. "Sometimes it's good to talk. It's just that the one who controls history makes himself the lead character. And if Germany... it feels strange now not saying East or West...but if Germany doesn't support the Americans, the media will have a field day. There'll be headlines of 'Nazis Back!' But when America invades Iraq, they will hail themselves as the heroes, fighting for peace, justice and freedom. It makes me sick."

"Do you think there'll be another Hitler?"

The question surprised Fischer and he looked at Eric curiously, seeming to wonder where it had come from.

"Maybe. Hitler came to power for economic reasons. He promised jobs, an improved economy, a return to greatness, and he delivered. If it turns out a united Germany, or any other country for that matter, falls into an economic mess, the situation might call for drastic change, and if the right man comes along, who knows?" He paused to gauge Eric's response, then added, "But Hitler was a one off, a special character who came at an ideal time. The chances of it happening again are slim, but we still see nationalism, patriotism or whatever it's called, in all its disgusting forms, especially in our own backyard."

Silence fell on the kitchen, like drawing heavy curtains on a sunlit room. Appropriately, the sun went behind a cloud and the kitchen became darker. Fischer watched the birds eating on the windowsill. There was the lightest of taps as beaks hit the glass. Again, Fischer tapped the glass with a finger and the birds, still not wise to the window, tried to wrap their beaks around the finger only to be denied.

"I guess it doesn't matter anyway," Fischer said. "I'll be dead soon and the meek shall inherit this earth. They already have. The whole human race is meek."

***

Eric trundled home, the wind ruffling his shirt and blowing his hair into his eyes. He tried to process everything Fischer had said, comparing it, and sometimes confusing it, with what Baum had said. He thought the two old men held similar views about America, and both seemed resigned to their age, that the world had passed them by and they were no longer responsible for it. That attitude angered him, for it was he who would have to clean up the mess left behind by the preceding generations. He was the civilian left to rebuild the battered city after the war, the lone gardener left to plant acres of trees, the one scientist trying to save the environment ruined by the previous generations. He would put the broken pieces together and attempt to make the world a better place, and then he too would be old, perhaps also resigned to the fact that there was no longer a point.

The sharp corners of the envelope dug into his leg as he walked. He had tried to read the letter, deciphering the complex script into words and sentences the meaning of which he could not comprehend. He would show the letter to Baum, who would understand it, know what to do with it and reward Eric for his successful thievery. But still he felt guilty, convinced now that Fischer was not a Nazi, because he talked with such hate and spite about his father, the Nazis and nationalism in general. No, thought Eric, the old man had just been a simple soldier, and how boring was that.

Jammed into the pocket with the letter and the stolen condom were two $20 bills. He would take his savings to the surf shop on Saturday. If the board was still there, he would put a deposit on it. Maybe they might even let him take it and pay the rest later. He would ask Pepper to come too, and in his wallet would be the crumpled bills of Fischer, the crisp notes of Baum, and the protective circle of the stolen condom.

Fifteen

From the comfortable confines of his bedroom, where he lay reading another book about the Nazis – one detailing the search for Nazi criminals and the secret organisation, the ODESSA, which protected them – Eric reluctantly answered the call for dinner, but not without some dawdling to make it seem he was coming of his own accord. His father was working on his third beer, the other two cans scrunched up on the coffee table. After dinner, as was the routine now, he would take his fourth into the study and work away the evening hours. Eric wondered if he just sat in there, staring at the wall or reading old magazines. Since his father had spent the night in the hotel, the dinners had been strained, as if all three were guests who had overstayed their welcome in the house the company owned.

Eric knew his father wasn't a bad man, but he was stubborn, almost completely unable to admit his faults and mistakes, and Eric still refused to talk with him. And now, Eric's mother was also wordless. All three were thankful for the television that filled the room with background noise. His father chewed fast, looking at the television when he wasn't looking at his plate. When he had eaten his fill, he quietly complimented the meal and excused himself. Eric watched his mother drop her face in her hands and feared his family was falling apart, and that he was powerless to stop it. More, he felt he had caused it.

That evening, rather than hiding himself in his room and burying his head in a book, Eric stayed in the kitchen and helped his mother with the dishes, hoping to remain, at the very least, on good terms with her.

"I saw dad a few days ago," he started, talking just above a whisper, but loud enough so his father might hear. He looked in the direction of the closed study door and raised his voice. "He said he was sorry."

His mother scrubbed at the old electric frying pan, keeping the electrical connection out of the water. Her face was red from the hot water and from the effort she exerted.

"Where did you see him?"

"Outside the hotel, where he stayed. That night you argued."

She stopped scrubbing, her hands nestling in the white suds which were tinged with brown. She did not attempt to hide her rather aggressive curiosity. "Which hotel?"

"Bayside, I think." Why was he so bad at remembering names? She continued looking at him in that demanding way of hers, so he gave her more information, hoping it would appease her. "Down on the beach. The blue one with the white roof."

She nodded slightly and then went back to the frying pan. When finished, she hauled it from the soupy water and handed it to Eric who dried it, the tea towel turning brown in the process.

"I wish he'd buy a new frying pan," she said absently, looking out of the window at the garden. Through the trees, Eric could just see the pink, orange and red of another beautiful summer sunset. "But stinginess is in his blood." She turned to Eric. "I hope it's not in yours."

Eric looked down at the floor. The tiles of the kitchen were rough and it gave him gooseflesh to walk on them barefoot. That was why he always wore socks in the house. He had already worn out a few pairs, but he didn't complain. The last thing he wanted was to go clothes shopping with his mother.

"How's it going, anyway, with the work? You've been going out every afternoon. You must have a bit of money by now."

"Almost enough for a board," Eric said.

"Don't tell me you're still serious about that. Maybe you should save it." But she caught her contradiction and laughed. "No. Don't do that. Spend it. Buy a surfboard. Buy whatever you want. It's your money, you earned it."

Eric forced himself to smile. Even in trying to give him freedom, her words still came out like an order. He put the old frying pan in its usual place next to the stove, ready to fry up the hot breakfast his father expected in the morning.

His mother dried her hands on a fresh dishcloth and then suddenly took hold of his shoulders, shaking him slightly, her eyes boring into his.

"You're almost a man now," she whispered, sneaking looks over Eric's shoulder at the closed study door. "You might have to make some hard decisions soon. We don't know what the future will bring. There could be another war for all we know. Frank's son might even be sent over to fight. But I want you to know that I care about you so much." She startled him by taking him in a firm and melodramatic embrace. "You're the most important person in my life and I'd hate to lose you."

"Don't worry, mum." He tried to pull himself from her clutches.

"Surfing's not that dangerous, and I'm not gonna join the army. I wanna go to university."

She nodded and collected herself. She pulled back her hair into a bun. Her cheekbones were high, and although she had a long, horsey face, when she pulled back her hair, Eric thought she was pretty. But she let her hair fall back down and again Eric was reminded of an old workhorse, big hooves, mangy mane and all.

"I trust you," she said, smiling with effort. Eric thought both her smile and her pledge of trust were unconvincing. "And I'm proud of the way you've got yourself together here. Much better than me, that's for sure."

Eric hung the wet tea towel on one of the hangers and, still hungry, took an apple from the fridge. He watched his mother rummaging through her handbag, spilling the contents over the side.

"By the way," she said, handing Eric some crisp bills, "I cashed the cheque from Mrs Canter today. It's not much, but I guess every little bit counts."

***

They had fresh glasses of milk and sat at the long dining table in the open front room of Baum's house. The curtains were open and sunlight streamed through the front windows. The light was so bright, the furniture cast long shadows on the tiled floor. But the air-conditioner hummed dutifully and the room was refrigerator cold. Eric wondered if his breath might cloud the room with steam. In the far corner, he heard Annie sliding the sofa and armchairs around, getting at the dust underneath. He was glad they seemed to be on the same schedule.

Baum sat with his elbows, rather pointy they were too, digging into the table, his reading glasses perched on his straight nose, the letter close to his face. He studied it with intense concentration and murmured to himself as he read. Once or twice, Eric saw the corners of the old man's mouth curl upward into a grin. The eyes smiled more than the mouth, as if Baum sought to hide his reactions. When finished, he folded the letter and slid it back into the envelope. He sipped his milk thoughtfully, leaving the faintest of moustaches on his upper lip. Like a thirsty dog, he licked it away with a dexterous tongue. Eric thought the old man would have no trouble touching the tip of his long nose with his equally long tongue.

238

"Curious," Baum said at last. "But I'm afraid there's nothing in there that anyone would be interested in. Just family stuff. Rather dull really."

Feeling his financial reward and his chance at heroism might be slipping away, Eric said, "Mr Fischer said his father was a doctor in a concentration camp." He spoke quietly, hating how his voice echoed in the open room. Baum on the other hand, seemed to enjoy the echo, always speaking loudly and relishing the sound of his voice bouncing off the walls. "He said he did experiments or something," Eric added, and then he remembered, "in the camp near Hamburg."

Baum raised his eyebrows slightly and took the letter back out of the envelope. He focused on the writing at the bottom of the page, tilting his glasses forward to magnify it.

"Josep Cazador." Then he laughed loudly. "A clever ruse," he said, wiggling his eyebrows up and down in that way that Eric now found repulsive.

"What do you mean?"

Baum waved him off. "Oh, it's not important." He stood up from the table, his chair scraping loudly on the tile floor. He checked his watch. Eric noticed it was a shiny, gold watch that looked like it cost more than any surfboard. "I've got some calls to make. You'll have to work alone today, I'm afraid."

Eric followed Baum into the room. He looked around and feared his days with Baum were numbered, for there didn't seem at first glance to be much work left.

"In these boxes," Baum said, striding to the far corner of the room and standing next to them, "there are a lot of old uniforms. Do your best to match the colours together. You're a clever boy. You'll see where the patterns are the same. And check the labels too, to match the sizes, when there are matches." He chuckled lightly. "Maybe we'll find one that fits you."

And with that leading sentence, Baum slipped from the room, closing the door behind him. Eric stopped to listen if the lock was turned, but it wasn't. He opened the first box, breathing in the musty, stale smell, but it wasn't sweet like Fischer's wardrobe. Again he felt guilty for stealing the letter. Now Baum had it, and was probably making calls because of it. He thought of the leather book bound by the short belt and he knew curiosity would drive him back to the shoebox, to the book he had stroked with the tips of his fingers. What was that piece of metal?

He worked diligently, but the sound of Baum's echoed voice sometimes made him stop. Once, he went to the door and edged it open. Baum was on the kitchen phone, speaking what Eric assumed was German. He barked into the phone, spitting his words, laughing at what seemed inappropriate moments, and then put the receiver down gently. To Eric, it sounded like a bizarre language, yet its form and delivery interested him, and it was also a connection to his own past, the language of his heritage.

He closed the door and went back to the uniforms. Familiar with the colours and patterns from the toy soldiers, he had little trouble matching the sets. He first separated them into piles according to colour and did his best to match the sizes. Sometimes, there were names on the tags – Schneider, Berghausen, Metzger – or just a set of initials. He checked these uniforms for bullet holes or blood stains and was disappointed when he found none. He guessed these uniforms had not been used, for they did not look worn. He marvelled at the swastikas and eagles stitched into the sleeves and on the lapels, and traced the stitching with his fingertips. Another world, completely far removed from his own, but yet not fully removed. This uniform was a part of his history as well, albeit indirectly.

The work took longer than he expected, but the time passed quickly. He heard Baum moving around the house, his ridiculous wooden clogs clapping loudly on the tiled floor. Baum talked on the telephone in German and in English. Eric wondered if the old man had forgotten about him. But when Baum came in to inspect Eric's work, he was full of praise.

"Good work," Baum said, rubbing his hands together, having a tremendous day. "We'll hang them up the day after tomorrow." He picked up a black jacket that had the twin lightning strikes of the SS on the collar and handled the material with care, almost caressing it. "Feel it."

Eric obeyed.

"Now feel the grey one."

"The black one is softer." Eric had already felt the difference during the sorting, but had thought nothing of it.

"And warmer," Baum added. "Cooler in summer, too. The elite soldiers of the Reich were treated accordingly." He held up the coat, inspecting it, turning it around, preening it. "This is a small one. Try it on."

Eric was reluctant, but did as he was told. He wanted to stay on Baum's good side, even with these rather disturbing episodes. He had yet to be paid for his last few days' work and needed to keep the money flowing. The board was almost within his reach. The jacket fell lightly onto his shoulders, gripping his elbows. But it was too big for him, with the cuffs almost over his thumbs.

Baum stepped back to admire him. "Do the buttons up, right to the top."

He reached out his long fingers to help, but Eric stumbled back and nervously did the buttons up himself. It was a winter jacket and he started to feel warm secured inside it, despite the air-conditioned room.

Baum smiled broadly and clapped his hands together. "Wunderbar. You look like a young Heydrich."

"Who's he?"

"A great man who was cut down in his prime. He probably would have succeeded Hitler otherwise."

Eric undid the buttons and slipped out of the jacket. It wasn't like wearing a normal costume, as he might to a fancy dress party. There was something sinister trapped in the material which he couldn't explain, an itchy evil that crept onto his skin, trying to force its way into his blood.

"Oh, what a shame. It would've made a wonderful photo. We could've put you next to your great grandfather."

"Maybe another day." He wanted to leave. It was moments like these that Baum scared him, as if the old man had designs on him and was cunningly trying to trap him. The way those long piano player's fingers had reached to do up the buttons had repulsed and frightened him, like Baum was reaching out to strangle him, or embrace him. He listened hard for a sound from Annie, but heard only the hum of the air-conditioner. "So, is that it for today?"

"I think so. I'm meeting Dorothy, Mrs Canter, at the club for dinner. We do it once a month."

"Um," Eric started, not knowing how to word the question. "Do you think you can, you know, pay me for the last two days? It's just that, I want to buy something special for my mum."

Baum smiled. "Very German to be devoted to your mother, Eric. It's one part of the German character the world could take on board, though there are most certainly more powerful traits."

Baum reached for his back pocket and pulled out the always full gold money clip. He slowly peeled off a straight-backed fifty and handed it to Eric. It was less than he had expected. He tried to hide his disappointment and appear grateful. He wondered if he should have allowed Baum to photograph him in the SS coat.

"Thanks. Thanks a lot." He pocketed the money and turned to go out of the room. Baum followed close behind. Eric could feel the old man's blue eyes boring into his back. He turned sharply and Baum was at arm's length. The old man reached out one of his slender, tanned tentacles and placed a hand lightly on Eric's shoulder, an inquisitive look carved into his aristocratic face. His gold watch glittered and his teeth more moist.

"Yes?"

"Can I have the letter back, too?" Eric asked, wanting to squirm out from under the old man's hand. He tried to move, but Baum tightened his grip, rooting Eric to the spot. He was thankful Annie was somewhere in the house. He just had to shout for her if anything went wrong. "I want to put it back before Mr Fischer knows it's missing."

"Very wise," Baum said, somewhat reluctant to move. He turned Eric around and the two went out of the room, side by side. The letter was next to the kitchen telephone. Baum picked it up and handed it to Eric, gripping it slightly as Eric tried to take it, so that he nearly had to wrest it from the old man's grasp.

"Tell Mr Fischer for me that his father was a brilliant man, a man whose genius the world has missed out on."

"Okay. Where's Annie? She said she might give me a ride home."

Baum smiled thinly, just showing the upper line of his teeth. "Oh, I sent her home hours ago."

Eric shivered. He bid Baum goodbye and dashed for the door, relieved to be finally outside in the windy, warm afternoon. He ran down to the beach and then sprinted on the sand as fast as he could. When he came to the beach he surfed at with Pepper in the mornings, he stripped down to his underwear and plunged in, wading against the strong current that sought to drag him north and back towards Baum's house. He rubbed hard at this arms and shoulders, hoping the itch of the uniform and the lingering smell of Baum's cologne would be washed away.

***

242

He paddled hard, driving his arms through the crystal blue as the wave sucked up more and more water. He felt that stomach-dropping feeling as the wave took hold of the board. It shot him forward and he jumped to his feet, throwing out his arms to balance himself. He took the wave left, as was his preference, swerving the board over the face. He kicked some spray off the lip and pulled out before the wave turned to mush in the shallows. He paddled back out, duck-diving easily under the breakers, and handed the pink board back to Pepper.

"Do you mean I get to use it?" She secured the leg rope around her thin ankle and jumped onto the board.

"Just this once."

She took the next wave and Eric waited, treading water or floating on his back and staring at the cloudless sky. He noticed then it was a different shade of blue than what he had grown up with in the country, where the dust of the desert, the smoke of summer fires and the blown away top soil combined to tinge the blue sky a hazy yellow. Here, the sky was pure, as if it were a giant mirror reflecting the ocean.

"Nest egg blue," he said, not knowing where the words came from. Once again, he was at his happiest and most content when he was at the beach with Pepper. Everything else, all those problems and insecurities, the old men and their stories, his parents fighting, it just all seemed to drift away.

After surfing for a time, Pepper gave her board back to Eric and started swimming in.

"Where're you going?"

Even during these content moments, he never lost the fear that Pepper was just using him for something, that she would cancel their relationship just as quickly as she had consented to it, that one day she would stop meeting him at the beach.

"I'm gonna run to the shops and get us some breakfast. I'm starved."

"That sounds great. Should I come with you?"

"Nah. Keep surfing." And a smile so sweet and cheeky appeared on her face that Eric's heart almost melted. He couldn't believe that this girl was his girlfriend. "I think pink might be your colour."

Pepper swam in, her freestyle so slow and easy that it made Eric wonder if she had been a competitive swimmer at some point, before the waves started to rule her life and getting up for swim training before school had become a chore.

He wasted the time riding a few waves, but got out to wait for Pepper. He stood the board up – it looked like a pink lighthouse – and then sat down close enough to the water that if a big wave rolled in, the whitewash might just tickle his feet. The sand was cooler here, harder too. His stomach rumbled. The mention of food reminded him that he too was hungry, was always hungry, and he kept looking at the path to see if Pepper was coming. He thought about passing the time by building one of his famous dams, but decided Pepper might think it childish. So he listened to the sound of the waves crashing, watching them peel left or right, and tried to picture himself riding the crest with the dolphin board. Lost in his thoughts, he didn't hear the group approaching.

"Looks like our friend's got himself a new board. A nice gay, pink one."

He jumped up and tried to run from them, tried to dodge their tackles and leap over their trips, but there were too many of them and soon he was cornered and brought down, face-first into the sand. They formed a tight circle around him and Josh started kicking him. But once again, there wasn't much in it, and Eric was able to roll with the kicks and shimmy deeper into the sand to protect himself a little. But then he saw Robbie with Pepper's board in his hands. Robbie was stroking it, tracing the patterns with his fingertips, perhaps deciding whether to break it or not. He said something and all the boys laughed, and they broke from the circle to crowd around him. Eric jumped up quickly and snatched the board from Robbie. He wrapped his arms around the board, protecting it with his body, and then fell on top of it. Robbie laughed loudly and the other boys echoed him, calling Eric a fag, a gay lover and a poof. They kicked him, and one kick was especially hard. He saw that one had come from Robbie. Then he felt the sand piling on top of him, over his head as well. He closed his eyes and mouth and held his breath, feeling the sand in his ears and going up his nose. He counted to a hundred, still holding his breath, and then tentatively raised his head. He saw the bikers heading south down the beach.

He emerged from under the sand and checked the board to see if it was damaged. It wasn't, so he shook the sand from his ears and hair and blew it out of his nose. A few grains were grinding between his teeth and he tried to spit these out. His ribs hurt and he clutched that side of his chest as he staggered into the water to wash off the sand.

He struggled out, head down, wondering if the rest of the summer would continue like this. He stopped when he saw Pepper sitting next to her pink board. He removed the arm that was clutching at his ribs and tried to act normally, like he had just taken a quick swim. How much had she seen?

"Come on," she said brightly, zipping open the top of her backpack. "It's getting cold."

He tried not to grimace as he sat down next to her.

"You want a pie or a sausage roll first?" She reached into her backpack and pulled out the grease-stained paper bags.

"Sausage roll."

She gave him one and he took big, hungry bites. They ate in silence, staring out over the ocean and listening to its rhythmical, calming sounds. When they were finished, Pepper leaned close and started kissing him passionately. Her tongue dived into his mouth, probing and tasting. She climbed on top of him and Eric felt the firm roundness of her breasts pushing against his chest, hurting his side, and making him wince slightly. She giggled when she felt his burgeoning manhood. For the first time, he wasn't embarrassed by it. If anything, he thought it seemed rather natural in this situation. The world drifted away and Eric rode the wave again. But it ended as quickly as it had started and Pepper jumped to her feet and ran for the water. Eric chased her, and in his pursuit, forgot about his pain. They had an intense splashing fight until Eric wrestled her down and they kissed in the shallows. The whitewash threw them around, but Eric held her in a strong embrace. Pepper seemed to like the hard hug, being held in his arms.

When it was time for Eric to go to work, he was very slow getting his things together.

"There's a party at my house tonight," Pepper said. "Drew and Mel'll be there. Wanna come?"

"Absolutely. When?"

"Come with Drew. I think Adam's coming as well. He knows my sister."

"Great," he said, his enthusiasm waning slightly. If Drew was coming, then Eric would be forced to confront him and Adam with the broken board. But he had some money now and could offer to buy a new one.

They held hands as they walked up the beach path. It seemed quite comfortable now for them to do so and that felt good. But Pepper stopped before they turned towards her house.

"You don't have to walk me home today," she said lightly, screwing her face up a bit in a way that Eric found so sexy. Though after the morning on the beach, everything she did now made her look sexy. Even the appearance of a scabby pink ear was a sensual invitation. "I mean, I like it, but most of my family's there. They don't know I have a boyfriend."

"That's okay. I can't believe I have you for a girlfriend."

Pepper smiled. "You're sweet. I wish more boys were like you."

They kissed once more and then Pepper started walking towards her house. Eric watched her. He admired her thin, shapely legs even though they were slightly knock-kneed, her narrow hips, and firm, round behind. She stopped, turned and smiled when she saw him staring.

"Hey," she called out, "thanks for saving my board."

***

How the afternoon dragged. Eric sweated and toiled, this time cleaning the back gutters, which looked like they hadn't been cleaned in his lifetime. He even pulled out a rusted Matchbox car, made in 1973. His arms and shoulders ached from reaching up to the gutters and yanking out the stinking mess of old leaves and sticks. And every time he reached above his head, the pain in his side was so intense, he sometimes had to stop and rest until it subsided. He felt the point of the pain, trying to feel the shattered outline of a broken rib, but the bones felt intact. He wondered if he should go to the doctor, but that would mean having to tell his mum and he didn't want his parents to think he was fighting again.

He kept checking his watch, but the time between checks became shorter and shorter and the afternoon longer and longer. Fischer was in high spirits. Wonder drugs, he had explained when Eric had arrived. His eyes had a glazed look and he had the false energy of stimulants: jerky movements, jumpy steps, speaking too fast, jumbling his words together and sometimes repeating himself. He often came around to the back of the house to monitor Eric's progress and talk some more, as he did now.

"These pills have got my old heart going again," Fischer said.

Eric wondered if the old man had perhaps taken one miracle drug too many. Fischer held the ladder and Eric took the opportunity to have a short break. His shoulders were killing him because the ladder wasn't high enough to reach the gutter. He thought it would be easier, and less painful, if he climbed onto the roof, but Fischer was against that idea. He climbed down and started putting all the sticks and leaves he had dropped into the big canvas bag that Barry had left a few days earlier. Fischer held the bag open. Eric sneaked a look at his watch and groaned.

"What's up with you today?" Fischer asked. "You normally come here full of energy and questions, jumping around like a kangaroo on steroids. I know, I know, cleaning the gutters is nasty work, but you'll get a little extra today, if that's any motivation for you."

"Thanks." Eric rubbed at his sore shoulders, but felt somewhat inspired by the increase in muscle size he was sure he could feel. The surfing and labour were making him stronger.

"By the way, forget what I said the other day, about the meek inheriting the earth. It's true, of course, but that doesn't mean those who know better, who see things in a different way, shouldn't try to change things."

Eric sat down under the shade of the neighbour's tree, which grew so far over the fence, it was more a part of Fischer's garden than the neighbour's. The bedroom window was in front of him and he could just make out the shadowy outline of the wardrobe. He thought of the leather book and wondered if he would be the meek who would steal that earth.

"Change the world," Fischer went on, "make it better for those who come after you. It's the wrong attitude just to accept things as they are when really we're just afraid to do our own thing and alienate ourselves. It's not easy, but maybe if a few do it today, more will do it in the future. I wish I'd done it, but I'm a product of my upbringing like everyone is."

"But you did a lot of good things," Eric said, staring up at the old man. Fischer loomed above him like a giant, albeit, a friendly one. He wanted to console the old man, especially because he had wronged him by stealing the letter. "You helped the kids in the footy team, tried to get the Aboriginals to play."

The old man nodded, but it seemed something else bothered him.

"Oh, I completely forgot," Eric said, jumping excitedly to his feet. "I met a man in Geraldton who knows you."

Fischer looked hopefully at Eric, his loneliness written in the lines that drooped and looped around his floppy mouth. It had never occurred to Eric that Fischer might be lonely, that maybe that was the reason the old man had him in his employ.

Eric closed his eyes and tried to remember the man's name. He could see him, the big hands, the jowly cheeks, the wide mouth that could have swallowed the glass whole. Then he thought of the family.

"Tomicich. That's it. My father knows his son. They worked together in Merredin."

"Ivan."

"He said you played football together."

Fischer chuckled, his shoulders bouncing slightly. "Will wonders never cease. Greedy Ivan is still alive, and probably still living in his old house, still drinking every night at the club and pointing to his name on the boards above the bar."

"Did he get that nickname because he was a goal kicker?"

"Well, he was greedy in other ways, too. But he did play the game with blinkers on and saw the goals and nothing else."

"He's huge, with a big fat stomach, and he drank beer like it was water."

"Still Greedy Ivan then."

"And he had massive hands." Eric held out his own skinny fingers, spreading them wide to try to give some idea of the size of Ivan's hands, then he caught himself. "I'm sorry. I didn't mean that…"

Fischer used his mangled right hand to wave it off. "It's all right. I lost my fingers a long time ago. I've learned to live without them. Lots of other soldiers lost arms and legs. Many of them lost their lives. I guess I should consider myself lucky."

"Mr Tomicich said you were a great player," Eric said, looking up at the old man with awe. He tried to glimpse the big ruckman that Fischer had been forty years ago. His size was imposing, even now, but he seemed hardly the competitive, aggressive type. "I saw your name on the board as the club's best player four years straight. How did you manage it, with your hand, I mean? How did you catch the ball?"

Fischer held up his right hand. The sight of it still shocked and intrigued Eric. He tried not to recoil when he saw it. But it was funny too, because it looked like Fischer was forever giving the peace sign. Fischer demonstrated his technique for marking the ball: he spread the fingers of his left hand as wide as possible, forming a kind of net, then closed his right hand over the top of the imaginary ball.

"But that was just for overhead marks," Fischer explained. "I took a lot of my marks on the chest. You don't need hands for that."

Eric looked at the hand in wonder, hoping that staring was all right because the hand was the topic of the conversation. "Wow. No wonder Mr Tomicich didn't like you so much. You had one bad hand and were still the best player on the team."

"Greedy and I had other problems. Historical problems." His voice turned sour: "He never even gave me a chance. Held me responsible for every friend, relative and passing acquaintance who died in the war. In a way, he was right to blame me. Every German who lived then was guilty. We went out into the world as a nation, with an elected leader mind you, and committed hideous crimes."

Eric stared at the hand again, grimacing a little at the pointy bones bulging out of the side of the hand, stretching the skin. Sometimes these pointy ends moved, like there was something alive underneath the skin. It was scary.

"How did it happen? The hand, I mean."

"Let's go into the kitchen and have a drink," Fischer said, leading the way around the house. "I think it's time I told somebody the truth."

They sat opposite each other at the kitchen table. Over glasses of Apfelschorle, Fischer recounted to Eric his time in the war, but it was a jumbled mess, with no chronology. Fischer described each memory as it came to him, and switched between years and seasons, sometimes correcting himself when he got the years mixed up. He spoke about the early triumphs of the Russian campaign, the stunning encirclements, how they had almost taken Moscow only for winter to deny them, with the merciless Russians burning their own city so the Germans couldn't survive there. They set out for Stalingrad and Fischer spoke fondly of the Cossack land on the River Don – the one part of their Lebensraum that was liveable – and the noble people who lived there. Bitterly, he criticised his comrades for being too harsh with the civilians in the conquered lands. They had been received and welcomed as liberators, he said, only to behave like pirates and barbarians.

"It was a big mistake to occupy the lands we conquered," Fischer said, his voice low. Eric listened intently, hanging on the old man's every word. "We could've raised an army from those who were against the Bolsheviks. Instead, we had another lot to battle against. They poisoned their water, bombed their own roads, shot us while we slept. And they had a right to because we behaved like animals. Hitler made some good tactical decisions early on, but his knowledge of people was severely limited. He was just a commoner. He couldn't envision how people would respond to his invaders. He made great, great errors which cost thousands, almost millions of lives."

Prompted by Eric's questions, Fischer went into deeper detail of the fighting, and even lifted his shirt to show the long scar of the stomach wound he had received in Stalingrad. He tried to explain how it had felt to be lying on the ground, the earth shaking beneath him, the life slowly seeping out of him. He said it had felt good, the relief of long suffering coming to an end. Eric sat forward in his chair as Fischer told how the doctors had operated with no anaesthetic and he had recovered to join the fighting again. But the old man turned solemn as he spoke of the last months of the war, that terminable winter where more died of starvation and exposure than from bullets and bombs. He told about the explosion that injured his hand and how he then deserted. It was almost fifty years ago, but still he hung his head in shame. Then, with a sad smile on his face, he described the Polish farmers who took him in and showed him kindness even though he was the enemy. He burned his uniform and his documents, and when his hand had healed and the Russians were advancing, he disguised himself as a refugee and joined the long lines marching west. A few tears rolled down his wrinkled and lined face as he spoke of Dresden, and the words came with difficulty. Eric was shocked to hear that the heroic allies had bombed the city so callously, killing many innocent civilians. Then he remembered the stamps in the passport.

"Have you ever been back?"

The old man nodded. "After my wife died. I went to Dresden, which then was in East Germany. Funny, it was easier for me to get a visa because I was Australian than it would've been if I'd kept my German nationality." He laughed sadly. "It's an ugly city now, full of Stalinist blocks. You know, those long apartment buildings they made in big pieces and then assembled like a child's jigsaw. I went to Poland too, and found the remains of the farm. Everything was almost exactly as I'd left it, because it had been abandoned. I never found out what happened to Josef and Elsie. I guess they were absorbed into the Soviet system, as corpses or as workers. Not much difference really."

Fischer paused and looked out of the window. His eyes narrowed and Eric could see the old man's jaw working back and forth, grinding his teeth, recalling the memories, events and images which he had carried his whole life.

"But it was all a long time ago. It still hurts, not as much as it used to, but it still hurts. Actually, it's good to talk about it. Before you came along, it'd been years since I'd thought about it. My wife had no idea I fought in the war. But I think she guessed it. Everyone else just assumed."

"I'm sorry," Eric ventured, unsure what to say.

"Don't be. It's good I've said it all now, faced it a bit." He held up his mangled hand. "I've got to learn to handle things better."

Eric chuckled. Just then, he admired the old man. What a life he had led. He had gone through most of it with a handicapped hand and still made it a success. He had looked death in the face and travelled all over the world. But most of all, Eric admired Fischer's honesty, and hated himself for stealing and for sometimes stretching the truth as he had the habit of doing. From now on, he promised himself, he would be straight and honest, like the old man sitting opposite him.

Eric looked out the window and was surprised to see the shadows longer than he expected. He spied his watch; the afternoon had skipped by.

"I gotta go," he said, jumping up from the table, but somewhat reluctant to leave.

"Of course. Don't worry about the gutters. We'll get to it another day. Leave everything where it is."

The old man hauled himself to his feet and dug his wallet from his back pocket. He handed the bills to Eric, who put them absently into his pocket. On withdrawing his hand, a fingertip caught the corner of the envelope and the letter drifted to the floor. They both watched it fall and stared at it as it came to rest on the linoleum floor, covering a worn and faded tropical fish.

***

Eric sat in the back of Adam's car, trying to look relaxed and cool. For some reason, he felt uneasy and out of place, dressed the same as Adam and Drew but somehow different. The two brothers had laughed heartily when Eric had shown them the broken board. But their humour had died when Eric, sheepishly, and with quite a bit of truth twisting – no beating in his story, only Josh and Robbie breaking the board while he was swimming, too far out to stop them – explained the circumstances of the break. There had been no colossal wipe-out as Adam had joked, no shark attack like Drew had said, and their humour had turned sour. On the drive to Pepper's house, talk quickly focused on revenge. A plan was hatched to corner Josh so that Eric could then give his adversary a sound beating. Adam said some friends of his would come along for a laugh and Drew fixed the location by saying he often saw Josh and his group lounging under the trees in the park across the street from the supermarket.

"Then it's set," Adam said, smiling broadly. Eric thought the uni student seemed to miss these kinds of escapades, having already complained that he only had responsibilities these days. Still, Eric was envious of Adam's freedom. "But not tomorrow," Adam added. "I gotta date. Day after, okay?"

The boys agreed and were united by their collective desire for revenge. Eric wasn't as excited as he pretended to be, and he shrank in the back seat, the stereo speaker loud behind his head. The beating of Josh would either bring an end to his torment or worsen it. One gain would be that his friendship with Drew would be secure and, now a competent surfer almost with a board of his own, he would be absorbed into the surfers group and would then be untouchable. But he wasn't sure if that was what he wanted anymore. He and Drew didn't have much to say to each other. Eric didn't like his arrogance, including the way Drew looked down on him. He thought about Fischer, who he had come to respect, whose company he enjoyed more than Drew or the other surfers, and who was more of a man than his father could ever be. Fischer had opened his eyes to the world, to history, and had complimented him on his tendency to question things, which everyone else in his life criticised him for, saying that his questioning made him negative. Fischer had admired that quality, gone so far as to wish he had it himself. But here he was with Drew, about to become a member of the surfers, safe in the group, ready to follow their lead no matter where it took him. Not exactly questioning anymore, he thought. His last vision of the old man stayed in his eyes like a sunspot: Fischer standing in the kitchen, shoulders slumped, his lined head drooping forward with disappointment.

"I was wrong," he had said, the words cutting at the air like the swish-swash of a sword, backing Eric towards the door. "They would've liked you."

It was a short drive to Pepper's house, just long enough for them to hatch their plan for revenge. Adam parked his car among the lines of others, then led the way into the house. To Eric's surprise, the party was mostly for adults, hence the lines of white and blue family sedans and wagons outside. Melanie was there, as was Pepper's sister with her boyfriend whose name Eric swiftly forgot. He noticed that the sister and Adam had a rather long hug, and he saw them smiling at each other when they thought no one was looking. Pepper introduced Eric to her mother. She was short and slightly stout. Her brown hair was cut short and she wore massive heels, looking like she might topple over any minute. Eric wondered that Pepper looked nothing like her, but Sandra was the spitting image. He guessed that Pepper took after her father and, though he had never seen him, he thought that was a bit better than taking after her mother. Blair was a tall man, over two metres, with long limbs, wide, bony shoulders and legs like stilts. Even with his size, he didn't have much weight and seemed to take up as little space as possible, inverting his shoulders, hunching forward and often trying to hide behind his wife. He had a large head, elongated, with a long hooked nose, and a shot away chin that barely held his thin mouth together. The quiet voice suited his shy, almost timid bearing, but he made a clear effort to engage Eric in conversation. Perhaps Blair was screening him, checking him out. He certainly was standing very close, making Eric lean back or take short steps backwards. For some reason, Blair reminded him of Baum, and both men scared him for reasons he could not fathom. They weren't strangers. According to the logic of his parents and his teachers, they could both be trusted, but Eric was still wary.

The house was not dissimilar to his own, except that it had a second floor, with a narrow staircase leading to the bedrooms upstairs. Pepper's family also used a plastic dining table in the living room, and the two sofas were crowded around the television in the corner. There were photographs on the shelves. Eric spied these in the hope he might see a shot of Pepper's father but found none. There were books on the shelves too, a lot of self-help stuff with titles like *Willing your Will* and *Taking Control* or some such, mostly written by professors or doctors or both, with headshots of them on the spines. The adults crowded in the living room and the kitchen, the men with beers in their hands and the women with glasses of wine or clear bottles of wine cooler. They looked at Eric and smiled. He had trouble distinguishing the people. The gaps between them seemed to disappear so that they all blended into one mess of adulthood. Eric didn't have time to savour the future he wanted now, to be grown up, independent, part of that mess, because Pepper whisked him away upstairs to her room.

Drew and Melanie were already there, tongues rammed down each other's throat. They separated as Eric came in, but didn't seem embarrassed. Adam brought some beer upstairs and they all took a can. They sat in a circle, with Eric next to Pepper, and talked of nothing. Eric, only half listening to a gossipy conversation about people he didn't know or care about, glanced around the room. The surfboard wasn't the only pink item in Pepper's life. Most of her room was pink, be it in lighter or darker shades, and the stuffed animals and plastic dolls gave the impression that a girl of eight or nine slept in the room. The bed cover and pillowcase were also pink, and the white wallpaper had small pink bunny rabbits on it. For some reason, Eric thought the room even smelled pink. He drank his bitter beer and tried to look cool, drowning in this magenta sea.

Adam drank his beer quickly and soon left. Pepper said that her sister had the hots for him and both Pepper and Melanie giggled at this. Not long later, Drew and Melanie also sneaked out of the room, leaving Eric alone with Pepper. As always, forced to make witty and interesting conversation, he could think of nothing to say.

"Can you keep a secret?" Pepper whispered. She sat close to him and held his hand, securing their pact. Eric was nervous and expectant, as if the secrets of the universe were about to be revealed to him.

"Sure." Secrecy and honesty hadn't been his strong points lately.

"Mel and Drew. They, you know, they…do it."

"Uh-huh." He tried to act nonchalant, that such a thing was no big deal, like he did "it" all the time, but he was sure his blushing gave him away. He smiled though, wondering if Pepper could no longer see his face, the red camouflaged by all the pink.

"Would you, um, like to…you know, do it with me?" And she looked at him with such shy and insecure eyes, that Eric thought she had suddenly morphed into the nine year-old girl the room was designed for, and the womanly body she had was just a costume she wore, the way a young girl applies several layers of lipstick and make-up to look older. "You know, if you don't want to, it's no big deal," she added.

Eric almost dropped his beer. "No, I want to. You have no idea how much I want to."

Awkwardly, they came together and kissed. Pepper was a little too aggressive, perhaps as nervous as he was, and pushed her lips hard against Eric's. His top lip cut against his own teeth and he pulled away, slightly stunned and tasting his own blood. Pepper ran for the door and secured the lock. Then she turned around and lifted her dress over her head. She wore frilly pink underwear and Eric was surprised to see her chest was much smaller than he had envisioned. But that could have been the fault of his imagination and not her size. Still, the blood pumped into his groin and he felt his underwear might burst, snapping it against the wall like a rubber band. He felt dizzy too, amazed he was about to lose his virginity. But the dizziness may have been due to the loss of blood to his head, for to compensate for the extra blood flow down low, none was getting to his head. She skipped back to him and helped him out of his shirt, yanking it and almost dislocating his shoulder when one sleeve got caught on his watch band. She ran her hands over his thin, scrawny chest, tracing the scratches and slightly pressing the bruises.

"Do you have something?" she whispered.

Eric pulled his wallet from his shorts. From amongst the hard earned bills he plucked Fischer's condom and held it up to her proudly. She wriggled out of her underwear and Eric fumbled with the rubber, for some reason having visions of carrots and the sex education classes that had been such a riot in Merredin. He remembered Mr Reynolds, the sports teacher, struggling to keep the class from bursting into hysterics. He only restored order by announcing, somewhat proudly, that he had had a vasectomy. An explanation of what that meant left all the boys crossing their legs squeamishly and the girls giggling at their collective reaction. Eric remembered diagrams of the female anatomy, lit by the florescent light of the overhead projector; that cow's head that looked so unattractive, an organ no less, hardly the heavenly place of pleasure they had all imagined.

And suddenly he was inside that cow's head, not knowing what to do, where to put his hands, how to look or what to say. By the time he had run through these nervous thoughts, it was over. Pepper smiled and kissed Eric on the cheek. He felt he had just finished a distant last in a running race, and the kiss from Pepper said, "You did your best. Better luck next time." It wasn't like in the films, where the sex started and within ten seconds the girl was screaming out an orgasm, sweat beading from her forehead, her fingernails tearing the skin from the man's back with the man seemingly able to go on for hours. And in what movie did any man stop and fumble with a rubber?

They lay next to each other, their nakedness hidden under the pink sheet. Pepper nestled her head on Eric's shoulder and mumbled an informed comment about beer, how it made everything happen faster. To Eric, she seemed experienced, although she may have just acted that way to make him feel more relaxed, and the beer comment sounded like something from her sister, or from some women's magazine. Eric, having stood in so many supermarket checkout queues with his mother spying such magazines, could picture the headline: "Ten reasons to excuse away your man's hopelessness in bed."

Still, despite his complete failure at sex, he had enjoyed his brief tumble and wanted to do it again. Eric reached out his hand to stroke Pepper's side, working his way up to her breast. The knock on the door startled them both, with Eric's hand frozen on Pepper's chest. The knocker tried to open the door. From the bed, they watched the handle jiggle up and down, the lock holding the door shut.

"Pepper?" said a familiar voice, but this time softer in tone and more musical than when Eric had first heard it. Eric turned to Pepper and saw the blood drain from her face.

"Get dressed," she whispered, almost pushing him out of the bed. "Quick."

"I've been looking for you, Pep," the voice called, the words muffled by the door. "Melanie said you were up here."

"Just a minute."

They threw their clothes on. Eric panicked and put his tight underwear on backwards. The elastic rode up his behind painfully, but it was too late to change it; he already had his jeans on. Pepper wrapped the soiled condom in a tissue and dropped it in her trashcan. In the haste, she put her dress on without wearing a bra underneath and Eric was surprised at what a difference it made; she looked again like a girl almost half her age. She was about to open the door, but was suddenly inspired and grabbed a board game from one of her shelves. Eric helped set it up, moving pieces into place like the game was a long time played. Pepper jumped for the door, sprung the lock and edged the door open a fraction. The elongated head of Blair appeared in the crack, ducking down from the top of the doorway, making Eric think it was one man sitting on another's shoulders. He looked first down at

Pepper, a smile forming on his timid face, but the smile disappeared when he saw Eric sitting on the floor, shaking dice loudly in a plastic cup.

"You wanna play?" he asked.

Blair looked down at Pepper and frowned. "No, no. You kids continue. I was just worried, that's all." He tried to edge into the room, turning his thin body sideways, getting some of his torso inside, but Pepper held the door firmly with her foot. "You need anything?"

"We're fine, thanks," Pepper said.

Blair twisted himself out of the crack and Pepper closed the door. She waited for a few seconds, listening to Blair's big feet hitting the carpet stairs, then sat down behind Eric. She hugged him hard, but there was nothing sexual about it. She wrapped her thin arms, strong from surfing, around him and Eric thought she might crush him. The pain in his ribs throbbed, but he let her embrace him nonetheless.

"Maybe I should go," he said at length, unsure of his place now. Pepper's reaction to Blair's visit had made him think something was wrong between them.

"No," Pepper pleaded, her voice muffled by Eric's shirt. He felt her breath go through his shirt and it tickled him. "Don't go. Stay, just for a bit longer."

"Okay. But I gotta be home at eleven."

Pepper whined a bit more about wanting Eric to stay, to have him in her bedroom always.

"You can protect me like you protected my board."

Eric breathed in the pink air and wondered what she meant.

Sixteen

The sea breeze was blowing itself into its usual afternoon hurricane as Eric walked along the beach-side road to Baum's house. The sand blew up the short funnels of the narrow beach paths and onto the road, some of it whipping nastily against his bare calves and the more adventurous grains finding their way into his mouth. Grinding his teeth and spitting, he detoured past Pepper's house and looked up at her window. The pink curtains were drawn and the window closed. She had not met him at the beach that morning and he was convinced his pathetic effort between the pink sheets was the cause of her absence. He sniffed, the sand grinding inside his nose, thinking their relationship was probably over.

He stepped up to the front door of Baum's stately domain in no mood for the old man's sickeningly sweet smiles and over-powering cologne, but rang the bell anyway because Baum was now his only employer. He needed to hang onto Baum or he would lose all the independence he had gained from earning money of his own.

"What do you want?" Josh said, opening the door.

Baum appeared behind him, seeming to emerge from the shadows. "Ah, Eric. Good to see you." He pushed Josh rather roughly aside. "Come inside, quick. You're letting in all the heat."

Josh closed the door. "What's he doing here?"

With the bright sunlight streaming through the white curtains, and the cream and yellow colours of the furniture, Eric was taken aback by the darkness of Josh's skin and by the black of his hair. It was as if he was seeing Josh for the first time, with Eric no longer confusing Josh with all the nameless faces of his group. Eric saw now that Josh was actually quite good looking, and in no way threatening.

"He's helping me with one of my rooms," Baum said airily. He stood next to Eric and put a rather grandfatherly arm around his shoulder. "Run along now, Josh. We've got work to do."

The rejection, the utter exclusion, was written all over Josh's face. Eric saw Baum smirk at Josh's reaction.

"Why didn't you ask me to help?"

"You said working was for losers. And let me assure you, Eric works and he's a winner in every sense of the word."

Eric, despite feeling uncomfortable under Baum's arm, couldn't suppress his rather smug smile.

"And I discussed it with your mother," Baum added, his voice more authoritative now, "and she didn't approve. Come along, Eric." Still clutching his shoulder, Baum turned Eric around, like leading him in a dance, and the two walked across the open floor. "Close the door on your way out, there's a good boy."

The slam of the door echoed through the house. Baum grimaced.

"Don't mind him," Baum said, smiling down at Eric. The old man's breath smelled of coconut and his smooth face glistened with moisturiser. It was put on lightly so Eric only noticed it up close, when the light caught Baum's face. "He's just jealous. And he should be. You're not only better looking than he is, you're also a much nicer person. It's true what they say about good breeding."

Baum withdrew his arm to unlock the door. He moved inside eagerly, almost slipping out of his house clogs.

"I've got something to show you. It arrived this morning by express post. An old friend sent it to me as a gift. He's on his deathbed, and this was one of his most prized possessions."

He pointed at a large rectangular package, white but covered with the exotic stickers and markings of a round-the-world journey. From the shape of the box, Eric guessed it was a painting, like the others he had helped Baum take out of boxes and hang on the walls. The package had already been opened. Baum lifted the painting out slowly. Eric held the box. Once free, Baum held up the painting for them both to admire. It was a portrait of Hitler. He looked strong and mean, with cold, deep-set eyes and that ugly moustache that made him instantly recognisable the world over. Eric looked at the picture with disgust, beholding who he had learned was history's most evil man. Baum held it back from himself, smiling with admiration.

"You've no idea how much this is worth." Baum traced his finger along a line that went through the middle of the picture. "Look. See how it was destroyed?"

Eric looked closely at the marks were the canvas had been torn. It had been repaired, but the scars were clear, as if it was intended that way as some kind of reminder.

"The inscription says, 'The German people is a young and strong people, a people with its future before it.' Stirring stuff, isn't it?"

Eric nodded, hearing Baum's words, but lost in Hitler eyes, hypnotised by the cold, grey stare. He had something Eric could not

259

explain, and it went deeper than just a historical legacy or a reputation. The shadow of a smile, so leading, like a promise made only when something is given in return, gave the ashen grey face a hint of its devilish intent.

"Where will you put it?" Eric asked at last, keeping his eyes fixed on Hitler.

Baum looked around the room, his eyes settling on the two cabinets. "We'll move one of these aside and put the portrait in the middle. A centrepiece if you will. It will set off the whole room. I'm starting to think I may be better off opening a museum, but culture is lost on these people. The day's cricket scores are more interesting than art or history. Give them wheat figures, not the Mona Lisa."

Eric began shifting the cabinet, careful not to knock any of its contents over. Baum put down the picture and helped. The cabinet was made of thick wood and was very heavy. They shifted it slowly, with Baum grunting and groaning a few times. They made just enough space for the portrait to fit. Baum leaned his hands on his knees and then tried to straighten himself, grabbing at his lower back.

"I'm not as young as I used to be." He tried moving his back, swivelling his pelvis in the hope he might loosen his spine a little and let out a girlish shriek. He crumpled to the floor like he had been shot.

"Are you all right?" Eric asked, trying not to laugh.

"I just need to lie down a bit. Get Annie, quick."

Eric dashed from the room and called out Annie's name. The word echoed and she was there before the last echo had sounded. She looked at Eric with great concern and worry.

"Everything okay?" she asked, and Eric was surprised by how hard her face was.

"Mr Baum's hurt his back," Eric said, leading the way into the room. But Annie wouldn't go inside. She stood tentatively in the doorway, her dark eyes shifting quickly from object to object.

"It's okay, Annie," Baum said from the floor. "Come in and help."

They managed to haul Baum to his feet, but not without substantial moaning, complaining and ordering from the old man. Annie and Eric stationed themselves under each armpit, taking almost all of the old man's weight so that his big feet dragged along the ground, the clogs clapping against the floor. They slowly moved out of the room, edged down the hall and then laid him carefully onto his bed. Baum groaned loudly as he tried to stretch out. Annie slipped the house clogs off, putting them neatly next to the bed. The flat position seemed to relieve Baum and he pulled himself together somewhat.

"Call Dr Stone," he said to Annie. "Get him here as soon as possible."

Annie scurried out of the room, leaving Eric looking down at the bed-ridden figure. Eric recalled his final visit to his grandfather in the hospital: the way the old man had been attached to machines, the ghastly noises those machines had made, and how wasted and pathetic he had looked, waiting to die, no longer jovial or full of humour. Baum looked the same, minus the machines. But Baum wasn't dying. The face was still proud and strong, the eyes not vacant like his grandfather's had been.

"You'll have to go on without me today," Baum said bravely. "Give the room a good cleaning and put the boxes in the garage."

"Do you need anything?" Eric asked. He tried not to look around the room. It was the first time he had seen Baum's bedroom and its cold stuffiness and closed curtains gave it a stale, uninviting feel. There was a built-in wardrobe that had sliding doors, and another door in the far corner that led to what Eric guessed was an en-suite bathroom. He thought of Fischer's shaded cell, with the mismatched furniture and the musty smell of the wardrobe, the condoms in the bedside drawer and the much-stamped passport. Amazing how much you could tell from a person by their bedroom, he thought.

Baum offered a weak smile. "Maybe a glass of milk."

Annie was in the kitchen on the phone and smiled at Eric as he came in.

"He can be such a woman sometimes," she whispered, one hand covering the mouthpiece.

Eric poured the milk into a long glass and tried to suppress his laughter. He brought Baum the milk and then went back into the room to commence the cleaning. First, he put all the empty boxes together, folding them flat in a large pile. Hitler watched him all the while. Eric did his best to avoid the cold stare, but the eyes followed him all around the room. He came to the box that had arrived in the morning, the vessel that had carried Hitler across the globe. He spied the address slip and noticed that the package was addressed to Christoph Baum and not Christian. Probably just a mistake, he thought.

He took the boxes into the garage and briefly admired the cream Mercedes, running his fingers along the bonnet; it was still slightly warm from the morning's drive. Back inside, he swept the floor and dusted the shelves. Hitler watched. Eric thought he saw a frown on the man's face, disappointed that Eric worked so slowly and made so many simple mistakes. The old leader was impossible to please and, despite Eric's diligent work ethic, he kept coming back at him with that cold, unsatisfied stare, the glimmer of a smile mocking him.

Eric folded all the uniforms into neat piles and put them on the floor according to their sizes and colours. It looked like Baum had rummaged through them, perhaps searching for pants to match the jacket he had forced Eric to wear. That jacket was hooked over the desk chair. He took it in his hands, stroking the smooth material, tracing the twin lightning strikes on the collar with his fingertips. He was tempted to try it on. Maybe then Hitler would stop scowling at him. Defiantly, he hooked it on the chair again and stormed from the room, giving Hitler the finger as he went out.

He knocked on Baum's bedroom door. The doctor had been and gone and the old man had recovered slightly. Eric helped him into a sitting position. He looked extremely weak stretched out on the bed, and his arms were limp at his sides.

"It's happened a few times before. My back just goes out on me sometimes. I had polio, you know, when I was young, and I think that stunted the development of my spine."

Eric wondered how many times Baum had mentioned the polio, making it sound like an incurable disease only he had had the power to survive, but it had left its mark. Any time he had physical problems or wanted to excuse away something from his past, Baum always played the polio ace.

"I cleaned everything like you said. I put the boxes in the garage too. The room looks really good."

Baum's thin mouth worked itself into a smile. "Yes. It's taking shape, and you deserve a lot of credit for that." Grimacing, he reached into his front pocket for his money clip and, to Eric's wide-eyed shock, handed him a crisp $100 note.

"Thank you, but that's way too much," Eric exclaimed, holding up the big green bill and looking at it with wonder.

"Now, that's a bonus. I think we might have to take a break for a week or two, until I'm fit enough for us to work in there together. You're most welcome to visit, and to look through the photographs and enjoy the room."

"Thanks, Mr Baum. Thanks a lot."

Baum reached out a slender arm and lightly stroked Eric's bare forearm. "The world needs more boys like you, Eric. But, I fear you're a rare breed."

Eric bit his lower lip, the skin on his forearm tingling from Baum's touch. He took the compliment awkwardly, forcing a smile, and backed towards the door.

"Get better soon."

He left the room and sprang through the front door, rubbing at his forearm, trying to rub away that sickeningly cool touch. He took out the $100 note and looked at it. He had enough for a board now, maybe not the dolphin one he preferred, but if he had a good board, did it really matter what was on it?

He ran home, his feet thumping the pavement as he barrelled along. At home, he greeted his mother brightly in the kitchen and darted for his room. From its place hidden in his chest of drawers, he pulled out his secret sock and dropped all the bills on his bed. He arranged them in order according to value and counted them again and again, amazed by his sudden wealth. He slid the $280 into his wallet. It made a healthy bulge. He heard his mother call out to him as he ran from the house and he shouted he would be back for dinner.

The bus trundled to the mall, picking up mostly old ladies, those too old to drive, en route to their weekly shopping or trip to the hairdresser. Eric was fidgety, impatient to be at the mall. He gave up his seat for an old lady, but got no thank you in return. She clearly felt it was her right to have the seat. That's fine, Eric thought, but a little gratitude wouldn't hurt.

The dolphin board was on sale, but still out of reach at $349. Brad's brother was there again and smiled as he remembered Eric. Shane even knew him by name. Eric guessed Brad had said a few nasty things about him.

"That board's too short for you." Shane put the dolphins back on the rack and pulled off a longer one, white with green slashes in no defined pattern. "You should take a longer board, because you'll probably grow a bit too."

Eric took the board in his hands, stroking the fibreglass and trying to act like an expert. The board was much bigger than him, but also very light, and the $200 price tag clinched it. He slammed the money down on the counter. He thought about buying some clothes too, but decided to save at least some of his hard-earned money. He bought a small surfboard key ring for Pepper – in purple because they had none in pink – and the cash register clanged.

"Maybe I'll see you down at Souths."

"Yeah, sure," Eric lied, still not ready for that nasty break.

He sprang from the shop and walked self-consciously through the mall, the big board tucked under his arm. Mothers pushing full shopping carts scowled at him because he took up so much space and nearly hit their children with the board, but he didn't care. He walked through the mall with his head held high. He had his prize and couldn't wait to show it to Pepper the next morning. He prayed she would come down to the beach.

***

"Eric, I'm really proud of you. I was against you surfing, but you worked for this board, you earned the money, and now you have it. One day, you'll thank me for teaching you the value of a dollar."

"Thanks, dad." They were the first words he had spoken to his father since Christmas.

They sat together at the plastic dining table. Eric couldn't contain his happiness. It was just like old times in Merredin. He had missed talking with his father, who wasn't such a bad old guy, and he had been stupid to think he could go the rest of his life with never speaking to him. His mother was beaming in the kitchen, frying big steaks in her new frying pan. Things were back to normal again. No, they were better, and Eric, in his high spirits, even apologised for his behaviour, explaining he had been having trouble with some local kids, but that was over now. He would get his revenge tomorrow and then his life in Crescent Bay would be set. He could work just for Baum and forget about Fischer.

"Maybe I'll come down with you tomorrow morning before work," his father said. "I used to surf a bit when I was your age. Maybe I could show you a trick or two."

Eric recoiled in shock, fearing his private teenage world was about to be invaded. He pictured his father meeting Pepper, and wondered if he would stare at her with glassy eyes and a slimy smile on his face, like he did at most girls.

"Let him go on his own," his mother said, rescuing him. "He's got his friends there. He doesn't want to have us around."

His father gave him a wink. "Quite right. You might embarrass us."

And they all laughed. What a great evening it was, the best they had had in ages. Eric locked the haunting spectre of divorce back in the closet. His mother had her hair up and looked lovely, like she did in Eric's earliest memories, when her smile brightened up rooms and all the kids in the kindergarten had loved her and had all wished she could be their mother.

The steaks were delicious. His mother said that the new frying pan did all the work. They followed dinner with cheesecake and ice cream and sat down together to watch a film on television. Eric lounged on one sofa, his parents sat arm and arm on the other, and his board leaned against the wall in the corner. Everything was as it should be.

***

He rose at dawn, packed his bag with a bottle of water, a hat and some sunscreen, grabbed his board and galloped from the house. The streets were deserted. The warm, still night had hung on until dawn. It was already thirty degrees and the temperature would keep rising until the sea breeze picked up in the afternoon. It would be hours before Pepper would come down, if she came that is, but he was so anxious to try out his new board, he couldn't sleep another minute.

The water was cool and, as was the weather pattern, a dry easterly blew off the desert but not strongly enough to ruin the surf or cause any nasty backwash or rips. His hands shook a little as he secured the leg rope to his ankle. He looked up and down the beach. Nobody in sight, not even any dawn runners. Still, he stretched self-consciously, going through the movements as if watched by thousands. He tried to savour the moment, staring over the water and sighing a couple of times. He copied Drew by running for the water and landing on his board in one movement. He did it, and the board skipped over the top of the water, sliding easily under the breakers and seeming to require no paddling at all. Out past the breakers, he sat on his board and waited for the first set. The solitude was comforting and liberating. He could try things with this board knowing no one was watching.

His first wave was a small, heavy one that had a low crest but plenty of punch. The board responded to his will, and by accident, although he tried not to make it look that way despite his lack of spectators, he completed a 360° turn that he had seen Drew accomplish at South

Corner. With this board, he thought, he would soon be able to take on that break and conquer his fear of the rocks. He would show Drew, Brad, Shane and the others what surfing was all about.

He took wave after wave, never tiring, oblivious to the world around him. World War Three could have started in the Gulf and half the planet could have been blown away for all he cared. Others came down to the beach for a quick swim to ward off the early heat, but Eric barely noticed them. He even turned in surprise when Pepper paddled up next to him.

"Hey," he said, flicking his wet hair back. "When did you get here?"

"I was watching you from the beach," she said, perhaps as unsure of their relationship as he was. "You look like a pro."

"Hardly." He pointed at his board, tapping the fibreglass. "This thing goes by itself. I'm just a passenger."

Pepper admired the board, smiling and frowning. Eric had no idea what she thought about it, and was reminded how he seldom had any idea of how she felt about things. The night of the party, she had barely said two words to him, seemed bored sitting next to him, and then asked him to have sex, wanting him to stay always in her room. Now, he had his board and they could surf together, but she seemed disappointed by it.

"What happened to the dolphins?"

"Shane said it was too small for me, especially if I grow a bit more."

She pouted. "I hope this big board doesn't give you a big head."

Unsure how to handle her bad mood and let down by her reaction – why wasn't she happy for him? – Eric did his best to ignore her and kept surfing, enjoying his triumph. Still, she was here and that was something, even if she surfed without enjoyment, taking waves with lacklustre sweeps of her arms and barely making any turns. Eric continued to surf with all of his energy until he had none left. They got out together and sat on the beach. Eric had brought some fruit and he offered some of it to Pepper. She ate an apple forlornly, looking over the water. Then, she threw the core aside, climbed on top of him and started kissing him, her salty lips all over his face. Eric was stunned but kissed her back, thinking it better to enjoy her change in mood rather than question it or try to understand it.

"Watcha doin tonight?" she asked, leaning back, her thin arms around his neck. She smiled and tried to look coy, but Eric couldn't help thinking he saw something desperate in her eyes, a kind of insecurity he thought beautiful people didn't have.

"Not much."

"Wanna meet me down here?"

"Sure. Should I bring anything?"

"Maybe a blanket and…" She looked down at the sand. "And maybe a few, you know, wet suits."

Eric matched her childish giggles and said he would sneak out of his house at around ten. They departed with nervous kisses, with Pepper hip shaking her way up the beach path and looking behind her as Eric put his leg rope back on. He suddenly had more energy and wanted to waste it on his new board. Pepper waved from the top of the beach path. Eric promised himself that this time, he would make an effort to be better at sex. He paddled past the breakers wondering if it was worth going to the library to look at more pictures of cow heads.

***

The skateboards clicked and clacked on the driveway, but Adam and Drew stopped their competition to look at Eric's new board. Adam smiled and made subtle jokes about Eric buying him one just like it, which Eric almost took seriously, his face dropping at the thought of having to fork out another $200 just for Adam. But Adam laughed and waved him off.

"Don't worry," Adam said. "There's not much surf where I'm living. And besides, I don't wanna do something my baby brother is better at than me."

He grabbed Drew and easily wrestled him to the ground, using his weight and superior strength to pin him down. Drew wriggled on the ground, trying to break free, but Adam held him, and tickled him viciously in the side so Drew squealed with laughter as much as with pain. Drew shouted out a code word between the two and Adam let him up. Drew jumped quickly to his feet and got back on his skateboard. He performed a few tricks, trying to redeem himself. Bored, Adam went inside the house.

"You ready?" Drew asked.

"Let me dump my board."

Eric was surprised to find the garage door locked and the house empty. It seemed strangely quiet without his mother there and again he felt like he was walking through someone else's house. The weeks were passing and still this company owned abode had yet to feel like home. It was amazing to think that he knew Baum's house almost as well as his own, and felt as uncomfortable there too. He washed down his board, stood it up in his room and changed clothes. He toyed with the idea of wearing sunglasses, but the pair he had was childish and too small for his face. He threw them in the garbage. He wasn't a child anymore.

Back outside, Eric was surprised to see two of Adam's friends leaning against Adam's beat up car. Shane from the surf shop recognised him and nonchalantly nodded hello. He made a funny comment about Eric being a feisty one, and explained how Brad and Eric had almost come to blows in the shop.

"You country kids sure are tough," Adam said. "There's guys like you at uni, always trying to show what men they are. They look at the Asians like they're from another planet."

They were big boys, both a head taller than Eric, muscular too, and he should have felt more relaxed by their presence. But he only felt more pressure, especially with Shane present; to be accepted by these boys and prove himself as manly as them. Adam and his friends remained aloof, and when they were all in the car, only those three spoke, with Drew knowing his place and Eric too shy.

They drove towards the park, which was only at the end of the street. They could have walked, but the car lent them a certain menace and they would be able to make a quick getaway if necessary. Eric tried to hide his nerves, especially because the older boys thought the whole escapade a great lark. He tried to laugh with them, desperate not to seem like a wimp or a sissy in front of them. They might just as easily turn on him as help him, for he and Drew were hardly the best of friends.

It was a stinker of a day. The sea breeze still hadn't come in, but the easterly had dropped which meant the south-westerly wasn't far away. Drew spotted the bikers lounging under a big tree in the park, the same tree Eric had sat under on the last day of school. Adam parked the car nearby and they all piled out. Spurred on by their size and number, they crossed the park, a gang looking for trouble. Eric and Drew walked side by side towards the big tree, with the three older boys walking behind and cracking jokes. Eric kept sneaking glances over his shoulder to be sure the boys were still there. He feared that their greatest joke would be abandoning him and Drew, turning and running back to the car, laughing all the way. But they stayed behind. Adam was regaling his friends with a funny story about his sexual escapade of last night. Eric heard Sandra's name a couple of times.

When the bikers saw them crossing the park, heading in their direction, they all stood up. Josh fidgeted with his hands, running them through his dark hair and brushing grass from his shirt and shorts. He edged to the front of the group with little Robbie standing next to him. The two groups faced each other, the bikers stronger in number but intimidated by the three older boys.

"What do you want?" Josh demanded, trying to sound mean and fearless. But his voice, the same that had tormented and teased Eric, no longer had assurance and confidence. The voice cracked.

"The rest of you idiots go home," Drew said. "We only want Josh." And he pointed the boy out, perhaps thinking the others would step away. But Eric knew they would only respond to Robbie. Without question, most of the group looked past Drew and Eric, saw the three burly boys, and wanted to run for it. Their fears were made worse when Adam and his friends, relaxed and in control of the situation – enjoying their dominance and perhaps remembering themselves on the receiving end of such a situation – moved in between the bikers and separated Josh from the group, pushing him towards Eric.

No one spoke. Then Robbie surprised everyone by lunging at Adam, who was at least half a metre taller, attacking him with his hands open like a cat. He got a grip on Adam's shirt and the older boy tried to pull the younger off. But Robbie's grip was strong and the shirt ripped loudly, exposing Adam's pale chest that was covered with scabby pink marks. He picked Robbie up like a rag doll and tossed him a good two metres to the side. The two older boys chuckled, pointing at Adam's ripped shirt.

"This midget's psycho," Adam said, inspecting his ripped shirt, arranging it so it covered some of his spots.

He walked towards his friends, but Robbie jumped onto his back and started pounding Adam's head with his small fists. Adam screamed with pain and lost control. He spun around and around trying to shrug Robbie off. Shane came over to help, punching Robbie lightly in the side – a warning punch but hard enough to make Robbie stop – and then pushed Robbie off Adam's back. It was a long way back down for the little boy and he fell hard to the ground. Adam turned and gave him a hard kick in the stomach. The small boy recoiled and rolled with the kick, grunting as he took it.

Eric looked down at Robbie, saw the tight grimace on his face, and was somewhat impressed by the courage he himself lacked. But that didn't undo all the beatings and humiliation Robbie and Josh had marked Eric with. Sensing his advantage, he went in for the kill.

"He broke your board," he said to Adam, unable to suppress the smile that crept onto his face.

Drew's brother, who seemed to grow in size with each breath he took in, and who looked even meaner and more vicious with his shirt ripped, turned to the crumpled mess lying on the ground. He stood over him, trying to decide whether he should give him another kick.

"I'd say my board was worth about as much as you are. I guess that means I get to break you in half and then we're even." He pulled his leg back to kick Robbie, but Shane laid a calming hand on his shoulder.

"Come on," Shane said, his voice steady, his enjoyment gone. "He's not worth it."

Adam paused in mid-kick, then laughed his agreement. He turned to walk away, but his laughter turned into a scream. He looked down and saw Robbie biting his leg, already with blood trickling from his mouth. Adam hopped around, almost comically, like he had stepped in a fire, but Robbie was like a pit bull. His jaw had locked and he would not let go. Adam shouted with pain and cursed loudly. He bent over and punched Robbie hard in the face. There was a resounding crack and Robbie relinquished his grip. He lay on the grass in the foetal position, his eyes closed, blood trickling from his mouth and his lower jaw disgustingly askew. Shane pulled Adam back.

"What the hell is wrong with him?" Adam fought against Shane so that his other friend had to help restrain him. He shrugged the boys off and bent over to inspect the bite. The blood trickled down his leg. "Am I gonna need a tetanus shot for this?" He spat on Robbie. "You crazy little shit." Then he turned to Eric, his face twisted with anger and annoyance, perhaps now missing the adult world of university. "Your turn."

Eric swung around to face Josh, who was still looking down at the unmoving figure of Robbie on the ground. There was fear in his eyes, but also concern. Eric wondered if Robbie would blame Josh for all of this mess.

"Hit him for me, Rick," Drew said, leaning close to Eric, his arms folded, an arrogant smirk on his face.

"Yeah," Adam added, still angry. "Break his face like this psycho midget broke my board." He took his keys from his pocket and spun them around his finger, eager to get back in the car and drive away.

Eric looked at the three older boys. There was no turning back now. He had to hit Josh or the boys would never respect him. He tried to catch Shane's eyes, but he had turned around and was facing the sun, the first breaths of the sea breeze blowing his shirt and ruffling his hair.

"We thought it was his board," Josh said to Adam, his voice unsteady. "If we'd known it was yours, we wouldn't've broken it."

"Too late for that now," Adam said. From the corners of his eyes, he looked worriedly down at Robbie, who still hadn't stirred. "Come on, Rick. Get it over with."

Eric took a deep breath, clenched his fists and faced Josh, who was also looking down at Robbie. Eric's head hurt. He felt dizzy, having spent the whole morning in the surf. He took a swing at Josh, catching him in the left eye. Josh fell to the ground, clutching his face with his hands, groaning and acting it up so that Eric might spare him. The other bikers, eager to impress the older boys and be spared themselves, laughed at Josh.

"Cry baby," one of them said.

"Hit him, Rick," Drew shouted. The bikers picked up the chant, closing in on the two and making a tight circle.

Eric looked around the circle, the faces eager and hungry for violence, not caring who received it. He was stuck in the circle, and the "Hit him, Rick" chant burned his ears, loud and demanding. He looked down at Josh. The fallen boy peered through a gap in his fingers and the look in his eye almost took away the last of Eric's courage. If not for the other boys, he would have run away. But the tight circle imprisoned him, and the older boys had taken up the chant too, their deeper voices louder than the others. Eric gritted his teeth and gave Josh a hard kick in the stomach. Everyone cheered. Eric kicked again, and again. Josh squealed on the ground, rolling with the kicks. Eric felt that he couldn't stop. He kicked and punched at the boy who had done the same to him, who had humiliated him in front of Pepper. The cheers and laughter spurred him on, and he tried to ignore the crying groans coming from Josh.

"You boys," a voice shouted. "Stop that."

Eric stopped and all the boys turned to watch the old man limping over. He waved his cane in the air and tried to look threatening.

"Run," shouted one of the bikers. "It's the old Nazi."

The boys fled in all directions. One biker even tripped over Robbie, but got quickly to his feet and sprinted across the park. Even the three older boys ran, with Drew following behind them. But Eric stood frozen to his place, standing over the fallen Josh. He was hypnotised by the shiny cane swinging in the gloved right hand. He thought he heard Drew shout for him, but the words didn't register, or got lost in the blustery wind now blowing in from the beach. Fischer's face was red and his breath came in short, stunted gasps. His face drooped with sadness and disappointment, and it cut at Eric's heart.

"Go on," Fischer said, frowning, his eyes watery. "Run."

Eric turned and ran across the park, pumping his legs so fast he thought he might fall over. He jumped into the waiting car and they sped off down the street. Eric looked through the window and saw Fischer help Josh to his feet and then try to rouse the still unconscious Robbie. In the car, the older boys cheered, slapping Eric on the back, calling him Rocky instead of Ricky and making jokes which their nerves made all the more hysterical. Adam almost hit another car and this was further cause for merriment. They honked the horn and yelled obscenities at the people in the street, shocking old ladies and scaring small children. Eric sat grimacing in the back seat. He did his best to play along and shouted his own obscenities; one of the group.

***

"Mr Baum called," his mother said as he closed the garage door despondently behind him. "He said he has a special job for you today, if you have the time."

He leaned against the kitchen counter, wondering if Baum already knew. Perhaps Josh had already told about the beating and Baum wanted revenge, or an explanation, or maybe he wanted to congratulate Eric, for Baum seemed to have little liking for his grandson.

"It sounded pretty urgent," she added. "He was very excited on the phone."

Then she turned from the sink to face him. She smiled brightly, her eyes shining, her whole face lighting up.

"I wanted to wait until tonight, but I can't keep it a secret any longer. I've got a job at the kindergarten down the street, the one attached to the primary school. I met the principal at the golf club. I start at the end of the month, when school starts."

272

Eric's forced smile hardly complimented his mother's beaming expression. He dragged out one of the plastic dining chairs and slumped into it.

"That's great."

His mother pursed her lips and put her hands theatrically on her hips. "You might want to be a little more pleased than that."

"That's great!" Eric tried, making his voice louder and trying to sound happy. It was good news. At least now she would be out of the house and he would get some peace. Maybe she would even buy herself a car, one that he might use in the coming years.

"If you see your father, don't tell him. I want to tell him myself." She moved the new frying pan into place and dropped a hunk of meat into it, the evening's celebratory roast dinner. "Things are going to change around here."

***

Baum smiled at Eric as he opened the door, greeting him brightly, seemingly oblivious to the day's events. "What a boiler today was," he said, closing the door on the afternoon heat that was finally being abated by the sea breeze. "This kind of heat makes me homesick."

"How's your back?" Eric was surprised to see the old man so nimble, stepping lightly in his house clogs and in a sprightly mood.

"Much better, thank you."

Baum unlocked the door to the war room and Eric followed him inside, in no mood for work or for any of Baum's games.

"My doctor gave me some painkillers and they've worked their magic."

"What are we gonna do today?" Eric asked. His voice was lacklustre, his energy low, but Baum seemed unperturbed. Every time Eric closed his eyes, he saw Josh lying on the ground and heard the boys chanting, "Hit him, Rick."

"Oh, there'll be no work today." He laughed, a great guffaw that made him throw his head back. "I've called a truce between us and the war room. Hah! No, I was thumbing through some old photo albums and I found something particularly interesting, something that might surprise you." He wiggled his eyebrows up and down. "It might even amaze you."

Eric's curiosity was sparked, but the old man's behaviour, especially his bright mood, was suspicious. Had he not screamed like a girl yesterday and then lay in bed like an invalid? And Eric found the room creepy now. Hitler dominated, framed by the two cabinets. He noticed that Baum had hung the picture on the wall, and it was the centrepiece the old man had said it would be. Hitler saw the whole room, judged it, seemed happy with it, but was forever asking for more. Hitler stared at Eric, who was so low in confidence and racked with guilt that he had to look away. Was Hitler proud of the way he had behaved today?

Baum moved over to the desk and pointed at the open photo album, at a black and white photo wedged behind a clear sleeve. Eric bent over to look.

"Come closer or you won't see it clearly enough," Baum ordered, his voice friendly and light. He raised an arm and Eric reluctantly sidled up next to the old man. He felt the arm land across his shoulders, drawing him even nearer. He hoped Annie was in the house somewhere. But this was a day when he would normally have worked for Fischer, and Baum knew he was free which meant Baum also knew he no longer worked for Fischer.

"Doesn't he look familiar?" Baum pointed at one of the men in the photo.

Eric looked closely, trying to forget Baum's tentacle that had him trapped. In the photograph was an SS soldier. Eric recognised the black uniform. The soldier stood casually, staring straight at the camera. He was next to a large open grave, which had a mess of naked, twisted and broken bodies piled on top of each other. It was like a tourist photo. The soldier did everything but point at the mass grave and smile. Eric leaned forward and looked closely at the soldier, studying his blurred features and the shape of his shoulders. He thought back to the photographs of the football team he had looked at in Geraldton, when Fischer was a tall, strong-faced young man dominating the game. This soldier looked similar, but seemed shorter, perhaps hunching forward. There was a resemblance, he thought, but if this was Fischer, then it would mean that a lot of what the old man had said were lies, and that Baum had been right by saying Fischer was a Nazi.

"Yes, I also think this is our friend Mr Fischer," Baum whispered, his breath tickling Eric's ears. "It would make sense that he was in the SS because of his father."

Eric continued staring at the photograph, trying to carve a young Fischer out of the blurred outline. The soldier stared back at him, his face blank, the blurry eyes hollow and revealing a sadness that looked all too familiar.

"This was taken near Kaiserwald," Baum said. "The camp near Riga. There was an outbreak of typhoid in the Jewish settlement and thousands died. Those people could never keep themselves clean. I guess he was responsible for disposing of the bodies." He curled his top lip in disgust. "A hideous job."

"What does it mean? If it's him, that is." For some reason, he was unwilling to go along with Baum's supposition. He was tired of the old man, sick of both of them in fact, of hearing about the war and having them both fill his head with lies. "Should we go to the police?"

"An old photograph is hardly concrete evidence. I suggest you show it to him and his reaction will convict him."

Baum reached back his arm, releasing Eric, who gratefully took a few short steps back from the desk. The old man slid the photo into a small envelope and handed it to Eric. He tucked it into his pocket.

"By the way," Baum said airily, flipping the album shut, "why aren't you working for him today?"

Eric looked down at his feet. "He found out about the letter."

"Oh, that's a shame. Maybe the photograph will get you back in his good books."

Eric looked at the floor, aware Hitler's eyes were on him. He wanted to shrink into the floor, turn to liquid and slip through the cracks in the wood.

"Look here," Baum continued, moving around the desk to the window. "I put together an SS uniform." It hung in front of the drawn curtains and Baum pulled it down. "Would you like to try it on?"

Eric was tempted. He looked at the shiny material, the same jacket as before but now with matching trousers. He wanted to feel the smooth material against his skin, get that feeling of empowerment the uniform lent him, and perhaps emulate his great grandfather. But the expectant look on Baum's face and the cunning twinkle in his shining blue eyes scared him. The old man wiggled his eyebrows up and down, trying to make light of it, but in doing so only looked more devious and sinister.

"I promised to help my mum clean the house," Eric said, looking at his watch and backing towards the door. "I better go."

He edged away from the desk, but seemed reluctant to leave without Baum's approval. Baum was his last source of money and he couldn't afford to lose him. Baum hung the uniform back on the curtain rail. Its blackness was startling against the white curtains and the twin lightning strikes of the SS on the collar shined and sparkled like silver. Eric wondered how he hadn't noticed it when he had entered the room. It seemed now it was all that he could see.

"If you don't want to wear it, Eric, you just have to say so," Baum said, his back turned. With his long, piano player fingers, he preened the uniform, plucking at small pieces of cotton and brushing away flecks of dust. "It's no crime to stand up for your convictions."

"I gotta go." Eric backed towards the door. Hitler caught his eye, ordering him to stay. The red of the swastika stopped him short and he stared at it. Baum caught him staring and moved quickly around the desk.

"He stood up for his convictions," Baum said, walking towards Eric, the clogs clicking on the floor. Eric noticed the old man's hips swayed a little and the front of his pants bulged slightly. Eric wondered if perhaps Baum had his money clip in the front pocket today. Eric reached behind for the door handle, missing with the first try. Baum came near, extending a tentacle to grab at Eric, but doing it slowly, like he meant no harm.

"There's no need to rush off, Eric." Baum's voice was soft and fatherly. He smiled, the same sugary smile Eric remembered that Baum had given Mrs Canter that first day they had met. Eric recognised that the voice was the same too, so sweet and fake.

Baum was close. Eric could smell the flowery cologne the man always wore, could see the old face glistening with moisturiser. He reached behind and got the door handle this time. It turned. Baum reached to grab his shoulder, but he slipped through the crack and ran through the open room. The clogs didn't click the floor behind him like he expected and he stopped short at the front door and turned. Baum stood in the kitchen, behind the counter.

"Give my best to Fischer when you see him." Baum smiled and waved, as if it was just a normal workday goodbye for them. "Show him the picture. I'll call you next week. You can tell me how he reacts."

Eric forced a smile, not knowing where he stood with the old man. He clicked the lock of the front door and went out into the now windblown afternoon.

**

He rummaged through the drawers, sifting through the personal items he knew well from bored afternoons he had spent alone in the house in Merredin, when his mother had worked the afternoon shift. On the pretence of looking for a pair of tweezers, he left his mother smiling over the new frying pan and now searched the bathroom for the condoms he needed. A part of him didn't want to find them. But he had walked in on his parents having sex before. He had to admit they did it, disgusting as the idea was, and probably still did it, despite their age and occasional differences. He went through the drawers, listening hard for footsteps in the hall. He panicked. If he didn't find any, he would be forced to get some from the shop, and how embarrassing would that be. He would have to shoplift them. But what if he was caught?

He eventually found the box in the bedside table on his father's side of the bed. He tore two off the long line and inspected a tube of cream that was next to the box. It was almost squeezed empty and Eric wondered what it was for. He stuffed the condoms into his pocket and appeared in the living room just as his father arrived home. His mother had just told her news, and his father smiled his winning, big-sale smile before retrieving a bottle of champagne – normally reserved as emergency gifts for clients – from the garage refrigerator. The cork was popped, and even Eric was given a glass. The sweet bubbly made him feel dizzy. He couldn't finish it and his father made some rather crude jokes at his expense.

"You certainly don't take after your mother," his father said, laughing loudly.

Eric went to bed early, sick of his father's comments, claiming he was tired from surfing so long that day. He read his book impatiently, watching the clock most of the time as it ticked slowly towards ten. He heard a few shouts coming from the living room, his father complaining that, while it was good to have a second income, he didn't want her working too much so that the house turned into disarray. Eric's mother protested, and even claimed that Eric could do some of the housework, if they gave him some pocket money. But his father was against this idea. They continued to argue, mostly about money, but trying to keep their voices down. Eventually, they took it into the bedroom where Eric could no longer decipher their words. He hoped they had made up. Maybe his father was even reaching for the drawer, putting that strange cream to use as well. He listened hard, trying to hear the sounds of sex but also not wanting to. He checked his watch. It was nine thirty.

He packed a blanket into his backpack and edged his window open. It creaked loudly. He saw the black outlines of spiders scurrying back to their webs. He unlatched the fly-screen and climbed out of the window, putting the screen back in place, but not securing it so he could get back in later. He ducked under the still bright kitchen window and then jumped over the locked side gate. Through the big front windows of Drew's house came the flickering blue light of the television, and it was loud enough that Eric heard gunshots and the shouts of the actors. He walked past Adam's car, which was parked sideways on the grass. He recalled the madness of the afternoon, the shouts, cheers and laughter, Robbie wild like an animal, and Josh crying helplessly on the ground.

Dogs barked to each other across the neighbourhood as he walked along the deserted streets. All the residents of Crescent Bay were safely locked inside their homes and the streets were a dangerous place to be, a lot of shadows and dark places the streetlights didn't reach. The blue and red lights of alarm systems flashed intermittently and every window was lit by the flickering of televisions.

He sweated as he walked, from the oppressive evening heat, with the wind having dropped after sundown, and from nerves. He had rolled on some deodorant, but still the sweat trickled down his sides and in long drops down his back. He smelled himself, testing his armpits. He smelled okay, he thought, but if necessary, he could have a swim when he got to the beach, but then he would be all salty. He wondered what Pepper would prefer, him smelling of sweat or tasting of dried salt. Probably neither.

He was early. The beach was deserted and black, with only the phosphorous white foam of the waves visible. The sand on the path was still warm and he edged down it, scared he would trip over. The darkness of the beach made him nervous – it seemed a completely different and foreign place at night – and the loud crash of the waves was like the wind rushing past his ears, blocking out all other sounds.

"Rick?"

"It's me."

"I'm down here. Next to the big rock at the bottom of the path."

He followed the sound of the voice, tripping over and stumbling in the darkness until he saw the whites of Pepper's eyes and the red glow of her cigarette. It was then he smelled the smoke.

"Hey."

He sat down next to her. He was so nervous he was almost shaking, his jiggling legs rippling the sand. Despite the warm evening, Pepper seemed cold, with her knees pulled under her chin and her arms wrapped around them.

"I didn't think you were gonna come." She took a drag and blew smoke from the side of her mouth. It was supposed to be a cool, seductive gesture, but Eric thought it looked anything but sexy. He had always found something pathetic about the contrived movements of smoking.

"I'm early."

"I've been down here for a while," Pepper said. "I've kind of run away again."

"Everything all right?" He was concerned, more so because it seemed his chance at sex redemption was looking less and less likely.

"Do you like me, Rick?"

"Of course I do."

Her voice was softer, quieter: "Do you love me?"

Eric was tongue-tied. He liked Pepper, thought she was beautiful and fun to be with, but what did he know about love?

"Of course I do," he repeated, trying to sound convincing. He worried that he had paused too long and that in pausing, she would guess his fallacy. He put his hand in his pocket to check the condoms were still there, but thought he wouldn't need them tonight. To his surprise, Pepper leaned close and put her thin arms around him. Eric heard her sniff in the darkness.

"I brought a blanket," he said, plucking it from his bag.

He stood up and spread it on the ground self-consciously, Pepper watching him all the while. His hands fumbled with the corners, trying to separate the folds. Pepper made no movement to help him. With the blanket laid, she took off her clothes and lay down. Eric asked no questions and did the same.

Again it was over pretty quickly. He wondered if it was like this for all men. She seemed to enjoy it, but it was hard enough to read her expression in the daytime let alone in the dark. Eric pulled out the second condom, showed it to Pepper. She smiled weakly and they tried again. It lasted longer this time and Eric even extracted a few pleasurable groans from Pepper that unfortunately only succeeded in making him faster. They lay together on the blanket, secure with their nakedness in the dark. Again, it had been nice, but Eric couldn't help feeling that Pepper was distant this time, almost letting him do it to her.

"Can you do me a favour, Rick?" she asked, puffing on another cigarette.

"Name it." He felt sleepy, sick of the day, wanting his own bed and to wake up tomorrow and start again.

"Come to my house tomorrow afternoon, at around four. I need your help."

"I'll be there." He hoped he wouldn't have to sit down to dinner with Pepper's mother and her preying-mantas husband Blair.

"I might not make it for a surf tomorrow morning," she said.

"It's okay. The way I'm feeling, I might sleep all day."

***

He didn't. His mother woke him early, Baum on the phone. Fischer had suffered a heart attack and was in hospital. Baum suggested Eric should pay him a visit.

"An excellent time to show him that photograph," Baum said. "It might put him over the hill." And then he laughed one his boisterous guffaws. "Shall I tell Mrs Canter to get her dress out?"

Seventeen

The neon lit hallways twisted and turned in a labyrinth of sickness. The smell of bleach burned his nostrils as he ran. When he stopped and peered into rooms, sick heads popped up expectantly, thinking he was there to visit them. Disappointed, the head flopped back on the pillow or refocused on the television suspended from the ceiling. He should have listened more carefully to the receptionist, but she had told him the room number and he had just started running, flying down the white halls, dodging doctors and nurses, only to discover that the same room number was in every different ward. So he ran around, spinning from one ward to the next, asking questions of pale nurses, and following their outstretched arms to the next ward, or up the next flight of stairs.

The hospital reminded him of a prison, especially the way the nurses marched up and down the hallways, so bossy and commanding, like he imagined cell wardens to be. But it wasn't just the nurses that lent a feeling of imprisonment; most doors to the hallways were closed and had eye-level porthole windows to look through, so that the wardens could watch their prisoners from outside the room. He didn't stop to look, but wondered, as he ran, if the doors also had a thin slot to pass a tray of food through. In the hall, footsteps and voices echoed, the squeaks of wheelchairs and mobile beds were loud, and all the patients were ordered to stay in bed and get better; a health sentence. Eric hated the place.

Fischer had his own room, and both the old man and Josh looked up when Eric burst in. Josh had plaster attached to his bushy eyebrows and his left eye was ringed with purple and blue. He looked away and got up to leave.

"Don't worry," Fischer said, extending an arm to make Josh sit back down. "He won't bite."

Eric and Josh exchanged a look, for neither knew to whom Fischer was referring. Josh slowly lowered himself back into his chair and Eric took short steps until he was at the end of the bed.

"Are you all right?" His voice was quiet and shy, the way his mother had told him to speak when they had visited his grandfather in the hospital a few days before he died. He also made an effort not to breathe too loudly despite having run through the hospital.

Fischer ventured a tired smile. "It doesn't look like it. The doctors are trying to be positive but the body knows the truth. My heart is kaput, though it's been broken a long time. It's been nothing but an ordinary pump for the last few years."

Eric swallowed the sobs caught in his throat. It was just like with his grandfather: the old man lying in bed, shrivelled up and lost in the white sheets, dying, and there was nothing he could do to stop it.

"Does that mean you're gonna die?" He looked down at the floor, turning away from Josh slightly, not wanting his adversary to see him crying over this old man.

"We're all gonna die, Eric. We're born with a terminal illness."

"What happened?"

Fischer tried to breathe deeply, but seemed only to get half way, his chest unable to take any more air. "Young Josh here rescued me in the park. Despite his injuries, he ran across the road to get some help. He helped the other boy too, who was in a very bad way. I hope he'll be all right."

"I didn't hit Robbie," Eric said, perhaps too defiantly.

"Does it really matter who hit him?" Fischer lifted himself up from the bed as far as he could, which was not very far, and he dropped back down on the pillows, blowing the air out of them. "The boy was unconscious. He was lucky Josh was there to help."

Josh looked down at the floor. "It's no big deal. And Robbie deserved it, in a way."

"Now that's the first wrong thing you've said since I met you, Josh." Fischer turned and directed his words at Eric. "The others ran, but you stayed and helped. And no one deserves to get hit the way that boy was. His jaw was almost crushed. You saw the way the ambulance men crowded around him."

Eric told himself to turn around and walk out of the room. He had conquered Josh, old Fischer would die, and in a few days he could get on with his life. The school holidays would be over soon and then there would be another long year of learning. He had his surfboard, his girlfriend and his cricket team. He certainly didn't need this depressing hospital and this dying, insulting old man, who had probably been a Nazi and had therefore done much worse things than hit a boy a few times in revenge. But he stayed rooted to the spot. If anything, he took a few short steps towards the bed so that his hands could grip the metal frame. Something kept him there, the inquisitive part of him that wanted to confirm whether Fischer had lied to him or not. The old man was connected to a variety of machines which were wheezing and sucking and beeping. The wires stretched from the machines to the nodes on his chest, almost as if they were securing him to the bed.

"I'm sorry," he said. "For taking the letter, I mean."

Fischer turned his head towards the window, away from the two boys. He frowned as he looked out at the bright morning. A flock of pink and grey galahs shrieked and fled from one tree to the next. Fischer followed the flutter of the birds with his eyes.

"Apologies reveal your shortcomings," he said, smiling bitterly. He turned back to Josh. "My father used to say that. He was a real Nazi, a doctor at Neuengamme Camp. During the war," he added, when the words didn't register on Josh's face. "He still sends me letters every year. One found its way into Eric's pocket and no doubt into your grandfather's hands." His head swivelled slightly and he lowered his eyes on Eric. "That's right, isn't it? Baum put you up to it. Well? What did he say?"

"Said there was nothing in it. Just boring family stuff."

Fischer's face went flat and turned a paler shade of grey. "He didn't say anything?"

Eric shook his head.

Fischer turned in the bed so that the wires went with him, yanking at some of the machines and pulling them closer to the bed. "Josh, what do you know about your grandfather?"

Josh shrugged. "Not much. He came from Austria after the war, and was a professor at a university in Perth. I always forget which one."

"What did he do during the war? Was he in the army? Austria was part of Germany then."

"He said he worked in an office or something, economic stuff I think." Josh scowled at Eric. "Maybe you should ask him. They worked together."

Fischer turned to Eric. The face was hard and demanding, and Eric stepped back from the bed, suddenly as afraid of the old man as he had been when they had first met in the park. There was a darkness there he couldn't explain, the shadow of violence hiding itself, biding its time.

"Well, Eric? What do you know about Baum?"

"He's got lots of stuff from the war. Toy soldiers and model planes and tanks and things like that. He's got lots of uniforms too, and stacks of photographs."

Eric dug his hand into his pocket, feeling the sharp corners of the envelope Baum had given him yesterday.

Fischer sighed and settled himself back on his many pillows. The stiff sheets crinkled loudly, as if he was lying on a bed of plastic.

"Well, that's interesting, but hardly proves he was a Nazi. The only curious thing is that he wants to protect my father. He must know how high up he was. I mean, you wouldn't believe the kinds of things the old bastard wrote in his letters."

Eric pulled the envelope from his pocket and slid the photograph out. He stepped around the bed and handed it to Fischer. "He says this is you."

Fischer looked at the photograph closely, squinting his eyes almost shut. His face changed and he was suddenly sad, a pathetic, dying old man. "But I was never in the SS," he mumbled, his eyebrows knitting together.

Eric saw a flash pass through Fischer's eyes. The stare was supposed to prove his honesty, but Eric's instinct told him Fischer was deceiving him. He wondered what other lies the old man might have told.

"Mr Baum said it ran in the family," Eric said, wanting the truth. "That if the father was involved, then the son would be too."

"That's true, but not in every case. The SS didn't want me. They thought I was soft, and they were right. I could never have hanged a fellow German from a tree, even if he was a so-called traitor, and I could never have participated in the slaughter of thousands of Jews, like in this picture."

"Mr Baum said they all died from some disease, typhoid I think."

Fischer sneered. "He has no idea what he's talking about. Diseases? That's Holocaust denial, that is." He pointed at the twisted and naked bodies in the open grave. "These poor people were murdered, gassed, or shoved into trucks where the exhaust was pumped back inside. I could never have stood by and let that happen."

Fischer's anger made the spit dribble over his lips, blown out with the words. A machine beeped faster, a red light flashing briefly, until Fischer controlled his breathing again and the machine returned to its regular rhythm. Fischer wiped the drool from his mouth with the back of his ravaged right hand.

"So, it's not you?" Eric asked, still unconvinced.

Fischer frowned and his voice was steady. "Like his picture of your supposed great grandfather, Baum sees what he wants to see. The Nazis were always good at that. Anyway, this soldier is far too short to be me, and I was never in the SS."

Eric turned and walked to the window. He was surprised to see clouds in the sky, grey, black and threatening, perhaps the final remnants of a cyclone which had drifted down from the north. The storm would make the surf bigger and he wished he was down at the beach, carving his name into the waves with his new board. Why didn't Fischer believe that his great grandfather was Georg Messer? It was possible. How could he find out? How could he prove it?

"Eric?" Fischer called from the bed, making him turn around. "I think you know me well enough to know that's not me in the picture. I'm not sure what kind of lies Baum has filled your head with, but you should at least trust your own feelings and not take everything he says as truth."

Eric looked at the floor. Again this word truth. If he couldn't trust Baum to tell the truth, or Fischer, or his own parents, then who could he trust? When he was honest, he couldn't even trust himself. He often lied and twisted the truth to suit himself.

"It's difficult knowing what to believe," Fischer said. "You can't imagine what rubbish I had to swallow when I was growing up, that the Jews were responsible for everything wrong in Germany and had to be shipped out as a result. Asian hordes, Aryan superiority, natural selection, Mein Kampf, what a load of garbage, but when you're young, how do you know that this is not the truth? It's coming from your teachers, parents, grandparents, politicians, your sports coaches and your friends, everyone who has a guiding influence on you. It must be right."

Both boys went quiet. Eric was lost in his own familial world, wondering what lies he had been told, what prejudices he had unknowingly inherited.

"But what about this room with all the memorabilia?" Fischer asked. "Is Baum obsessed with war? Tell me about it, Eric."

"Well, he's got this big picture of Hitler," he said, spreading his arms wide to give an idea of the size, exaggerating a little. "It came a few days ago. He said an old friend had sent it to him. Strange present if you ask me. The picture's really creepy, and not even perfect. It was damaged, split down the middle and badly repaired."

Fischer's mouth dropped open. His face went blank and his body was motionless. Not even his withered chest moved up and down. "Was it framed?"

Eric nodded.

"Was something written on the frame?"

Eric looked at the old man quizzically, amazed that he might know the picture. Perhaps it was a common picture at that time, he thought. "I can't remember the exact words. Something about how great the German people are, 'a people with…'"

"'…Its future before it,'" Fischer finished.

"That's it."

"Good lord."

The room fell silent except for the wheezes and beeps of the machines and the laboured sound of Fischer's breathing. His pale chest, peppered with nodes and wires, like a join-the-dots picture gone wrong, struggled up and down, blowing out each breath as if it was the last. He stared into space.

"What does it mean?" Josh asked. He seemed uncomfortable with the silence, and leaned over Fischer to look at the photograph.

"It means that Baum knows my father, or knows of him. I guess he contacted him after Eric showed him the letter. It also means that Baum must be well connected, or perhaps was. Not many are still alive, but that's no great loss."

"Do you mean the painting belonged to your father?" Eric asked.

Fischer nodded, grimacing as he did so. He tried to laugh, but didn't seem to have the energy. "The picture is ripped because I smashed it over his head the last time I saw him."

"I'd like to do that to my father," Josh said.

"Me too," Eric added.

"I guess that's the problem," Fischer said. "Our fathers are human, like us, despite what they make themselves out to be in our eyes, always dressing themselves up as a god we should worship, and hope to emulate. Your generation's no different than any other. But how does Baum know my father?" He turned to Josh. "What did you say he did in the war?"

"He worked in an economic office," Josh said, shrugging again.

"Where? In Berlin?"

"I think so. He used to tell me stories about the air raids when I was younger, before he lost interest in me."

"He worked in the Reich Economic Administration Office," Eric said, trying to better his adversary. Josh snarled at him, but there was no malice. Eric knew then they would never trade blows again, and they now only kept up the pretence of hate not to seem weaker than the other.

"You're joking." Fischer's voice was loud and echoed in the room. A nurse poked her head around the door and ordered them to keep quiet, warning the boys not to excite the ailing Mr Fischer.

"The office sounds innocent," Fischer said when the door closed. "But they were responsible for the riches the Nazis collected over the years. Think of it as a government organised mafia. The Nazis were just a bunch of gangsters after all, thugs with worldly ambitions."

"What did they do?" Josh asked.

"They exploited the Jews. Took their property, money and businesses, sold the people as slave labour, even yanked out their gold teeth, melted them down, and made mountains of gold bars with it."

"Wow," Eric and Josh exclaimed in unison.

"They were responsible for pilfering the conquered lands of treasures, too. Art, wine, money, buildings, people, anything of value they simply stole. Their efforts were much more successful than the army's because they provided the means with which to fight the war, and to continue the fight after all the men had been killed. It's interesting. Hitler claimed the Jews tried to take over the world economically and so the Nazis went out and tried to do the same, but as professional pirates. Baum fits the type. Clever, sinister, bookish, but without the murderous streak to kill millions with his own hand. He was better suited to signing them to their deaths."

Eric grabbed a chair and sat next to the bed, opposite Josh.

"I'm not sure if it means anything," he said, "but the box the picture of Hitler came in was addressed to Christoph Baum and not Christian."

Fischer sucked at the air with difficulty and stared at Eric. He gave the boy one of his old smiles, when the floppy face turned jovial and the shadow of violence disappeared. The face was proud and full of admiration, as if once again Eric had defied expectations.

"So, you snooped around his house, too," Fischer said, but he didn't have the energy to laugh too hard, and could only manage a pathetic, wheezed chuckle. Then his face turned blank and he stared straight ahead. "Can't see the forest for the trees," he mumbled, his eyes glazed over. His mouth hung open and there was the slightest trickle of drool coming from one corner. Behind the glassy eyes, the brain seemed to be struggling with the effort it was being put under.

"Mr Fischer?" Eric asked, wondering if the old man was turning senile before his eyes.

Fischer turned to him, his eyes bright and gleaming. "In the shoebox. There's a diary. A leather book held together by a short belt. Bring it here. Josh, my keys are in the wardrobe. Go together and bring that diary back. No. Bring the whole shoebox."

Josh did as he was told and held the keys up triumphantly.

"Wait," Eric said. "What's this all about?"

Fischer's eyes went cold and his smile was thin and nasty. Eric saw the glimmer of violence again, ducking out of the shadows and carving itself into the old man's face.

"I know who Baum is." And he took up the photograph and stared at it as the Eric and Josh darted from the room.

In the hallway, Josh said, "Follow me."

Reluctantly, Eric ran behind Josh. They moved through the prison-like corridors, from one bleach-cleaned ward to another. Josh was quick on his feet and knew the way. He led Eric into the children's section of the hospital and into a room with five beds. Robbie, his head swathed in bandages, looked up when they walked in.

"Goway," he mumbled through his teeth. He turned away, his face set in pain from the movement. The narrow bed made it hard for him to move from side to side. Through the sheets, Eric could see that Robbie still had one arm clutched around his stomach.

Eric looked down at Robbie, the tough leader of the bikers, stretched out on the bed and imprisoned by his injuries. He looked so small lying there, like a child half his age. Eric wondered how such a small kid could be so intimidating and inspire such fear. All three turned to see the middle-aged woman come in. Her face was small and lined, but her body was broad, with large breasts crammed into a tight shirt. Her flabby mid-riff was showing, made even flabbier by the painted-on stonewash jeans she wore which bundled the fat in rolls at her waist. She flicked back a bleached, permed lock of hair from her made up face with fingers that had long red nails. A plastic coffee cup was clutched within one red set of talons and the other landed on her protruding hips. Robbie groaned at the sight of her.

"You the boy what did this?" she asked, spitting her words at

Eric. She unhooked her tiger skin handbag from under her elbow and dumped it on a chair. She went up close to Eric, dousing him in flowery perfume and old cigarette smoke. "Well? Did you bully my little Robbie?'

Robbie groaned from the bed again, kicking loudly at the walled sides, trying to get his mother's attention.

Eric held up his hands. The woman frightened him. "It wasn't me."

"Oh, yeah?" She turned to Josh. "Come on, Joshua, you were there, supposed to be protecting Robbie too."

"It wasn't him," Josh said, also intimidated.

"Then who was it?" She looked questioningly from boy to boy, acting like some barbaric, whorish school principal.

"I hit meself," Robbie mumbled through his teeth.

"That's nothing to what you're gonna get when I get you home." She leaned over the bed like she was going to hit him then and there. "And there'll be no more visits from ya father either. It's his influence that gets you into trouble."

"Oh, mum."

The woman shimmied her bundled bulk alongside the bed and sat down in a chair. She sipped her coffee anxiously, her long, sharp nails scratching the plastic. She downed the cup quickly, but then it slipped from her grasp, landing on the floor and spilling the remaining brown liquid.

"Now look what you've done," she said, trying to wipe away the coffee with the heels of her sheepskin boots. "I shoulda sent you to remedial school like I was told. Then none of this woulda happened."

Josh signalled to Eric for them to go. They both wished Robbie well. Eric took one last look at the boy in the bed. He was surprised to see the small boy, who had seemed so tough and confident, look at Eric with a rather embarrassing plea for help.

They said nothing as they ran from the hospital, and both took lusty gulps of air when they were outside. The clouds had rolled over and the sky was its usual boring blue. The hospital was several kilometres from Crescent Bay and they were hot and sweaty by the time they got to Fischer's house, having quietly competed on the way to see who was the faster runner. Josh opened the door and Eric led them through the house to the bedroom. He pulled the old shoebox from underneath the wardrobe. The streaks in the dust his fingers had left were gone; all the dust had been wiped away. He flipped off the lid, pulled the leather book out and then started to unlatch the short belt.

"I think we should do that at the hospital."

They hadn't said a word since leaving Robbie's room and Josh's voice was low and timid, sounding like he was still unsure where he was with Eric.

Eric looked at the diary, feeling the worn leather in his hands, toying with some strands of stitching that had come loose with time. He stroked the rough buckle that was orange with rust and then dropped the diary back in the shoebox.

"You're right," he said, putting the lid back on. "It's probably all in German anyway so what chance would we have to read it."

"I know some German," Josh said, and Eric saw his former tormentor blush, making the black eye even more prominent. "My grandmother always speaks German with me. My father's mother. She's from Poland, but she grew up speaking German."

Eric looked Josh up and down in the shaded darkness of the bedroom. He remembered how, during the last weeks of school, Josh had often turned away from the war documentaries they had watched, preferring to draw violent pictures which he handed to Eric.

Eric chewed on his bottom lip. His head felt muddled, his brain wobbling like a slab of pink jelly. The present was colliding with the past and within the both of them, the truth ran through their veins.

"I'm sorry for yesterday," Eric said. "But you got me more than I got you."

"The group put me up to it." Josh grimaced, squinting at his shoes. "You know what it's like."

Eric nodded. "Come on. Let's get back to the hospital."

They pumped their tired legs through the suburban banality of Crescent Bay, the houses carbon copies of each other and the front gardens in immaculate condition, with residents forever competing to outdo their neighbours and secure garden supremacy. As they ran through the entrance gate, Josh waved at the security guard who was sitting on the bonnet of his little white car. Eric stopped to look at his father's face on the billboard. Josh came to a halt and looked up at the billboard as well, seeing the resemblance.

"Your dad?"

"Yeah. But let's not waste time over him."

They ran down the wide highway to the hospital, but there was no competition this time and they ran easily. They even joked and talked along the way, finding a few things in common, and Eric was surprised how easily the words came. At the hospital, they both froze when they saw the two-door, cream coloured Mercedes parked in the disabled zone in front of the entrance.

***

The blurred face in the photograph stared back at him. He frowned at the weak shoulders, the way he hunched in on himself that was so characteristically un-SS. It could simply have been hunger, for they had all – SS or Wehrmacht – been hungry in those days, their stomachs inverted like shallow bowls. He looked closer at the picture, studying the out-of-focus face, until the photo was inches from his own face. He didn't see the naked bodies piled awkwardly in the grave and the loose limbs grabbing at each other, the bodies huddling together even in death; nor did he see the skeletal trees weeping in the winter background. He saw only the soldier, tracing the outline of the uniform with his eyes and resting on the bulge made by a thick book crammed into the breast pocket.

"Guten Tag, Herr Jäger."

He lowered the picture. The visitor wore well-pressed pants of lime green and a light pink golf shirt. The collar was turned up and the green alligator stood out clearly against the pink background. Above the usual smell of bleach and disinfectant came a waft of fresh lawn clippings.

"Was willst du?" He had always read in German, but now the words seemed to come with difficulty, the language of another person, spoken by a foreigner.

"Wie geht's dir? I wanted to see how you are." He took a chair close to the bed and sat down. "May I?"

He reached a long arm across the bed and snatched the photograph. He looked at it as if seeing it for the first time, to the point of unfolding a pair of spectacles to see it more clearly.

"You look good in this picture. So young and full of life. I guess the successes of the army made you feel better about yourself."

"It's not me."

"Are you sure about that?" He pointed a long index finger at the soldier in the photo. "He has the same weak face, the same drooping shoulders. You only got in because of your father, didn't you? The SS were the elite. They never would've taken you without the help of the Herr Doktor."

"How do you know my father?"

He sat back in the chair and eased one lime green leg over the other. He sighed whimsically, recalling the memories. "It was long ago. I often went to see your father when he was in Berlin. A brilliant man. Charming, handsome, and the girls fawned on him as much as the men admired him."

"The man's insane. Always was."

"The uneducated often confuse genius and insanity, but are only really rebelling against that which they are unable to understand. They shout insanity to hide their own inability to comprehend and appreciate genius."

He tossed the photograph carelessly back onto the bed. It got caught between the stiff folds of the sheets. "One for your album, I think. Not mine." He sighed brightly, like a man sitting on a park bench on a sunny afternoon. "So, what news? How long have they given you? Dorothy is hungry for information."

"That old bat had my funeral planned years ago. She's probably sitting at home in her black dress as we speak."

Baum laughed, his mouth open, light chuckles that showed the whiteness of his back teeth. "I guess I might have told her a few things about you."

"No doubt."

Baum smiled and glanced around the room. He looked at the machines knowingly, reading the numbers. "Will they operate?"

"What do you want, Wald?"

On the hearing this name, Baum's face contorted itself in an expression of confusion. He inspected his fingernails. "Wald? Who is Wald? Sounds like you're reflecting your own demons onto me. I'm not the one you want." He held out his manicured hands, palms up. "I have nothing to hide."

Silence fell on the room. A nurse came in to change the water jug and scolded Fischer for not finishing his lunch. She spoke in a matronly manner, almost like a grandmother would to reproach a wayward grandchild.

"Your father is a great man," Baum said when the nurse had left the room. "He deserves to outlive you." He sighed rather dramatically, eager to make his point, and then spoke with theatrical melancholy:

"It's such a shame that the sons and daughters of great men never reach the same heights."

"I never wanted to emulate him."

"You couldn't get close anyway. But why didn't you write back? I spoke to him a few days ago and he said what hurt the most was that you never wrote back to him. He sent so many letters. Why didn't you respond?"

"Probably because this son never reached the same heights."

Baum smiled his agreement.

"But probably because that time was over. I wanted to close that book. He killed my mother. I could never forgive him for that."

Baum narrowed his pale blue eyes. "But you never turned him in either."

"Well, despite everything, he's still my father. I thought they'd catch him. And if I had turned him in, then I'd be just as bad as he was with my mother."

"Ah, Prussian loyalty never dies."

"No. Only people do."

"And it looks like your time has come. You will join your dishonoured and defeated brothers."

Fischer took the photograph in his hand again. "I think I'd rather join the members of this grave."

"That's why we failed," Baum said, standing up quickly, his chair scraping loudly across the floor. "We put our faith in a people who were unworthy. Offered them a great future, but you failed us."

"We may have failed, but we certainly left our mark."

Baum waved away this remark. "The figures are grossly over-estimated. They wrote the history and just added a few more zeros. More ethnic Germans died at the hands of the Russians than in that so-called Holocaust. The Americans came up with that word anyway, and they write their own version of history, as you well know."

Fischer grunted, hating the conversation. "That's no different to what you're doing now. The Nazis had their own version of history as well. God, they had their own version of the present, and a future only they thought possible. But the Jews were killed. I was there, I saw what happened. And it's a legacy I'm none too proud of."

Baum paced around the room. "Those people had it coming. We weren't the first to think so either. And you confuse legacy with destiny."

"I hope you meet yours."

Baum stopped pacing and grabbed the back of the chair with his hands, leaning on it. "Take my advice. Leave the past where it is. You'll gain nothing from digging around in it. If anything, you should quietly revel in it, that once the world cowered before us. You are German, a pure Aryan. Greatness flows in your blood, despite your frailties as a human."

He turned and stepped towards the stack of machines lined up next to the bed.

"I know who you are," Fischer said.

"It makes no difference. I'm not wanted because I never escaped. The Australian government helped me emigrate, gave me a nice house and a professorship at the university. And I've been an exemplary citizen. They won't go after me because then they'll have to explain themselves, and if you give me up, you'll be exposed as well. I'm sure you've done far worse things than me."

With his eyes, Baum followed the white and grey electrical cords to where they were connected to the wall.

"Go on," Fischer said. "Do it."

Fishcer wondered how many others had escaped so easily. How many had the Australian government, or other governments for that matter, helped to emigrate? Like von Braun and the others, who had been whisked away to America in private planes. Had the Nazi elite been dispersed to bolster the floundering ranks of the intelligentsia of less intellectual countries? It was too sick a thought to ponder.

"Go on," he repeated. "It's the Nazi way, to kill those weaker, those who no longer have any use. You killed all the old people, the disabled, the crazy, the homosexual too. Killed anyone who protested against you. But not you. You're no killer. Your violence isn't physical."

Baum bent down and picked up the cords, gripping them in his long, slender fingers. He stroked them, massaging the plastic, and then took a firm grip to yank the cords from the sockets. He turned and scowled at Fischer slumped against a mound of pillows.

"You don't deserve such a noble death," he said, dropping the cords. "You deserve to die slowly and painfully, without dignity and honour, suffering from the weaknesses of your own body."

"You always hated it that I beat you at golf, didn't you?"

"But I will win in the end."

"What a marvellous victory it'll be. I wouldn't want to change places with you."

"Well, then we're both glad we are who we are."

"You Nazi filth," Fischer shouted, lifting himself from the pillows. "Get out."

Baum raised his eyebrows, untouched by the insult. "You should be nicer to your visitors. I can't imagine you get many, if any."

"I've had one, your grandson no less."

"Probably came to ask for a reward for saving you." Baum headed for the door.

"He's a good kid. Guess he gets it from his father's side of the family."

Baum snarled, snorting loudly through his nose. He shook his head bitterly and opened the door. "Good riddance to you, though I should say good luck, because you will hardly be well-received on the other side."

The door closed with a gentle, quiet click that was more spiteful than any loud slam.

***

Eric tasted his own salty sweat as it trickled down the side of his face and into his mouth. They waited, peering around the corner of the hallway like two hunters pursuing an elusive animal. Eric had the shoebox tucked firmly under his arm and was eager to know more about its contents, so much so that Josh had to grab him sometimes to hold him back, pulling at his shirt and whispering that they couldn't go in until his grandfather was gone. Eric knew Josh was right, but his impatience, his desire for action and to know the truth sucked him around the corner and towards the door to Fischer's room.

They saw the door open, the green legs striding through, and ducked quickly back around the corner. The leather slip-ons slapped against the floor and Eric could just make out a soft squeaking; Baum sock-less, like always. The straight-backed figure passed them but stared ahead and did not see them plastered against the wall. To Eric, Baum looked like ice cream, all green and pink and yellow, the special super-sweet Trio flavour he had loved so much when he was younger. He smelled the familiar cologne of the old man, but got a whiff a cut grass as well. He looked at Josh, whose eyes were firmly fixed on his grandfather's back. Josh had a confused look on his face, and was biting his top lip, sucking it down and moving it between his teeth.

"Come on," Eric said, grabbing Josh's arm. He had to pull and drag him towards the room. "What's up with you?" Eric asked.

Josh looked back at the corner Baum had just walked around. "It's just that…well, he's my grandfather. If it turns out he did bad things and is a wanted war criminal, can I really turn him in?"

Eric reached for the door handle. "You'll have to decide pretty soon."

"But it was all nearly fifty years ago. And what does any of this have to do with us? Most people have forgotten anyway."

"Has your grandmother forgotten?"

Josh shook his head.

"I think that's reason enough," Eric said. "We can't let him get away with it, whatever it was."

"Maybe we should ask Mr Fischer. He'll know what to do."

Eric opened the door and they went in. Fischer's face was turned away, but he looked quickly at the door. He saw the white shoebox tucked under Eric's arm.

"Well done," he said. "Sit down and let's take a look at it."

The boys took their seats. Eric's chair was still warm from when Baum had sat on it, and the room still had the lingering smell of cut grass. He placed the shoebox on the bed and opened it. The leather book lay on top of the pile of letters. He picked it up, unbuckled the short belt and the diary sprang open. The jagged piece of metal that was secure under the belt fell amongst the envelopes.

"Careful," Fischer said. "There's loose papers and photographs inside. Don't let them fall out."

Eric handed the book to Fischer. The old man's hands shook as he took it, and Eric got gooseflesh as his left hand brushed the leathery skin of Fischer's gnarled right hand.

"I haven't read this in years." Fischer thumbed slowly through the pages. He stopped to read short passages and then skipped chunks of pages to find other passages he was looking for, going through the book like it was a road map and he was trying to plan his route, or find his way. He smiled and frowned, knitting his eyebrows together, but he seemed to have none of the enthusiasm of earlier. This change was not lost on Eric, who rummaged through the box, sifting through the envelopes and plucking a name tag from among them.

"What's this?" he asked, holding it up.

Fischer took it in his hands. "My father's name tag. From the camp." He put it to the side, out of Eric's reach.

"Can I read one of the letters?" Josh asked.

"Sprichst du Deutsch?"

Josh nodded.

"I can't believe that Baum taught you, or did you learn it at school?"

"My grandma taught me. My father's mother. She's from Poland."

Fischer turned to Eric. "A lot of Polish people could speak German in those days. Up until a few years before, most of the country had belonged to Prussia. The German settlers and ethnics had the run of the place during the war and a lot of people learned the language to deal better with the conqueror."

He picked up the shoebox and put it on Josh's side of the bed, leaving Eric to sit helplessly while they both read. He looked at his watch. It was two thirty. He had promised to be at Pepper's house at four.

"It's Sütterlin," Fischer said to Josh. "Don't worry if you can't read it."

But Josh seemed to understand what he read, at least some of it. "Your father's a real fanatic. My gran reckons there wasn't so many of those. She said only a couple of bad guys forced everyone else to do bad stuff."

Fischer looked up from the diary. He had been on the same page for about five minutes and seemed to be going over the words again and again, as if he was missing something of vital importance written between the lines.

"She's right. A lot of people were nationalists but not Nazis, and if they were when they joined the party, probably became disillusioned by Nazi practice. But by then it was too late. Most people just got swept up by it all. Baum acts like a Nazi but he was probably just another careerist who sought his own gain by siding with the bullies in charge. And to me, that's almost worse than being a fanatic."

Silence fell on the room. Fischer and Josh read and Eric fidgeted. He picked up the photograph he had given Fischer earlier and wondered if the two old men had talked about it. Fischer was right, he thought. The soldier didn't look anything like him.

"It's not me. But in a way, it is. That soldier is a witness and a participant, like I was. He stood by and let everything happen and I did the same. They killed millions, and even though I didn't agree with it, like many others I didn't have the courage to stand up and protest. I would've been killed for it anyway so it would have made no difference. But guilt isn't collective, it's individual. I did some terrible things during the war and I saw others do much worse. Baum never saw any of it. He pushed pens and shuffled papers. In a sick way, he probably did more damage than any of the soldiers."

A nurse bustled in, a short bird-like creature with starched white plumage. She jumped around with short steps and moved quickly around the bed. She even had the face of a bird, with a small, round mouth that she seemed to hold tightly together, and a long, hooked nose that looked like a short beak.

"Now it's nice that you boys are visiting your granddad, but don't go exciting him. He needs his rest."

She tidied up the table and removed the plates from the lunch that Fischer had barely touched. Eric looked at his watch again. It was now close to three.

"Not too long now," the nurse said as she bustled back out. She closed the door too quickly, with a slither of white uniform caught in the door. But instead of opening the door again she tugged at it, and all three of them watched the white feather slowly get yanked to the other side.

"Here," Fischer said. "I've found what I was looking for."

He unfolded a piece of paper, tan with age, and pointed at the signature at the bottom of the page.

"Christoph Wald. That's who Baum really is."

Josh took the thin paper in his hands and studied the page. He read it out loud, translating what he understood. Eric was impressed.

"Think of it as a delivery docket," Fischer explained. "All the belongings and money taken from Jews had to be signed for and catalogued when it was received at the other end. The Nazis were extremely diligent and meticulous when it came to paperwork, almost as if they wanted to show succeeding generations how brilliant their thievery had been. Baum, or Wald, worked in that department, which was part of the Reich Economic Administration. It also means that he must've been pretty high up in the department if he was signing for deliveries."

Josh's eyes brightened. "That's what you meant by not seeing the forest for the trees."

"What?" Eric asked. He hated to be left out of revelations. Normally he was the one who figured things out quicker. "I don't understand."

"Baum means tree and Wald means forest," Josh said condescendingly.

"The Nazis loved their symbolism and imagery." Fischer leaned over and patted Josh's shoulder. "My father made a direct translation of his name from German into Spanish. Jäger to Cazador, which in English is Hunter."

"And that's your name too," Eric said, surprised by his own anger. "You want us to chase after Baum or Wald or whatever his name is, but we don't know about you. How can we trust you? And what are the chances that Baum is Wald? It was probably just a mistake on the box. Your father is the wanted criminal, that could be you in the photo, and you wrote this diary. Who are you really?"

Fischer blew out a long breath. His chest sagged and it seemed to take quite a lot of effort for him to breathe in again.

"Okay. My name is Jäger. I was born in Thöby, which is a small farming village in Schleswig Holstein. Hitler came to power when I was twelve and my father made me join the Hitler Youth as soon as it was formed. When war broke out, he took me out of university in Hamburg and pushed me into the SS." He turned to Eric. "I'm sorry I lied about that, but I'm extremely ashamed that I was in the SS. I was sent to the eastern front and my unit was responsible for cleansing the villages and cities of enemies. In the battle for Stalingrad, I was wounded in the stomach. That was just before the Sixth Army was encircled and Hitler gave them up for dead. When I recovered, I fought on the eastern front again as the Russians pushed us back towards Germany. After the last Christmas of the war, my hand was wounded and then I deserted. I stole a regular army uniform and spent a few weeks with some Polish farmers. When the Russians came, I dressed as a peasant and joined the lines of refugees walking west. I was in Dresden when it was so callously bombed and then made my way back to Hamburg. When the war was over, I turned myself in at the prisoner-of-war camp. I came out two years later with a new name. I took a ship to Australia, met an Italian on board, and went with him to work on the banana plantations in Carnarvon. Things didn't work out, so I drifted down to Geraldton. I worked, got married, started my own business, did my best to forget, and every year got two letters from my bloody father. When my wife died, I moved down here. Baum and I were never friends, and he always hated it that I beat him at golf. I'm not proud of what I've done and I've never told anyone the truth about my life. And I never turned my father in because I feared I'd be caught as well."

Eric and Josh sat in silence and stared at the old man. Despite Fischer's actions and lies, Eric couldn't help but be impressed. Fischer had lived a long and exciting life, one that made his own suburban existence seem dull and meaningless by comparison. Fischer's life had been one long battle, and though he now lay on a hospital bed dying, Eric couldn't help but think Fischer had won the fight simply by surviving this long. But even with that admiration and respect, Eric frowned, thinking of all the lies Fischer had told him. All along he had been an old Nazi. The rumours were true.

"What do we do now?" Josh asked.

"Probably the best thing is to make copies of the important documents and then we'll send all the stuff to the right authorities. If you've got a picture of Baum at home, Josh, you should include that too."

Fischer looked wearily at the diary he held in his hands. He was breathless and seemed to be struggling to stay awake, his eyelids drooping at the sides. The monologue had knocked the wind out of him.

"The Australian government has a special department which hunts for war criminals. Their address is in my address book. It's in the top kitchen drawer, next to the sink. Send it all to them." He inhaled with effort and then sighed heavily. "There's not much else we can do really."

"What about your father?" Eric asked. "You said he lives in Spain."

"Yes, of course. In the address book you'll find a place in Vienna called the Simon Wiesenthal Documentation Center. They probably have a file several inches thick on my father, perhaps one on me too. These letters will help. Send the name tag too."

"That's it?"

"We can't just go to the police with a diary, some old letters and a bunch of ghost stories. We've got to do this the right way. If we expose Baum, he'll just run. We have to keep him where he is. And," he added after a reluctant pause, "we have to be sure that he is actually Wald."

"What about you?"

Fischer let out another heavy sigh, expelling the air like it was poison. "Look at me. I'm hardly worth saving. I should've done this a long time ago. You've no idea how hard it is to sleep at night with what I've seen."

But Eric didn't care about the old man's nightmares or his lack of sleep. Fischer, who had always spoken of honesty and truth, had lied to him. He had talked about helping others, about sacrifice, but had spent his lifetime saving himself, lying for his own preservation. He was hardly the courageous football star he had made himself out to be, succeeding at life despite his disabled hand. Eric looked at his watch and saw that it was past four.

"Where are you going?" Fischer demanded as Eric headed for the door.

"I gotta be somewhere. I'll be back tomorrow, maybe."

"I'll come too," Josh said, jumping up. "I'll photocopy this stuff, find the address book, and send it all away."

But Fischer didn't seem to want to be left alone and sat up in bed. "Can't you stay just a little bit longer? There's still so much to tell."

Eric and Josh both shrugged and looked down at their feet. Eric already had the door open and the sounds of the hospital were a refreshing break from the noises of the machines and Fischer's fading monotone and laboured breathing.

"We'll be back tomorrow," Josh said.

Fischer dropped himself back on his pillows. Eric closed the door.

Eighteen

They separated at the old bridge that crossed the river. As every afternoon, men in faded flannel shirts were set up for an evening's fishing. They had stinking buckets, big tackle boxes that rattled when they walked, and long nets to catch the fish in case they wriggled off the hook on the haul from the water to the bridge. Eric already recognised some of the men, saw the familiar bicycles with the big boxes attached, and other bikes with small trailers connected. Some of the men smiled at him as he walked along the bridge, calling him "Little Johnny" or some such and holding up their long rods as if they would be temptation enough to make him sit down and fish with them. He did his best to ignore the men and put his head down to the sea breeze. The wind rifled past his ears and he didn't hear the calls of the fishermen, nor the quiet conversation they made with each other. He frowned at the bird shit splattered pavement. He was late, he had no condoms, he smelled of hospital bleach and old sweat, and his head was filled to burst with the stories and lies he had heard. All he wanted was to have a long hot shower, a cold drink and to sit down and stare at the television.

But once across the bridge, he started running for Crescent Bay, not wanting to keep Pepper waiting while hoping that the exercise might clear his mind. He waved at the guard still sitting on his car at the entrance gate and then manoeuvred through the streets, past the green gardens and the large, bulky houses that seemed far too big for the small families which inhabited them. Watering systems were going at full blast despite the summer restrictions and the tips of his shoes got wet enough from the puddles on the footpath for his toes to feel the moisture. He stuck to the main road that curved around the bay. He saw the breakers smashing against the rocks at South Corner. A few scattered surfers were braving the afternoon winds, their stretched out figures bobbing up and down as the white caps rolled under their boards. Josh's house loomed high over the beach. Eric stopped to marvel at its size and wondered what secrets were secured inside. It was just like Merredin, he thought; the houses hiding a myriad of family problems, where every other family looked better and was more normal, but only from the outside. Because of the fronts put up, the scripted and costumed show, rehearsed to perfection until someone forgot their lines or fell out of character. He wondered why they tried so desperately to show their family as normal and nice, and decided that the need for acceptance was no different from Josh and the bikers, from himself and the surfers. This need to belong was poisoning every part of his life. His family had it too, and both his father and mother had always been desperate not to be different, even trying valiantly to show up the other families by being so perfect, with both his parents sometimes scripting what Eric should say.

He knew now there were no perfect families, and when people tried to present their family as such, it could only be a construction; a performance staged for outsiders to envy. But despite everything, all the fallacies and cover-ups, he was glad that, at the very least, his family was still intact.

He ran north along Bayside Drive, the wind at his back now and driving him forward, billowing his shirt about him, almost blowing it over his head. Baum's house was as still and silent as ever. He slowed down to look at it. From the outside, he could never know if the old man was home or not. He could just hear the steady drone of the air-conditioner and thought to knock on the door and confront Baum with everything. If Baum was who Fischer said he was, then that would mean that Baum had also lied to protect himself. Eric didn't know what to believe anymore and was sick of it all. Trust your elders, he had been taught, but they were all a bunch of fakes and liars. If only his father had just bought him a surfboard, he would never have had to get involved with the old men. Nevertheless, he still wished he could read Fischer's diary, which seemed to hold all the answers. Or had Fischer lied in that as well? Maybe Josh would translate some of it for him. It would be a good reason for them to get together again, he thought.

The shadow of a figure, tall and thin, passed across the curtains. Eric turned and ran down the road. It was Baum who had stroked the SS uniform lovingly, fondled it with his long fingers, and Baum who revelled in the glory of war and spoke of Hitler's greatness. Fischer had denounced all of it, haunted by the nameless, faceless people he had killed and the others he had watched die, unable to save them. Both men had lied, both had changed their names, both had come to Australia to make a new life and forget: both were Nazis. The only difference was the line that separated criminal from follower. If Baum was a war criminal, he wondered, why not go to the police? Why send the diary to some government office in Canberra and the letters to some obscure place in Vienna? And if Baum was such a criminal, why hadn't anyone hunted him down?

The driveway to Pepper's house was empty. A tractor sprinkler chugged along the grass, spraying the windows and as far as the road, leaving a perfect half circle on the bitumen which was slowly forming itself into a puddle, the water being replenished faster than the wind and sun could dry it.

It was just after five.

Eric stood in front of the door. He found the empty driveway strange. Every time he had passed the house or been there, at least one car had been parked in front, usually two or three. The wind rushed past his ears and his shirt billowed around him. How sick he was of the afternoon winds, the way they blew the tops off waves, whipped the sand against his legs and made it almost impossible to go outside and enjoy the afternoon. He missed Merredin's dry plains and the dusty easterly winds which swirled the sun-dried grass into small willy-willys which he could jump inside; they would spin him around and around until he fell to the ground dizzy and sick. He missed the uncomplicated farming world where the weather meant success or failure and where his father had been a local cricket star, Eric the drinks boy. When it rained, it poured. When the sheep were heavy with wool, the shearing season started and burly men from around the state would congregate in Merredin, filling the bars and fighting with each other. When the wheat was high, it was cut, and when there was no rain, everyone suffered. Eric missed that fixed, basic life when his family had convinced the town they were normal and nice, and he was firmly entrenched at school.

He reached out and pressed the doorbell. He just heard the faint chime echoing through the house. When no response came he turned to walk down the drive, thinking he was too late, that he had missed his chance and let Pepper down.

He headed for the beach, hoping the wind and salt might clear out his head some more. From a distance, he saw Pepper sitting on the rocks at the north end of the bay.

He went slowly up to her. "Hey. What's going on?"

"Where were you?"

"Sorry I'm late."

Pepper wiped the tears from her face. "Forget it," she said, her voice hoarse from crying. Then she jumped off the rock and clutched him with all off her strength, squeezing him so tight he struggled to breathe.

"You all right?"

"Just family problems. I hate Blair."

"Why don't you tell me what's wrong? Maybe you'll feel better."

But she shook her head and looked down at the sand.

"Well, what do we do now?" Eric asked.

Pepper sniffed and shrugged her thin shoulders. "I dunno."

They started walking south down the beach, holding hands, their hair and clothes blustered by the strong south-westerly. But with the sun edging towards the horizon, the wind was starting to slowly die down. By sunset it would barely be a breath.

Neither spoke.

When they got to South Corner, they sat down and watched the surfers trying to milk the pushed-over waves, but it seemed they spent most of their time paddling against the current. It looked to Eric like hard work.

"Hey, Eric."

They both turned as Josh came clambering down the rocks, his house behind him like a backdrop.

"I thought that was you." He blushed when he saw Pepper. "Hi."

Pepper looked briefly at the purple that ringed Josh's eye, then turned to Eric. "Are you two friends now?"

Eric smiled back. "Yeah, weird, isn't it?" He looked at Josh. "Did you send the stuff away?"

"I'll do it tomorrow."

"Not that it means much," Eric said. "But I guess it's something. If you ask me, the chance that Baum is Wald is really small."

"You wanna go together to see Mr Fischer tomorrow?" Josh asked.

"I don't know." Eric spied the leather diary clutched in Josh's hands. "I'm kinda sick of it all. What do you think? You think he's a Nazi?"

"Who's a Nazi? Mr Fischer?" Pepper said. "My gran thinks so. She reckons all Germans are. But I think he's just a harmless old man. Bit weird, and that hand is freaky." She pointed a finger at Eric scathingly yet jokingly. "You can't go around calling every German a Nazi. That's not fair."

"I reckon he is," Josh said. He sat down next to them. The wind blew back his hair and Eric could see the dark hairs which connected the two eyebrows into one. Josh unbuckled the short belt and opened the diary, careful not to let any loose papers blow away.

"Who cares?" Eric said.

"Look," Josh said, pointing at the front page. "He said his name was Jäger."

Eric looked closely and saw the name "Reinhard Jäger" written in the broad and blotchy strokes of a fountain pen.

"So he wrote the diary. So what."

"You can't believe what's in here," Josh said, talking quickly, seemingly unable to get all the words out fast enough. "You can't read it because it makes you sick. He did it all. He was in the SS, he killed women and children, hanged German soldiers. Shit, he even met Himmler. He wrote about his time as a guard at a concentration camp."

"What are you talking about?" Pepper asked.

Eric closed the book emphatically and pulled the short buckle tight. "History. But we're supposed to be on holiday. Why are we talking about school?"

"I think we should go for a swim," Pepper said.

They waited for Josh to go home and change and then walked down to the swimming beach. Brad and Drew walked from the other direction, with Drew looking quizzically at Eric, seeing him walking next to Josh. Eric knew then he and Drew would never be friends. Brad called Eric a sheep lover and Josh countered quickly by calling Brad a dumb waxhead. But no one broke stride, and Eric, Josh and Pepper felt comfortable and strong in their little group. At the beach, they fought against the current and splashed water at each other. With the sun low, they separated. Josh walked back up the beach to his house and Eric walked Pepper home.

"Are you gonna be okay?" Eric asked when they stood out the front, staring at the cars now parked in the driveway.

"Yeah. I think it's time I told my mum the truth."

Eric slowly put the pieces together. "The truth's important."

Pepper walked to the front door and disappeared into the house.

Eric started for home, walking slowly into the wind. He saw Baum standing in the front garden watering with the hose. From Eric's point of view, it looked like the old man was pissing on his own lawn. Baum saw him and gave the hose a turn. The water stopped.

"Eric," he called out, waving a hand expectantly.

But Eric kept his head down and walked quickly along the pavement, almost running. He hadn't even acknowledge the old man, but he still felt eyes boring into his back the whole way until he took the first corner left and headed for home. He dragged his tired feet along the footpath, down the streets that were now as familiar to him as the streets of Merredin had been. He could walk along in a daze and still find his way home. He thought of Pepper and hoped she would come through it.

He passed the Bayside Hotel and stopped to stare at the company Ford parked in the lot, the lone car. He went up to the door nearest to the car and knocked loudly. The aqua blue paint was cracked and peeling up close, chipped away at the keyhole by so many missed keys. The door swung open. His father stood there with his white business shirt open, his pale chest showing, his tie hanging loosely around his neck.

"Is that the wine you ordered?" asked a woman's voice from inside.

His father looked at him sheepishly, his shoulders dropping, his face weak and pathetic. Eric tried to look past him, at the figure lying on the bed. He could see a pair of slender, naked legs, but his father blocked the doorway.

"It's not what you think, sport," his father said, snatching at the buttons of his shirt, trying to do them up but his hands were shaking too much.

Eric turned and walked away from the door. The old receptionist with the blue hair came trundling towards the door, a tray in her arms with a bottle of wine and two glasses on it. She stopped when she saw Eric. He saw her shake her head slightly, her painted lips pursed. Then she shrugged her shoulders at him and kept walking forward.

Eric picked up a large rock and threw it at the white Ford. The driver-side window smashed and flecks of bluish glass piled on the ground. The alarm made its loud and offensive blaring and this caused the receptionist to drop the tray. But Eric didn't hear the wine bottle breaking, or the shouts of his father. He ran from the hotel and down the familiar streets to the house the company owned.

***

He lay back on the bed and stared out the window. The sun was going down and he could see the first traces of pink and orange painting the sky. The wheeze and suck of the respirator sounded like the boom and groan of the Russian rocket launchers they had nicknamed Stalin Organs. He saw the putrid plains of the Don Steppe, the scoured remnants of a Poland picked cleaned, the corpse-littered Stalingrad. Rats scurried over the bodies and crows scraped every morsel of exposed flesh from the bones, digging their sharp beaks under the uniforms in search of more. He saw the faces of soldiers, German, Russian, Romanian, Italian, all the nationalities of Europe, frozen in anguish as their lives were ripped from them by rifle bullets and bombs. He saw himself, young and proud in his SS uniform. How his father had cheered and clapped when he had marched off to war. In venturing east to kill innocent people and a nameless enemy, he had finally won the approval of his father. He saw the fast friends he had made – soldiers from his unit or from others – tumble to the earth, bent backward by bullets or blown to pieces by shells. Lying in the trenches, he jumped as shrapnel whizzed past his head and dug into the dirt or struck others. The screams of pain echoed through the long nights, men wounded but unable to be rescued, and others in the medical tent shouting and cursing as operations were done with only vodka for anaesthetic. During those terminal nights, the sky was lit by explosions, the plane fights their only source of entertainment. But nobody cheered when a supply plane caught fire and plunged to earth in a shower of flames, taking months of precious supplies with it.

He heard the jungle cry of the enemy as they charged from their trenches, running like madmen into a sea of machine gun bullets. And when that wave had been cut down, the cry came again and the process repeated itself until the field couldn't be seen for the number of corpses which covered it. The dead fell onto the wounded, and in the madness, he could hear the muffled cries of those still alive, now trapped under a blanket of bodies, their blood mixing with that of their fallen comrades. And yet still more came, from deep within the bowels of Russia, an endless supply of manhood which outnumbered the German army ten to one. But those valiant Germans, his remarkable comrades, held on for three more years, sending back wave after wave, capturing those they didn't kill and leaving them to starve in POW camps that were even more inhumane than the concentration camps.

He saw himself walking across the maze of bodies, their faces twisted and frozen. He watched his comrades pillage the fallen soldiers of their precious valuables. He did the same, not wanting to earn the ire of the fervent fanatics who watched him suspiciously from the corners of their eyes. So he played along, copying the others and pocketing the few wedding rings he found. The Bolsheviks had little which was worth stealing, with mere trinkets for watches and money that looked home-made and had no value in the real world. Their rations were their most prized possession and the SS took these too, leaving the food they did not prefer scattered on the ground.

He saw the local peasant women emerge from nowhere to drag the bodies off the field and into mass graves dug by old men. The women wore kerchiefs on their heads and had thick calves and wide hips. Some of the SS men raped these old women and they submitted to this degradation quietly as if it was just another invasion, the victor getting his spoils.

They marched across Russia, stealing and looting from the local people when they should have been rousing them to join the fight against Bolshevism. The locals poisoned their own water and brought it to the Germans to drink. In the battle for Stalingrad, that ruined town on the Volga – he could never understand why Hitler prized it so fiercely – he felt the bullet pierce his side and he crashed to earth, the life seeping out of him. What a relief it had been. He hoped he would die quickly. His blank face stared up at the pale blue sky. It had been a most beautiful day when he had been shot. That was strange; there had not been the usual explosions which clouded the sky, the powder that burned his nostrils and the dust that prevented him from seeing the sun. That day, it was clear and the air was clean. He lay looking up at the sky's stark, almost cheeky blueness, the bright sun hurting his eyes, knowing that it was all over and he would die a soldier's death. His father would be proud. But the strong alcohol passed his lips. He tried to spit it out, but the orderly, barely a teenager, forced him to drink again, covering his mouth with a dirty hand and holding his nose until he swallowed. He was quickly drunk and watched in a daze as the butcher went to work, trying to put his intestines back inside and make him whole again. The doctor's hands were red with blood, the same deep red that was on their Nazi flag, and he kept having to stop his work to brush the flies from his face. The pain ran through him, hot and white, and he felt he had gone blind. He hated then the uniform he had worn, the royal treatment it had got him. The fresh blood pumped into his veins; the doctor had checked under his left armpit for the tattooed blood group. Betty had always asked about that tattoo and he had stuck with his lie, that his father was a doctor and had been overprotective of his only son. The tight stitches left him hunched over, with the scar long and ragged, like a doll mended by a child. The side of his stomach remained indented slightly, his spine bent a little. A farming accident, he had always said, the same that had taken two fingers and part of his right hand.

He saw himself being shipped back to the front to rejoin the slowly retreating Germans. The mood in the ranks had turned sour since Hitler had abandoned the Sixth Army and all the soldiers knew the war was lost, that their great leader would leave them to die as well, given the choice. He smelled the burned-out crater where he lay with his hand partly blown off, and saw the comrade next to him, his insides spilling onto the dirt, like a can of worms tipped over, only bigger. The comrade smiled and said "Moin", the common greeting of northern Germany. Then he saw the comrade had his own face, and with that recognition, the comrade was absorbed by the earth and the battered leather diary lay in his place. He picked it up, brushed away the dirt, wiped off the blood and jammed it back in his pocket, feeling the familiar belt buckle rubbing against his ribs. And then he ran, past the trenches still populated by the emaciated master race, behind the line of rusted tanks and up over the hill. He covered kilometres with each stride, bursting through the fire storm of Dresden, leaping over the scorched plains of the fatherland until he found himself standing over the mass grave from the photograph Eric had shown him. He was back in his SS uniform and the material felt smooth against his skin. The wounds were gone and his hand was whole. He was younger, stronger, and they were winning the war. He stroked his rifle with his complete right hand, wiggling the fingers inside the leather glove. He peered down inside the grave, as the other soldiers did. In amongst the twisted and broken bodies he saw the face of his mother. She pleaded with her eyes and extended a bony arm towards him. He was about to jump into the grave and rescue her when three of his comrades sidled up next to him. They put their hands on his shoulders, slapped his back and made jokes about the naked and pale corpses. They held him to the ground. He could only stand and watch as his mother's face disappeared under the pile of bodies, with more being thrown on top. Michaela was thrown into the pit, Remo too, the siblings staring up at him with their dark eyes until more bodies covered them as well.

The tears came easily and his right thumb edged onto the emergency button. So many mistakes. So much weakness. In his left hand, he gripped the thin piece of shrapnel that had killed Michaela.

He felt his chest expanding, the heat rising from his heart and into his head. It was like holding his breath under water, the way he and Ernst had done when they had gone swimming in the Schlei, having contests to see who could stay under water the longest, contests which Ernst had always won. When under water, with Ernst smiling at him, pretending to look at his watch with nonchalance, he had feared he would try to breathe, take in only water and die, and had always swum for the surface. Now, he held his breath again, still competing with Ernst, and not wanting to breathe in the lake of death he was immersed in. His cheeks burned with the effort and he felt the sharp metal digging into his left hand, drawing blood. His right thumb went to press the button. But he dropped it, the gadget slipping through his injured hand, where the last two fingers would have secured it. He opened his mouth and breathed in death. He heard a pop like a burst balloon. He lifted his mangled right hand and his bleeding left hand to his chest, clutching the bloody piece of shrapnel to his heart.

Nineteen

He put down his pencil and let out a long sigh. He looked over at Josh, who made a confused, comical face and promptly broke his pencil in half. Josh picked up the broken end and went back to marking the answers, filling in the small circles, most of the time just guessing and marking every answer as C.

Eric spent a few minutes playing with his own pencil and then raised his hand. The old examiner struggled over and collected his paper. He stood up to go, waited for the examiner to turn around, the white and yellow sheets clutched in her shrivelled hands, and then dropped the pencil on the floor near Josh's table. Josh, looking like a post-modern punk with his hair bleached blond, grinned and leaned down to pick up the pencil. He inspected it closely, reading the letters that Eric had scratched into the side with his thumbnail, and went back at his exam with renewed vigour.

The fresh afternoon air brought Eric out of his daze. He lingered, talking with the other students about the exam, discussing it. Some students, like Eric, revelled that it was their last exam and all the madness and stress was over. Drew was there, laughing heartily at his abject failure in all of his exams, and saying he would probably have to do the year again. His blond hair was very long, halfway down his back and working itself into dreadlocks. His skin had cleared up and he was quite good looking now, in a roguish sort of way, Eric thought, but he was playing the typical surfer boy like it was a character from a film. A rather plump Melanie, no longer Drew's girlfriend, worked hard to stay by his side, pathetic in the way she was striving for his attention. Eric and Drew got along, but apart from surfing, they had little to say to each other. It was last year that Eric had replaced Drew as captain of the cricket team, and Drew had never forgiven his former neighbour. In protest, he had dropped out of the team. He was suspended that year for bringing ecstasy tablets to the school ball and it was only his mother's influence in the Parents and Teachers Association that prevented him from being expelled.

"Go okay?" Eric asked.

Drew flicked the hair from his face and snarled. "What do you reckon?"

Josh came out with the others, cracking jokes and flirting with the girls. He sidled up next to Eric and handed him the remains of the pencil. Eric looked down at the pieces in his hand.

"Thanks," Josh said. "But I had to destroy the evidence."

"I hope that bleach didn't poison your brain, man," Drew said, getting snickers from those around him.

Josh, who had taken to being the class clown, did his renowned California surfer impression: "Like, man, the answers just, like, totally came to me, dude."

Everyone laughed, and the attention caused Josh to go on. Drew cursed at Josh and then turned in his sandals and walked away, his few friends following behind him as if attached by rope.

"Stupid waxhead," Josh said. He turned to Eric and smiled. "Sorry, you're one of them dudes, too."

"Like, man, it's just totally fine to call me that." Eric gave his hair a shake and then ran a hand slowly through it, pretending to let it catch the wind. The few people remaining laughed.

"I'm so glad that's over," Josh said.

Eric nodded. He was exhausted from the hours of cramming he had done; the nights spent in his small room in the duplex he shared with his mother, when he thought the walls were closing in. It was like the small house Fischer had lived in, on the hill near the golf course. His mother had gone out most nights so that he could study in peace. She was dating Martin, the latest divorcee she had met at the kindergarten. Like the others, Martin was working hard to become friends with Eric, thinking that to win his approval was to win hers. They kept the Messer name, simply because it saved a lot of hassle, and Eric saw his dad once a month in Perth, as was agreed. Now that Eric had his own car, half of which had been paid for by his father and the other half from stacking supermarket shelves, the trip took a lot less time than on the bus. His father had married again and had a small, golden-haired daughter. Eric had little to say to his father and both were glad that Kristy was there to occupy their attention. Eric looked like his father, acted like him too, and he knew their similarities made it harder for them to find some common ground.

Eric and Josh climbed into Eric's old Nissan. Josh had failed his driving test – the written, not the practical – and was anxious to get behind the wheel. His father had promised him a new car if he passed his final exams and he was due to take the test again next week. Josh had talked incessantly about trading the car for a year abroad. He wanted to go to Europe and track Fischer's course, as it was written in the diary, and perhaps write about it.

"By the way," Josh said. "Did you see the news last night? That guy Wagner, you know, the one in Adelaide who killed all the Ukrainian kids? He got out of his trial."

"I know. The same will probably happen to your grandfather."

"You know he still writes to me. I think he's starting to lose it. At least Wagner's already in prison, whether he gets tried as a war criminal or not."

"I guess his remorse is catching up with him," Eric said. "I don't know how he did it, but I know he killed old Fischer. Pulled his plug or something."

"Maybe we can get one old Nazi for murdering another, hang him from a tree with traitor around his neck."

"Have you been reading that stupid diary again?"

"Only to practise for my German exam," Josh said.

"Like you needed it. At least that's one you passed."

They drove along the main road towards Crescent Bay. Eric was an impatient driver, staying close to the car in front, honking his horn even when it wasn't necessary.

School was out and kids walked home with heavy bags weighing down their backs, causing them to hunch over as they walked. Eric sighed. Thank God that's all over, he thought, looking with pity at the younger kids who still had three or four years left. He thought of himself at the same age, with skinny legs and an army-sized backpack weighing him down. But school was over for him. All year he had been motivated by getting to this point, when he could leave this provincial trap and his life could really begin.

"I got another letter from Pepper," he said. "She's applied for the unis in Perth, but she reckons she won't get in. Didn't study enough."

Josh looked at Eric. He leaned over and turned the music off. "Are you still gonna fly to Sydney?"

"I don't know yet. I should be saving my money for uni next year, spend the whole summer working. I wanna see her, but she's got a new life, probably a new boyfriend. She never says that, but...I had other girls so I guess she had other boys. Maybe I'll wait and see if she gets into uni over here."

"Good idea. Then you and I can tear this place up this summer, if I can pry you away from that surfboard of yours."

"I see you spying through your curtains down at Souths, writing down every mistake I make."

"As if you make any."

They crossed the bridge and passed through the walled entrance into Crescent Bay. They stopped at Eric's house for a quick snack. Eric's mother had her hair in a bun, like she always had now, and her face was almost line-less, despite her middle-age. Her skin was drawn tight across her prominent cheekbones, making her look young and pretty. She agreed that Eric could go out and party with the others, celebrate the end of school, but he wasn't allowed to drive. He would hand her his car keys later, as was their agreement. She even made Eric write down Martin's phone number in case there was trouble.

"The boyfriend to the rescue," Josh said. "Maybe he has a weekend gig as Superman."

Eric grabbed his board and they drove to the beach. They passed Fischer's old house. A retired couple had moved in last year. After Fischer's death, the house had been renovated and sold for a high price. Eric's father had handled the deal, his last before applying for a transfer to Perth.

At South Corner, Eric continued his competition with Drew and Brad. The boys said few words to each other, apart from a mumbled compliment for a good ride or a mocking insult for wiping out. Eric paddled hard for his first wave of the day, the water washing away the stress of the last few months. The green and white board burned across the wave. Eric saw the dark outlines of rocks under the water and bent low to ride the tube. The wind rushed past his ears and when the wave died out, he went hard for the lip, getting a lift off the top and flying into the air. He plunged into the water, the refreshing coldness stinging his body. He regathered his board and paddled out past the breakers, where he got a monotone compliment from Drew.

The waves rolled in and the water was sucked back out. The surfers fought for waves, sticking to their groups. Sometimes tempers flared, with fights erupting over who had the wave first. Eric, a known and respected surfer here, did his best to steer clear from such entanglements.

Eric sat on his board and waited. He saw the speck of Josh on the beach, the black camera in his hands. Having lied about his age and credentials, Josh had already sold a few photos to surf magazines. The photos were more comic than extreme, and he had a good eye and excellent timing. Josh will make it, Eric thought, even if he failed all his exams. Not for the first time he felt jealous that Josh's family had money. But he fought those feelings, trying to remind himself that he was stronger for having earned everything he had. He hoped Josh would fail his driving test and take the trip to Europe. Perhaps then his mother would let him go as well. As always, it was just a question of money. He wanted to see all those famous places and research his own background: the Messers, farmers from Saxony, and the van der Mergens in Amsterdam. There was so much to see and do; spending four years at university only prolonged the wait. He wanted to get started with life, to go overseas and experience what he had only heard about. Fischer had often said he should go to Germany and see it.

"A lot of it's still there," the old man had said once, during one of the afternoons they had sat together at the kitchen table. "Not just the scars of war, the camps and bunkers and what not, but the feelings of the people. Everyone remembers and they all deal with it in different ways. But go and see for yourself. It's your history too. It's also your fatherland."

It was that idea that had lodged itself in Eric's head, the concept of fatherland. He was born in Australia, but for some reason he couldn't separate his link to Germany and didn't want to. The warnings Fischer had made about nationalism had left him forever critical of how nationalistic Australians were. It left him swinging in the middle, like so many other immigrants and the sons and daughters of immigrants, claiming whatever nationality is convenient at the time, but never really one and not completely the other. He remained thoughtful of his country, this land of immigrants with an identity that seemed like a construction, something thrown together to fit the space: the Anzac spirit and the fair go. But what did these things mean, and how did they relate to immigrants, to him? Perhaps if he went to Germany, he might understand more about Australia, that he would find things in Europe that were missing here, clues that would give him a clearer idea of what it meant to be Australian. If anything, the distance would allow him to remove himself from Australian society and all its influences. Maybe then he would see it for what it really was.

He paddled against the current, the wind blowing back his hair and chilling the water against his skin. He scanned the ocean, trying to predict where the next set of waves would come from. The ocean asked no questions, held no prejudices, didn't care who rode the waves or swam in the water. It simply flowed. He saw the waves coming and paddled into position. He had beaten Drew and Brad to the spot and had first ride. The wave lifted him up, shot him forward and he eased into the void.

Postscript

In Australia, the Employment of Scientific and Technical Aliens Scheme ran between 1946 and 1951. In 1987, after the report by ABC radio journalist Mark Aarons on Nazis in Australia sparked the Menzies Inquiry, the Special Investigations Unit (SIU) was set up to find former war criminals, gather evidence against them and bring them to trial. When the unit was shut down in 1992, some 800 cases were still open. Robert Greenwood, former head of the SIU, estimated that at least 27 of those cases could have gone to trial. But prosecuting these criminals would have highlighted the mistakes of former governments and how they had muddied the waters of justice. *Sanctuary: Nazi Fugitives in Australia*, by Mark Aarons, documents the immigration of Nazis to Australia.

In August 1999, the *Sydney Morning Herald* uncovered documents detailing how a number of known Nazis and Nazi Party members had been brought to Australia. No doubt, there were many others who had renounced their Nazi affiliations or had taken other identities who also came in via the supported immigration route, and still more who were migrants. The result was that a large number of Nazis entered Australia after the war and started new lives. Few were hunted down and none were caught and put on trial. The Jerusalem Post once called Australia "a haven for some of Hitler's worst henchmen."

Travel Page (cont.)